ALSO BY STEPHEN DAVIS
(as author or coauthor)

Fleetwood
Bob Marley
Hammer of the Gods
Say Kids! What Time Is It?
Reggae Bloodlines
Moonwalk

JAJOUKA ROLLING STONE

RANDOM HOUSE   NEW YORK

JAJOUKA
ROLLING STONE

A FABLE OF GODS AND HEROES

Stephen Davis

Grateful acknowledgment is made to Times Newspapers Limited for
permission to reprint "Jajouka" (music review) by Richard William
(TT 24 September 1980). Copyright © 1980 by Times Newspapers
Ltd. Reprinted by permission.

All interior photographs except the dancing boy on p. 190 are
reprinted with the permission of the photographer, A. J. Rubiner.
Copyright © A. J. Rubiner.

The photograph of the dancing boy on p. 190 is reprinted with the
permission of the photographer, Michael Mendizza. Copyright ©
Michael Mendizza.

Library of Congress Cataloging-in-Publication Data
Davis, Stephen
Jajouka rolling stone: a fable of gods and heroes/Stephen
Davis.—1st ed.
p.   cm.
ISBN 0-679-42119-X
1. Morocco—Fiction. I. Title.
PS3554.A937735J3   1993
813'.54—dc20   92-56809

Manufactured in the United States of America
24689753
First Edition

Book Design by Oksana Kushnir

for Jude

What men or gods are these? What maidens loath?
What mad pursuit? What struggle to escape?
What pipes and timbrels? What wild ecstasy?

—John Keats
"Ode on a Grecian Urn"

Ah Brahim Jones
Jajouka Rolling Stone
Ah Brahim Jones
Jajouka really stoned!

CONTENTS

BOOK ONE

Over the Hills and Far Away

Meet Bou Jeloud

For a hundred years stories have been told about the secrets of Jajouka, an old village perched above a long valley in the blue Djebala foothills of the Rif Mountains in northern Morocco. Jajouka isn't on any map, and many of its legends originated with foreigners like myself who have managed to visit the remote and hidden area.

But the Master Musicians of Jajouka, of the hill tribe Ahl Sherif, have their own stories preserved in the folklore of their clans. At night, around glowing braziers, the people of the Ahl Sherif—"The Saintly"—tell their children how Bou Jeloud came down the mountain to dance with them and bless their village.

They tell of their ancestor, Attar, whose forefathers had come from the East to conquer and settle these wild Berber mountains. Like his cousins and uncles, Attar was a goatherd who prospered amidst Jajouka's highland pastures and abundant water. One day, while grazing his flocks on the side of Owl Mountain, his lead goat wandered into a forest cave. People usually stayed out of caves, since they were entrances to the underworld realm of the Djinn, but Attar was a new kind of man. He was unafraid. Inside the cave, he was astonished to find a passage leading to lush grass, rippling springs, and azure pools. Soon the rest of the flock entered the cave and began to graze on grass as green as emeralds. Feeling fatigued, Attar lay on a tuft of moss and fell into a deep sleep. When he awoke, there was an unfamiliar sound. It was like the wind in the trees, but Attar could feel no wind. It was like rain, but the sky was clear. It was like a river, but the hills were dry. Attar knew only that it was the most beautiful sound he had ever heard.

It was music.

Evening came. Attar gathered his flocks and went home. The next day he returned to the cave, to listen to the sound that no one else had ever known. Attar spent almost all his time at the cave, which he kept secret until his goats became impossibly sleek and fat, and his own face shone with radiance. The other villagers began to ask if he was bewitched. (You know how small towns are.)

Attar could keep the secret no longer; he told the elders of the Ahl Sherif about the cave. They were aghast at what they considered blasphemy, and forbade Attar to reenter the cave.

But he could not stay away.

One afternoon, as his goats fed contentedly, Attar fell into his usual sleep. He awoke in a panic. Before him stood a huge, horrible thing—half man, half goat. Attar was terrified and tried to run, but the beast stopped him.

I am Bou Jeloud, the creature said. *Father of Flocks. Master of Skins.* Attar, shaking like a petal, was soothed when the creature produced a bamboo stick with holes in it and began to play the music that Attar loved with all his heart. Bou Jeloud handed the flute to Attar, who couldn't make it work. This made Bou Jeloud very happy. He made Attar swear to tell no one of their meeting before allowing him to leave in safety.

Attar came every day to Bou Jeloud's cave until, little by little, he learned to play the flute. One evening after his lesson, Attar asked if Bou Jeloud had a wife. No, the creature replied sadly. So Attar offered a trade. "I will find you the prettiest black-eyed girl in Jajouka," Attar proposed, "if you give me your flute."

Done, said Bou Jeloud.

Attar returned to the village and played the flute for his people. They were ecstatic! Give us your flute, they pleaded, and we will make new ones so we can all play together. Attar gave them the flute, and the secret was out like sparks in the wind.

From that day forth, the Ahl Sherif played their flutes in the evenings when they returned from pasture and field. Their music became so beautiful and strong that the breezes carried it up Owl Mountain and into Bou Jeloud's cave.

Bou Jeloud became restless and excited, and very angry, when he realized that Attar had betrayed him. One night he could stand the music no longer and rushed down to Jajouka to force Attar to give him his wife. But Bou Jeloud was a rustic, a bumpkin who knew nothing of humans and their towns. He hesitated on the upper outskirts of the village, not knowing where to go. His rank scent panicked the village goats in their blue cactus pens. Then the dogs caught whiff of him: their howling confused Bou Jeloud even more, and he ran amok, destroying pens and killing animals, looking for his wife.

Jajouka erupted in fear and panic. The music stopped. Women and girls screamed as the beast dashed amongst them. Attar was hiding in his house when Bou Jeloud broke down the door and seized him.

"Wait, Master!" begged Attar. "The music you hear? It is for your wedding tomorrow!!"

Bou Jeloud demanded his wife immediately.

"She is being prepared for you, Master, if only you return tomorrow for the wedding."

Bou Jeloud knew nothing of the wiles of people, and he believed Attar. The next evening, when he heard the music, he danced down the mountain and entered Jajouka for what he thought was his

6   wedding. He danced before the musicians, whipping them with flails to produce the wildest music. When they were exhausted, Bou Jeloud danced with the women as they sang for him and played their drums. To placate Bou Jeloud, Attar convinced a toothless hag named Aisha Hamoka to dance with Bou Jeloud as if she were his bride. But Crazy Aisha was crafty, and always managed to elude the creature's grasp.

At last, after a night of wild dancing, unable to carry off his bride, Bou Jeloud was exhausted. He left Jajouka, promising to return another day. Before he left, he named the villagers the caretakers of his music, bestowing upon them his powerful *baraka,* his blessing.

Through the centuries, Bou Jeloud danced in Jajouka one night every year, during the time of the Great Feast when the moon shone full over the mountains. Jajouka's herds thrived, the fields were fertile, and the women bore the musicians many children.

Some time later, Bou Jeloud disappeared from his cave, and Aisha Hamoka vanished from Jajouka. A distraught Attar took his flocks and set off to find them. Each week, to sustain himself, he would slaughter and eat one of the goats.

After years of searching, Attar had only four goats left. He could not return to Jajouka and live as before. Instead, he slaughtered and flayed his remaining animals and dressed himself in their skins. That evening, he entered Jajouka in this disguise. The joyous villagers believed that Bou Jeloud had returned to them and that the blessing would continue. That night, they played their music, and Attar danced amongst them as Bou Jeloud.

After that, Attar lived in Bou Jeloud's cave, coming down the mountain only when he heard his special music. Before his death at a very old age, Attar passed on the secret of his disguise to his sons. This tradition continued among the Ahl Sherif in Jajouka down through the generations, according to the Master Musicians. Some travelers who claim to have seen him dancing insist that Bou Jeloud survives into our present time.

.   .   .

BRIAN JONES, a name to conjure with, was the founder and essence of the Rolling Stones. He was the flower of his generation of English *artistes*, at least until his considerable decline and murder. In the early years of the Stones, say 1963 to 1966, it was Brian at whom the girls came to scream.

If Brian Jones had merely been a teen idol and pop godling, his saga would be of little interest. But Lewis Brian Jones, born 1942 in Cheltenham, is also remembered as an important sonic artist and composer. Although his name does not appear on song credits of the period, his brilliant palette vividly colors the Stones' best music. Think of the marimba lick on "Under My Thumb"; the dulcimer on "Lady Jane"; the flute on "Ruby Tuesday"; the dangerous sitar on "Paint It Black." Bells like chimes at midnight. Wailing saxophone. Stride piano. Slide guitar à la Elmore James on "Little Red Rooster." Brian Jones rolled the bones. He could play rings around everyone else, and was a genius in the grand atelier of the sixties—the recording studio.

In 1968, a year before his death, Brian Jones visited Morocco and recorded some tapes of native songs in an obscure place called Jajouka.

"Pan the goat god is still dancing up there," a voice had whispered seductively in Jones's ear. *"You must see it and hear the music."* Brian Jones was listening now. *"It's a tribe of musicians . . . priests of Pan . . . smoke kif all day, music all night, dancing boys . . ."*

This was all he needed to hear: he was bored to death with the Rolling Stones.

"I can take you up their mountain to see them," the voice whispered to Jones. It belonged to Brion Gysin, an artist who lived in Tangier. And Gysin was *quite* insistent about it.

"It's important for you to be turned on to this music," Brion Gysin said to Brian Jones. *"I mean, my dear, it will change your life. It changed mine. It changes everyone who comes into contact with it. It's a trip and a half. Take my word for it. We can go anytime, whenever you're ready. I'm here to go. Say the word. Let me take you there."*

chapter 1

Thirty-five Djellabas for Jajouka

The Pan American 747 landed at Casablanca in a grey dawn mist, and I felt a spiritual jolt when my feet touched Africa for the first time, as if I'd been plugged into some ineffable continental juju. It was late December 1973, and I had managed to persuade *National Geographic* magazine to send me to Morocco to report on an obscure tribe whose Arcadian rites and rituals were said to be in danger of extinction. Walking away from the steaming jet, I saw a crowd of Moroccans on the terminal's observation deck. All wore *djellabas,* ankle-length woolen robes with pointed hoods drawn up against the morning chill. "They look like monks," observed Morgan, the photographer the *Geographic* had assigned to the story. So began our journey back in time.

Inside the terminal all was hijack, bomb threat, police state security. We gaped in disgust as helmeted gendarmes performed a lewd public search of an American hippie girl, which stopped when

10   we intervened. I noticed the customs police looking at Morgan's aluminum camera cases with lurid visions of massive bribes. But they were deeply disappointed when Morgan flashed a heavily berib-boned credential explaining that we were on "official assignment" for the National Geographic Society, and their sergeant let us through without inspection. (These impressive-looking papers al-most never failed, and were affectionately known as "dago-dazzlers" back in Washington.)

Exhausted from the night flight, we sipped inky cups of espresso before boarding a Royal Air Maroc Caravelle jet to Tangier, thirty minutes up the Atlantic coast. The old port city soon appeared under the portholes of the descending jet, in which we were the only passengers, as a vivid cluster of white buildings clinging to a steep hillside overlooking one of the most dramatic landscapes in the world—Tangier Bay, the Strait of Gibraltar, and the massive wall of the Rif crashing in headlands to the wine-dark Mediterranean Sea, along the very shoulder of Africa itself.

Tangier airport was narcoleptic at nine on a Sunday morning. We loaded into an old metal-flake Ford taxi that roared down the airport road, scattering peasants and their flocks and blanket-wrapped mountain women carrying heavy baskets on their heads. We careened through city streets to the Hotel El Minzeh, where liveried fez-wearing doormen ushered us and our luggage into the hushed vestibule of the former sultanic palace. Jet-lagged, Morgan went to his room to sleep. I was too excited to rest and presently left to explore the ancient town. The Boulevard Pasteur was the main avenue of the newer, European quarter. Just off the café-lined street, I stood on a broad terrace bristling with old cannon and gazed at the high jagged sierra of Spain that towered in the distance across the strait. Since the days of Delacroix, of Matisse, Tangier has been the place where Western artists intersected with the Muslim world. Could I possibly hope to comprehend this world in the three months the *Geographic* had allotted for my research? Lined with late-nineteenth-century Spanish provincial architecture, the boulevard turned right at the Place de France, past the French legation and the Café Paris, and descended past the El Minzeh to the great public square and bus terminal, the Socco Grande, which divides European Tangier from the ancient warren of the Moorish *medina* and port. Gagging on black fumes spewing from dusty grey autobuses, jostling with wizened peasants on their way to and from market, I kept walking downhill through the streets and alleys of the medina. Soon I was lost and overwhelmed by the data my senses were transmitting—the smell of untanned leather, brass, urine, cumin; the sight of mysterious figures in djellabas with hoods pulled down over their eyes; the sound of the *muezzin*'s call to prayer from a forbidding, green-doored mosque.

Disoriented and fighting malaise, I stumbled down to the modern port, full of tourists and hotels, taxis and professional hustlers who targeted me in an instant and proceeded to vie for the honor of showing me the market and selling me hashish. "Hey," I said to one, "not so close, not so fast," and shoved him a little. He shoved me back, much harder. We looked at each other. "Fuck your mother," he said in English. "I can get mucho crazier than you." In his red eye was murder and bloodshed, and I believed him. I jumped into a little green mini-cab, which took me up the steep hill, back to the hotel, where I collapsed into the arms of Morpheus.

Many hours later, I woke up with no idea where I was. Then I focused on the persistent knocking at my door. When I opened it, Joel Fischer came into my room, pale and unsteady, almost in shock.

I HAD MET JOEL in New York a week before. He came to my flat carrying slides he'd taken and audio tapes he'd made in Jajouka earlier in the year, when Ornette Coleman had recorded there. Joel was about a year older than me, maybe twenty-six. He had lived on the Balearic Island of Ibiza during the late sixties, where he sold sandals and other leather goods to the German kids who used the island as their connection to heroin in the sun. He was fluent in Spanish and Arabic, and extremely eager to get back to Jajouka.

"When I was there with Ornette," he said, "he was making the Jajouka Masters do all sorts of strange things to their music, like playing in weird instrumental combinations, things they normally would never do, but did in this case because someone was paying them—or at least paying Hamsa, who said he was their manager. After Ornette left the village, I could see the musicians were still buzzing, and I stuck around for a few days and kept my Nagra recorder running at night. I got some great tapes of music they were making in the wake of Ornette's crazy experimental stuff, as if they were now playing it the *right* way, to reprogram their system. Now I want to go back, play the tapes for them, and then try to get a record deal. See you next week in Morocco."

NOW, STANDING IN my room, Joel Fischer looked so pale that I thought he needed a medicinal drink. I took a pint of non-*Geographic* issue Rémy-Martin from my valise and offered it to him. "Thanks, no," he said and sat down at the desk. From a plastic film canister he produced a fresh chunk of hash, took out a pocket knife, and whittled off some shavings, which he rolled with tobacco from a Kebir cigarette into a joint. After a few hits, he was ready to tell his story:

"I'm crazed," he said. "I feel like I've been assaulted. It was surreal, almost. Look, I've been traveling up to Jajouka for two years now and thought I'd gotten into a routine. You arrive in Tangier, and check in with Hamsa at his house here in town before you go up to the village. And that's what I tried to do this morning.

"I've always considered myself more a friend of Jajouka than of Hamsa," he continued. "The musicians are mostly sweet, simple country people; next to them Hamsa, with his booze and his foreign clients, tends to look slimy. Maybe Hamsa picked up on my feelings, because when he opened his door and saw me, not an hour ago, he let out a ferocious yell, grabbed my lapels, and dragged me inside. I could see right away that something was wrong. The place was in disarray. His French wife Simone was slumped in a corner. Their young daughter was crying, and Hamsa had worked himself into a rage. Have you met him? Well, he's a brute of a man: short, dark, incredibly strong. A tough little minotaur.

"As I stood there, he stormed around screaming at me about those 'sons of bitches up in Jajouka,' and about how they owed everything to him, and about some kid stabbing him, and that he was going to show them what their lives would be like without Ahmed Hamsa. Then he stopped for a moment and looked at me hard. He had been shouting and was foaming at the mouth. My own Arabic could barely keep pace with what he was saying. 'What are you doing here?' he says in English. 'What do you want from me? YOU WANT TO STEAL JAJOUKA!' And he grabs my jacket and starts to push me around the room. It began to hurt. I looked at the wife for some help, but she'd been terrorized. Hamsa had been drinking. I could smell the alcohol in the room. It was a horrible scene, so I pushed him away as best I could and made for the door. He jumped to block the door, but I got there first. As I ran through the hall down the stairs I could hear him screaming curses behind me. I felt really bad for his wife, who never seemed like a bad sort to me." He stopped and relit the dead joint.

"Well," I said, "what does all this mean?"

"Something *bad* has happened up in Jajouka," he said. "I don't know what it is, but I guess we'll find out when we get there."

THERE WAS A KNOCK at the door. Ace *National Geographic* contract photographer Morgan Robbins entered and smiled at the scent of the joint, which he took from Joel. I introduced them and dropped a Coltrane tape into the *Geographic*'s Sony TC-224. We smoked in silence as "Giant Steps" played and we pondered our mission.

That evening we dined in the Minzeh's tiled restaurant on an

14   enormous *tagine,* a platter of stewed chicken and vegetables piled on couscous. Joel went over his ordeal with Hamsa for Morgan, who was worried that our access to Jajouka might now be impaired.

"I wouldn't be too concerned," Joel assured. "The Masters probably need you right now more than you need them. I promise they'll be happy to see us. It's all a question of *baraka.* Do you know what that is?" When the photographer said no, Joel went on. "Baraka literally means 'blessing.' In Morocco baraka is something that exists, something that can be bestowed or lost. Baraka is very serious business here, because if you have it, you're okay. If you don't have it, you're considered worthless, and despised. How do you get baraka? You can be born with it, especially if you're related to the *Sherifs,* the local saintly families that claim descent from the Prophet. The king of Morocco"—Joel indicated the unsmiling photo of Hassan II that hung on the restaurant wall—"has the most baraka of all, since he's a direct descendant of Mohammed. Or you can absorb baraka, which is why people in Morocco make pilgrimages to the shrines of local saints. By praying to the saint, they seek intercession and blessing the same way Christians do when they visit Lourdes or any holy place. The tribe that lives in Jajouka and its environs is called Ahl Sherif—'The Saintly.' The village guards the shrine of a powerful saint named Sidi Hamid Sherq, and people from all over Morocco visit his tomb to pray and receive his blessing. For hundreds of years the Jajouka musicians played music for pilgrims on Friday mornings—the Muslim sabbath—and on feast days. The musicians have old royal decrees granting them the right to collect tithes on the crops and livestock of the Djebel, but some are resentful of this ancient tradition. Now it's, 'Those Jajoukans don't do anything but sit on their mountain, smoke kif, and play their music. Why should we tithe to these hippies?'

"Then, five years ago, Hamsa and his buddy Brion Gysin bring Brian Jones of the Rolling Stones up the mountain. Jones made a record of their music, and suddenly Jajouka was famous. Then a cult grew around the recording, and foreigners started appearing at the bottom of the mountain, wondering how to get to the top. They all wanted to smoke kif, which is extremely illegal in Morocco even though everyone smokes. Pretty soon, the locals started getting jealous of Jajouka. They see Hamsa importing foreigners and whiskey to Jajouka. Word gets around that there's drinking and girls dancing up in the village. People naturally figure that if blasphemous stuff is going on, Jajouka will lose its baraka.

"And I've gotta say, that's what it felt like on my last two visits. Hamsa and his friends are drinking, and Hamsa is ordering the Master Musicians around like they're his servants. I could tell the Masters were unhappy—they're very proud, very conscious of their Arabness in a conquered Berber land, and don't like to take orders from anyone. Sidi Hamid Sherq is revered because he introduced Islam to the valley in the first place.

"Meanwhile Hamsa is sucking the baraka out of Jajouka like a cancer. The more I think about it, the less I'm surprised there's a tribal feud up there."

We adjourned to my suite. Joel rolled another bomber. I put on Coltrane and we unwound. "See you in the morning," he said as he left for his hotel. "We'll go to Jajouka and see what in hell is going on."

ON THE MORNING OF the last day of the year, I met Joel Fischer for *café con leche* on the terrace of the Gran Café Paris. He brought a bag of croissants, which we devoured as Benz taxis polluted the clear and sunny winter air. For the holiday, the streets had been festooned with strings of lights and pictures of the king, who stared like Big Brother from every lamppost. I wanted to rent a villa in the suburbs of Tangier, a place where we could recover in privacy from life in the mountains, which I anticipated would be rigorous. The Minzeh's concierge directed us to a little office around the corner that housed Anglo-American Properties Ltd., a real estate firm operated by a very pink Englishman, Mr. Aspinall.

He drove us up the Djemaa el Mokhra, the fashionable Old Mountain that overlooks the city, parked his Renault, and herded us through a shrubbery-covered garden gate into the front door of a stucco villa from the 1920s. "It belongs to Lord Ravenscourt, Tory MP from Hampshire. It has three bedrooms, an empty pool, a living-room fireplace that doesn't work, and a caretaker named Mohammed who lives downstairs. And a woman comes in daily. The name of the house is Villa Elizabeth. Yes, the telephone works most of the time. The rent is a hundred and fifty pounds a month."

I walked through French doors onto a sunny terrace surrounded by carefully tended vegetation. I could see other villas on the mountain but could not hear a sound. It felt peaceful, quiet, safe.

"Hey, look up here!" It was Joel, calling from the roof. Up a narrow whitewashed flight of stairs was a little platform equipped with grass mats and wide-brimmed straw hats that hinted this was a place for tanning. The view was panoramic, and I told Mr. Aspinall we would take it.

After lunch we tried to rent a Land Rover, a difficult task on New Year's Eve. One rental agent told us we'd have to go to Gibraltar to get one. Another said he had one, and to meet him in the coffeehouse on the Rue Fez after the siesta that shuts down Tangier in the afternoon. But he didn't show up. The photographer looked glum, and Joel tried to cheer him up. "Look man, Tangier has been here for five thousand years, and *nobody's* in a hurry. Things happen here very, very slowly. You feel like moving around in a dream. You want something, but you can't have it because a shop is closed for siesta or the owner has gone to the mosque to pray. But if you're patient, Tangier usually manages to provide. Let's go have dinner and we'll try Hertz tomorrow. They won't have any Land Rovers, but they'll have something that'll get us to Jajouka."

NEW YEAR'S EVE in Tangier. The solar year 1973 was ending in a blare of car horns and the din of twenty thousand Tangerines teeming on the brightly lit Boulevard Pasteur. God knows what was happening down in the medina, but uptown the throngs of celebrants screamed and called to one another. Young men promenaded down the street hand in hand, kissing each other in greeting. Normally shy young women, having left their veils at home, paraded in platform shoes and heavy makeup, but instinctively covered their faces with their hands when one of the handsome Euro-style Moroccans looked them in the eye. They walked in groups for protection, which was necessary because most of them are stunning, all almond-shaped, kohl-rimmed eyes and flashing white teeth under garish, painted red lips. As Morgan and I walked the streets, we came upon a huge throng of men dancing and singing in the Place de France. All were wearing traditional clothes, djellaba and fez, and chanting orgasmically over some object in the center of the circle, their voices rising and falling in an almost sexual rhythm. They were blocking traffic and their song was accompanied by honking Peugeots, squeaking Simcas, and four-toned Benz blasts—a thousand cars bleating at once. It was bedlam, and I felt a moment of panic. Urchins, beggars, and hustlers importuned us at every turn. The din became louder as the Moroccans really worked themselves up. We were jostled and shoved by maddened swirling crowds until I felt caught in a dangerous riptide of humanity. Over my shoulder I saw a familiar lamp-lit doorway, and Joel Fischer reached into the mob and pulled us into the Minzeh. In the hotel's nightclub, a lounge singer named Bob Destiny crooned in 1974, which we celebrated with several bottles of Valpierre Blanc Sec and a couple of Joel's hash joints.

Later, alone in my room, I was writing some notes and listening to Miles play "Pan Piper" when I felt a sub-audible frequency in the middle of my head. I turned off the tape: in a second the frequency turned into sound, then into music. Somewhere, far beyond my shuttered hotel window, someone was playing a *rhaita*. I leaned out the window to catch the wild bagpipe sound, but the wind had changed. It was gone. In that instant all the fatigue and jet lag seemed to clot my blood. I trembled violently for a moment, understanding that I'd come a long way in pursuit of something perhaps frighteningly beyond my ignorant grasp. What did I know about Roman gods and Muslim saints, Rolling Stones and Moroccan tribes? Was I—a minute particle hunched on the shoulder of Africa—even worthy to seek the old mysteries of Jajouka? It was a question whose probable answer really scared me.

ON THE FIRST MORNING of the year I walked down the Boulevard Pasteur and fetched Joel Fischer at his *pensión,* the Villa Mouneriya, a local literary landmark where William Burroughs had written the early drafts of *Naked Lunch.* "I was over at Hertz an hour ago," Joel said, "and it looks like they may have something for us." We walked back up to the boulevard just as Tangier's synagogue was letting out its Saturday morning congregation.

"The Jews of Tangier are an old community," Joel said. "They were expelled from Spain in 1492, along with the Muslims, and the two peoples have lived here ever since, at least until Israel became a state. In 1948, mindful of what had happened to the Jews of Europe, the wealthier Sephardic Jews here in Morocco gathered the poor from their ghettoes—there were even tribes of nomadic Jews living in tents down in the Sahara—and shipped them wholesale to Israel, en masse. Quite a few stayed behind, protected by the king. His father, the old sultan Mohammed V, was said to be *quite* fond of the Jews."

We jumped into one of the green mini-cabs that plied the upper city and got out at the Hertz office on the Place d'Espagne. The proprietor, Madame Cohen, leased us an almost-new Volkswagen bus. "Don't worry," Joel whispered when I fretted that the notoriously underpowered bus might not make it up Jajouka's mountain road. "I've driven up the mountain in a *lot* less."

I went out to inspect the bus, and when I returned Joel was quizzing Madame Cohen on life in an Arab nation technically at war with Israel. (The fighting of the big war of October 1973 was over, but Moroccan troops were still deployed on the·Syrian side of the cease-fire line.) The middle-aged, businesslike Madame Cohen looked at us carefully before answering. "It's not bad yet," she said. "Life has been very nice here."

"Do you ever think of leaving?" I asked.

"Of course," she answered as she prepared the insurance forms. "Everyone does. I myself would go to Canada where our children live, but my husband says it's too late for us to leave."

Joel remarked that he'd heard that the king had ordered special protection for Morocco's Jewish community during the height of the war.

"The king . . . Ah, look at it like this: When those who oppose the king want to rile the people up and get them excited, they always blame the Jews first. It's always the same. Now sign here. And here. And your initials there. Thank you very much. Please be careful with the bus, and bring it back in three months. *Bonne chance.*"

LATE THAT SAME EVENING I was packing my gear when Joel urgently knocked on my door. He had been running and was breathless. "Get dressed," he panted, "and hurry. There's something you'll want to see." Soon I was half-running behind him through shuttered medina streets before he turned into a winding covered passage that gave onto a hidden square and Achmed's Café. Incredible music poured out like honey. We found an empty table in the back, bathed in ghastly fluorescent light. But the music was sublime. An *oud* player and a fiddler sat among a half-dozen drummers and singers, who passed pipes of kif to each other as they sang chorus upon chorus of a beautiful, mournful song whose melody flowed like an old Moorish river. "They're singing *Andaluz,*" Joel said. "I ran back to get you because this music rarely gets played in public anymore. It's from the courts of the caliphs of Islamic Spain—Granada,

20   Córdoba, Seville. After 1492, the music migrated to North Africa, where it now survives only in the cities of northern Morocco—here in Tangier, in Tetuan, and Fez. It's incredible! Listen to that!''

The music *was* glorious, violins and banjos, the lost classical modes of vanished medieval Andalusia. The vocals were call-and-response, with the elderly lead singer answered by a passionate chorus of men who chanted with their eyes closed, transported somewhere else. They sang for an hour, until the lead singer came back to earth, focused his eyes on Joel and me sitting in the back of the café, and signaled the oud player to cool it. The sumptuous melody faded into coughing and the tinkling of tea glasses as the musicians sat back with their kif pipes. Two teenagers dressed in the white gowns and the cowrie-adorned red hats of Gnaoua musicians from the desert entered the café and began a horrible racket with brass clappers. ''These kids are fake,'' Joel said. ''Strictly tourist stuff.'' Nevertheless, the old Andaluz singer dug into his pocket with a bemused smile and gave the boys some coins. They kissed his hand and left. A deaf-mute came to our table and began to draw in the air with his eloquent hands, trying to sell us kif.

The old singer wrapped himself in his djellaba; music was finished for the night. Outside I almost stumbled into a girl and a youth leaning into each other in the shadows. I could hear him passionately whispering to her. Both were dressed in black, and their faces were invisible. Suddenly the girl let out a short, sharp cry. The youth hissed at her and she shied away like a spooked pony. He aimed a vicious kick, which glanced off her leg, and she disappeared into a door in the wall. Then he looked at me, the evil spirit of Tango in his pockmarked tomcat face. Glad for my companions, I walked with them fast uphill through the deserted streets.

Early the next morning, Joel brought our bus round to the front of the Minzeh, where the doormen helped Morgan load his twenty metal cases. I paid our bill, tipped everyone in sight, and was about to climb into the bus when Joel quietly said, ''Don't look now, but here comes Hamsa!''

Cruising down the Rue de Liberté like a powerful shark, Ahmed Hamsa appeared in a blue blazer, smiling, with a crazed gleam in his eye. He stopped at the open gate of the bus and inspected the gear and Morgan and me, like an undertaker mentally making notes for our coffins. "Ha!" he laughed, without mirth. "You are going to Jajouka today?"

"Yes, Hamsa," Joel said.

"*Mabruq,*" he said, wishing us good luck, his hand resting on the door of the bus. He paused, as if waiting for something, before disappearing into the crowded street. We drove a hundred yards to the Socco Grande, where Joel parked the bus, gave a coin to an old parking warden to watch our things, and trooped Morgan and me into a doorway under a sign that advertised PRACTICANTE.

"Last time I was in Jajouka, I heard about some hepatitis," he said, "so I'm treating us all to a shot of gamma globulin." We waited while the old Spanish woman who called herself a practical nurse filled three enormous glass syringes with amber fluid. When it was my turn, I dropped my pants and gazed at the picture of a bleeding Christ on the wall as the crone gave me an injection. It hurt going in, and I was sore for the following week.

Next we stopped at the Fez market and bought provisions—vegetables, coffee, pastries, various kinds of teas. Finally, the bus filled to its ceiling, we drove down the boulevard and on out of town. There were few cars on the road as we headed south along the coast, but everywhere shepherds were walking huge flocks toward Tangier. Sometimes the road looked more like a woolly river than Morocco's main north-south highway, and more than once we had to stop while dun-colored herdsmen shooed their animals out of our way. In the back, photographer Morgan was snapping away furiously; a smiling man with a beard and a straw hat noticed him and drew his finger along his neck in a cut-throat motion. "What does he mean?" Morgan asked. "Is he mad because I'm shooting pictures?"

Joel laughed. "He's referring to the sheep. He's taking them to

22 town where they'll be slaughtered when *Aid el Kebir* starts in a day or two.''

"Tell me about it. This is my first assignment in a Muslim country.''

"Well, let's see. Aid el Kebir means 'The Great Feast,' and it's the principal holiday on the Muslim calender. The feast commemorates the prophet Abraham's willingness to sacrifice his son to the glory of Jehovah, who was for once kind enough to stop the killing just as Abraham raised his knife. To mark the Aid el Kebir, Muslims all over the world slaughter a ram as a symbol of Abraham's devotion. It's also a time of pilgrimage, what the Islamic world calls the *hajj*. Every Muslim should go to Mecca once in his life, ideally during this feast. If you can't make it to Mecca, a local religious pilgrimage will suffice, which is why Jajouka is usually jumping at this time of the year. People make their hajj to honor Jajouka's saint. Villagers who have left for the cities or the factories of Europe also come home for the Aid el Kebir. And of course this is when Bou Jeloud does his thing.''

"Which is?'' Morgan prompted.

"Which is to dance around a bonfire all night, cast away the evil vibes that have accumulated during the year, and get the local girls ready to bear strong children.''

"Sounds like fun,'' the photographer commented, dryly.

"It is,'' Joel said as he accelerated down the now open and empty road. "That is, if you have the stamina to keep up with him.''

For the next hour we drove along the broad Atlantic beach road, crossing estuaries and tidal basins on long bridges. We passed the large town of Asilah, which Joel remarked had a reputation for discouraging Christians from living there. Then the road turned inland and ran through rolling hills of black earth plowed for spring planting. Joel said that this part of Morocco was known to agronomists for the high quality of its topsoil, which was said to extend an extraordinary ten feet into the ground. Following produce trucks belching inky black soot, we crossed a broad tidal river, the Oued

Loukos, before heading into Larache, a seaside fishing port that had been fortified by the Portuguese five centuries ago. Here the road again turned inland toward the ancient Moorish city of Ksar el Kebir. Morgan remarked that he'd traveled all over the Third World on *National Geographic* assignments, and that this two-lane highway was uncommonly well maintained.

"There's a reason for that," Joel said. "The king is very nervous about his safety. Only last year, he was flying back to Morocco from France when his plane was attacked by Moroccan air force jets. It took some hits, but the king, who's a pilot himself, took the controls and radioed the attacking jets that he'd been killed and begged to be allowed to land. There've been other attempts on him but oh God, the heads rolled after *that* one. But this is why the roads are so well maintained: The king no longer relishes flying over Morocco. Now he drives everywhere in armed convoys. They say he usually drives himself, and that's why the roads are so good."

"Who wants to kill him?" I asked.

"I'm not sure. Certainly there are Moroccan nationalists around who never wanted the monarchy to survive after Morocco became independent from France and Spain in 1956. There are probably people in the army who sympathize with Colonel Qaddafi, who threw out the king in Libya. There are also Muslim elements that don't appreciate Hassan's former reputation as a playboy on the French Riviera, and the way he's tried to modernize Morocco. All I know is that if the king has to get from Casablanca to Marrakech, he drives. If he wants to get from Meknes to Fez, he goes by car."

IN KSAR EL KEBIR, which looked to me like a dusty adobe town in New Mexico, Joel parked by the produce market. It had started to rain. "We'll stop here and get some fish, which is a treat up in the hills. And it looks like we could use some mud boots as well." We haggled in the market for three pairs of cheap Wellingtons, found ten kilos of fresh sardines, and picked up a half-dozen chickens.

24 Tired from the drive, we sat in a café under an arcade and drank mint tea until the continuing downpour sent us back on the road. Instead of continuing south on the main route, we turned northeast onto a gravel road marked TATOFT. "That's where the *caid* lives," Joel explained. "He's the king's representative for the area we're entering, the Djebala, or 'Little Hills' as they're called. He's like a tribal chief, a judge, a Big Man, and a real son of a bitch if he's the same one they had earlier in the year.

"See that mountain over there, at the end of the road?" Joel asked. "If you look about halfway up, you can just make out the village." I saw nothing but a massive green mountain looming before us in the rain, its summit obscured by grey clouds. Joel deftly rolled a joint with one hand in his lap, and drove on.

At Tatoft we turned into the caid's compound, guarded by soldiers in berets and olive-colored wool fatigues. The place was quiet under its dripping acacia trees; one of the soldiers told us the caid was away and to return later. So we drove on through an empty market area and onto a rutted dirt road that ran upward into the hills. The rain filled the deep ruts with mud, and it took an hour to go five miles.

Joel shouted as we rounded a bend and the road began a steep incline, "Up there! Jajouka!" Midway up the mountain, perched on an escarpment that jutted from its slopes, I could see a tin-roofed, white-walled village of low buildings whose metal caps glistened in the rain, surrounded by walls of giant blue-green cactus that, from a distance, obscured all but the tops of the houses. Joel veered onto an unmarked track of sharply pointed stones. "Follow the yellow brick road," he called as he struggled with the wheel. "*This* is the way to the village?" I gasped. "I *never* would have found it."

"Most people who come here don't," he said. "They miss the turn, because you gotta know where it is. There aren't any signs pointing to Jajouka because they don't want any unexpected visitors up there."

Our bus began to lurch and shake ominously as it rounded a

hairpin turn, its suspension sorely tested by the jagged track that was rising at an improbably steep angle toward the village high above. Suddenly an aluminum light case crashed to the deck, followed by the box carrying Morgan's lenses. "Holy shit!" he screamed. "Are we gonna make it in this thing? I knew we should have gone to Gibraltar for the Rover!"

"No problem," Joel grunted, as he slammed down to first and began to climb. The engine in the back of the bus whined like an animal in pain, and in ten minutes the conical hills receded beneath us as we ascended above the valley of the Ahl Sherif. Once we lost traction on the rain-slicked paving stones and skidded toward oblivion. Joel went white, but held on. I lit a cigarette for the first time in my life. Half an hour later, to alleviate some of the weight, Morgan and I got out of the bus and walked until we reached the outskirts of town, consisting of a few tumbledown rustic huts and the whitewashed graves of lesser saints under a grove of gnarled and weathered oaks. At that point, the track disappeared into a goat path amid giant boulders. We had reached the plateau of the village and were once again on level ground, so we rejoined Joel in the bus for the ride into Jajouka.

Soon we came upon a wide plaza surrounded by large blue-washed houses. Jajouka was larger than I had expected. From under a wooden awning, where they had been sheltering from the rain, a young man and two boys dashed toward the car. Joel wound down his window, and they stuck their heads in the bus to kiss their old friend, and looked at Morgan and myself with big, welcoming smiles full of promise and hope. At that moment, I knew that everything was going to work out.

"ANOTHER HUNDRED YARDS and we'll be there," Joel said with an elation I hadn't heard from him before. Clearly he was as thrilled to be here as I was.

"Where's 'there'?" Morgan asked.

"The *madrassah*," he replied. "The clubhouse where they train their sons, cook, hang out. Brion Gysin built it for them about fifteen years ago."

"Is that where we'll be staying?"

"You got it. Don't worry, they'll see to it that you're comfortable while you're here."

"I'm not worried," the photographer said. "In fact, I think I'm going to like this place."

Joel headed the bus out of the plaza and farther up the hill. More djellaba-clad figures appeared from houses to wave and call to us. Above the plaza was a huge open area where a wet soccer game was in progress in front of a tiny modern building made of green corrugated plastic. "That's the little government school where the village children are taught," Joel said. "And look, that's the madrassah." It was a long adobe house with a tin roof, flying the Moroccan flag, surrounded by a low fieldstone wall. As we approached, the house came alive: robed men rose from the porch and surrounded the bus. Others converged from points throughout the village, which seemed to be divided into upper and lower neighborhoods.

As we drove through the narrow gate, rough hands flung the bus doors open. Our cheeks were smothered by grizzled kisses from men in their fifties and boys in their teens. There were perhaps two dozen Master Musicians milling about, unloading our gear and passing it hand over hand into the house, being introduced so quickly that I couldn't get *any* of their names. Then they almost carried us into the main chamber, whose floor was below ground level. Despite the rain and wind outside, the room was warm and cozy, protected from the elements by thick blue-washed walls. We were seated on low couches that lined the room's perimeter while glasses of hot mint tea materialized on a tray before us. I took a sip and almost went into a diabetic coma, so sugary was the amber fluid.

"That's country-style," Joel said. "Up in the mountains they like it sweet."

Morgan grimaced and whispered, "It's like sucking glucose!"

When our gear had been been loaded into one end of the room and the dictates of Moroccan hospitality had been fulfilled with a big plate of crispy eggs fried in green olive oil, we commenced negotiations with the Master Musicians. There were maybe twenty-five of them in one room. Three of the elder musicians did most of the speaking. The first was Jnuin, the chief. About sixty, he wore a golden turban to denote his rank and a heavy silver ring in the lobe of his left ear. Handsome, slender, kindly, intense-looking, he delivered a long discourse in Arabic that I couldn't follow, aided and abetted by his big deputy, Fudul, a rotund bear of a man. Like the rest of the senior musicians, Fudul wore a white turban wound around his shaved head, and he punctuated Jnuin's narrative with tough, sarcastic observations of his own. Seated next to them was the chief of the drummers, Berdouz. Tiny, like a pixie, like Fudul around fifty, he was darker than the other light-skinned Masters, and carried himself with authority. Occasionally he would interrupt the chief to offer an indignant observation.

"They're very upset," Joel told us. "They've just had a revolution up here. I'll tell you everything when they calm down."

While the chief continued his story, I had a chance to survey the Master Musicians' lair. The room, perhaps forty feet long, was carpeted in bright tribal rugs. The ceiling was painted in geometric patterns that reminded me of Amish hex signs. Drums and stringed instruments hung from pegs on the walls, along with framed photographs of Berdouz standing in front of a line of dancing boys from the village. In a place of honor on the rear wall hung a framed Rolling Stones Records publicity photo of Brian Jones, backlit, smiling eternally. A low table held two brass candlesticks, a copy of Bob Dylan's book, *Tarantula,* and a large ledger that I wanted to open, but of course didn't. Feeling the call of nature, I excused myself, slipping into my boots that had been left at the doorway, the custom in Morocco. A half-dozen boys and young men on the porch smiled at me shyly. They had been pressed against the door and windows, listening to the story their uncles had been telling us inside. A teenager, who introduced himself as Bashir, one of the chief's sons, took me around to the side of the madrassah and showed me the *hammam,* a little out-building with a hole in its concrete floor and a pail of water for flushing. My business done, I stepped back outside and surveyed the main building. It had four rooms in a line: the main room, a large bedroom to the right, a kitchen to the left, and another room lined with straw mats between the kitchen and the hammam. The madrassah was fronted by a covered porch or terrace, now crowded with white-turbaned musicians in brown homespun djellabas, curious about our arrival. They parted to let me through, murmuring *Salaam Aleikum* and *La bess* in greeting.

The room had become smoky in my absence. Joel and Morgan were pulling on long kif pipes and drinking mint tea. A distinguished-looking senior musician, Malim ("Master") Ali, came and sat next to me. He took a leather pouch called a *mutwi* and displayed an abundance of newly cut kif—two parts finely chopped marijuana blended with one part black tobacco, which he said was grown here in the village. A narrow leather case contained the two halves of Ali's *sebsi,* an eighteen-inch-long kif pipe joined by a gleaming brass rifle cartridge and tipped at the end by a small pink clay bowl. With an avuncular smile, Ali filled the bowl and lit it with a blue-tipped wax match. He sampled a puff and handed the pipe over to me with a soft *"B'saha."* Cheers. The smoke was harsh, delicious; I held it for a second, then coughed like a horse. Everyone laughed at this, and the kif made the laughter echo in my head like a tape loop. Suddenly I began to fly out of the top of my skull, and it took all my will to reel my astral self back in. *Better watch this stuff,* I thought, handing the pipe to Ali, who lit the expired coal and spat it into a ceramic ashtray designed for that purpose.

By now the Master Musicians of Jajouka were engaged in heavy intramural discussions. Morgan and I demanded that Joel translate for us. "It's quite a saga," he said, accepting another pipe from

Berdouz, who hovered solicitously as Joel related what they'd told him. "As I mentioned, they had a revolt up here," Joel said. "They threw Hamsa out of town about ten days ago, and he came back at night and stole all their formal djellabas."

"I think you better rewind for me," Morgan said.

"Well, they say that a few years ago, with some of the money he got from Brian Jones's album, Hamsa had a set of new djellabas made for the Masters. He really lorded it over these people, constantly reminding them who brought the rich foreigners to the village, who was responsible for their good fortune. He was like a manager who keeps telling his client, 'You'll never be anything without me.' Know what I mean? Now these are very *proud* people. They're a clan, the musicians. They all have the same last name— Attar. It means 'perfume maker.' It's a Sufi watchword and a deeply mystical name. Only an Attar, the son of a Master Musician, can be one of them, can be taught the music. Only an Attar can play at the tomb of Sidi Hamid Sherq. Hamsa's mother was an Attar, but she married outside the village, so Hamsa's one of them, but then again . . . There's always been resentment about this, heightened by the musicians' feeling that they were getting too little of the money Hamsa extorted from his guests. It was pretty basic manager-client stuff.

"Then, a couple weeks ago, there was a fight between one of Hamsa's sons and Bashir, the son of the chief."

I looked over at Jnuin, who smiled sweetly and tapped the ash of his cigarette.

"Hamsa intervened, and Bashir pulled a knife and threatened him. So Hamsa upped and left, and everyone thought, 'Yes, that's too bad, but at least now we'll be left in peace for a while.' Well, Hamsa came back in the middle of the night, used his key to the madrassah, and stole the djellabas that the musicians wore when they played, which turned up a few days later in the used djellaba market in Tangier."

I asked what all this meant.

30   "Well, the Masters are upset," Joel answered. "They're not sorry to see Hamsa go, but they're worried how they're going to pay for new djellabas. I mean, these were like their parade uniforms. They were beautiful—striped grey wool with very intricate embroidered piping along the seam that runs down the front. They wore them on Friday when they played for the saint. They wore them for weddings and other local events for which they're hired to supply music. If they played in Tangier or Tetuan or at the annual folk festival in Marrakech, they wore these things. I explained to them that you represent an important scientific society in America and you want to live among them and record their music and take photographs of their lives for a magazine. Jnuin said they'd be embarrassed to work with you right now because they don't have anything proper to wear when the photographs are taken. As you can imagine," Joel added, "Morgan's little black boxes—those cameras—are taken pretty seriously up here. Morgan, you've gotta be careful who you shoot, and when."

"Look, why don't we just buy them *new* djellabas?" suggested the photographer. "Is that a big deal? I mean, could we unclean infidels perform this service for these righteous Sufis or whatever they are?"

Speaking to the assembled Masters for the first time, I asked in French how many djellabas they needed. The musicians, whose number had increased in the past few minutes, put their heads together and calculated. After five minutes, Jnuin said, *"Trente-cinq,"* and went on a bit in Arabic.

"The chief says they need thirty-five djellabas," Joel translated. "There are twenty rhaita players, ten drummers, a couple of dancing boys, and someone might come home from the army and want to play with the band."

Morgan asked, "What's the bottom line on thirty-five djellabas?" Buzzing from the Masters, who came up with twelve thousand dirhams. "Let's see . . . eight dirhams to the dollar, so about fifteen hundred dollars. We can afford it, if we pool our expense advances."

We asked how long it would take, and there was much buzzing, disputation, and counting on fingers. I noticed that a gaunt old man with a great beak of a nose was now talking. "They say it would take about two months," Joel reported. "They want to buy the wool in one place, the thread in another, and use a tailor somewhere else. There'd be some traveling, that's for certain."

"Tell them," I said, "that with their permission we would be honored to help them buy new djellabas."

Joel again translated, which was met by more excited buzz. The crowd of younger musicians out on the porch went buzz-buzz too. Then they all broke into applause; their happiness wasn't just tangible, it was radiant. I looked from whiskered face to face and saw tension and strife momentarily vanish. They were all talking at once, shouting at us. The impish drummer Berdouz came over and kissed both my cheeks. He confronted me with his one working eye and said, in splendid *turista inglés,* "Berry gut! Yes! Eberryting outasight!"

Jnuin delivered a short discourse in which the word "baraka" was mentioned many times. "The chief says that your generosity will bring you and your family the baraka of Jajouka forever," Joel said. "He says that they will pray to Sidi Hamid Sherq and the saint will intercede for you for the rest of your life."

"Tell him," I replied, "that we wish nothing other than to be allowed to take some photographs and ask some questions while we are here. And that, if all goes to plan, our magazine will make them and their music and Sidi Hamid Sherq famous all over the world."

Joel translated, and the Master Musicians of Jajouka all uttered the same word in unison.

"Insh'Allah."

God willing.

SPIRITS RAN HIGH in the Masters' house. Berdouz took up his bass drum as Fudul grabbed a primitive oud and began to tune up. A young man, extremely handsome, slid quietly into the room and

32 began to unpack an old violin. "That's Tahir," Joel explained. "He's the lead singer and local superstar around here." As Tahir began to play, bowing a fiddle held vertically in his lap, another old man began to sing in a penetrating soprano voice, like an old bluegrass singer. As he wailed, he played a large flat circular drum, developing an astounding backbeat within seconds. I started to twitch, involuntarily. Other musicians sat down, clapped in time. Suddenly Berdouz put down the drum and stood up, the beat never faltering as another, younger musician raced in from the porch and took up the drum. Berdouz shed his short djellaba, came over to us, and bowed deeply, a broad grin creasing his features. Then he began to dance. He was about fifty, but was soon moving so quickly that his steps were hard to follow; his feet were a blur. From the old singer came a shrill, exultant cry: *"Eeeeeeewwaaa!"* As the dance rhythm approached its climax, Berdouz seized his bass drum and began to whirl with it, ecstatically. "Outasight," he called to us. "Eberryting!"

A bustle outside the door, and the music stopped on five short strokes. Big round metal tables were set up on low tripods. Young men brought in kettles and towels and washed our hands. Steaming rounds of fresh bread, sixteen inches in diameter, were followed by heavy enamel dishes full of stewed chicken, vegetables, and spices. Famished, we ate like wolves. Morgan wished he'd brought a fork.

"Up here you eat with your right hand and a piece of bread," Joel said. "When you eat with these guys, it's important to remember to keep your left hand out of the dish."

"Why is that?"

"Because you're only supposed to use your left hand to wipe yourself," he replied.

We were seated at one table with the chief. Perhaps twenty-five musicians were clustered around two other tables, smacking lips and chewing noisily, enjoying the hot, savory cooking. At the point when we were full and beginning to relax, more boys carried in more platters of crispy fish, fried in a batter of cumin and breading.

"Come on," Joel said with a laugh. "There's no refrigeration up here, and the fish won't keep. It's got to be eaten." The Masters scarfed fifty fish in five minutes. Soon mint tea came to wash the meal down. The musicians took out their pipes and a fragrant blue cloud of kif smoke perfumed the room.

We were quiet for a while, listening to the older musicians talk among themselves. Gradually, one by one, the elders said good-night—*"Sl'ama"*—and left, to be immediately replaced by one or more of their sons. These young guys wanted to pick up the drums and play music, but Berdouz wouldn't let them. "He's telling them to save their strength and let us get some rest," Joel said. "He's reminding them that the Aid el Kebir starts tomorrow and that everyone will need all their energy."

Eventually, they all left except the chief, who saw that we were comfortably bedded down in sleeping bags and had sufficient blankets. The hissing gas lamp was extinguished; candle shadows flickered dimly on the thick walls. Three stout young men were camped outside our closed door, the chief assured us, as guardians.

I lay in the dark, enjoying the fuzzy glow between consciousness and sleep. Joel was quiet, and Morgan snored slightly, a very human sound. *I made it,* I thought. *I'm here.* More important, there was something I could actually do for these people. What a relief, I thought, to have a cause.

In the night the rain came, hitting the tin roof above the ceiling like a million tacks. In my bag behind those adobe walls, I felt as secure as an infant, and fell back into dreamless sleep.

chapter 2

Aid el Kebir

I woke just after dawn to the muffled coughing of the men who had slept outside our door. Joel Fischer was awake too. He dressed and stepped outside, piercing the gloom of the chamber with a shaft of red early morning sun. The door closed and it was pitch black again. I slept until the aromas of coffee and kif tickled my nose. When I emerged, rumpled, into the morning glare, the musicians laughed at my hung-over state. *"Sba'al ghair,"* they called, saying good morning. In their pointy-headed djellabas they seemed like Snow White's dwarves. A donkey ambled by under a punishing load of firewood, driven by a straw-hatted peasant with a switch. Two country women followed, swathed in white home-spun blankets. Rural Morocco was medieval Europe. Except for the VW van looming in the foreground, this was a poor monastery in thirteenth-century England. Then someone switched on a battery-operated radio and caught a skein of Egyptian soul music, and my

36   reverie was at an end. A glass of sweet black coffee was put into my
hand, followed by a platter of eggs in oil and a fresh loaf of bread
that steamed when Joel broke it open. Then pungent kif was offered
by the gaunt older Master who did much of the figuring over the
djellabas yesterday. "This guy is a special friend of mine," Joel said.
"His name is Ahmed Skirkin, and he does the cooking for the
Malimin, as the Masters refer to themselves. If there's anything you
need while you're here, speak with him; Spanish or French will
do."

I washed and shaved, and began to look around. The madrassah
sat on the down side of the village's plateau, overlooking a lush
alpine vale carved by a roaring brook a thousand yards down the hill.
What lay a thousand yards farther beyond the stream stopped me
cold. It was a sharp granite escarpment jutting out of the bare
mountainside, a massive jagged plug of rock thrust up out of the
magma by primeval volcanism. The face of this awesome formation
was pocked by the black opening of a cave. Looking into it, even
from a mile away, made me shiver. Bashir, the chief's son, was
standing next to me and saw me staring at the cave. "Casa Bou
Jeloud," he commented. So *this* was Bou Jeloud's cave. I told Bashir
I wanted to visit Casa Bou Jeloud immediately.

Joel and Morgan were enthusiastic. The latter recruited some
youths—Berdouz's son Mohammed, Bashir's older brother Amin,
the ever-smiling Achmido—as Sherpas, and we ambled down the
hill toward the brook, threading through paths between gardens and
houses surrounded by cactus fences. The winter sun was rising in
the sky. We forded the roaring valley stream on giant boulders and
then started up the hill toward the cave that now loomed ahead like
a giant holy dolmen.

The mouth of the cave was eight feet off the ground. We had to
scramble up worn footholds to haul ourselves up. The cave itself
was a large hole in the crag, big enough to hold the six of us and
some camera cases—uncomfortably. There was something magic
and marvelous in the air. "I always have the feeling," Joel whis-

pered, "that rituals have been performed here since the beginning of human time. It's a shaman's cave, a power spot for sure."

"This is Casa Bou Jeloud," said Mohammed in schoolboy Spanish. "Tonight my cousin Abdsalam will return here. He will black his face, put on the skins and the hat, smoke a sebsi, and pray. Then he will be Bou Jeloud. That's the way we do it."

I asked if Bou Jeloud came here every night.

"No," answered Amin, who would dance the role himself later in the week. "We come *here* only the first night of the *Boujeloudiya* to honor the tradition of our people. The other nights we change at the madrassah."

"Casa Bou Jeloud used to be in the forest," Mohammed told us. "When our first Attar came here, there were trees everywhere. But over time they were cut for firewood, and our goats grazed down the land around it, so it stands by itself." The other boys nodded and smiled. Achmido said it was going to rain, so Morgan took some snaps from the rim of the cave and we scrambled back to the village, feeling exalted. As we passed through gardens and fields, some people smiled and waved; others seemed annoyed that strangers were in their midst, and Morgan's cameras dangling from the necks of his bearers drew cold stares. Not everyone in this hardscrabble hill community was thrilled to have us there.

A girl appeared on the path; she was about seventeen and was wrapped in light blue. In the instant before she saw us and covered the lower half of her face, we noticed that she was beautiful, with large oval black eyes and a trace of shy humor in her involuntary smile. She passed silently, quietly greeting the three Moroccan kids and properly ignoring us. A few steps later Morgan said, "Did you see her smile?" Achmido winked at me and kept walking.

BACK AT THE MADRASSAH we were greeted like long-lost relatives. Other musicians from outlying farms had arrived to welcome us, and we were showered with more stubbly kisses and introduced to more Mohammeds, Achmeds, Abdsalams, and Abdullahs than I could remember. Reed mats, cushions, and low tables furnished the covered porch; Malim Ali, master of rituals, was brewing mint tea in a big aluminum kettle. Skirkin, the cook, handed Ali a big paper-wrapped cone of white sugar, which he unwrapped and broke into large chunks with a wooden mallet. Selecting five *big* chunks, he dropped them into the kettle already stuffed with fresh mint leaves. Boiling water was poured in, and a metal tray appeared with two dozen small glasses. After a few minutes, Ali began to pour tea into a glass, which he quickly inverted and poured back in the kettle. This he repeated until the tea was the proper shade of amber. He filled the glasses, holding the kettle high above the tray to aerate the brew.

One of the older Masters, like his confreres tall and hawk-nosed, sat down next to me and regarded me warily. "La bess?" I asked. How's it going? "Aha," he grunted, unrolling a dread-looking mutwi and filling his pipe, which he lit and handed over to me. Thirty seconds later I was more stoned than I'd ever been in the daytime. *"Baraka l'aufic,"* I mumbled in thanks as Joel had taught me. "Aha," he replied, and got up and left. His kif left me so high I wondered whether my eyes were crossed.

After an hour staring at the stupendous white cumulonimbus clouds that shipped ponderously across the sky, the cook served the afternoon meal: chickens stewed in lemons and prunes, served with eggs in a rich gravy, sopped with fresh rounds of wheat bread. After lunch, the musicians relaxed with their kif pipes, and the afternoon's siesta commenced as figures sprawled in sleep everywhere, some in shade, some in the winter sunlight, their faces invariably covered by the voluminous hoods of their djellabas.

I awoke late in the afternoon. The sky to the west of Jajouka was turning purple, and a noisy soccer game raged. Joel was in a heated discussion with the chief and the cook concerning the album he wanted to make from the tapes he had recorded in the village the year before. Morgan was loading film. Just then, three well-dressed young men, obviously city people, walked through the gate. "Larbi," the musicians said, referring to the one in the middle. Blind yet prepossessing, he was led to the porch by two companions. Musicians shifted respectfully to make a place for them.

"You are from America," Rtobe Larbi said, when we had been introduced. "We heard you had arrived." I remarked that it was our good luck to meet someone in Jajouka who spoke English so fluently. "No," said Larbi, "it is *my* good luck, because I am studying the teaching of English at the university in Rabat, where my teachers are Englishmen. I am most looking forward to hearing, for the first time, what an American accent sounds like."

"Are you from Jajouka?" Morgan asked. "I mean, is this your hometown?"

"Hometown," the blind man repeated. "Hohm towun. Yes, I like this accent. I can almost not understand it, but I think I like it! Yes, this is my village. There are two major families here. The Attar are the musicians. The Rtobe are the family of Sidi Hamid Sherq."

"And you are here for the holiday?" I asked.

"Yes. The holiday. Aid el Kebir. I always come to the 'hohm towun' for Aid el Kebir." Everyone laughed, most of all Larbi, his eyes hidden by dark glasses. "I cannot stay now," Larbi went on, "but I wish to make an appointment to speak with you again tomorrow, if that is convenient."

We'll be here, I said. Larbi and his friends left, and the musicians spoke of him among themselves with evident respect.

At eight o'clock they served another feast, couscous with vegetables and succulent goat meat, which the ravenous musicians noisily sucked off the bones. Afterwards Morgan gave them 250 dollars in *National Geographic* "hello" money, which worked out to two thousand dirhams, a considerable sum in those parts. Gas lamps were lit, a place was cleared in the middle of the floor for dancing, hand-drums were held up to the flame to tighten the skins for playing, and the young Master Tahir meticulously tuned his *gimbri,* a three-stringed lute made of goatskin stretched over a gourd with a neck attached. Soon he was tracing soulful arabesques; the drummers and clappers fell in and began a song with wailing vocals and dance rhythms that can only be described as interplanetary, a backbeat bold as love.

After half an hour, there was a shout and the young dancing boy, Achmido, came in *dressed as a girl*. He began to shimmy to the music, which had risen in pitch. Dressed in flowing pink silk and chiffon, crowned and belted with intricate red embroidery, Achmido moved with the sexual undulation of a cobra, a sweet but enigmatic smile on his lips. The music, goosed by Tahir, became more frenetic, and broke into a speedy reel whose rollicking chorus, sung in English, absolutely floored me:

Ah, Brahim Jones, they sang. *Jajouka Rolling Stone. Ah, Brahim Jones, Jajouka really stoned!*

I looked at the picture of Brian Jones on the wall of the madrassah. Maybe it was the beat, maybe it was all the kif I'd smoked, maybe it was a trick of the light of the flickering, hissing lamp . . . but that picture seemed to jump in its frame as they sang that song. *Ah, Brahim Jones, Jajouka really stoned!*

THIS WENT ON for *hours*. One by one, the Malimin got up to dance, some enthusiastically, some with violent prodding. Often Berdouz would command one of the younger men lurking on the porch to come in and do a few special bumps and grinds. The sexier the dancing, the louder the old men laughed, showing outrageous gaps in what remained of their teeth after forty years of sweet mint tea. Then one of the older guys would parody Achmido or whatever younger blade had just given up the dance floor. Through it all, Tahir strummed his gimbri like a Moorish John Lee Hooker, throwing down killer licks, singing in a masculine falsetto that cut through the dusky atmosphere like a ratchet knife.

"What they're playing is called *Djibli*," Joel said. "It's the local after-dinner music of the Djebala. Gysin says it's descended from the old Andalusian songs. I know that some of them are pop tunes you hear on the radio, but most are strictly local.''

Between numbers everyone rested, and the kif pipes came out, producing clouds of blue vapor and catarrhal coughing. Achmido the dancing boy had pulled Morgan out of his seat and dragged him to the middle of the circle, where the photographer performed a disgracefully spastic frug for fifteen minutes. Now he sprawled out, exhausted. In came a tray of fresh tea, which he guzzled as though it were a restorative tonic. I had set up my tape recorder and a couple of microphones to test the levels. Tahir sat staring at the thing with his gimbri in his lap, mesmerized by the red needles indicating sound levels as they danced in time to the thumping bass string he was plucking while he warmed up for the next song.

This proved to be a deep, sonorous *cante jondo* titled ''Jajouka Black Eyes.'' As soon as he heard the opening notes, Joel leaned over and whispered, ''This is my favorite of all the songs they do here.'' It was a beautiful, darkling melody that expressed a powerful, fruitless yearning. ''Oh where, oh where are you, my black-eyed lover?'' asked the lyric, which flowed from the handsome singer like a sonic skein of yellow silk. It was magic. It made me think of my beloved girlfriend, five thousand miles and seemingly centuries away. Sitting in that adobe longhouse in the foothills of the Rif mountains, I once again felt that I had slipped back in time. I also felt that there was *no* time, and at the same time, there was no time to waste. I looked at the empty pegs on the wall where the stolen djellabas had hung, and felt relieved to have arrived in time . . . to replace these garments and play a miniscule part in the conservation of the Master Musicians of Jajouka.

''Jajouka Black Eyes'' evolved into an extended dance sequence. Two more dancing boys started off, both under twelve, both dressed as girls. Then Berdouz got up, handed off his drum, and took two bright scarves from a brass mirror hanging next to a very old picture of the king. He tied one over his bald head, babushka-style; the other he wound around his buttocks. As the rhythm came forward, Berdouz began a thoroughly lewd parody of a woman's dance that was, *à la fois,* brilliant in itself. This was punctuated by various comedy routines, for which he abruptly stopped the music with a flick of his hand. Berdouz was a gifted mimic, whose art— much of it clearly obscene—provoked gales of hilarity from the musicians. At one point he waddled over to me, handed me a glowing pipe, and said something to the others. I pressed Joel for a translation. "He told them you are a troublemaker," Joel said, "but that you bring good luck."

Winded, Berdouz finally sat down again, and the piece crashed to a halt after a series of dynamic climaxes that would have exhausted the early Led Zeppelin. More trays of tea, more kif. Some of the older musicians left and were immediately replaced by their sons. "What's going on?" Morgan asked. "Why don't the sons sit in here with the elders?"

"It's taboo," Joel replied. "Sons don't socialize with their fathers in public. They can't be seen smoking in the presence of their fathers either, whether it's kif or tobacco."

Tahir tuned his violin; more older masters said goodnight. Except for Jnuin, Fudul, Berdouz, and the old cook, the musicians were now all younger, and the house really shook when they began to play. The drumming reached a plateau of African polyrhythms that were beyond comprehension. I got up to dance and they howled—"EEEEEWWAAAA." I spun and spun until I felt sick and staggered out into the night. The cold air hit me like a heart attack, and I gasped at the dazzling silver curtain of stars that crowned the immense cobalt sky. From the madrassah I could hear the music rising higher, and made out the shadows of the dancer who had taken my place inside.

You'd better be careful, a voice inside my head advised. *You could get very lost in all this.*

·   ·   ·

IT RAINED AGAIN during the night, the five-hour interval between the reluctant cessation of the evening music and the serving of coffee an hour after dawn. The steaming earth was sodden and redolent of an almost obscene fertility, and the massive mountain sky was painted in watercolor shades of grey. I begged the cook for a bucket of hot water, which appeared after twenty minutes, carried by one of the younger kitchen-*cum*-dancing boys to the hammam. I stripped off the sweaty clothes in which I had slept, squatted on the floor and upended half the tin pail over my head. I lathered with the castile soap I'd brought from home, and rinsed with the other half of the water. I stood up, naked and shivering in the morning chill, and toweled myself. As my eyes got used to the gloom of the hammam, I noticed something dark and fuzzy lurking in the corner. At first it seemed like a sleeping dog or the corpse of some animal. But when I looked closer, I could see it was a pile of goatskins, sewn into a costume—Bou Jeloud's ragged pagan cloak, now lying mysteriously lifeless. I shuddered, involuntarily, and made my way to the terrace.

There I found my traveling companions drinking coffee sweetened with canned milk and chatting about camera f-stops. Berdouz arrived, bade us Salaam Aleikum, and unwrapped from the folds of his djellaba five big rounds of aromatic caraway-seed bread, just removed from the communal oven. We breakfasted, and considered ourselves very lucky that the sun was now beginning to peer through the dense cloud cover. "If it had rained much more," Joel mused, "the whole village would have turned to mud, making it doubtful Bou Jeloud would do much dancing tonight."

After we ate, Morgan grabbed a camera and Achmido, saying he wanted to photograph some of the village's children. I tagged along, and we soon found ourselves surrounded by two dozen urchins led by Fatima, Jnuin's ten-year-old daughter. As the giggling, chattery throng pressed around us, Fatima kept the bolder ones from getting too close and the younger ones from being squashed in the crush. Motor-drive clicking like an assault rifle,

44 Morgan fired off three rolls, pausing only to exchange cameras with Achmido, who took his key-grip duties ultra-seriously. Soon the growing crowd of children was overwhelming, and civilized exploration of Jajouka's byways became impossible. Morgan went back to the madrassah to reload, and gradually the children drifted off in different directions to tell their families about their meeting with the strangers in town.

I got involved in a hot little soccer game with some nine-year-olds who were on recess from the little government schoolhouse. Two young male teachers came out to watch, and whistled their approval when the most agile of their pupils stole the battered, worn-out ball from me and scored a goal between two small cairns of stone. We smiled and waved to each other, and I resolved to try to interview them later; as literate outsiders, they might have an interesting perspective on things around here.

AT THE MADRASSAH, the blind English student Larbi was sitting on the terrace, drinking tea with Jnuin, who chain-smoked from a pack of Casa Sport filter cigarettes. "I have been very much looking toward this meeting," Larbi said. "So many topics I desire to discuss, one does not know how one should commence."

"Well," I tried to help, "what do you want to know about?"

"It is not only me," the blind youth said. "So many of my friends in Salé, where I live near Rabat, will be very cross with me if I tell them I have met an American journalist and did not ask him certain questions. Such as: Why do you have so much racism in the United States? Why do your white people kill your black people? Why is America destroying the people of Vietnam? Why do you support General Pinochet in Chile? Most of all, what everyone in our university department of English wants most to know: What is the meaning of this 'Watergate'?"

By mid-morning we had covered the field of American foreign policy, before Larbi announced he had to leave for a family gathering. On cue his two cousins appeared. "Thank you for the information you provided," he said. "Perhaps tonight I will come back and help you with some of your researches here in my village." I said I would appreciate it, and he walked off between his escorts.

MOST OF THE MUSICIANS drifted off while I was speaking with Larbi, and I could hear the high skirling of rhaitas coming from below the plaza. They sounded more majestic than bagpipes from Valhalla.

Accompanied by Achmido, I grabbed my notebook and hurried across the village to the large blue tabernacle that housed the tomb and shrine of Sidi Hamid Sherq, Jajouka's *tout puissant* patron saint.

At the gate of the sanctuary stood the sherif, the guardian of the shrine of Sidi Hamid Sherq. Tall, slender, dressed in a white djellaba and a stained, loosely wound turban, he was gossiping with some local women on their way to prayer. I approached timidly, since walking into a religious site in Morocco is frowned upon if one is an infidel. But the sherif seemed glad to see me. In fact, to my delight, he stuck out his right hand in introduction and said, "Saint!" Relieved, I took it. "Sherif" means saint, and as a descendant of Sidi Hamid Sherq, this man was indeed a *fqih* of the local saintly family. He opened the gate and Achmido and I slipped inside.

Seated in a long line on a straw mat were a dozen of the oldest Malimin, playing the rhaita in what sounded like solemn processional, the Moorish equivalent of a Bach organ prelude. Eight drummers stood in a line perpendicular to the rhaitas, led by Berdouz. They beat a muffled tattoo in intricate counterpoint to the declaiming oboes. All wore white djellabas, turbans, and pointed slippers of bright yellow leather. Several boy drummers came in late, and kissed each seated rhaita player on the cheek before taking their places on the line of drummers. As the piece built to an ethnosonic climax, I noticed Joel and Morgan lurking in a corner beside the rear door, trying to look inconspicuous. I crossed the

46 open courtyard to sit with them and hear out the awesome religious offering.

Glancing around the sanctuary, I saw it was designed to accommodate pilgrims. One wall of the enclosed area supported a metal awning that sheltered the donkeys and mules that ferried some of the devout up Jajouka's road. Rooms along the third wall could be occupied by overnight visitors. The fourth wall supported a second storey, where the sherif and his family lived. In the middle of the courtyard was the oldest tree I've ever seen, an ancient fig whose thick, gnarled trunk was bound by heavy black iron chains with huge links. The branches of the tree, bare of leaves on that winter morning, reached up to the sky like the fingers of bony, supplicating hands. The tree was a presence as immediate as that of a king or a sultan. It reeked of power and mystery, and I longed to go over and touch its hoary bark. But, by that time, I was so riveted by the soaring flight of the music, which suddenly halted in a final waterfall of fluttery piping, that I could barely move. Immediately Berdouz slung his drum over the back of his shoulder, stepped out into the courtyard and began to offer prayers, holding his hands cupped in front of him. After every phrase, the other musicians and pilgrims would mutter ''Amin,'' and Berdouz gradually picked up the pace until one could hear only a low murmur of Amin Amin Amin Amin Amin Amin . . .

One by one, pilgrims dropped money into Berdouz's palm. He would nod and request baraka and saintly protection for the donor. Deciding this was exactly what I needed, I found a fifty-dirham note in my jeans and gave it to Berdouz. Just hearing him say my name felt like a shot of spiritual B_{12}, and I felt sanctified. Joel told me later that Sidi Hamid Sherq's baraka was famous for being fast-acting.

Prayers finished, there was a bustle as the Masters stood up and a group of female pilgrims stepped into the courtyard. *Something was about to happen.* The musicians began to play, but the sherif opened the wooden door in the wall behind us, and politely *threw us out.* The heavy door thunked shut at our backs. The rear of the sanctuary abutted the village cemetery, a millennium of rough rectangles of jagged stones. We were cheerfully greeted by a pair of extremely dread beggars clothed in the most piteous rags; they evidently existed in a rude lean-to against the back wall of the tomb. Our quick exit had caught them by surprise, and they smiled toothlessly as they brewed tea in a filthy can over a sputtering fire.

Five minutes later, the back door opened and the Master Musicians filed out, playing a sprightly recessional theme. Jnuin, at the head of the line, motioned us to follow them. They led the way into the graveyard, among groves of old olive trees, and assembled in a line facing the long sweeping view of the Ahl Sherif valley and mountains that lay to the east. For five minutes more, they played for their ancestors and dead loved ones, and for the air and the winds that swirled about their mountain. At the end of the piece they dispersed, each musician visiting a grave and murmuring prayers.

Then a group of younger musicians, led by Berdouz, strolled toward the wide village plaza, playing as they made their way from Islam to Pan in less than five minutes.

"THE AID EL KEBIR began very early this morning," Joel was saying. We were sitting on a rock overlooking the village plaza, where four rhaita players and three drummers, all young, were conducting a rehearsal and invitational Bou Jeloud tryouts. "The feast is a lunar calender event," he added. "It doesn't begin until religious authorities in Mecca see the sliver of the new moon from the tallest minaret. That first sighting is announced on the radio and beamed all over the world."

"When does Bou Jeloud make his appearance?" Morgan inquired.

"We'll probably see him now, because they're auditioning different boys to see who gets the job for the big pilgrimage, in five or six days. Several thousand people show up, so Bou Jeloud has to grind out a very hot performance that day."

"What about the light?" the photographer asked. "I hate using flash. Does any of this stuff happen during the day?"

"Yeah, but the real action is at night. They build a big bonfire."

"Doesn't sound great for pictures," Morgan groused.

A little later that afternoon a shout rose from the several dozen villagers who were watching the young piper band, and Bou Jeloud materialized out of an alley, six feet of shaggy quivering brown goatskins topped by a ragged straw bonnet. Dancing barefoot on the hard rock ground before the line of singing rhaitas, his face blackened with charcoal, Bou Jeloud twitched his butt lasciviously to a compulsive slow backbeat and waved a big stick in the air. This was accompanied by a frantic trilling from the rhaitas as Bou Jeloud began his rampage, hitting, threatening, shouting, and abusing anyone who got in his way. I realized that this crazy music was descended from furthest antiquity, that it must be among the oldest still heard on the planet. Then the lead piper, a chunky young master we called Fat Mohammed, signaled the band back to slinky Moroccan roll; Bou Jeloud, as if on command, ceased his depredations and meekly slithered back to the line of pipers to dance. The goat god, it seemed, was at the disposal of the musicians.

"These slower dance tunes are variations on music for Bou Jeloud's girlfriend, Aisha Hamoka," Joel told us. "Her job is to seduce Bou Jeloud into town so his baraka will benefit the tribe. This music is her stand-in, and is of course irresistible to our furry friend."

Now the rhaitas were playing Oriental cobra-charming melodies in time to an Andalusian waltz from the drummers. Some of the drone-playing pipers, I noticed, had been holding the same note for fifteen minutes. "It's called circular breathing," Joel said. "They're trained to inhale through the nose and exhale through the rhaita. They've got a complicated swallowing technique worked out in the muscles of the neck and throat. There are stories that some of the older men can sustain certain notes almost indefinitely."

The drummers picked up the beat and the band kicked into Bou

Jeloud's chase music, fibrillating blasts—sheets of sound—that generated fear, fright, attacks of p-p-p-panic! It was the music of chaos,
a soundtrack for a desert war in olden times, and it hit me like a
heat wave.

Suddenly the drums dropped out; the abrupt change of rhythm
altered the beat of my heart. The lead rhaita played a cue change that
sounded like Morse code, and the other rhaitas blasted into Aisha
Variation no. 1, wild Persian snake lines. Several youths now
danced alongside Bou Jeloud, who shimmied elastically before the
line of musicians, holding aloft two leafy green branches of oleander, while the players indulged in a call-and-response jam with
several funk-style percussive tricks in the mix.

Wham! Just like *that,* the band shifted into Bou Jeloud's music,
half the rhaitas braying out a cosmic drone. The shaggy beast came
straight at us. *HUT* he shouted into the microphones I thought I had
set up inconspicuously. *HUT* he screamed at Morgan, whose motor-
driven Nikons were crackling like small-arms fire. He raised his
whips above his head and quivered with rage as the horns did a
blood-boiling screech. Then he drew back to strike, and we cringed.
He had been hitting people, some of them hard. I could smell the
awful stink of the boy and the skins, and could not bring myself to
look under the brim of the ragged straw bonnet he wore tied around
his head. But no blow ever came, and I could hear Bou Jeloud
chuckle under his rank breath as he skittered away from us, seeking
a more appropriate target for his wrath.

Zap! Back went the band into hip-curling Aisha Variation no. 2,
and the goat god immediately fell into line. For an hour or so, the
musicians went back and forth between dance music and panic
soundtrack. As Bou Jeloud chased a pack of laughing children
around the plaza to the tune of Aisha Variation no. 3, another
"character" appeared. This was a dancer wearing a red fez and
dressed in white, his face covered by fuzzy cotton whiskers to signify
great age.

"That's Old Man Hajj," Joel whispered. "He's the personifica-

50   tion of the pilgrimage to Mecca or some other holy place, which every devout Muslim undertakes this time of year.'' Yet Bou Jeloud evinced very little respect for Hajj, butting and menacing him and chasing him to the the fringes of the plaza; I soon realized that Hajj was comic relief, the clown at the rodeo.

I also noticed that Bou Jeloud, as danced by the chief's son Amin, would occasionally go ''out of character'' to assist tiny boys in miniature djellabas who had gotten tangled up with him on the dancing ground. Confronted by the goat god, the faces of the children contorted in terror until soft-hearted Amin stopped dancing and led them by the hand out of danger. Then he was back into it, hips swiveling lubriciously to martial camel music.

Suddenly panic mode kicked in again, and Bou Jeloud ran straight at me. I looked briefly into the black hole underneath the straw hat and saw two vertical yellow slits. Jesus! I blinked and he was all over me, scattering me, recorder, and microphone in three directions. I came up for air crouching by the rough wall and people scampered away in fright as Bou Jeloud crowned me on the head with his oleander switches. I heard him laugh as he skittered away to his next target.

Morgan and Joel picked me up, dusted me off, and escorted me back to the madrassah, where mint tea and a pipe were waiting. As the reddened western sky was turning to deepest blue, I looked back over my shoulder a final time to make sure it was all real and saw Bou Jeloud leaping through the flames of the bonfire.

THE FINNISH ANTHROPOLOGIST Edward Westermarck published his two-volume masterpiece, *Ritual and Belief in Morocco,* in 1927. Westermarck described Bou Jelouds dancing all over the northern Moroccan landscape during the seven days of the Great Feast at the turn of the century, when his principal research took place. He concluded the dance must be a survival of the Roman festival of the Lupercal, which was celebrated in the first two weeks of February, when Morocco was one of Rome's Punic colonies, but which later syncretized to the principal Muslim feast when Arab invaders turned the calender back to the lunar year in the eighth century A.D. The Lupercalia itself was an extremely important Roman celebration of purgation and fertility. Noble youths of the city dressed in wolf or goat skins and raced through the streets of Rome and its provincial cities, carrying whips or flails. Women who wished to conceive children that year positioned themselves on street corners to be whipped by the savage beast-men running the wild stampede of the Lupercal. The whips were called *februa*. The days of the Lupercal were the *dies februatus*. Hence the month of February.

Westermarck wrote very little about Bou Jeloud, never claimed to have seen the dances, and indeed surmised that the old custom had died out. But, fifty years later, Brion Gysin understood. When he saw Bou Jeloud whipping girls during the Aid el Kebir in Jajouka, he realized that Bou Jeloud was running the same "holy chase" that Shakespeare described in Act I, scene 2, of *Julius Caesar*. Marc Antony is dressed for the Lupercal in skins, whips ready, and Caesar instructs him:

> *Forget not in your haste, Antonius, to touch Calpurnia; for our elders say the barren, touched in this holy chase, shake off their sterile curse.*

Caesar was telling Antony to whip his wife, to purge her inability to conceive an heir. Two thousand years later, Bou Jeloud was still chasing around Jajouka, whipping girls with branches of oleander. It was the real thing!

AN HOUR LATER we were on the porch of the madrassah, eating brochettes of sheep's liver. From the kitchen wafted the savory vapors of mutton stew in progress. The blind student Rtobe Larbi had joined us, and he spoke in careful English after I pressed him to provide me with an outline of the local history.

Sidi Hamid Sherq, he told us, was expelled from Baghdad, in

what is now Iraq, sometime in the eighth century. The reasons for his exile are unclear, but it might have involved the schism between the Shiite branch of Islam and the Sunni, which is predominant in Morocco and most of the Arab world. Hamid Sherq stayed at one of the caliphal courts in Andalusia for several years, making a name for himself as a preacher, healer, and converter of Christians. Eventually, he was invited to Jajouka by the Attar family, who had founded the village after emigrating from India.

But why, I asked, would Hamid Sherq have come to Jajouka? This is, after all, an out-of-the-way mountain village. What was going on that would have enticed a well-known cleric from sophisticated Granada or Córdoba to settle here? Was he "assigned" to curb paganism and idolatry?

"Sidi Hamid Sherq was a great lover of music," Larbi replied. "Some say he was a great musician himself. Our tradition is derived from a bond that formed between him and the Attars in which secrets were exchanged. In return for teaching him their old music, Sidi Hamid Sherq taught them metaphysical techniques of spiritual healing. *Tu m'as compris?*"

I assured him, yes, I understood.

"When Sidi Hamid Sherq died, he was buried here. My family, the Rtobe, are his descendants. And every Friday morning, the day of our sabbath, the musicians play for pilgrims who visit his shrine to be healed."

"Healed of what?"

"They come because their minds are . . . *malade,*" Larbi groped for the English word, ". . . sick. That was Sidi Hamid Sherq's *specialité*. He was called 'the healer of sick minds and the cultivator with lions,' because his baraka enabled him to yoke mountain lions to his plow."

Please go on, I begged.

"At some point in time, long before the present Alouite dynasty of Moroccan sultans, musicians from Jajouka traveled with the sultans as royal musicians. They rode at the head of the army and heralded the sultan's arrival in a new city. They had very old papers from the king that spelled out their duties and their rights at the palace, which were: to play him to bed at night; to play for him in the morning; and to play him to the mosque when he went to pray.''

Larbi consulted for a moment in Arabic with the chief, whom he referred to by his real name. ''Malim Abdsalam now tells me that the papers were renewed when the Alouiya, the ancestors of our king, came to power. These papers address the musicians with extraordinary respect and, *en effet,* set them free from all labor forever. The musicians are allowed to collect a tithe on all the crops grown around here. It is a very special privilege.''

''Do the musicians still do either of these things?'' I asked.

Larbi conferred with the Malimin. ''Not exactly,'' he replied after quite a hubbub. ''It has been many years since Masters from Jajouka exercised their rights to play for the royal family. The oldest man in the village played for Sultan Moulay Hafid at Marrakech. That was the last known time our musicians were regularly employed at court.''

''When would that have been?''

''Moulay Hafid was deposed by the French in 1912,'' Larbi replied.

''But to finish my answer to your question,'' he continued, ''musicians from this village still played for colonialists who ruled here under French and Spanish 'protection,' as it was called until we were granted our independence in 1956. There was no more work for them and they came back to the hills here and have stayed ever since.

''You asked also if the traditional tithe was still collected. The answer is yes, but not without difficulty. Here, in hard times, there is some resentment toward Jajouka. 'Why should they not work?' 'Why should I give them some wheat or a goat or a little money?' That's what they say. People have forgotten that Jajouka is very important, and some do not want to support the musicians, who like to rest and smoke kif all day and play all night. I myself remember a few years ago that the musicians were stoned by some stupid farmers when they went to the fields to collect what they said was due them. So it is still a difficult situation.''

Just then some boys appeared with basins and towels for washing before the meal, and our conversation came to a halt. An hour after supper, the Djibli band re-formed and played dance music into my microphones until three in the morning. The black tobacco in the kif kept me wide awake, yet thoroughly wasted. When they finally turned out the light and let us sleep, it was as if we were dead, so dark and still was the night.

I WOKE A FEW hours later at dawn, went outside and almost stumbled over the old chief, who was bent over in front of the door in the deep devotions of his morning prayers. After I washed, I found him sitting on the terrace. He smiled in his incredibly kind way and motioned me to join him. The cook brought us little tea glasses filled with boiling black coffee that took the chill of daybreak from my bones. We communicated in Spanish. ''I need a djellaba like yours,'' I told him, ''a woolen envelope to keep me warm up here.'' Yes, he said, we'll take care of that tomorrow. He wanted me to write to him when I returned to America and laboriously inscribed his address on a pad of paper.

Larbi arrived a bit later, this time unescorted, to share our breakfast of boiled eggs and tangerines. There was more talk of the lineage of the Ahl Sherif tribe. After some argument, Larbi explained the musicians were insisting that their ancestor Attar was from Persia (now Iran) as opposed to India or Iraq. He came, they said, in the first wave of invaders from the East who took old Barbary and imposed Islam on the Berber people. A bit later, talk turned to the future, and Larbi murmured that he could not be optimistic about his future. *"C'est une grande différence entre vous et moi,"* he said, reminding me that he was *aveugle*, blind.

I didn't know what to say exactly, so I reminded him of something he'd told me the previous night: "Up in the mountains we have a . . . how do you say it? Legend? We have a legend that if the music of Jajouka stops for some reason, then the whole world stops as well. Finish." Larbi had spoken with conviction, not the condescending irony of the educated man.

"Look Larbi," I tried to assuage, "if what you told me about Jajouka last night—that the music is keeping the world turning—if that is true, then we must dedicate ourselves to the musicians' well-being, isn't that so?"

The blind man only laughed sadly.

I slept on the terrace after lunch, awakening late in the afternoon to the metallic sounds of Morgan loading his three Nikons. The drums and rhaitas had already begun down in the village plaza, so I slit the cellophane seals on a pair of C-90 cassettes, deployed one in the recorder, pushed the REC button (relying on Sony's built-in condenser mikes) and set off down the hill where the 4000th Annual Bou Jeloud Tryouts and B-Team Band Rehearsals were under way. A crowd of kids dispersed as a good spot was cleared for us, and I handed off the recorder to assistant engineer Achmido who instinctively knew the machine should be placed as far from Berdouz's bass drum as possible. Meanwhile the oboes were wailing like crazy for two Bou Jelouds. They were Amin and Mustapha, both sons of the chief, and they danced for hours as the sun slid behind an impressive cloudbank and the sky turned half scarlet. A bonfire was lit in the center of the plaza, around which the two Bou Jelouds cavorted like prehistoric creatures.

When the sky went completely black but for twinkling stars, the rhaitas stopped. One of the Bou Jelouds disappeared down an alley; the other walked slowly in bare feet through the fresh coals of the bonfire. Joel and I had been smoking all evening, and now looked at each other in disbelief. Had we just seen this happen? The drums kept up their brutal, primordial beat, and again the goat god scampered through the fire, sending a shower of orange

56   sparks flying upward. Tahir, who had been leading the drummers,
got up without losing the beat and led Bou Jeloud into a cluster of
perhaps fifty white-blanketed girls and women, who ululated and
yodeled in high wild voices as the drummer and Bou Jeloud entered their pulsating circle. I couldn't see the mystery that was
unfolding in the crowd of women, who chanted an ethereal song
of pastoral seduction.

"They're teasing him," Joel said to me. "They're teasing Bou
Jeloud just the way Aisha used to. And, I'm told, it can get very
lewd. I've never seen this before." Just then, firm hands pulled on
our jackets, and we were led up the hill, back to the madrassah.
"Maybe next time," Joel said. "Some of these mysteries must be
too sensitive to be seen by outsiders."

I felt torn. I didn't want to be intrusive in the life of this village.
I didn't want our presence as journalists to change, in any way, what
was going on here. "Yeah, that's very enlightened of you," Morgan
said with sarcasm. "But what are we gonna show the editors back
in Washington when they wanna see what happened here? They'll
laugh when you tell 'em you didn't want to be intrusive."

Later that evening, Larbi reappeared and invited us to his family's
house for lunch the following day, but I explained that we were
leaving for a few days in order to begin the quest for new djellabas
for the musicians. "It's good work you are doing here," Larbi said.
I asked if we could accept his invitation later, but he said he was
returning to Rabat and wouldn't be in Jajouka when we came back.
The blind student embraced each of us, slipped into his pointed
yellow slippers and vanished into the night. On subsequent visits to
Rabat we were never able to find his house, and mail sent to the
address Larbi had given me was returned unopened. I never saw him
again.

THE NEXT MORNING dawned with black rain clouds scudding across
a grey sky. After coffee, kif, and two dozen grizzled kisses, we were

off on our own holy chase to procure replacement djellabas for the Master Musicians. Along for the ride were the chief, Malim Ali, and a thirtyish local wool expert named Rikki Rotobe. As our van scrabbled down the perilous mountain track, I felt like we were descending from Shangri-La, an enchanted place sheltered from the cares of the real world.

With Joel at the wheel and the three Jajoukans in back, the drive was quite spirited, as Malim Ali kept filling his intricately carved sebsi with his personally blended and especially strong kif, before passing it forward to us. We skirted the city of Wazzan without entering it. "It's a strange place," Joel said as he drove the nearly empty road. "The Masters have their rhaitas made here. Before they're sold, the horns are blessed by the sherifs of Wazzan, who have a reputation for powerful blessings."

An hour later we reached our first destination, Chaouen. Like most cities in northern Morocco, it appeared suddenly around a bend in the road, clustered like a group of mushrooms. Chaouen lay at the foot of a giant granite mountain that was home to one of the last big families of Gibraltar apes.

As we made our way to the center of town, I was *dazzled* by the special shade of aqua covering the walls of the entire city, giving the town a blue aura of surreal airiness. At a café in the *centre ville,* we took mint tea and listened to the amplified groaning of the mid-morning call to prayer. Jnuin and Ali went to inquire about buying djellabas, but returned empty-handed after an hour. Everything was closed for the Aid el Kebir, so we loaded up and drove off to the bigger djellaba market in Tetuan, deeper in the Rif.

"Tetuan—have you ever been there?" Joel asked. "Tetuan is a *very* tough town and always has been. When the French and Spanish partitioned Morocco in 1912, the Rifians refused to go along, and Tetuan became a garrison town in the midst of rebel country. Maybe you've heard of the bandit Raisouli? He led the resistance to the Europeans, and at one point kidnapped Mrs. Pedikaris, the wife of the American consul in Tangier, and carried her back to Tetuan.

58   Teddy Roosevelt sent in the marines and there was fighting that
eventually lasted until sometime in the 1930s.''

"What about now?" Morgan asked.

"It's still a dangerous town, the gateway to Ketama, where the
best hashish is made. A smuggler's city, full of roadblocks and
betrayal and bribery. Keep your hand on your wallet when you're
in the marketplace, and don't buy anything from a stranger.''

"Right," Morgan said. I noticed he looked a little bleary, having
gobbled a *National Geographic* Nembutal the night before in an effort
to get some sleep, but I thought nothing of it. An hour later, we
entered the sinister-looking, Spanish-provincial part of Tetuan and
parked on the main boulevard amid the crowded Sunday prome-
nade. All the locals were on display: the young men in suits and
stacked-heeled boots, the women in heavy makeup and black
dresses. It looked like a scene from *Carmen,* that of Prosper Mérimée
as opposed to Bizet. We walked to the clothes market in the medina
of the town, behind a pitted medieval wall. There the Jajoukans
bought three brown wool djellabas cut in the shorter mountain style
they desired. Before we could find any more, evening closed in and
the Tetuan djellaba haberdashery began to slam shut for the night.
Within ten minutes, a bustling, shouting market square became a
deserted, shuttered space occupied only by our party of five and a
pair of cats scrounging in the garbage. Faced with having to spend
the night, we ate country-style, with our hands, in a restaurant in
the Spanish part of town, and then tried to check into a hotel, which
proved impossible since Morgan, in a Nembutal fog, had left his
passport back in Jajouka and the desk clerk refused him a room
without it.

"Christ, Morgan!" Joel was exasperated. "You can't travel
without papers in this country. We have to go to the police now and
ask permission for you to stay here tonight. You don't speak the
languages, so I have to hassle for you.''

"Look, I'm sorry," the photographer said. "I couldn't sleep so
I took this pill and it turned me into a zombie. *C'mon.* It won't
happen again.''

We proceeded to the nearest *comisaría* without the terrified musicians, who loathed any contact with the cops and preferred to wait in the lobby of the hotel. The police station was right out of *The Battle of Algiers:* night interrogations, muffled cries from underground cells, plainclothes goon-squads and paramilitaries moving in and out. After filling out endless paperwork, the sergeant reluctantly issued Morgan a pass that would allow our hotel to accept him for one night only. They all but told us to get the hell out of town.

It had been a long day, and we were exhausted. We sat in a café and drank tea, then retired to the suite in which we had installed the Jajoukans. Malim Ali kept us plied with kif, whose delicious aroma soon permeated the entire hotel. "They're glad they didn't have to deal with the police," Joel said. "These are mountain people, almost hillbillies really, and they don't like the law at all. In fact, when I was playing back some of the tapes I recorded last year, they got very upset about a prayer that was on one of the reels. It turned out that part of the prayer suggested that red-hot irons be inserted in the rectums of certain important persons in the region. What if that had made it onto the record I want to put out? What would have happened? I don't even want to think about it."

AT EIGHT O'CLOCK we breakfasted on harsh blood-orange juice, oily black coffee, and great croissants. Then we totally immersed ourselves into the Tetuan medina and the stall of a henna-bearded djellaba merchant who dispatched his four sons to all points of the compass searching for garments the color and quality the Master Musicians required. By mid-morning they had returned with nine; we now had a dozen. The call to prayer sounded, and the bright orange—whiskered man slipped into chrome yellow slippers and disappeared round the corner to pray in the neighborhood mosque.

Business suspended, I bought my own djellaba, from a twelve-year-old named Mohammed. It was a long brown number that came

60 to my ankle and fit like an old friend. "One hundred dirhams," the boy said. "That's too much," Joel said behind me. "Offer him fifty." In the end I paid seventy, and Morgan and Joel each bought one from the same kid. By then the merchant with the bright orange beard had returned from his devotions. His eldest son, he said, had scoured the city: there were no more ready-to-wear, off-the-rack brown djellabas to be had. So we bought twenty-three bolts of brown wool cloth, which the musicians decided could be tailored in Ksar el Kebir, close to home. This transaction took hours to haggle through, during which time we became famished.

Following his nose, Joel led us into the medina, past mounds of nougat candy piled in the street for sale, to a soup kitchen that specialized in *bisar,* the national soul dish of Morocco. The thick, porridge-like grey soup was ladled into plastic bowls and served with a hunk of bread and a cup of water. "It's basically fava bean soup that poor people eat all over the Mediterranean world," Joel said. "It's soul food for working people." Indeed, as I spooned the delicious mush into my mouth I could see that our fellow diners were craftsmen, students, beggars, and the elderly. At one point a young cat in a cheap suit stuck his head in to check out the action. He saw us and his eyes widened with glee. "Amerikani!" he shouted. "Tzoupe? You wanna tzoupe? You like-a Snuppy?" He opened his jacket to show that he was wearing a T-shirt featuring Charlie Brown and his dog. "Ignore him," Joel said. "Maybe he'll go away." No such luck. He came over, sat down, and tried to sell us sticky black hash for twenty minutes until the owner threw him out.

On the way back to the central square of the medina, Joel told us to wait and ducked down a dim side street, emerging a few minutes later. "When I was here a few years ago there was an artisan at the end of this street who was famous among kif smokers for his *zhqafs,* the little clay bowls at the end of the pipes. He sculpted zhqafs in the shape of elephants, rhinos, lions, apes, all sorts of tiny and exquisite figurines. I just knocked on his door and his wife said he had died. I asked who was doing that sort of work now, and she said nobody, that the craft had died with her husband. It's incredible how an art that existed for hundreds of years can dwindle down to one guy, and then just flicker out like a candle when he goes.''

"Maybe that's the whole story of the modern world," Morgan said.

"Maybe so," Joel said with resignation and a laugh. "The tragedy of the contemporary world is that we have to smoke out of undecorated bowls.''

By three o'clock we had loaded our djellabas and wool into the van and were leaving Tetuan, heading down from the Rif. The three Jajoukans were pleased. Jnuin and Ali smoked and chatted excitedly. Gradually the mountains unwound along the empty road and turned into foothills, and then flatlands under cultivation as we neared the coast. We arrived in Ksar el Kebir in the early evening, where we spent another two hours in the market bargaining for multicolored silk thread that would be embroidered onto the front of the new djellabas to give them geometric flash and Moroccan showbiz authority. On the way back to Jajouka, with every cubic inch of van crammed with cloth and fresh tangerines, the chief ordered Joel to stop after we passed a pair of boys holding dead rabbits by the side of the road. For four and a half dirhams Jnuin bought the rabbits for the next day's stewpot.

It was dark when our van lurched between the boulders and wheel ruts that constituted the last bit of track before entering the village. As we passed the plaza, we saw a crowd and the sparks of Bou Jeloud's bonfire. When we pulled up to the madrassah a shout went up from the assembled musicians, who saw the cloth we'd brought and realized that they would soon be back in business and looking good. They stuffed us with left-over chicken and mutton on huge plates of couscous, and discussed how the cloth would be tailored and by whom, and how and where the proposed embroidery would be displayed.

Joel, Morgan, and I ate quietly and listened. "This is great," Joel said. "At least we're making a tiny contribution to keeping this thing going. There's so much pressure on the sons of the musicians to join the army, or drive a taxi in France. Maybe these new costumes will keep one or two more young kids here, people who might have split for the bright lights otherwise."

I remembered what one *National Geographic* editor had said about this expedition being a salvage job. I'd mocked this notion at the time, but maybe he was right. In any case, sitting there that night, with the cloth bolts piled high in the corner, gave me the greatest sense of accomplishment I've ever felt.

"THE CAID THEY'VE GOT down at Tatoft is a real prick," Joel was saying, "if it's still the same one that's been there for the last few years." We were in the van the next morning, lurching off the edge of Jajouka's plateau, about to begin the controlled free-fall down the mountain track. In the back were our wool team, less Morgan who had stayed in the village, plus several village women headed to Ksar el Kebir. Word had reached Jajouka early that morning that "the Nazarenes" in the village were overdue to present themselves to the caid for inspection.

"Anyone who passes the caid's fort and enters the valley is technically under the caid's protection and jurisdiction," Joel continued. "The present caid is an army officer, a big drinker easily bought off; a couple bottles of scotch under the table enabled Hamsa to get away with a lot around here."

When we got to Tatoft an hour later, soldiers showed us into the caid's office. He was a swarthy chain-smoking forty-year-old in a Spanish leather jacket who accepted, without comment, the discreetly wrapped bottle of cognac Joel handed him. The caid made no eye contact, ordered an aide to scribble our passport numbers, and listened to the chief's rambling explanation that we were working with them on a folkloric project. The visit was uneventful, a blessing because the caid was the king's representative in the Djebala, called upon to judge all disputes and feuds. "You don't wanna rile him," Joel said, when we were driving through the undulating fields toward Ksar. Spring wheat was just up, and the entire ancient sea floor was bright green.

In town we found a dark café and drank cold orange juice while the wool team dissolved into the covered souks to find someone to embroider the djellabas. We were back in Jajouka by five o'clock, being served the rabbits we'd bought the previous day. Stewed with preserved lemons and ginger, plus cumin seed and cardamom, they were my first rabbits, and they were superb.

WE HEARD BOU JELOUD's music begin at four o'clock in the afternoon, heard the squealing rhaitas like Eastern melodies in a dream. We followed our ears out of the madrassah enclosure and across the upper campo, as the adjoining big field was called, and down to the lower plaza, where the goat god was holding court before four rhaitas and four drummers. The crowd got bigger as the village began to swell with pilgrims. The music was correspondingly more propulsive, the goatish dance more frenzied. Watching the shaggy figure cavorting before me, occasionally digressing to wade into a crowd brandishing his whips, I had a strange moment of terror, a sensation of hot blood sacrifice. *This* god is the god of chaos, the god of frenzy and panic, the god of the bonfire, the god of dance fever, the god of jealousy and sexual rage. I tried to see who was dancing, but Bou Jeloud's face was occluded, an empty black hole in a basket atop a jittery boy's body. The harder the music, the better the dance, feet flying like cloven hooves, gliding along like an automaton.

I had been careful not to smoke during the day. I wanted all my senses to be clear. I wasn't taping this session, just watching and listening and trying to take the whole tribal ritual straight up. Yet watching the Boujeloudiya I felt completely muzzy and stoned after no more than ten minutes. I felt the psychotic tranquillity of the mouse who has been caught by the belled cat and is being played with. Some strange gland had squirted anti-fear juice into my system, allowing an easy kill along the food chain. They say the man being eaten by the lion feels no pain. Something like that is the spell that comes over the outsider who experiences the Aid el Kebir in Jajouka.

Bonfire lit, the goat god leaps through the flames. At six o'clock an invisible cue stops the rhaitas dead. The women near the musicians began their shrill yodel and Bou Jeloud disappears into their midst as the drummers continue to play. Then the drummers stop, with the rhythms continuing from within the pulsing white cluster of women, who keep their own distinctive, hip-swinging time on hourglass-shaped hand-drums. Yow! What a beat! I felt an irresistible urge to dance, but just as I stood up, gentle hands were laid on my djellaba and we were again pulled away from the scene of the Teasing of Bou Jeloud.

"This is frustrating," Joel mumbled in a rare complaint as we walked up an alley between dark houses. Sitting on the terrace of the madrassah, drinking tea, we could hear the women screaming for an hour more to the staccato rattle of their private rhythms. *Lllulululululululu,* they yodeled at the pitch of a shriek. I wanted to disappear to the hammam, leap over the wall, pull up the hood of my djellaba, and sneak down for a look. "That wouldn't do," Joel sniffed when I told him. "They'd throw you off the mountain if they caught you."

NO SUPPER WAS SERVED at the madrassah the following night, because the old cook's daughter had recently birthed a son. Instead he cooked for us at his house in the oldest part of the village, an old Attar family precinct to which we had not previously been invited. We arrived after dark and were shown into a lovely whitewashed bedroom whose walls were covered with lush fabric. Inside were the mother and child, amid a writhing mass of more than a dozen little girls. The beautiful mother, aged sixteen or so, unveiled the baby for us.

"His name is Kerim," Joel said, "and the cook says the father is away somewhere. He was probably born about a week ago, because they usually wait seven days to see if the baby lives, before giving it a name."

Mother smiled at our strange-sounding words, and the bevy of girls giggled and tittered. Kerim was swaddled again and we were transferred to a salon where the chief and other local dignitaries were waiting to eat. The cook, barking orders in his raspy voice, served a groaning feast consisting of couscous in chicken broth, a tagine of mutton and vegetables, crispy fried whiting and cinammon-dusted orange sections. Eating out of a large common dish, I soon became bloated as Berdouz insisted on prying succulent chunks of meat off the bone and placing them invitingly on my side of the plate. As the umpteenth morsel was placed in front of me I began to fear for my digestive tract. *"Safi!"* I cried. Enough!

We could hear music coming from the madrassah as we walked back up the hill after supper, picking our way along the unfamiliar path in the dark. The normally quiet village was filling with relatives and pilgrims, and our way was made easier by light and laughter from many of the houses. Sounds of revelry greeted our arrival as Tahir led a cadre of younger musicians in a spirited Afro-funk jam. After every song, each lasting twenty minutes to half an hour, they filled their pipes with kif and rested until the dancing boys caught their breath. Much later, the only two remaining older musicians, Big Fudul and Little Mohammed Stitu, sat down to play the flute together. No drums, dancing, or distractions, just two veteran pipers playing the *lira,* weaving ethereal countertones and scientific microtones that bore deep. I closed my eyes; it was like Ali Baba and Aladdin having a session. I switched on a microphone and made a tape, but when I played it back later, I could hear only two flutes in beautiful unison. The

66 partials that were so magical, those imaginary sounds that only existed in the listener's inner ear, were beyond modern technology.

That night I ended up in the boys' chamber, a nearly bare room on the other side of the kitchen with a few straw mats and some sardine-tin ashtrays. The younger men hung out here while waiting for their fathers to withdraw from the main chamber. Somewhat bewildered, I stumbled in on the way back from the hammam. Young Berdouz, Amin Attar, Achmido, and a new kid named 'Slimou were playing a game in which they held their breaths until one gave in and breathed. The loser had to answer a series of questions accompanied by a semi-violent sequence of pinches, pokes, and spanks. They thought this hilarious, and held their breaths until they turned blue, these sons of the priests of Pan, whose livelihoods as pipers would someday depend on the breath they were holding fast in their chests.

THE FOLLOWING DAY marked the zenith of the Aid el Kebir. After staying up all night, traditional during the feast days, listening to young Bashir and the other boys practicing on flutes, I emerged from the musicians' compound to find Jajouka almost unrecognizable. During the night the village had been transformed into a pilgrim encampment. White conical tents had sprouted in every corner to shelter hundreds of the faithful who had made their little hajj to the tomb of Sidi Hamid Sherq. Their cookfires, and those of the vendors servicing the crowds, sent grey plumes into the still winter air. I took a deep breath. Mules and donkeys and their droppings added another fragrance to the smell of grilling brochettes.

Back at the madrassah, I found Joel chopping a bit of cocaine on a mirror. "It's gonna be a long day," he said.

Now we were wide awake, but the old masters were slumped into woolen bundles, having passed out from the night's exertions.

Joel and I spent the morning scanning the radio for news and
watching the sky turn twenty different shades of blue.

Bashir Attar came for us at noon. "Come on," he said in English,
and then said *"Agi,"* which means the same thing in Arabic.

"Fain?" I said. "Where?"

"La Fantasía," Bashir said.

A throng of several thousand had encircled the big campo, at
whose other end, two stadia away, gathered a dozen men on big
brown Arabian horses. At a signal they charged the crowd in a line
at top speed while passing their silver-banded muskets under the
necks of their flying horses. At the climactic, near-fatal moment
they reined in, narrowly avoiding trampling the skittish crowd, and
fired smoky rounds from their desert flintlocks. What a scene! Then
they proudly trotted back, heads held high, bells jingling on the
golden caparisons of their steaming ponies.

These Fantasía *caballeros* performed intricate rifle acrobatics for
another hour. Magnificent riders, they wore all white except for
bright yellow slippers. Their chief wore the same kind of woven
gold turban as Jnuin. With each cavalry charge they got nearer to
the crowd until it began to look dangerous. The final explosion of
their muskets signaled the end of the show. After the performance,
Jnuin gave their leader a wad of bills and heartfelt thanks. *"Baraka
l'aufic."*

BOU JELOUD'S MUSIC started around three o'clock. Two Bou Jelouds were working today, joined by a white-bearded boy wearing
a red fez who was dancing the part of Hajj, as well as a chiffon-
laden boy dancing Aisha Hamoka. After only a few minutes, there
was an incident. One of the Bou Jelouds took a less-than-playful
swipe at a young outsider who was insolently crossing the dancing
ground. The stranger tried to punch Bou Jeloud, which turned
out to be a capital crime. Ten villagers were on the perpetrator
within seconds, then a hundred. *Skreeeee* went the music from the

pipes as they began to beat him. Amid the jostling, I could just
glimpse him go down, like he'd been poleaxed. Then they
scraped him up and thrust him in the dusty vanguard of a howling
mob that ran him to the edge of town and threw him over the
cliff. The pipes never stopped. The drums just got louder. No one
else got in Bou Jeloud's way.

Three "gun dancers" showed up in immaculate white robes and
canary yellow slippers, with golden turbans and intricately stitched
leather ammunition bags. Like the riders, they made acrobatic
motions with their flintlocks: twirling, handing off, and behind-the-
back before firing in unison at the dance's final step. Then they did
it again and again, each time ending in a puff of acrid gunsmoke.
"These gun dances have a lot of meaning," Joel said, "although the
musicians haven't told me exactly what it is. I believe it has to do
with the old wars against the Christians. The stitching on their
leather bags represents symbols that protect against incoming bul-
lets. I'd bet there was a cult of Islamic warriors that took assassins'
vows or suicide oaths, and this dance is some kind of survival of all
that."

Just then we were hustled back uphill to the madrassah to meet
with some honored guests—the caid's representative and the sherif
of the shrine at Tatoft. The former was a respected local bureaucrat
who often intervened on behalf of the hill tribes, while the sherif
was a black-toothed little man who commanded *enormous* respect
and deference in Jajouka. ("He's an *extremely* holy dude," Joel
whispered.) The sherif offered kif out of a worn leather mutwi that
had been in his family for generations, and the musicians flocked to
him with their long sebsi pipes, all the while making flattering
comments about the potency and full-headedness of the sherif's
mixture.

After a decent interval, I slipped away from this happy group and
back down to the plaza where the two Bon Jelouds were jumping
through the bonfire and chasing shrieking young women. The rhaitas
and drums had been going for two hours in shifts with no sign of

letting up. The sun was down and the air was dusty and humid. The rites of Pan would continue for hours. I settled in, watching young men home for the feast shed their shoes and join in the dancing until their slick city clothes were soaked and filthy. The Moroccan women who were visiting from town were mostly unveiled, and I realized these were the first female faces (other than the cook's daughter) that I had seen in a couple of weeks.

I allowed myself to settle into Bou Jeloud's rapid groove when a pair of hands pulled at my djellaba. "Agi," said young Abdsalam Fudul, indicating that I follow him.

As we approached the madrassah I knew there was trouble. Parked next to our bus was a beat-up old Morris, an English car. Leaving the compound at a fast walk was Hamsa's wife, Simone, followed by several older musicians telling her she wasn't welcome. She smiled at me despite the hostility of the musicians, and turned left up the hill to another part of the village.

Consternation filled the madrassah. The Masters, livid, were gathered in one end of the room. I looked at Joel; he rolled his eyes toward the far corner where three English travelers in their twenties were huddled miserably for protection. They introduced themselves as Jim, Jane, and their friend Gee. They had stumbled up here, discovered they'd come with someone the musicians didn't like, and were now being shown an extremely cold shoulder after an over-land journey of a thousand miles.

"Pretty deadly vibes in here," I mused.

"I can't believe this," Jim moaned. "We're friends of William Burroughs!"

LATER I HEARD from Joel what had happened. "I was chatting with the Tatoft Sherif when their car pulled up. Hamsa's wife got out and they freaked. They called her a witch and other worse names. It was a bad moment. I was afraid they were going to start throwing stones at her. Then these three climbed out and somehow I got everyone

70   inside and talking, or actually shouting would be more accurate. Mrs. Hamsa explained that these people had been recommended by Burroughs, had driven all the way from England, and were very tired. She obviously knew the musicians couldn't refuse hospitality. So the chief told her she could stay one night, but must leave in the morning.''

"Where did she go?"

"Up to Mohammed Stitu's house. He's Hamsa's uncle. Then Jnuin asked me to tell the Brits that Jajouka was working with us for the time being and to forgive them, but they were 'finish' with Hamsa forever and please come back some other time.''

"Joel, I feel sorry for them.''

"I do too. They're tired, their car was robbed of the usual passports and money in Tangier, and they have colds. I told them we'd see they were taken care of, but they should be off in the morning.''

"How did they take it?''

"Let's just say they're not too thrilled, and I've got a feeling it's gonna get worse. The Malimin are not happy at all about them being here and just want them out.''

Back in the madrassah, the vibes were brutal. The windows had been thrown open and the young men on the terrace—Achmido, Berdouz Junior, Amin, 'Slimou—were alternately scowling at the men and leering at Jane, a pretty girl who obviously didn't want to be there. The two men, on the other hand, were thrilled to follow in the footsteps of the late Brian Jones. They tried to ignore the hostile stares of the boys and pleaded with us.

"Look," said Gee, "can you tell us what's going on? We're completely in the dark.''

I explained about Hamsa and the stolen djellabas. I told them they had the ill fortune to arrive with the wife of the Masters' sworn enemy. It was guilt by association.

"That's a relief," Gee said. "But do we really have to leave tomorrow?

"Well, Simone has to leave in the morning, and since you brought her here, you must take her away," Joel said. "We feel bad about it, but there's nothing we can do."

It was six o'clock. In the distance I could hear Bou Jeloud's music. I wanted to be down there, but the musicians wouldn't let the English kids see anything.

"This is *absurd,*" the girl said. "Are we under arrest or anything? I'd like to leave *now*. I *never* wanted to come up here anyway. I should have flown home after the car was broken into." Her boyfriend Jim said he was too tired to drive down the mountain in the dark, and begged her to be patient until morning.

An hour later tables and gas lamps were brought in and set up. Achmido circulated with warm water and towels. Supper was terrific—big tagines of chicken and goat cooked with almonds. The English trio was famished and made a great show of eating with their right hands. The men asked a thousand questions; we tried to answer. Seeing Hamsa's wife had produced indigestion in the older musicians. They told us she was a *haramia,* a sorceress, and the village would have to be exorcised after she left.

After supper, the musicians smoked a few pipes and began to relax, stretching their worn bare feet on the thick carpet. As a special treat for the Aid el Kebir, Joel had bought two quarts each of Coca-Cola and Fanta orange soda from a vendor. Malim Ali mixed a toxic cocktail in their tea glasses, two parts coke to one part Fanta. This ultra-sweet elixir was savored like a vintage port, as looks of great contentment spread over the rapt features of the old men.

Tahir put on a show for the pretty English girl that night. After presiding over the drumming for Bou Jeloud, and dancing with the women later on, he had gone home, washed, slicked his hair, and put on a clean white shirt and tie, over which he wore a soft white woolen djellaba. He entered the madrassah with the flair of a Moroccan gigolo. He greeted the English formally, lingering slightly over the hand of the girl. He took his place at the head of the room and picked up the gimbri, which he began to tune. Within ten minutes he had the primitive lute purring like a leopard in heat. His goathorn pick flew over the strings in a blur, and his high-pitched voice began to wail a horny love aria.

Joel leaned over to relate a story. "About a year ago, around the time Ornette was here, a crew from Swedish television came and stayed a few days. One of the Swedes was a young girl, and she and Tahir got it on. He really fell for her, but she went back to Stockholm. He wanted to follow her but couldn't. That was when I learned that Tahir isn't from Jajouka," he added. "His name isn't Attar like most of the others, it's Bokazar. His family lives down in Ksar el Kebir."

By then the drums had started and Tahir got up to dance. After displaying some astonishing Al Green moves, he took the English girl's hand and bade her dance with him. It was a brazen thing for Tahir to dance with a woman in Jajouka, but Joel explained that any woman allowed in the madrassah was considered an honorary man, so it was all right. To her absolute credit, the girl shook with a willowy grace and, after a few moments, some pleasure. In the end, she got a rousing burst of applause from the Malimin when she sat down. They appreciated her effort.

"There hasn't been an attractive foreign woman here in a long time," Joel said. "At least one that would dance for them."

For the rest of the evening, the atmosphere was more relaxed. A dancing boy in full drag entertained. The two English guys loved it. The room gradually filled with people, and the music got quite hot; Jim tried to set up a little tape recorder, but Berdouz told him to put it away, explaining that we alone were permitted to tape. I told him I was sorry, and that if he left his address, I'd send him a cassette someday.

The far room had been opened up for the extra visitors, who retired around midnight, grey from fatigue. I was tired too, but the madrassah was still full of young blood who played music all night in shifts, sustained by tea and kif. I stayed awake with them as long as I could.

HAMSA'S WIFE APPEARED at the wall the next day just before noon, putting on a brave face. She seemed interesting, knew everyone on a first-name basis, and I regretted not being able to speak with her. Her companions loaded themselves into their car after Berdouz conspicuously fondled the girl's breasts as he was bidding them a compassionate good-bye. Then they drove off, much to everyone's relief.

THE HOLIDAY HAD peaked the day before, but there were still crowds of pilgrims in Jajouka. Bou Jeloud would dance for several more evenings, and many visitors stayed to pay their respects to the Masters.

Late that day I smoked with nervous young Mohammed as he dressed in Bou Jeloud's skins in the damp shade of the hammam. Mohammed was tall and skinny, a supple dancer who suggested a lot with little turns of his head or rear. Of all the Bou Jelouds I saw, he was the best. We had no common language, but he smiled and commented in dialect as I watched him put on the costume, feeding him kif so he would tolerate my being there. His ears pricked up like an animal's when he heard the rhaitas and drums commence in the village square down below.

Bou Jeloud *stinks*. The odor of the old goatskins commingled with the accumulated sweat and body protein of the last hundred boys to dance in the skins is appalling.

Bou Jeloud finished blacking his face with burnt cork. He motioned for another pipe, took a big hit, spat out the coal, handed the long wooden tube back, and was out the door without a word, like a savage beast. I dropped everything and ran after him, the music blazing in my ears. I followed him down the hill overlooking the blue valley, through a stony alley between houses. He hit the top of the plaza at a dead run, having acquired two stalks of leafy oleander on the way. Women screamed, children cried,

74   the rhaitas went mad, and the crowd parted to let the day's festival begin. Bou Jeloud was on the prowl, and panic filled my heart.

I sat with Joel and Morgan and a group of young men from the village and watched as Bou Jeloud pranced around offering comic threat displays. From the cluster of white-blanketed women and girls on the hillock across the plaza, one of them stared at me with intense curiosity. She was about my age and very pretty, with long unveiled black hair gathered in braids. Her prominent cheekbones were rosy and her black eyes were shaded with kohl. Around her neck she wore a wonderful display of necklaces—old amber, red coral, silver, turquoise and jade-green amazonite. Her caftan was light blue, with dark blue piping. She regarded me directly, without shame. She was probably married, but I fell for her immediately. This must be, I thought to myself, Jajouka Black Eyes herself. After a few minutes, with Bou Jeloud about to wade into the women, she put on her mindle and I lost track of her.

This night, instead of being led away, we were allowed to stay; supple Tahir and his drum disappeared into the throng of dancing women along with Bou Jeloud, and the women of Jajouka seemed to heave together and breathe as one. The mystery that unfolded at the center of the circle was still forbidden to infidel eyes, but the rhythms these women generated were otherworldly, totally penetrating, and like nothing I had ever heard. I wanted to tape this bit, but was gently discouraged. Evidently the women's part of the Boujeloudiya was going to remain private.

That night I took a gas lamp to the hammam where I found Bou Jeloud's steaming skins and bonnet discarded next to the bog hole, as if, after dancing, the goat god had apotheosized into pure organic shit and been subsumed into the ground. The smell was awful, half human and half goat. Mohammed wouldn't be seen again that night; the boy who danced the goat god was himself somewhat taboo for the duration of the Aid el Kebir. Sometimes Bou Jeloud died. It had happened a few years earlier, right after Ramadan. A boy had danced for a week, gone home and drunk many liters of water, and died in his skins. Apparently, it wasn't that uncommon. That night in the hammam, the lank goatskin costume seemed to breathe in the flickering lamplight, as if it were alive and waiting for the next boy to come along, put it on, and dance.

chapter 3

Malim Ashmi Speaks

Down the mountain, across the plain, up the coastline through the *bled,* or countryside, unpopulated and enormous, and into the white city. After two weeks in the mountains, returning to Tangier was a feast of small pleasures, first among them a hot bath at the Villa Elizabeth. (What a luxury to turn a tap for hot water!) The house came with a caretaker named Mohammed, who lived in a hovel in the bowels of the house, and a perky Fatima who arrived, veiled, in the morning, brewed coffee and heated milk, cleaned and washed, served lunch and went home to her family. It was paradise. A starving mother cat with a brawling brood of kittens lived under the kitchen and devoured our table scraps, providing entertainment.

I spent the afternoons in the Café Paris reading the papers: *Times* of London, Paris *Herald Tribune,* and the *Matin du Sahara,* published by the government in Casablanca. I alternated mint tea with *café con leche* until the sun set behind the portico of the French consulate across the Place de France. Then Joel and I crossed the Socco Grande and dove into the medina, its main streets full of gaily lit shops, its alleys a dark maze of furtive courtyards and dead ends. Joel led me to the house of an old friend, Mohammed Yusufi.

"You like smoke kif?" Mohammed asked gleefully the first day I met him.

"I think I've become an addict," I told him.

"Well, you *do* get habituated to it," Joel said. "You wake up in the morning and your mouth tingles, first thing. You want a pipe. After meals, you think about the pipe. The grass in Jajouka is world class, and the tobacco gives you a craving for more."

"Pass the pipe," I said.

IN THE EARLY EVENING we'd go back to the cafés along the Boulevard Pasteur, maybe Claridge's or the Koutoubia, and watch the girls as they left work. I always looked in at the European bookstore, Librairie des Colonnes, to see if anything new had come in. We took supper in restaurants or Joel would cook us chicken if we had provisioned that day at the European market in the Rue Fez. At night we sat around the salon of the villa and cruised the shortwave radio or played tapes we'd brought, especially Joel's soul music cassette, with Marvin Gaye pleading and begging, "Let's get it on."

THE WEATHER TURNED rough in the Strait of Gibraltar later that week, and we all got sick. As floods of black rain clouds scudded eastbound through the narrow pass between Europe and Africa, we were brought down with abdominal cramps. "It was something we ate somewhere," Joel said. "It's a rite of passage, *la turista.*" While it rained, the terraces of the cafés were soaked and empty; inside the tables were packed and the air was so thick with black tobacco that respiration was difficult. So we stayed in the villa, huddled

around an electric fire, and planned our next visit to Jajouka. I told
Joel that I wanted to start interviewing individual musicians. "My
suggestion," Joel said, "would be to hire Mohammed Yusufi as
official interpreter. He's out of work, the fishing is bad these days,
and he could use some cash."

That night Mohammed arrived with a roar at the gate of the Villa
Elizabeth on a motorbike with his wife Aisha on the back seat, her
arms full of bundles. The caretaker wouldn't open the gate for his
fellow Moroccans until Joel intervened, explaining that these were
our guests. He protested that no Moroccan had ever been a guest
in this house before, and went down to his hovel to sulk. The
bundles held the makings of a Tangerine bouillabaisse, which sim-
mered for the next few hours while Mohammed Yusufi cut some
fresh kif and held forth. "I am a Muslim, a musician, and a fishing-
man, in this order," he said proudly. He was about thirty, with
close-cropped grey hair and one of the saddest faces I ever saw, even
when he smiled. You could see by looking at him that he had
suffered terribly at an early age. He told me later he was an orphan
from the Rif who lost his whole family during a famine, but would
say no more. Aisha was older, about forty-five, with a kind smile
and gold teeth.

After we had feasted on the herbed red shellfish stew, Mohammed produced a four-stringed African banjo, and Aisha a tambourine; they sang for us beautifully, sad old Moorish love songs,
until Morgan fell asleep on the sofa and the Moroccan couple
apologized for keeping us up so late.

No, we protested, keep playing, stay the night, we have lots of
rooms. Instead, they cleaned the kitchen and got on their Honda
125 bike and drove home. But before he left, Mohammed said he
would meet us in the morning and return with us to Jajouka for one
week. Then he looked at me and said, "You have Muslim face. Very
Muslim, Berber face."

.   .   .

80 FIVE MILES SOUTH of Tangier, on the Atlantic coastal road, the clouds broke and we were plunged back into wicked North African sunlight. Om Kalthoum was on the radio, wailing one of her volcanic Egyptian odes, Joel was at the wheel, and Yusufi was in the back, making opinionated Moroccan proclamations like, "Womens is nothing and good for nothing. The washing . . . the cleaning . . . the children. Safi. Don't do nothing but sit in house and clean. Soon you will see it: *No more mini-skirts in Tanja!* Womens go back to veil and tradition dress!"

"But Mohammed," protested Morgan. "I like to see a woman's legs."

"Ha, you are a Nazrani, a Nazarene, and thus ill in your head. You should become a Muslim. You have a Muslim face."

Jajouka had emptied of the faithful and returned to its sleepy self. We were greeted by shouts and running children as we drove through the town to the madrassah and into the walled courtyard with its hundred-mile view. A dozen pairs of eager hands reached for the luggage and the load of groceries we'd picked up in the markets. A dozen smiling faces appeared in the windows to kiss and be kissed. Mohammed Yusufi was welcomed like a brother, and soon we were under the muzzy spell of Jajouka, prone on cushions with a pipe and a glass of tea, while Tahir whittled gimbri picks out of a black goat horn, and Berdouz badgered Yusufi about life in Tangier.

Tahir leaned over and told us that everything was *tranquilo.* "When you are here," he said, "everyone forgets their troubles and no one fights. The musicians smoke, eat, drink tea, make music. No complaining, no arguments, everyone behaves. *B'saha,*" he said, meaning so be it, *enjoy it.*

It was splendid to be back among the brotherhood. With the holiday over, it felt like we had them to ourselves.

The chief appeared after an hour in his white woolen djellaba and golden turban, the big silver drop dangling from his left ear like a talisman. Some issues had been debated in our absence, Jnuin said, and he wanted to clarify Jajouka's position. "You have lived with us," he said, "and you see how the Malimin exist. No one here drinks tea unless all are served. No one is allowed a sour face. We are a family. Though we have some new djellabas, thanks be to God, no one will wear his until *all* are sewn. This is all I have to say."

AFTER THE HOLIDAY the Master Musicians assumed the routines of life in the mountains. The more prosperous older musicians had some agriculture going; in the morning they sent their wives and daughters out to the fields and their younger sons up to higher pastures with the flocks. We heard them early in the day, goat bells clapping amid the trilling cane flutes of the young shepherds. Some of the more fit musicians carried out communal tasks for the brotherhood, tending their clubhouse, preparing meals and making new instruments. There were several Attar bachelors who did no work at all. They spent their days at the madrassah playing cards, smoking and waiting for the call to play at some wedding or festival down in the valley of the Ahl Sherif. The most imperious of these celibatos was a tall rhaita player named Achmed Attar, who we called Achmed Sicko because of his grotesque black humor. If Malim Ali scalded himself while making tea, Achmed Sicko unleashed a harsh peal of laughter. If Morgan burned his fingers by holding a wax match too long, Achmed Sicko dissolved in scornful glee. He loved suffering, thought it was a scream. He spent all his time with us during our residence, squatting near where we sat, we were sure, in hopes of seeing us do damage to ourselves, watching us like a hawk.

"You know," Morgan said after a while, "the pace here is kinda slow. In fact, if I do much more sitting around I'm gonna go nuts. I gotta shoot some rolls for Washington or they'll be pissed."

Joel said, "I think Malim Ali here just said he was cutting some kif this afternoon. He's like the master of rituals around here. He does all the wood carving too. Why don't you concentrate on him for a few days?'' And indeed, later in the day, Ali showed up with the tools and product of the kif-cutter's craft and permitted Morgan to make a series of photos with the stipulation that only his hands were pictured.

"Oh yeah," Morgan said. "After a while you forget this stuff is illegal."

"It's not only the kif that's a problem," Joel said. "It's the home-grown tobacco they mix with it. Tobacco is the king's monopoly here and is heavily taxed. You can do more jail time for the tobacco than for the kif."

In the shade of the metal roof that covered the terrace, Ali set up his cutting board. From stalks of heavily budded dried marijuana plants, Ali began to pluck leaves, stems and twigs until only the green bract that surrounded the hempen seed remained. This he gingerly harvested into a numinous pile, separating the glistening black seeds. Using his leathern fingers to tamp down the moist, oily flowers, he diced them with a mean-looking curved black knife. An old knife. Finished chopping, he spread out the diced herb to check for color. Then he gathered it and chopped it again. "Check the leaves, which we smoke back home with pleasure," Joel said, gesturing toward the discarded stuff at the side of the board. "It's called *shira,* or shit; *they throw it away.*"

After more obsessive cutting, Ali had a couple of ounces of kif in front of him. Malim Titi appeared with some long, dark brown leaves, which he placed on the cutting board.

"Titi grows the tobacco," Joel said. "He has the only tobacco patch in the village, and it's said that the reason his product tastes so hot and sweet is that Titi farts on the plants."

"God, that's revolting," Morgan observed. Tall Titi smiled his widest gap-toothed grin and said, "B'saha."

Ali diced the black tobacco the way he cut the kif, slowly and thoroughly, until it formed a little pile. "This is the hardest part," Joel said. "Mixing is always a matter of taste. The proportions have to be just right, and they're usually sixty/forty, kif to tobacco."

When the color of the mix satisfied Ali, he took a carved sebsi from its leather *zhwah* and sampled the kif. Then he corrected the taste with more tobacco. "Too little tobacco is bad form," Joel said. "You don't want kif that's *m'suss*—weak."

"Kif alone mek you krazee," Mohammed Yusufi chimed in. An expert cutter himself, or so he felt, he had been closely observing Malim Ali's technique. "Americans smoke kif with no *tabac,*" he said laughing. "No wonder they all krazee."

Berdouz walked by, comically clearing his throat while waiting to be invited to test-smoke Malim Ali's fresh batch. He filled his big pipe and pronounced the kif fresh and satisfying. "Outasight!" he exclaimed. "Eberryting! Berry gut!"

Ali made sure our communal *National Geographic* pouch was filled with kif; then he filled his own mutwi and slipped away to a corner of the compound to pray.

THE NEXT MORNING we were up before the sun in order to climb the big mountain that overlooked Jajouka's promontory and the valley of the Ahl Sherif.

"My editors like to see overview shots," Morgan had announced the day before, "so the reader can get 'the big picture.' Any volunteers?"

A trek was organized. Outside the old green doors were three of the boys, whom we burdened with cameras, oranges, and water bags. We made our way down through the dark cultivated fields, over the boulder-mad roaring stream, up the bare hillside past Bou Jeloud's cave until we found a goat track that threaded up the mountain. We climbed for another hour through a conifer forest until we reached the treeline and the sun broke like glory over the taller peaks to the east. We watched the immense valley beneath us illumined, inch by inch, by new light flooding into it. Morgan snapped away. Joel chatted with the boys, while I looked at the squat, impassive face of Ahmed Aribou and tried to figure him out.

Aribou was a mystery to us because he was so despised by his own senior generation of musicians. He was always neatly dressed in a short brown mountain djellaba, impeccable white shirt and breeches, a snowy turban carefully wound on his head. He was short of stature, quiet, and very subservient for one his age, performing most of the menial tasks and dirty work. He played the drum in the shrine of Sidi Hamid Sherq, and took a lot of shit from the other musicians. There had been an incident the previous evening involving him, which was captured on the tape I was recording of a flute piece. The music had suddenly faltered when Berdouz stopped playing and the other drummers, playing hourglass-shaped ceramic *drabougas* and round flat *bendirs,* piddled out as well. The clappers stopped and the pipers trilled at the high end of their pipes and quit.

"Aribou stinks," Berdouz spat. "He can't play."

Aribou looked mortified. His eyes widened in dismay. "That isn't true, Malim Berdouz," he said. "Enough!"

"He doesn't know the beat," Berdouz complained. "The voice is wrong. He plays the drabouga like my old mule fucks!"

Much lighting up, coughing, and laughter accompanied this declaration. Aribou flushed slightly, but seemed used to this kind of treatment. "This isn't right, Malim, in front of the Nazarenes like this. The time was *Ntata Ntata Ntata Ntata.*"

"*Uminta Uminta Uminta,* you turd." Berdouz was disgusted and blew the coal from his sebsi into the ashtray with contempt. "Give the drum to your little brother and go play with the boys next door," Berdouz commanded. "And bring in a *mizhmar,* my hands are cold." And Aribou meekly did as he was told. When he left the room his seat was assumed by his son, who was treated with all due respect.

What transgression, we wondered, had the senior Aribou committed, to bring such scorn and derision upon his head? Almost every night the musicians made sport of him. Sometimes, after making him play the dancing boy for an evening, which he did with a disgruntled smile, the others would stand up at the end of a

frenzied bout and mockingly chant, "AR-RI-BOU, AR-RI-BOU,"
until they collapsed in derisive laughter and glee. The fact that he
trekked up the mountain with us was an indication of his low social
status, but to me he seemed stolid and incredibly strong, and I was
quite happy to have him along.

After an hour on our perch we began to hear the distant ululation
of Jajouka's young female population. They had spread out around
us in the mountain forest with axes to gather firewood. Spying us
at the crest of their mountain, they called to us, teasing with that
ululating tribal yodel.

The landscape that stretched to the ocean, thirty or so kliks away,
was a plain of green fields humped by chains of small hills that rolled
in orderly undulations.

"There's no doubt in my mind that we're looking at a prehistoric
seafloor. It's like *this* spot was once the edge of the African continent, and the waves once broke on the rocks below Jajouka," Joel
mused.

"Maybe you're smoking too much of that weed," Morgan said
absently, as he rewound his fifth roll of film.

BREAKFAST WAS WAITING when we returned, dirty and tired from
our trek. (The young Moroccans were unwinded and seemed not
to perspire in their djellabas.) Coffee, hot wheat bread with honey,
and eggs fried crisp in oil brought us back to life. I spent the rest
of the day twirling the dial of the radio between the weak U.S.
Armed Forces station in Kenitra (which had news on the hour), the
Moroccan station from Casablanca (with its Islamic sonorities), and
a flash of the BBC World Service on short-wave: " '. . . *seems like
a dream, you got me hyp-no-tized*'. . . That was Fleetwood Mac,
number eight on our survey . . .''

After lunch, a group of young men arrived at the madrassah. The
previous afternoon, the tribal soccer ball, already in tatters, had
been destroyed in a hard-fought battle between the Attars and the

86   Rotobes. Now there was consternation involving the current afternoon game on the campo, which was the major energy burner for the youth of the area: not only was there no ball, but there was massive disagreement about who bore responsibility for replacing it. "No problem," I told them, and volunteered to drive into Ksar that afternoon and let the National Geographic Society have the honor of replacing the damaged ball.

We piled a big gang into the van and bumped down the mountain to the dirt road that led towards Alcazar. Mohammed Yusufi and I spent the afternoon at the Café Central drinking orange juice while the Malimin went shopping. They found a soccer ball, imported from France and prohibitively expensive even after an epic Moroccan haggle. I ducked into the food market, black with flies, for coffee, chocolate, the freshest tangerines in the world, a dozen rolls of pink, devastatingly coarse toilet paper, plus the last five kilos of silver sardines left in the fish market.

There was singing in the van on the rutted paved road out of town. I was struck by the brilliant light on the greening hills of new wheat and sugar beets, which had been brown soil only two weeks before. Now long lines of stooped weeding peasants moved up the hills, leaving darker cultivated earth in their wake. At the end of the day we'd see them returning to their settlements on big farm trucks, crammed like animals, singing and waving as we drove by. As we lurched back up the mountain, the setting sun rouged the rocky road.

Jubilation greeted the new soccer ball and a huge game was organized: the Jajoukans against the Americans. I played in my mud boots, and even the teachers put on track suits and running shoes and came out to play in an epic contest that featured four goals scored by slim barefoot Mohammed Bou Jeloud (that's what we called him) against the most ferocious checking since England beat Germany in the 1966 World Cup.

Night fell. Musicians came and went. "I'm always curious about the social structure up here," Joel said, "the segregation of fathers from sons. Not even a thirty-year-old man can be in the same room with his fifty-year-old father.''

"Yeah," Morgan said, "if the father walks in and sits down, the son checks out right away."

"I know that the same structure doesn't apply with the women. When my girlfriend was living here with me, she was taken in by the women, and said that they all lived happily together in their homes on the other side of Jajouka.''

THE NEXT MORNING was Tuesday, market day in Tatoft. At nine I watched Joel and Morgan drive off in our van crammed with market-bound musicians, their families and chickens. I took an escort of boys and descended the mountain by foot. The ancient trail that traced the mountain's watercourses and geosynclines was already busy with traffic from villages higher in the hills, and we walked briskly among donkeys and mules laden with high loads of produce. Despite my djellaba, some old country women noticed my un-Moroccan gait and made some evidently hilarious comments at my expense. But I didn't mind: it felt fine to be part of this trickle of humans and animals headed for the country market.

After two hours, we arrived at Tatoft. We heard a commotion and discovered Berdouz shouting at the owner of the corral. The little drummer was livid because the guy wanted ten francs to park Berdouz's mule for an hour. (The mule was eventually parked for free after Berdouz threatened the wrath of Sidi Hamid Sherq.) I found Morgan among the market stalls, shooting colorful mounds of spices heaped in the open air. We wandered over to the pens to look at the goats and sheep, lean and ribby in their winter coats. "A summer in the high pastures will fatten them up," Joel observed.

Shopping was over by noon. I followed Jnuin, Fudul, and Malim Ali to the dark, cool house of their friend, the Sherif of Tatoft, whose kif was of such high octane that even the Masters were in awe of him. Even the cynical Yusufi later admitted that the sherif was

88   "very holy man." I liked the sherif's saintly smile that displayed his rotting black teeth.

I walked back to Jajouka in yellow sunlight with my boys and some of the musicians who couldn't fit in the van because of all that had been purchased. There were funny traffic jams in Jajouka when market people heading up-country were caught among tinkling goat flocks coming down from pasture. Some of my fellow travelers would walk ten miles farther into the Djebel before reaching their hamlets.

The cook served a big tagine of chicken, carrots, and couscous that evening, and we filled our mouths with the steaming, cumin-spiced mélange of grain, roots, and fowl.

Morgan had enjoyed a field day at the market and after a few pipes was in a ruminative mood.

"What would happen if you fell for one of the girls here?"

"Do you have anyone in mind?" Joel teased.

"Well no, not really, although there are some real beauties up here." That was true. As our presence in Jajouka became less of a novelty, some of the young women had stopped covering themselves as we passed by.

"I don't know what would happen," Joel said. "Maybe you could become a Muslim and get married. Maybe you'd be driven out of town at the point of a stick and the girl would be in a lot of trouble. I heard there was a case down in Marrakech back in '69 where a Dutch hippie boy with long blond hair started cavorting with his Moroccan girlfriend in public. She was a stunning tattooed sixteen-year-old chick from somewhere in the Atlas, and somehow she hooked up with this guy in Marrakech. Anyway, they started living together and being outrageous in the street. One day, the Dutch kid was arrested and thrown out of Morocco on the first plane. The girl was stoned to death by the neighbors."

"Nice story," Morgan grunted.

"So don't get any ideas," Joel said.

The night was cold, the stars shone like lanterns, and the Master

Musicians of Jajouka huddled around the *mizhmar,* a clay pot containing a simmering charcoal fire. Some warmed their hands, some fanned the low flames, and some immersed the ceramic bowls of their kif pipes in the glowing embers to sear out the tar and ash for a smoother draw. The little clay bowls turned into red embers themselves, molten and nearly transparent, before being plucked out of the inferno and laid among grey ash at the side of the brazier to cool.

I spent most of the evening with the younger men—Amin and Bashir Attar, their brother Abdallah (who had been an extravagantly wild Bou Jeloud), Berdouz Junior, Achmido, Mohammed Bou Jeloud. They had their own mizhmar going in the room next to the kitchen, where they reclined on reed mats, smoked, and occasionally produced some hip-shaking Moroccan-roll of their own, generally more out of control than the Djibli produced in the big room next door. These young kids also played more raunchy games of a good-natured sadistic bent. "Building a House" was a favorite. Everyone stacked thumbs and held their breath until some player cracked up. The whole premise of the game was so carnal that it was hard to keep a straight face. The one who cracked up had to get down on all fours and submit to general humiliation and a beating.

Most of the young men were under twenty-five. Most of the Malimin were in their fifties and early sixties. Where, I asked them, were their older brothers? Where were the men in their thirties? In the army, they answered. When you go, it's for twenty years, then you come back to Jajouka and retire. Others were in Europe, making cars or driving trucks. Or sweeping streets, I said. No, they said, not possible. No one from Jajouka would do that kind of work.

Amin asked, "Have you seen Malim Ashmi?"

I hadn't. "Who is he?"

"Malim Ashmi is the oldest malim. He is the teacher of all the musicians. They say he's over a hundred years old. Tell my father you want to see Malim Ashmi!"

THE NEXT MORNING I asked Joel about Malim Ashmi. "Is he still alive?" he wondered. "I've never seen him, only heard about him. I thought he had died."

"Well, Amin said he was among the living, and that we should ask to see him."

"If he is alive," Joel said, "I don't know that he could be much help to you. When I was first told about him, they said he was a hundred and ten. They also said he didn't go out of his house and didn't like Europeans."

The chief smiled when he heard our request. "Malim Ashmi? Of course he's alive. He's a hundred fifteen years. Was he our teacher? *Never.* He's too old to have paid much attention to us. He taught our *grandfathers,* and they taught us! You want to talk to him? If God wills it. Today I'll go to his house and ask his son. How old is his son? Maybe ninety."

The next morning, a frail apparition appeared on the crest of the hill overlooking the madrassah. Tiny, stooped, covered in a pointy-hooded grey djellaba, the figure staggered along supported by a gnarled wooden staff much taller than the person who carried it. Several of the musicians lounging on the porch gasped with surprise. Malim Ashmi! Coming to the madrassah!

Jnuin and Achmed Skirkin, the cook, met the old man at the gate and escorted him to the warmest seat on the terrace. When he was settled on a divan, Malim Ashmi let his hood drop back, revealing a wizened but unwrinkled ancient face under a fresh, pure white turban. Malim Ashmi's shirt and breeches were also crisp and white, and he wore his best yellow slippers. He spoke toothlessly to Jnuin, who bent low to hear the old man's whisper. "Malim Ashmi says that he has come to visit the foreigners because he has been told that they are helping Jajouka," the chief related. "Malim Ashmi says he will smoke a pipe or two and drink a glass of tea, and will try to answer any question you pose to him. He also says he is unsure of his memory because he is almost with Allah, but not yet." The other musicians smiled fondly as Malim Ashmi withdrew a mutwi and a simple reed pipe from the folds of his robe, deftly tapped out a charge of kif from the lip of the shriveled leathern pouch, filled his pipe and, with the help of a light from the cook, took a short draw or two before laboriously ejecting the coal with a snort from his lungs. A glass of tea was reverently set in front of him, and Ashmi sat back between the chief and the cook, looking attentive and expectant. When I turned on the tape recorder, a brief look of dismay passed over his old features like a double exposure, but he regained his composure when assured that the machine would not harm him. Yusufi began to ask my questions, but Ashmi spoke first, peering at me intently.

"What do these children want? Achmed! Tell them our dancing boys had bums like ripe figs. God! I'll never forget it. Ha!"

The chief smiled wanly. "We can't tell them that, Malim Ashmi."

"Yes, all right. Ask the questions. Where is my pipe?"

"Right here, Malim Ashmi."

"Thank you. I want to tell them about the thousands of beautiful boys I made love to in the palace in Fez, in Meknes, in Marrakech. We ate the tongues of sheep every night. We were treated like kings! Only His Majesty the sultan lived better than we!"

"Malim Ashmi, do you know how old you are?"

"Well, yes. I was born in the last year of the reign of Sultan Abd er-Rahman [1859]. It was same year [1860], when the new sultan lost a big battle to the Spanish, that I was born here in Jajouka."

When did you go to court to play for the sultan?

Yes. Good. Let me think . . . there was a royal *dahir* [decree] that we had here in Jajouka. It said we had always played for the sultan. There were papers! We had them. A group of our best musicians lived with the sultan and traveled with him and his army and government from city to city. Eight thousand rifles!

"How long did we have our papers? We always had papers. We

92 had them from the Alouiya. [The Alouite sultans have ruled from 1630 until today.] And before then—from the Saadis at Marrakech, from the Merinids at Fez for hundreds of years, from the Almohads and Almoravids at Marrakech . . . all the way to the Idrissi in Fez a thousand years ago. Listen to me! We are the sultan's musicians and always have been!''

Joel asked the chief if he still had the royal papers, and it was explained that Spanish army officers came to Jajouka fifty years earlier and took the papers to Tetuan, where the governor still has them.

The interview continued after some delay because Malim Ashmi was haranguing the cook about some famous date vendor who claimed to have made love to Malim Ashmi a hundred years ago, when Ashmi was himself a young dancing boy. This was an outrageous lie, the old man stammered, because it was he, Malim Ashmi, who had somehow turned the tables and made love to the date vendor. Achmed Skirkin smiled indulgently, as he had heard all this many times already.

Malim Ashmi, I persisted, when did you go to court to play music?

''Listen! I will tell you!'' The old man paused for a minute, and then spoke. ''We lived at court in Fez. Six of us at any one time. We were paid by the month. Also at Marrakech. Don't forget that. I started late. It was the year that Sultan Moulay al-Hassan I received the English at Marrakech [1877]. Do they understand me? Good. Tell them exactly what I am telling you.''

Malim Ashmi, what did you do when you lived in the palace?

''We had two jobs, at least, every day, playing the rhaita. We played when His Majesty woke up in the morning, and the rhaita was the last sound he heard at night. Rhaitas and drums. Our papers also gave us the right to play his majesty to mosque on Friday. We preceded him in the streets, he followed on horseback, under his parasol, surrounded by his black slaves. But we went first to say he was coming.

"When the sultan and his *makhzan* [government] traveled in a great *harka* [army], we were the heralds. We rode ahead on horseback, playing away. When we came to a new city the sound of the rhaitas opened the gates and closed all the shops. We'd ride through the streets playing the rhaita while thirty thousand women would ululate in welcome for His Majesty. We always got the pick of the boys! Aaagghhh!'' At this point on the tape Malim Ashmi coughed for five minutes. Then he lit another sebsi and tried to focus his dim eyes in our direction.

Tell us more, Malim Ashmi.

But the old man was off on a tangent. "We ate sheep's tongues so we could stay hard for hours. There were contests in the boy harems back then. Every important tribe had one, and they vied in getting their most beautiful boys to the sultan, or maybe the vizier. Sometimes we got the ones the sultan didn't want. I had hundreds, thousands, more than anyone at the palace, except Sa Majesté. When there was a feast and they slaughtered the sheep, we'd steal the tongues and roast them. . . . Ask the foreigners if they would help me find a new wife. I've had four wives, but they're all finished now. Children? Dozens! *H'amdullah!*''

Malim Ashmi, which was your favorite sultan?

"What does he want? Favorite sultan? What a question. My first, Moulay Hassan I, was a warrior, a real *man*. Allah be praised!

"My father was with his father, Moulay Mohammed IV. After Hassan died coming back from Tafilalet [1894], we went with his son, Moulay Adb el-Aziz. He was a very big man, but he was weak. He gave Morocco to the English. We had an English caid at the palace and we had to play 'God Save the King' when His Majesty woke up in the morning. For five hundred years, maybe longer, we played *'Kaimonos'* when His Majesty got up. Now, it was 'God Save the King.'

"When they made Moulay Abd el-Aziz abdicate [in 1908, when Morocco was partitioned into a Franco-Spanish Protectorate], the sultan retired to Tanja [Tangier] and we were sent to Rabat to await the arrival of the new sultan, Moulay Hafid, who was the sultan's brother. But Moulay Hafid stayed in Fez and never came [to Rabat], so we went home to Jajouka in disgust. We looked at our papers. They are legal papers! Learned holy men in Fez drew them up long ago! The papers say that the musicians pass from one king to another, but we did not wish to go to Fez. To us, the *real* sultan was in Tanja. So we went to Tanja and worked for Abd el-Aziz, who liked our music. They were good times. I was fifty years old then. We had plenty of money and kif, plenty of boys to make love with. See these men [referring to the chief and the cook]? I made love with their grandfathers. And now *they* are grandfathers! HEE-hee-hee-hee.'' Malim Ashmi cackled like dry leaves burning.

Then what happened, Malim Ashmi?

There was a long pause, during which the old man appeared to doze. But then he nudged the chief and asked for tea. He looked at Yusufi, who had come with us from Tangier, and said, ''You are not from around here, not a Djibli. No? You are from the Rif. I know this face.''

We tried again. Did you ever play for Moulay Hafid?

''No, by God. Not once! Then his brother Moulay Yusuf was made sultan [in 1912], and he called the Jajouka musicians to Rabat, where the French had put him. We tried to go to him, but Jajouka was now enclosed by the Spanish Zone. We were cut off from our own sultan! The French had him! Then the caliph of Tetuan offered us good money to come play for him, so we went. Then he died and his son hired us. Then we played for Si B'raisul, the son of the pirate Raisouli. He was a brute of the streets who fought the Spanish from the Rif. He had his own army! We were with him! He needed our baraka for his war with the Spanish. But he lost. I think they killed him.''

Here the chief interjected that the Spanish authorities had taken a dim view of Jajouka's association with the constant rebellions in the Rif, which many Spaniards died trying to subdue. When the rebellion led by Abd el-Krim failed in 1924, the Spanish officers

came up to Jajouka to take the musicians' papers. The chief said that
it was the first time in a thousand years that a Christian had set foot
in Jajouka. He also maintained, vehemently supported by the cook,
that the Spanish confiscated two violins the musicians used, which
they said were made by a great Italian violin malim, "Stradivario."

What happened to these violins, Joel asked.

Jnuin said he didn't know. There was a silence as Malim Ashmi
dozed. A bee circled like a lumbering old fighter plane and then
plunged headlong into Ashmi's glass of tea, offering himself up to
a forty-minute orgasm and death. But Joel lifted the bee out by a
wing and laid him on the table to dry off. "Too decadent for me,"
he said.

Ashmi woke a few minutes later and looked around as if in a
daze, unsure of where he was or even if he were still in the land
of the living. Then he noticed Jnuin and the cook and smiled,
reassured. We sat there in awe and gaped at the old man, grateful
for his brief tour of the last century. Eventually, with much help
and cantilevering, Ashmi was raised to his feet. He filled and
smoked a pipe of kif, acknowledged our good-byes, and doddered
off in the direction of his house. It took him almost an hour to
travel the thirty yards between the terrace and the outer wall of
the madrassah.

We rewound the tape and began to translate. As the names of
long-dead sultans unreeled, we were amazed to realize that Ashmi's
life had encompassed the entire colonial era of Moroccan history.
Born when the Maghrib was anarchic and pirate-ridden, he had seen
the French, Spanish, and English fight each other to gather Morocco
into their own tinted area on the colonial map of Africa. Ironic, Joel
mused, that Morocco was the closest to Europe, but the last to be
tamed.

MOHAMMED BERDOUZ came over, lifted his grey Rifian djellaba over
his head, and sat down. He listened to Ashmi's voice on the tape

96 recorder and began telling stories of his own. I quickly popped in a fresh cassette and pushed the record button:

". . . you want to buy something, anything, I don't care what it is, you must buy it from a Christian or a Jew."

"Why do you say that, Malim?" asked Mohammed Yusufi with some annoyance.

"If you buy something from an Arab," Berdouz said, "there will always be some kind of trap!" The drummer smiled. Mohammed got up and went for a walk, bristling.

Berdouz went on with a story.

"Walking in the street in Alcazarquivir a few days ago, three shameless town girls began to follow me. They were walking behind me and speaking to each other in their horrible voices. 'Look at that man from the country,' one said to the others. 'He looks more like a cute wooden puppet [*muñeca*] than a man.' "

This was of course true, I realized, as I taped this tiny man with his wandering eye, curled yellow slippers, and shaved head.

"I turned around and yelled at the shameless ones. I told them I would show them I was no puppet! Before their dreadful eyes I pulled up my djellaba and was naked on the street and waving my horn at them in less than a few seconds."

What happened? Joel asked.

"They looked. They screamed. They fled," Berdouz laughed, holding his sides. On the terrace the other musicians thought this very funny. "Only Berdouz!" He was their grand trickster and wild spirit. In the sultan's court, he would have been jester, able to say anything with impunity.

THERE WAS EMPTY SPACE at the end of the afternoons for us in Jajouka in the days after the Aid el Kebir. No Bou Jeloud, no crowds, no spectacle, no rhaitas wailing like Chinese babies, no sound of screaming cave paintings. I found myself missing the shaggy creature, now safely back in the realm of myth, and spent hours making pen sketches of the quivering goat god holding his whips above his bonneted head.

Some of the ferocious local energy that was spent on Bou Jeloud was now taken up by the afternoon soccer game, which achieved epic and hilarious proportions as even some of the old men playfully took part. I fought for the ball and was brutally tackled by the teachers in their blue track suits, but I got my share of goals, which raised my status among the villagers beyond that of infidel tourist. The games were often interrupted for homeward-bound flocks of tiny brown goats. Tahir's younger brother, a squirrel-faced youth of about sixteen, would occasionally break off a brilliant striking charge on goal, pass the ball, and take out his kif pipe in the middle of the field for a smoke. When the sun set behind the sanctuary of Sidi Hamid Sherq, I slipped away from the game and back to the madrassah where Megaria, the associate cook, had a bucket of warm water waiting for my bath. Exhausted, I'd look at Joel and Morgan lounging on the terrace and wish I had the sense to conserve my energy.

Music continued every night after supper. The musicians arranged themselves in various groupings and poured out songs and dance music until all hours. The structure was always the same: tuning, which became an overture; verse-chorus singing led by Tahir, usually playing his violin as well; and long instrumental dance codas that encompassed both repetitive trance music and multi-climaxed ballets. Fudul, the affable giant, often put down his gimbri and got up to dance, beating his big feet on the carpet with a beatific smile. One night, after each musician took a turn dancing for the group, they spontaneously all rose and danced in a circle, ring-around-the-rosy, the rhythm never faltering as the old men swirled around the room.

"SO COLONIALISM FINISHED the Masters as royal musicians, right? And their status wasn't revived when the Moroccans got their independence in 1956. So where does that leave Jajouka?"

98   This was the question I asked Joel as we walked toward the
sanctuary of Sidi Hamid Sherq the next morning. It was early on a
Friday, New Year's Day 1394 by the Islamic calendar. As we walked
past the cemetery we could see a heavy mist unraveling in the valley
far below, revealing only the peaks of the tallest hills above a lush
carpet of dusty cloud.

        "It leaves Jajouka cash-poor, and marginally dependent on the
faith and tolerance of the people of the Djebel. Look, here's that
faith coming right toward you." Indeed, there was a procession of
white-blanketed women waiting outside the sanctuary, pilgrims
seeking the healing baraka of Jajouka's saint on this auspicious day.

        The Master Musicians were seated on reed mats under the tin
canopy, wearing white wool robes, formed into their right-angle
drum and rhaita corps. They played their most majestic music, at
once heraldic and deeply religious. "This piece is called *'Hamsa ou
Hamsin,'* " Joel whispered to me. "It means 'fifty-five' and derives
from the old royal music played for the king on his way to mosque
on the morning of the sabbath."

        The tin roof added echo and volume to the music that rent the
still air as veiled and shrouded women entered the courtyard where
the musicians were sitting. Many had walked great distances to
receive Hamid Sherq's blessing for the coming year.

        The music proceeded in sections, marking different stages in the
royal procession. The *'Kaimonos'* announced the king's arrival and
mounting his horse; a sustained note—loud like a siren—signaled
his departure and was called the *'Leimra';* the *'Tfardisha'* announced
that he had left the palace grounds; the *'Qalandri'* marked the
blessing of the population thronging the route. The piece finished
with the *'Gnouia,'* as the sultan descends from the saddle and enters
to pray.

        Halfway through, the drummers began to increase tempo and
punctuate the rhythm until a woman stood up, offered a symbolic
kiss to the musicians—kissing them good-bye—and whirled into a
possessed, arm-waving dance. Her long oiled hair tore loose and

waved around the manic dancer's head like a black flag. She was amok. But amok was clearly Sidi Hamid Sherq's specialty.

The blaring fanfare stopped suddenly. Something was in the air, but the cook was motioning us to leave the sanctuary. "Damnation," Morgan spat. "They're kicking us out." But I saw this scene for a few seconds before they closed the door behind us: a woman— very disturbed and obviously sedated—had been led in wearing a body-length sheer woolen veil. Berdouz, drum slung over his shoulder, led her gently to the musicians, before whom she lay on a mat, face down, while they placed their drums and a few rhaitas over her body until she disappeared under the instruments. Several of the older Masters had removed their yellow slippers and were about to step on her head and back when the door in the back wall slammed shut and the image was lost to us.

"That was incredible!" Joel looked at me. "I never saw that before. It looks like the musicians transmit baraka and curative blessings to the seriously ill through *actual contact* with the instruments. And what were they about to do when the door closed? Step on her? I wonder if Brion Gysin has seen all this. He never mentioned it."

Just then the door behind us opened. The sherif of the sanctuary came out to scold Achmed in a loud voice to impress the pilgrims, valued clients who preferred privacy. I moved back into the hazy sunlight of the graveyard and sat under a wizened olive tree to watch the fog disperse over the valleys toward Chaouen. Pipes were lit and we exchanged pleasantries with the local beggars. A dirham here and there kept everyone happy. I felt peace profound among Jajouka's dead, who had the best view of all.

Back at the madrassah a midday meal of bisar soup and rounds of hot bread was served. The sky had burst and rain was falling in sheets of sound. The chief had business in Tetuan, and we longed for the comforts of our villa in Tangier, so we packed the van and literally surfed down the mountain and sluiced through rivers of heavy mud before meeting the paved road at Tatoft. We stopped in Ksar el Kebir to let off the chief's flamboyant sister, a great musician in her own right, and flute-playing Little Mohammed, who had lost face for being Hamsa's uncle and who seemed to prefer town life anyway. Then we headed north, the only vehicle on the drenched roadway. The *douars,* or farms, clung to the vacant hills precariously, and bare ground stetched to the horizon, mute testimony to the chaos and anarchy that ruled the proud land until a few short years ago. I had the queasy, what-am-I-doing-here feeling that the bled was for gods, not men, that people had never been meant to live here.

We let off our dear friend the chief at the Tetuan cutoff. We tried to insist on waiting with him until the bus to Tetuan arrived, but he refused even though his djellaba was his only shelter from the driving rain. We felt terrible about leaving him, but before we rounded the next bend a car had picked Jnuin up, and he was gone.

THE WET STREETS of Tangier were quiet for the New Year holiday, the shops were mostly shuttered. We dropped Mohammed Yusufi in the Socco Grande. I paid him a thousand dirhams for his week in the hills; he accepted the money with great sadness, knowing it was more than he could ever make in several months. Back at the Villa Elizabeth, we found disarray. The phone had been taken away for repair, as had the water heaters in both kitchen and bathroom. "You won't believe this!" Morgan howled. "No bath! No calls to Washington!"

The next morning I stalked into Anglo-American Properties and confronted the horrid English proprietors, demanding the immediate return of the water heaters or another villa, tóod-sweet! No one should fuck with a dirty and disheveled journalist who needs a bath. Mr. Aspinall was delegated to show us the Villa Sarah, a tacky cottage owned by a Lord Bewley. It was in a crowded neighborhood down the hill, and had no view, so I told Mr. Aspinall that I wanted *both* villas. To my amazement, he agreed and gave me the keys to Sarah. I spent the next three hours trying to call my girlfriend, but the line crackled like a transmission from hell and I finally hung up.

Later we drove over to the Atlantic beach at Cap Spartel, the very corner of Africa. The perfect beach was empty, the sea so cold I could catch only one wave before fleeing to the embrace of the weak winter sun. The air, fresh after a three-thousand-mile journey over open water, was like a hit of pure oxygen. I lay out on my towel under the Pillars of Hercules, terrible granite cliffs that guarded the entrance to the Mediterranean, and again felt dwarfed by the gigantism of the awesome Moroccan landscape.

On the road back to Tangier squads of young boys tried to stop us on the switchbacks. They were hawking jasmine blossoms and pine nuts, which they thrust into our open windows. The oily nuts were a good snack after the beach. We stopped at a cliff-side café, and were led down a pine-tree path to tables overlooking the strait. Mint tea was brought and we spent an hour watching supertankers turning to starboard after their long trip around Africa.

In the evening, we parked in the Socco Grande and threaded through medina alleys to Yusufi's house at the end of a dark passage. The green door opened to admit us up a flight of cold stone steps and into a salon decorated with family photos and a portrait of King Hassan.

Aisha had been preparing Moroccan soul seafood—sardines baked in oil, deep-fried whiting, codfish stewed in basil and tomatoes; these were served with an olive-carrot-radish salad and rounds of crusty bread.

"Aisha," I said, in bad Arabic and with my mouth full of fish, "this isn't very good." She looked at me in horror before getting the joke, holding her hennaed hands palm-out to ward off evil, and calling out Berber oaths and curses that caused her husband to laugh and blush. Then she set out a deep blue platter of orange slices dusted with cinnamon and sugar. This dessert cut through the seafood, cleared our palates, and filled the little house with the scent of an orange grove. We sat back on cushions and drank tiny cups of coffee as Mohammed and Aisha played music together, banjo and drums.

. . .

THE SKY STAYED mostly grey over Tangier for the next few days. Since the three of us lived so close in the village, we tended to disperse when in town. Joel spent time with the Yusufis down in the medina. I prowled the casbah and the old sultan's palace, looking for the views Matisse sketched when he was in Tangier in 1912, or sat in the cafés of the Socco Chico, the little stagelike square in the heart of the medina, watching the improbable processions of tourists, hippies, donkeys, merchants, and boys carrying trays of coffee to shops in the side streets. The shop signs were in Arabic, French, English, Spanish, and German. I tried to be an invisible spectator, but it didn't work. Every Moroccan idling at the nearby tables watched me out of the corner of his eye.

Morgan liked to stay in the villa and worry about the first film he had shipped to the *Geographic* from the Iberia Airlines office on the Boulevard Pasteur. What, he obsessed, were they saying about him back in Washington? I'd bring him the Paris *Herald Tribune* and the international edition of *Time* from my forays into town and he'd disappear into his room for hours.

One day I had a cable from a friend of mine in New York: David Courage, an Englishman who worked as a producer for public television, wanted to join our expedition and shoot some film in Jajouka. Would this be possible? He also wanted to bring his wife. I invited Morgan and Joel to supper that night at a Chinese restaurant, and broached the subject over bowls of cellophane noodles.

"What's the wife like?" Morgan asked. When I told him she was one of the most beautiful women in New York, all he wanted to know was, how soon could she get here?

A FEW DAYS LATER Morgan announced he was heading back toward Jajouka by himself so he could photograph the market in Tatoft. "I wanna capture the musicians buying supplies and stuff," he told us, and took off in the mini-bus. Joel went off to town and I took advantage of a few hours of blue sky to sun on the villa's roof. Wearing an old broad-brimmed straw hat I found in the stairwell leading to the roof, I was soon deep into John Fowles's novel *The Magus,* a paperback I had stolen from Lord Bewley's library. I was astonished how the story of an English teacher's encounters with romantic, mythographic archetypes on a remote Greek island provided a perfect counterpoint to the scene here on the other side of the Mediterranean. The characters came instantly alive for me as the sun crossed the cool blue sky.

I heard Fatima leave for the day, far below me; her steps echoed up the walk, through our gate, and down the mountain road. On I read. Later I heard a taxi up the lane, and Joel's footsteps as he came into the house. He had been to the market in the Rue Fez and returned with a bundle of baguettes and the makings of serious omelettes—huge eggs, *chèvre,* scallions, mushrooms, bulbous green peppers and herbs, as well as half a case of Stork beer. We ate together at the villa's big dining table.

How's your story coming? he asked.

I told him I thought I was about halfway through.

"How do you know when you have enough?"

"I'll probably never have enough," I told him. "Not for years anyway. But I figure when the new djellabas are delivered, that will be the end of this chapter, and time to go home and write it."

MORGAN ARRIVED back at the villa the next day, with Jnuin in tow. The kindly chief of the Master Musicians spent the next two days bustling through the Tangerine bureaucracy, making arrangements for Jajouka's appearance at a big festival to be held that summer. This put the old virtuoso under a strain: booking gigs had previously been Hamsa's job but now the chief felt it was his responsibility.

"This band needs a manager," Joel said, after an exhausted Jnuin had retired to our guestroom for the night.

"Why don't *you* do it?" I suggested.

"I've thought about it. But I'm leery of getting that involved. I don't know . . . it's just an instinct . . . but I have a feeling it's better to be Jajouka's friend than her business partner."

chapter 4

The Saintly Folklore Association

$\mathcal{W}$e played our tapes of gimbri music as we drove south in heavy rain back to Jajouka. The road between Tatoft and the invisible exit to Jajouka was a sorry quagmire. I struggled to stay out of the deep ruts while the chief murmured prayers. The sky cleared at the last plateau before the village, and a tremendous double rainbow arched over Jajouka and the valley of the Ahl Sherif, stretching away to the east. *Welcome home, Malim Jnuin,* the rainbow seemed to say to the powerfully mystic man in the backseat. *And your friends are welcome too. At least for a while.* Over the next two hours, several dozen Master Musicians trooped in to say "La bess." Tea was served, and again there was little to do but sit quietly on the terrace and enjoy the afternoon sky.

Tahir played the gimbri that night, at our request. I began to put the tape recorder in front of him instead of just the microphone, so he could read the levels and pull back when he saw the meter

106   needles push into the red zone. Tahir proved to be a natural recording artist, ordering repeated takes of "Brahim Jones" when some element of the playback wasn't to his liking. He sat imperiously under my headphones, refusing to let anyone else listen, concentrating on the recorded sound of his band like some pampered rock star, his round, shining face a chiseled mask of self-communion. He didn't like the muffling effect the drums had on my simple recording system, and herded Berdouz and the other drummers around the room trying to get the bass levels down so the gimbri could be better heard.

When they finished, the Masters bade us goodnight—"*Sl'ama! Naz m'zien!*"—and filed out. A few of the boys stayed behind to smoke and chat, and I took a candle to my dark corner of the big chamber and read *The Magus* until all hours. The mythographic twists of the novel began to affect my subconscious: that night I dreamed I was confronted by Anubis, the god with the jackal's head who guarded the portals of Tartarus, realm of the dead. I woke in a feverish sweat, swallowed two aspirins, and fell into uneasy sleep.

"GOOD MORNING," Joel said when I staggered out into the hazy glare of the terrace. "Guess what? We've been here for a month." He poured a glass of murky black coffee for me and added some sweet canned milk. "Are you feeling all right?"

"Why do you ask?"

"Because you don't look well."

"As a matter of fact, I feel quite ill." My hand trembled slightly as I took the glass.

"Well, try to take it easy," he advised. "Body trips can be real heavy when you're on the road."

Indeed, it proved not to be my day. An hour later I was unloading some of Morgan's photo gear from our van, aided by Abdsalam Mezhdoubi, a huge jovial rhaita player with clear blue eyes who was one of my favorites among the older Masters. Thinking that I had finished, he slammed the van's heavy sliding door on my hand while I was leaning on the post for support. Within seconds my hand turned purple; my fingers swelled like bloated sausages.

Berdouz and several of the others ran to see the cause of the commotion. While several of them upbraided Mezhdoubi for his clumsiness, Berdouz led me into the madrassah. "Holy shit," Morgan said as we went in. "Your thumb looks like it could be broken." I felt like fainting.

Berdouz ordered everyone out and closed the windows so the room was almost black. Then he began to heal my wounded hand. First he poured mineral water on it from a bottle of Sidi Harazem. Then he held it between his hands and began to pray, rubbing my fingers and thumb as I begged him to stop. Then he spat into my palm and worked it into the skin. Then he prayed some more and spoke to me in words I couldn't understand.

After fifteen minutes, the sharp pain subsided, leaving only a dull throb. The spiritually potent little drummer continued his palaver until my hand stopped hurting completely. We sat quietly for a while, my hand cupped in his. "Gut, berry gut," Berdouz finally said and led me outside. In the sunlight, there wasn't even a bruise. All fingers flexed painlessly.

"That's hard to believe," Joel said.

"What did he do in there?" Morgan wanted to know.

MORGAN AND I trekked for an hour with Abdsalam Fudul and a few lads to a different "Casa Bou Jeloud," this one overlooking rock springs and wild oleander gardens. Abdsalam brought Bou Jeloud's skins so Morgan could shoot a couple of rolls. He'd had a cable from Washington complimenting his photographs thus far and asking to see more goat god.

While they worked I practiced my flute. I had loved music all my life, but usually as a listener rather than a player. But one day in Jajouka I tried one of the red-tipped lira flutes the Masters carved from local cane. Seven holes up top, a thumb hole underneath. I blew a low tone and held it. Ummm. Malim Ali woke up and smiled. *"M'zien b'zef,"* he said—very good—and taught me to trill. Two days later Mohammed Stitu gave me a freshly carved and hennaed lira. It had tiny red "racing stripes" and sounded like a bell at every tone on its scale. Slowly, and with patience, Ali and Little Mohammed began to show me a song called "Jilali," with a melody that fell like a trickling brook. Then they taught me "Jajouka Black Eyes," "Brahim Jones," and other post-Arcadian shepherd airs. After a week, they began to let me play with them sometimes when flutes were deployed after supper.

WE STAYED AT the cave and springs until Morgan ran out of film and I ran out of breath. During the long walk back to Jajouka, in a pool of a brook we were crossing, I saw a litter of newborn puppies that had been drowned and left to rot in the brown water. Depression set in, and I was barely able to suppress my rising gorge.

I was sick by the time we returned to the madrassah. I joined the afternoon soccer game, thinking that the jolting, good-natured competition might lift my spirit, but if anything I felt even more ill at the end of the day. I spent the rest of the evening, half-dead, watching Morgan play checkers with Fudul and Ali. The game was called *damasa* in Jajouka, and was played according to a shifting set of rules that allowed kings to make improbable jumps across jagged boundaries. Morgan and some of the older Masters had a fierce rivalry going, and their banter reminded me of the old crackerbarrel types from the porch of the general store in the town where my Missouri grandparents had lived in my childhood.

Soon my body began to shake with fever. When Joel returned from Ksar el Kebir, where he had spent the day with the musicians who had played for the Ashura observances, he ordered me to bed, fed me antibiotics, and had the cook make soup for me. But my appetite was gone. I lay down in the unused bedroom and fell into a damp coma for a few hours. I could hear the Malimin playing music through the thick adobe that separated the two rooms. I'd wake up for a few minutes and feel like I was sinking until I fell asleep again.

I got up around midnight. The evening music was over, and Joel and Morgan were asleep. On the terrace, Tahir and Abdallah Attar and Abdsalam Fudul were discussing their marriage plans. Tahir said that he had been saving his *flus* and expected to pay three thousand dirhams for a wife this year. That is, he added, if God wills it. Insh'Allah. His tone implied this plan probably wouldn't work.

Abdsalam Fudul had just gotten divorced. What was the problem? I asked.

"Grimble grimble," he said. His wife had complained all the time. The other young men laughed ruefully.

Jnuin's son Abdallah was exactly my age and was currently on his fourth wife, and asked me why I hadn't married yet. I said I lived with a woman who wasn't interested in marriage.

"You're married," they told me, "but without papers."

Eventually, I crept back into bed and prayed that the antibiotics did their job.

Insh'Allah.

THE NEXT DAY dawned sunny and cold, and I felt better. I got up to wash in the trough in front of the madrassah, and one of the boys, another young Mohammed, objected in French to my using bottled water to brush my teeth:

"Why waste your money on water from a bottle when our water here in Jajouka is so delicious?"

I explained that my American guts were not accustomed to the local microbes and that I was afraid of getting hepatitis.

"In a little while we go to the well," he said. "Come with us and see for yourself how clear the water is."

My appetite was still weak, and all I could manage for breakfast was a carrot or two. But when I saw a party of boys start off with the madrassah's metal buckets, I joined them. As we filed through the upper village, tiny children along the trail kissed the hands of the Masters' sons, seeking the blessing of the saintly musicians. Since I was last in line and wearing my djellaba, they kissed my hand too.

The well turned out to be a spring in the rocks above the village. The water was clear as a mirror and very cold, so I took a long drink and felt quite refreshed. According to what I had learned, the quality of the water was what caused the village to be settled in the first place, and it seemed ridiculous not to taste the liquid that gave life to the town.

I returned to my journalistic duties that morning, interviewing some of the other musicians. Malim Ali, avuncular master of rituals, blithely informed me that he served twenty years with the Moroccan colonial troops of the Spanish army. Along with Achmed the cook and others, he had been drafted when Spanish officers came up to the village. Ali pridefully said that he and others from Jajouka had been among the Moroccan troops Francisco Franco used to invade Spain and overthrow the Republic in the bloody 1935 Spanish civil war. Then he must have noticed Joel and me exchanging glances, and grew concerned. "Franco m'zien, eh?" he asked hopefully, checking for our approval.

What could we say? That we hated the old fascist who had kept Spain in the Dark Ages for forty subsequent years? That the atrocities inflicted upon the Spanish civilians by Franco's Moroccan troops were legendary? So we smiled sadly and said, "Sí, Malim Ali. Franco m'zien."

The cook was next.

Achmed Skirkin had an impossibly scratchy voice. He told us that he had been a dancing boy, a drummer, and a rhaita player in that order. No, he didn't know how old he was. (We guessed he was around seventy.) He had been in the army in Spain and then had worked for twenty-five years as a cook at a rich man's estate near Wazzan. Now he was back with his family and cooking for the

Malimin and playing the rhaita for Sidi Hamid Sherq. He had this little black and white sheepdog named Bitu, or "Egg," that he loved beyond anything else. Of all the curs in the village, with whom the villagers lived in a state of hostile dependency, only Bitu was allowed to pass within the boundaries of the madrassah. Only Bitu wasn't greeted by a hail of pebbles. Only Bitu was actually fed from the musicians' kitchen and lived a sleek and glossy, cared-for life. The cook wasn't interested in being interviewed, actually. Several times he said he had to prepare the midday meal, and we had to beg him to give us a minute more. This was frustrating, because we *loved* the cook. He went out of his way to look after us and see that we were fed and warm. He was like our mother in Jajouka.

There was one musician who wouldn't let me tape him. This was Achmido Twimi, one of the enigmatic stars of the band. He was perhaps thirty-five years old, and thus one of the few Masters between the older and younger generations. He was a prosperous farmer; we hardly ever saw him during the day. When he came to dine and sing in the clubhouse at night, he was always immaculately dressed. He played the drabouga and would do the lead singing when Berdouz called an old tune that Tahir didn't know.

"I think Twimi sings in an old-timey style," Joel said one night. "You know, like an old hillbilly." Twimi's voice was very high, a dry and forceful falsetto that soared over the pulse of the drums. But Twimi was extremely modest and, according to the others, very religious. "Maybe that's why he didn't want to be taped," Joel said.

"It's frustrating," I said. "Like having an older brother you really respect, but he's too busy to be interested in you."

"But he doesn't mind being photographed," Morgan put in. "A couple of days ago he asked me do some Polaroids of his children."

Twimi would remain a calm and dignified mystery. It should be added that he was a *great* rhaita player. He could play forty measures without a breath.

·   ·   ·

WE SPENT SEVERAL rainy days interviewing the musicians. By the early evening my strength would give out and I'd take to my bed in the candlelit side room, listening to the thump of the drums through the walls, sweating out the fever. One night it was quiet for a long period, and when Joel came with some food I asked what was going on.

"They're praying for you," he said.

The next morning I felt better. Sunlight was breaking through the woolen cloud cover for the first time in a week, and I emerged onto the terrace and back into the land of the living. After a few days of shivering delirium, it felt like a rebirth. The musicians greeted me kindly and expressed their concern.

"Joel," I said, "ask the chief how long until the new djellabas are ready."

The chief consulted with Ali and the cook and answered: one week.

"Tell them I want to go back to Tangier for a bit, to recuperate. When we return it will be with a television director from America and his wife, if that is all right. Then we'll pick up the djellabas, and our work here will be done."

This was duly announced, and the Malimin concurred. Morgan was running out of film stock anyway. So we packed up the van, and drove slowly down the side of the mountain, slippery and treacherous after saturating rain. Crammed in the back were several women who asked for a lift to the market in Alcazar. None had ever been in a car before, and all of them threw up.

Two hours later, we drove over a rise and Tangier lay before us, like a gleaming white jewel along its bayside beach. Joel steered the van up the Old Mountain road until we reached our villa, whose gardens were redolent of flowering bougainvillea and sweet narcissus even before the gate was opened. The phone and the water heaters now worked, but I was too out of it to care. I collected my mail and the clean laundry Fatima had done while we were in the hills. Joel helped Mohammed unpack the van, and I went up to my sun-washed white room with its single bed and fresh sheets, and went to sleep for two days.

WHEN I PULLED my curtains open after finally waking up, I was as frail as a petal. Joel kept me hydrated with broth from the Chinese restaurant near the boulevard, and Mohammed's wife Aisha cooked a restorative chick pea soufflé, which tasted so wonderful that my body must have decided life was worth living. I rested and read on the villa's sunny terrace, watching the kittens devour my untouched food and pursuing the plot of *The Magus* to its appalling climax. At night I listened to drumming, far away.

ONE AFTERNOON WE visited the little sebsi merchant who sat like a Capuchin monkey in his stall in the "head shop" souk near the used-djellaba market behind the Socco Grande. A craving for kif was returning along with my appetite for food, and all our pipe-bowls were broken from over use. The proprietor greeted us with a chimpish smile. Then he began to frantically fan the air as, behind us, two uniformed gendarmes had walked through the Moorish arch and begun to peruse his pipes, bowls, mutwis, and assorted paraphernalia.

"The worst thing that can happen to a foreigner in Morocco is to get mixed up in a kif bust," Joel whispered. "They throw you in a dungeon, the American consular people are contemptuous and do nothing except arrange for a lawyer, *if* you can pay for it—and it costs thousands. *Let's just buy our stuff and get out of here.*"

The cops were there to buy zhqafs for themselves. It was Friday, and the weekend was looming.

I paid for our stuff, exchanged nods with the police, and we beat a hasty retreat.

"Wait a minute," I said as we passed a big stall that sold appliances—washing machines and televisions. On the flickering

114   black-and-white TV a prizefight was just starting: Muhammad Ali
and George Frazier! We bellied up to the counter and watched the
live broadcast from Madison Square Garden in New York. The last
time these two heavyweights met, in 1971, both were undefeated
and both claimed title to the championship of the world. Back then,
Frazier had knocked the great Ali down, removing all doubt about
who was champ.

As the fight progressed, a highly partisan crowd gathered around
us. The physical pressure of all these people was so great that Joel
and I were actually bent forward, as they watched over our heads.
Muhammad Ali was a god in Morocco and every other Muslim
nation. The crowd cheered every punch he landed and groaned with
every one he took. "Ali!" they chanted, "Ali! Ali!" Neither man
held the title that day, January 28, 1974, but much to the satisfaction of the Tangerines, Ali was the clear victor and won the fight
after twelve moderately thrilling rounds.

A DAY LATER the little yellow mail truck came up the hill and
stopped at our villa. "Hey!" Morgan cried as he read his letter.
"Guess what? My girlfriend is coming."

"Good for you," Joel said with a smile. "But with all your gear,
your girlfriend, and the New York people, it's gonna be crowded
in our bus. Any chance the *National Geographic* would spring for a
second car?"

"No problem."

We drove to the Place d'Espagne and rented a big Renault sedan.
Morgan was in a great mood. "Executive seating, right this way,"
he barkered as he held the passenger door open for me. An hour
later our little fleet drove to Bouhalef Airport, on the beach outside
of town.

David and Red Courage were flying in from Casablanca, having
taken a Royal Air Maroc flight from New York the previous day. I
saw them descend the back staircase of the Caravelle after it pulled

up near the terminal. You couldn't miss them if you tried. David was slim and full of long blond curls. And Red was an American beauty. She had been a dancer until an injury forced her to change professions. She had immense almond eyes and flaming red hair, and drew stares wherever she went.

We embraced, the three of us. David drew back and looked at me. "My god, man! You've lost weight! Have you been ill?"

"I hate to admit it. But, yes. Quite sick."

"You poor thing," Red said. "I'm so glad we came, in that case. We can look after you." I wanted to cry. We waited for their baggage out under the palm trees that were swaying in the warm breeze.

"It was two degrees when we left New York, mate." David sounded tired. "This is Nirvana."

Red looked around at the porters and customs agents and gendarmes that surrounded us. They were staring at her in awe. The sun was warm and gentle, and she seemed so pleased to be here. "Is this Heaven?" she asked.

"No," I said. "This is Tangier."

On the way back toward the Djemaa el Mokhra, David filled my head with news of home: long gasoline lines supposedly caused by the Arab nations' sudden hike in the price of oil; Bob Dylan on tour with The Band; the affairs, intrigues, and ODs of mutual friends.

At the Villa Elizabeth I introduced them to my team, who were suitably impressed. "You were right," Morgan said when the couple had gone off to rest. "She's smashing. I can't wait to see the reaction to her in Jajouka."

That afternoon I told Joel Fischer I thought something was missing in our research, there was something we were overlooking, some area we had failed to penetrate.

"That's very true," he answered. "But the real question is: How far do you, as an outsider and an infidel, really *want* to 'penetrate,' as you put it? I think it might not be such a great idea to get too close. Jajouka has its secrets. Some of them might be dangerous to know."

"Do you mean the healing properties of the music, the instruments, and the musicians themselves?"

"Perhaps," he said, thoughtfully. "Then there's the 'Attar' of Jajouka. You know that the musicians all have the same surname— Attar. It means 'perfume maker.' Gysin claims there's an actual scent associated with Jajouka's music at its highest, most ecstatic level."

"You mean, the 'Attar' is real?"

"I don't know for sure, but I *think* it might be. Gysin hinted that the 'Attar' of Jajouka could possibly be detrimental to one who was not an Adept."

THERE WAS SOME BUSINESS to take care of the following day before we could leave for Jajouka. Tired of the sardines and whiting we'd been buying in Alcazar, we visited the big fish market near the Socco Grande, where giant moray eels gaped toothfully. We found sea bass, some of them thirty-five pounds, and shellfish beyond count and description. Then we were off to the Fez market for vegetables and Madame Porte's famous tearoom for several tons of butter cookies, which I had taken to passing around the madrassah after supper on days when we had returned from town. Soon we were racing the clock to get to the bank before the siesta. We expected to purchase the djellabas this trip and needed cash since they didn't take plastic in Tetuan.

As we came out of the Deutschbank, which offered the best exchange rates, Red Courage and I literally bumped into young Abdsalam Fudul coming the other way down the boulevard. Here was Bou Jeloud, I explained to Red, in his civvies. Abdsalam kissed me on both cheeks and shyly peeked at Red, who kissed him on impulse. I thought Abdsalam would either shit or go blind. Momentarily befuddled, he just smiled. "I'm sorry," Red said. "Maybe that's not polite to do here."

We sat on the terrace outside Claridge's restaurant. I knew the

Fuduls had family here in Tangier, and Abdsalam explained that he was trying to get work as a porter at the airport. "Come back to Jajouka with us now," I told him. "We have two cars, plenty of room, let us take you home."

"Baraka l'aufic," the Moroccan boy said, his dark eyes flashing sadly. "I *must* stay here for now. I *must* get work. We have so little *flus* right now. I will see you in the mountains in a few days. Tell my papa that you saw me and that I might have a job."

The situation sounded semi-desperate, so I didn't press our friend. I gave him fifty dirhams over his half-hearted protest, and we left to gas up the fleet and head for the hills. As we set out along the shining blue coastal road—Joel, Morgan, and the gear in the bus; me and the Courages in the Renault—I felt an aching sadness. Our mission for *National Geographic* was almost over, and I didn't expect to pass this way again.

TWO HOURS LATER we flashed past the Caid's little fortress at Tatoft, not pausing to check in. We figured we were a familiar enough sight by now.

The little blue hills, curiously conical like gigantic Moroccan sugar cones, rose immediately around us as the paved road turned to *piste*. In the valley, farmers plowed behind mules and oxen, overturning black earth still moist from the drenching spring rains. Half an hour later we turned left onto the hidden track to Jajouka and began to climb the yellow brick road. Just before the penultimate plateau, near the whitewashed lesser saints' graves that lay under immemorial olive trees, the Renault stalled out. "Sorry," I told the Courages, "but you two are bailing out here."

The sedan took heart and continued to climb. In the rearview mirror, I could see my friends admiring the hundred-mile view across the greening hills and plains toward the ocean. "This is breathtaking," David said when they caught up with me on foot a few minutes later.

The chief was waiting for us in the plaza, where Bou Jeloud had stomped and swirled eight weeks earlier. A swarm of children gathered as we stood chatting by the cars, fixing the modestly dressed but no less flamboyant American woman with a collective stare of astonishment. When we men had first walked through Jajouka, the children would chatter like little birds. Now they were quiet, dumb with awe.

"What's the big deal?" Red whispered. "Am I *that* strange to them?"

"Try to enjoy it," Joel counseled. "It means they like you already."

At the madrassah mint tea and kif quickly materialized. David was a goner at the first whiff of Jajouka kif. Red usually didn't smoke, but she accepted a pipe from Joel. "I should try it, right?" she said. "Just to be in the spirit." Unaccustomed to the rituals of the sebsi, David had trouble spitting out the spent coal; this predicament caused tremendous merriment in Achmed Sicko.

Gradually the whole clan of musicians showed up. "They are *very* excited to have you here," Joel told the Courages. "I believe they were experiencing the early stages of media-fatigue, with just the three of us."

Berdouz was the last to arrive. He sized up the situation and wasted no time in getting a little band together. Once the drums and gimbris and clappers were clicking to his satisfaction, he walked over and grabbed Red and made her dance for them. It took her no time to get in sync with their rhythmic thing, and she threw her hips to the beat and wiggled her shoulders and whirled with the grace of the ballet student she had been. The energy in the room was mind-boggling. The Malimin followed her every movement with rapt attention, immediately shifting the rhythm to her desires. They played until the gyrating woman seemed near collapse. Joel nodded to the chief, who was clapping along, and he signaled Berdouz, who crashed the music to a halt.

The Master Musicians broke into wild applause for their visitor's dance, and the irrepressible Berdouz jumped up and hugged her, trying to feel her heaving breasts until I shouted ''Safi!,'' which put a stop to it. From then on, Berdouz was completely charming and behaved himself. He delivered a long, passionate monologue to the Courages, who asked Joel for a translation. ''Berdouz said they're going to play music for you all night, and he will work hard to show your wife how great he is.''

After a while, needing a break from all this, I walked outside, noticing that the fig trees in the courtyard of the madrassah were beginning to bud. In the boys' room near the hammam, the boys were sitting around glumly, pissed off that their elders were with the American lady and they weren't. I sat down as commanded and was plied with questions about the new guests. Who were they? Were they married? Were they important? How long were they staying? ''Get the *mujer* to come and see us,'' Bashir begged, so I brought Red in, much to the younger generation's surprise and pleasure. She was good-humored about it. The boys were too shy to look at her after the first few moments anyway.

The assistant cooks, Megaria and Ayashi, were just outside the door, cleaning the sole we had brought. There would be a mighty fish fry that night. In the kitchen the old cook was mixing his spices and heating pans of olive oil. ''Mmmmm,'' sighed Red when I brought her in to see him. ''I *love* cumin!'' This declaration made the old man very happy. Next I showed her the spare bedroom where I had lain ill the week before. Now it was being aired out so the Courages could use it.

Tahir finally appeared at dinner time, dressed to kill in an off-white djellaba and a pair of the fancy stacked-heel boots that young Moroccans liked to wear in the city. He resined and tuned his fiddle for half an hour after supper, and proceeded to lead the band in a ferocious program of dance music that went on for hours. Red Courage danced until her legs gave out. Then Tahir got up and showed his stuff, the first time I'd seen him dance since the Aid el Kebir. And he was, of course, devastating, snaking his hips and pulling steps that would have killed James Brown, letting it all hang out, using every dancing-boy trick in the book.

After many hours, the big room veiled in kif smoke, the older masters began to tire and say goodnight. Everyone was exhausted except the younger band, who took their fathers' places and jammed eagerly. At four in the morning, we begged them to stop. "Gut nite," they said sheepishly, speaking our language. "Sl'ama." A dozen guardians slept outside the doors that night, and the dogs, energized by the music, howled until the first streaks of dawn.

EVERYONE SLEPT LONG and hard the next day, and nothing stirred around the madrassah until afternoon. At around four o'clock we were listening to Radio Cairo broadcast Om Kalthoum, the Morning Star of the East, warbling her intoxicating Islamic arias when a shout was heard from the bottom of the village. Then another, closer by; the chief and the cook exchanged glances. A minute later, all sebsis disappeared into the folds of djellabas and a kilo of kif was whisked away. A squat grey police jeep pulled up and stopped. Two gendarmes and a civilian dismounted and strode into the madrassah. The cops didn't bother to wipe their muddy black combat boots, much less take them off as manners required.

"What the fuck is this?" David whispered.

"I don't know," Joel answered, "But we better go in and find out."

We quickly learned that the Tatoft caid was very annoyed when his spies told him two vehicles had ascended his hills toward Jajouka, and this unconscious violation of protocol had brought these mean-looking dogs upon us. The two gendarmes were Rifians, strangers here. I looked at their numb cop faces and a chill went down my back. As they began the slow, laborious process of checking our passports and documents and writing down the numbers, they were treated with typical hospitality. Tea arrived. Plates of fried aggs and rounds of bread appeared before them. The chief was obsequious, but I knew he just wanted to be rid of the intruders.

"I feel guilty about this," Joel whispered. "It's our fault that these assholes are here. We should've stopped in Tatoft."

"But how were we to know?" Morgan asked. "We've been coming and going for a long time with no problems."

Joel looked disgusted as the gendarmes suggested a little music while they worked. *"I* should have known. The caid is responsible for foreigners in his territory; he wants to know who's up here."

Then the trouble began. While one of the cops and the *fonctionnaire* were copying our papers, the other cop began walking around the room, holding a lit stick of incense as if to ward off the negativity he knew was being beamed his way. (Earlier I'd been told that the police didn't like to come up here, since Sidi Hamid Sherq was known to curse Jajouka's enemies.) The cop looked at the pictures on the wall, stopping at Brian Jones to stare into the dead rock star's angelic face. Then he moved toward the long table at the end of the room and picked up a stack of Polaroids. All of them showed Megaria, the assistant cook, chopping kif! "Who is this man?" the cop demanded.

Shocked silence. Again, to me in French. "Who is this?"

"I don't know," I said. "Perhaps a man from the village." Out of the corner of my eye, I noticed Megaria, a stricken look on his face, begin to edge away from the nearby kitchen and move toward open ground.

"Where is he now?"

"Je ne sais pas." I told him I didn't know.

The cop began to rant. "Bring this man to me! We want to talk to him!" I could see that Megaria was long gone, and said nothing. Goddamned Morgan and his Polaroids. Now the chief intervened. No, he assured the police, it wasn't anyone from around here. Just some type who was here during Aid el Kebir. Long gone now. No, we don't know his name. So many people come and go for the holiday. The cops demanded we see the caid. They were looking at Red Courage and seemed eager to bring this trophy to the boss.

Somehow, the chief talked them out of it. Berdouz picked up his drum and the musicians began to play. The chief asked Red to

122   dance. Being a good sport, she bumped and swiveled and did her
thing, which made the cops forget themselves; soon they were
clapping along like any Moroccan, enjoying the show. Eventually
they took the kif Polaroids and instructed us to present ourselves to
the caid the next day. Then they roared off in their jeep under a dark
grey sky.

A few minutes later, the sky split open and dumped two hours
of heavy water on Jajouka. When Megaria felt safe enough to show
his face again, it was clear he had been severely traumatized. We
apologized profusely. I made Morgan give him a hundred dirhams
(in secret) for his pain, which seemed to cheer him just a little. Only
when he was able to supervise the destruction of the remaining
undiscovered pictures did he breathe easy again, poor man.

That night, five cane flutes trilled like a conference of birds. Red
swiveled her hips and gradually spirits were restored. During a
break, Berdouz told a story, which I got on tape: "It's no good for
a bad man to come up here. No good. Jajouka knows when something is evil. There are always consequences, praise be to God in the
highest. The day after Hamsa stole our djellabas, the very ground
under our feet began to exude a substance. It looked and smelled
like *shit*. That's right! Yes! It was like shit right from the ground.
The whole village stank. So we played the 'Kaimonos' for Sidi
Hamid Sherq in his sanctuary. Do you want to know what happened? Our saint interceded for us and the shit sank back into the
ground. Ha! What do you think of that?"

LATER THAT NIGHT, Joel brought out his dictionary of Moroccan
Arabic. "Look at this this," he urged me, holding the book up to
the hissing gas lantern so I could read the entry under "*Sherq.*"

The first meaning given for the word was "polytheism."

SEVERAL TIMES DURING our stay in Jajouka we had been invited to
a *sebaa,* a naming party for an infant that had survived its first week

of life. There was another sebaa held the night after our return to the village, but we weren't invited; the baby had been stillborn. But they went ahead with the party anyway. Jajouka's women had painted and dressed themselves and were already at the home of the bereaved family. There was no music in the madrassah that night. Instead the musicians gathered while Berdouz led an intense prayer that sounded like a scatting bebop-style rap. The Malimin were glum, *disconsolado,* as the cook put it in Spanish, explaining that every man was expected to sleep with his wife that night. More babies would be born; grief would be allayed.

Earlier that day several women, including Jnuin's formidable sister, had come to the wall and asked for Red. She went off with them and we didn't see her for many hours. When she returned, just before supper, our Manhattan hothouse flower had been transformed into a princess of the Djebel. She was dressed in a glittery silver dress, adorned with amber and red coral, an enormous embroidered belt cinched around her tiny waist. Her hair had been oiled, her face carefully rouged and painted, her hands tattooed with henna.

"My God!" her husband gasped. "This is incredible. You look like a doll!"

She was almost speechless. "I feel like I'm *glowing,*" she managed.

"You *are* glowing," I assured her. "Tell us what happened."

"They took me to a house where there must have been a hundred women and girls. They treated me like a queen. They fed and bathed me, took my clothes, washed them and dressed me like one of them. They were all talking to me at once, but I couldn't understand a thing. It was so frustrating. They all wanted to feel me up and see what I was like under my clothes, but they were very gentle. They worked on me all day, like they were preparing me for something. I felt like a bride! Then they sang and played music and had a party. Other women came in and out to visit and say hello. Oh! It was so *wonderful.* I can't explain how it felt, like they wanted me to be like them, to be one of them." Then she asked, "Do they do this for all the foreign women who come here?"

"I don't think so," Joel said. "My old girlfriend Anastasia was also dressed up the first time she came up here with me, but she spoke fluent Arabic and became a great favorite of the musicians' wives."

Red's question was also answered the next day, when Morgan returned from Tangier with his friend, June, a sweet, attractive girl, dazed from jet lag and culture shock. She too disappeared into the ample bosom of female Jajouka and returned gowned and done over. But the care and detail lavished on Red was missing in June, and I sensed that she had been "done" as a courtesy to Morgan.

SO THE DAYS went on, with vast sailing cloudscapes, marathon checker games, nightly feasts, singing and dancing.

One night while Malim Titi was singing and the drums pounded, a weird scent, like ripened fruit, suddenly permeated the air in the long room.

I looked at Joel, and our eyes locked. "Is that it?" I asked. "Is that the 'Attar'?"

"I don't know," he said. "Maybe. I hope it is. Whatever it may be, it's magic."

ONE FRIDAY MORNING in early March I woke up feeling enervated. I staggered to the hammam, wondering what was wrong this time. My urine was the color of strong tea. I looked in the mirror. The whites of my eyes were yellow.

Merde.

Over breakfast, David said, "Your eyes look like some old bluesman's, Sonny Boy Williamson or Bukka White."

"Your liver's going," Joel said.

Oh, Christ. "Do you think it's hepatitis?" I asked.

"It could be," Joel answered. "We did get those gamma globulin shots back in Tangier, though."

"That old witch probably *gave* us hepatitis," Morgan snorted.

"This means our time here is getting short. The chief says the djellabas should be ready in a day or two. Let's get 'em and get out of here."

From across the village we could hear the nasal rush of the massed rhaitas in the sanctuary of Sidi Hamid Sherq. We walked down the hill and were admitted to the courtyard, where I became intoxicated by the double-reeded music of the holy wooden horns. I thought, is anything in the world as beautiful as this music? The musicians were squatting under their canopy in their djellabas, their cheeks puffed out in the fierce concentration of circular breathing. Eventually, for the few pilgrims who had journeyed up the mountain that morning, Berdouz uttered a staccato rhythmic prayer. "Amin, Amin, Amin," echoed the musicians after every phrase. During the offering part of the ceremony, I walked over and handed Berdouz a large note, hoping it wouldn't contrast with the pittances brought by the local pilgrims. But Berdouz expertly palmed the money, and moments later I heard my name mentioned in dispatches to Allah. I felt my jaundiced eyeballs blaze inside my skull and hoped that venerable Sidi Hamid Sherq would intervene on my behalf.

A bit later, during the long afternoon siesta, David Courage asked for help in interviewing one of the musicians on camera. Three of the best, Achmed Sicko, the chief, and the cook, just happened to be sleeping while squatting on their haunches near the kitchen, so we said we'd try. Achmed Sicko hated having his picture taken, so he was out. The cook said no, thank you, called his dog Bitu, and departed. That left the chief. I switched my tape recorder on while David shot three reels of Super 8, and Joel translated.

"Malim Abdsalam, my friends tell me you know all the old songs."

"Ahh, yes. I know many of them," he said, lighting up a filtered Casa Sport cigarette.

"Are you teaching them to your sons?"

"Yes. Some of them. To some of my sons."

"Tell me about your sons."

"Which ones do you wish to know about?"

"All of them."

The chief smiled his kindly smile and sighed. "The eldest is Mohammed. He knows all the rhaita songs I know."

"Is he here in Jajouka?"

"Oh no," the chief said. "He lives in Germany."

"Is he a musician."

"Oh yes. A fine musician. A *malim kebir*. He drives a big truck as his job."

"And your second son?"

"Achmed. He lives in Francia. Paris. He drives a taxi. Then comes Abdallah. He lives here but he's going in the army. Then Amin. You know him, too. Then Bashir, who is just beginning. And the youngest is Mustapha."

"How did you get your name—'Jnuin'?"

"It came to me from my father. He was a Jnuin as well."

"What does it mean?"

For the first time, the chief looked uncomfortable.

"I don't think he wants to discuss it," Joel said. "The name has to do with, you know, fairies or Little People. Here they call them Djinn. We say, 'Genie,' right? Same thing."

The chief listened impassively, and then pulled something from the fold of his djellaba. It was a golden coin, very old and worn, with strange writing and bizarre, inhuman figures on it. "See this money?" he said. "One day many years ago I was sitting in my house. There had been rain for days. For *days*! The water was a meter high in the valley. A man I'd never seen before, in a very rich djellaba, rode up to my door on a mule. A *big* mule.

"This man said to me, 'I have been sent here by my masters, the Djinn. They are holding a festival nearby in honor of the governor of all the Djinn, who is visiting.'

"This man said to me, 'The Djinn command you to come and

play the rhaita at their festival.' I asked him where the festival was, but he would not say. So I told him it was raining too hard and I didn't want to go out. The man then took a big basket of fresh food from the back of the mule and gave it to me, but again I told him I would not come. Then he gave me this gold coin, and showed me that he had two saddlebags that were full of this golden Djinn money. 'Come to the festival and play!' That's what he told me. 'You can have all the money you want.' ''

"I thought about it, but I was frightened. If I played for the Djinn, I might as well play for the devil. So I told him it was raining too hard. 'What do you mean?' the man asked me. 'Look, it's not raining at all.' That's when I noticed his djellaba was as dry as dust, the rain had not wet him. Then he disappeared! I never saw him again. But I kept this money. H'amdullah!''

"Did you get all that?" Joel asked David.

"No," he said. "Something happened to the bloody camera. Can you ask him to tell the story again?"

But Jnuin had put the coin away and was already on his way out the door.

THE WINDS BLEW up the mountains so hard during the night that, but for the thick walls, it seemed the madrassah would be blown off its foundation. Then there was an explosion of rain whose intensity pressed me deep into my mattress. I'll never forget that feeling— warm, helpless, poisoned. Then came hail; on the tin roof it sounded like the bones of the storm, as though the African sky had nothing liquid left to give.

The day broke clear and bright, and Jajouka steamed as it dried under the rising sun. *"Caila b'zef"*—sunlight to spare—was the order of the day, and even Malim Ashmi doddered into the musi- cians' compound to smoke his sebsi and inspect the American woman whose exotic presence had permeated even his antique conscience. He squatted against the columns of the porch like a wizened old chimp and allowed himself to be filmed and interviewed by David Courage.

"What does this one want to know?" the old man shouted. "I already told them everything!"

"I believe he wants to hear about the old days, Malim," the cook said.

"I'll tell him something. Listen to me now. When I was young, the old men would gather all of us at a secret place back in the mountains. Great meetings were held among the Malimin in order to judge the bums of the boys in our tribe. Who had the roundest? The sweetest? The best of all? Then we'd decide whose bum was number one!" At this memory Malim Ashmi let out a hideous cross between a cough and a cackle.

"Then we played Smell the Donkey. The boys would lift their djellabas and present their bums for the oldest men to smell. If a boy was particularly sweet, one of the old men might kiss it. Heeee-hee-hee-hee. We had a rule. No one could laugh during these contests. No one could laugh! This was serious business in our village. If one of the musicians laughed, he had to take the place of one of the boys, and be judged himself. We laughed until we were sick.

"Then we played another game called Folded Palm. I loved this one. Palm leaves were folded and jumbled and a boy and a musician would select one end. When the palms were opened, whoever was holding the same leaf would disappear for hours into one of the caves that are hidden all over our hills. That's how it used to be around here." The old man's eyes glinted with mischief and tears. As an afterthought, he asked David, "Where is your wife? Bring her to me so I can see her!"

"She's off with the women," the cook explained.

"Ouacha," Ashmi said. "Give me my staff. I'm going home now. Tell her to come see me later." The old man staggered off.

The musicians shook their heads; there was nothing they could do about the old reprobate except keep him away from visitors. "We let him say whatever he wants," Abdsalam Mezhdoubi told me later. "We have no choice," his younger brother Mujahid added. "He was our grandfathers' teacher. We must respect him."

LATER ON I was resting by myself in the dark corner of the main room, when Malim Ali glided silently through the doorway and handed me a little package. Wrapped in plastic were two halves of a sixteen-inch, olive-wood sebsi, joined at the center by an old brass cartridge shell. Along the wooden tube were intricate carvings of serpents and stylized cannibis leaves. It was a stunning piece of craft, an artifact I knew would be my own private tunnel back into this mysterious place. "B'saha," Ali said with back-country simplicity, and glided out again.

The *frajia*—the nightly entertainment of music, dance, and comedy—was spectacular that evening; the hint of celebration was in the air. During a supper of goat tagine, the chief (he was called *"Moqadem"* ["chief"] by the other musicians) announced that the new djellabas were ready and that, Insh'Allah, we would depart in the morning for Tetuan.

COFFEE WAS SERVED EARLY, a bitter black syrup cut with canned sweet milk from the shop on the plaza. The sun was just over the mountain as our fully laden van lumbered down the stone track. The members of this mission were the three-man Djellaba Advisory Board—Jnuin, Ali, and Rikki Rotobe—plus myself, Joel, and the Courages. We followed the same route as before, stopping at Chaouen for tea in the busy market square between the baths and the red-tiled law courts. An hour later, through alpine passes, we were amidst Tetuan's dark, sinister Hispano-Moorish colonial architecture. In the back of the van the chief had been haranguing his fellows about the necessity of bartering the tailor's price down. We tried to stifle our laughter as the chief went into his little tirades of repeating everything he said at least three times, for emphasis.

We repaired to the shop of the tailor who was making the new djellabas and settled into several hours of tea and formalities prefatory to a long, difficult haggle. In the corner of the stall, the finished garments were stacked in overflowing white boxes. Several examples were unpacked and spread out. They were beautifully tailored from strong chocolate-colored wool. The rims of the flowing hoods were lined with soft, sky-blue cloth, while down the fronts and along the seams of the sleeves ran bright tufted embroidery that lit the cloaks like tiny Chinese fireworks. The general effect was pure charismatic flash. The wool team and the tailor finally agreed on a price, and the Jajoukans were anxious to get their precious cargo out of dangerous Tetuan and the uncertainties of the Rif. We headed toward Tangier in a cloud of blue smoke, and arrived at the Villa Elizabeth after dark. Yusufi and Aisha arrived with some food, and we stayed up late discussing how we might further help Jajouka.

The chief explained that Jajouka was recently registered with the government as a cultural organization entitled *Association Sherifiya Folklorique*—the Saintly Folklore Association. He suggested we form an American branch to look after their interests. We told the chief that his wish was our command.

We left early the next morning. "There was a bad jailbreak down at Kenitra last night," Joel said. "The radio said two guards were killed and the murderers are on the loose." There were police and army roadblocks all along the coastal road. Our van was finally pulled over near Larache by hard-looking gendarmes wearing combat helmets and pointing at us with machine guns. They made us get out and began to paw and body-frisk Red when Jnuin whispered something about Sidi Hamid Sherq to the sergeant, who turned pale white and immediately ordered his men to quit it and remove the heavy iron spikes they were using to hold up traffic.

We drove on, somewhat shaken, only to be stopped by armed customs officers five kilometers down the road. "This could be a bitch," Joel murmured. "They may make us pay 'tax' on the djellabas. I don't like this one bit.'' But their officer recognized the Malimin, and scowls turned to broad smiles.

''Where's that funny little one?'' the customs cop asked. ''You know, what's-his-name . . . Berdouz!'' Informed that Berdouz was up in the village, he waved us on and turned his wrath to the car behind ours.

Malim Ali passed his pipe as Joel turned the van inland.

We arrived at the madrassah at supper time. The finished djellabas were inspected and then blessed with a long thankful prayer by Berdouz. Then they were unfurled and hung on pegs all around the long room so that the scent of new wool filled the cozy, hermetic place. I felt exhausted. Refusing the meal, I collapsed into the bedroom and passed out. *Mission accomplished,* I thought to myself. *Now you can go home.*

IT WAS A GREY, low-energy day. We mostly sat around and moped, smoking and listening to the radio, while the whole troupe of musicians—the entire three dozen who I'd never seen all together at the same time—came around to try on their djellabas. Much hilarity ensued as elderly cousins staged mock battles over a preferred garment. Several of the cloaks were tiny, cut for the youngest dancing boys. One by one they came over to thank us. *''Shoukran,''* they said in Arabic. ''Baraka l'aufic,'' they cried, using the blessing-laden Moroccan term.

Mohammed Berdouz shed his handsome grey-striped djellaba and modeled his new one, pulling his right arm free from the hood to play the drum and lead the band. He walked over and shook my hand. ''Tomorrow,'' he said, ''we're going to play some good music for you. Insh'Allah. And we're going to play it so loud you'll still be hearing it when you get back to America.''

''Moqadem,'' I said to the chief the next morning, my voice quavering with *tristesse,* because I truly was sad, ''I regret to inform you that we are leaving tomorrow.''

132   He brightened measurably as his son Bashir translated my clumsy formulation in French. "Insh'Allah," he said, reminding me that our plans depended upon the will of the Highest. "Are you going to America right away?"

"First to Tangier, then to America. The others will stay in Tangier. Morgan might come back here to take some more pictures."

Then the chief said my name—it always sounded special when he said it—and sighed. "You have done good work here. We will miss you and your friends. When you write about us, tell them we want to come to America and play for them. Do you understand?"

"*Je comprends,* Moqadem."

"Good. We will see you again . . . Insh'Allah."

THE LAST FEW EVENINGS had been cold, and I had taken to spending them in the kitchen. I'd lie with several of the musicians around the glowing brazier. Sometimes I'd pull the hood of my djellaba over my head, lay my cheek on the straw mat, and fall asleep as Achmed the cook prepared dinner.

On my last night in Jajouka I was thus prone, with my feet near the fire. Big Malim Fudul began to warm his immense hands over the brazier, until they were very hot. He then took my feet in his hands, transferring the warmth. Although I was wearing woolen socks at the time, his hands were so hot that my feet began to perspire as he held them. This display of affection and caring touched me as deeply as anything else I experienced in Jajouka during that visit. I had a feeling this canny, tough old fighter was giving me strength for the thousands of miles that lay ahead of me.

THE MASTER MUSICIANS convened that evening for our last supper in the village. The main room of the madrassah was transformed, with low aluminum tables and cushions, into a banquet hall. A chicken couscous was served, rich in yellow gravy and firm white meat. There wasn't much talking at our table, so we listened to the lubricious smacking lips and resounding belches that marked the group's appreciation of Achmed Skirkin's cuisine.

"Sounds like they're enjoying themselves," Joel said.

Morgan, his mouth full of grain, somehow got out, "They're probably relieved to see the last of us by now. We've been here a long time. The djellabas are a big hit; why take a chance on ruining a good friendship?"

"You can say that," David Courage interjected, "because you've been here awhile. We've been here ten days or so. I really don't want to leave yet."

"The problem is," I told him, "that you're here as a guest of our little expedition, which has done business with the Malimin. We're about to wind it down, close the villa, turn in the cars, and leave. You'd have to make your own arrangements with the chief if you want to stay on."

David looked at Joel. "I have to agree," he said. "Especially if you were to return and film more material. They'll want to know what's in it for them. Are you prepared to come up with some cash?"

I knew the Courages were traveling on a budget, and I knew the answer would be no. "You're right, of course," David said. "It's just that this is such a Power Spot. I feel different just *being* here— more awake, more alert, extrasensory. It's a difficult place to tear yourself away from." David looked hopeful. "Didn't you say there was an English kid who lived up here for a while?"

"You're talking about Ricky Stone," Joel said.

At the mention of his name, about half the musicians stopped chewing. "Englis Ricky," one of the younger ones said.

"What about him?" David asked.

"He's a friend of Gysin's," Joel said. "He stayed here for six months. In the end he didn't get on with Hamsa and probably ran out of money and they threw him out in a friendly kind of way."

"Maybe we'll stay until they throw us out," David remarked sourly.

"I'm not sure it would be wise to overstay our welcome," Red said. "I have a feeling life is very hard here. How could you even think of imposing on them?"

"I should listen to my wife," David said. "She's usually right anyway." He looked at me. "What do you think?"

"I think I've got hepatitis," I said.

"I think I might have it too," Morgan said quietly. "My pee's the hue of the Potomac."

There was music that night, but it was half-hearted and it ended early, without any dancing. Everyone said Sl'ama and went off to their houses. Unable to sleep, Joel and I stayed out on the terrace and smoked kif under the moon and stars until dawn.

LATER THAT MORNING the chief announced they were going to bless the new djellabas that afternoon.

We were all invited to Fudul's big house for a luncheon. On a sheltered porch overlooking now-verdant rolling fields of new wheat, we feasted on *bisar* and huge soft pancakes, hot from the skillet, tasting of almonds and honey. Fudul was the perfect host, playing with his newest son, year-old Mustapha, a plump, roly-poly miniature of his big father.

Back at the madrassah, we found all the Malimin, beaming with pomp and pride in their new cloaks. The rhaitas and drums were taken from their cloth sacks. "They're going to play," Joel said as Morgan and David ran for their cameras.

The rhaitas and drummers lined up at a right angle and began to play wild flowing horn music that attracted first the village's children, then the adults. The tune was a flat-out piece of celebratory thunder called *"Johar,"* which meant jewel. As the drums galloped and jumped, the mouths of the wooden horns blared in unison salute. Malim Ashmi appeared over the hill, leaning on his staff.

Stirred by the music, he marched in review down both lines of musicians, right hand held aloft in blessing, his ancient face cracked in a smile. Then the sherif of Sidi Hamid Sherq added his blessing as well. Finally, the rhaitas cried out as Bou Jeloud himself turned up. The goat god immersed his head in the mouths of the horns and danced his purgative dance, shakin' 'em on down.

They played for an hour and then quit. Over tea and kif, we were thanked profusely by one and all. "Enjoy them!" we advised. "B'saha!"

MORGAN ANNOUNCED THAT he and his girlfriend had decided to stay on for a few extra days. He wanted to shoot some more rolls of film, just to be safe. So the rest of us loaded up the Renault. The skies were open and weeping as the several dozen Malimin came to offer embraces and grizzled kisses of farewell. Berdouz intoned a short prayer, everyone said "Amin," and we left.

We drove out of the madrassah, over the campo near the village school where our soccer games had raged, and through the plaza where Bou Jeloud danced. The sherif of the sanctuary ran out in the rain to say good-bye, an extraordinary gesture. In the lower part of the village, some waved and others glowered at us, as if they were quite content that the annoying foreigners were on their way. At the bottom plateau, a solitary figure in a good djellaba waved us to a stop. It turned out to be Amin Attar, one of the chief's sons; he asked for a ride out to the main road. He was going to Casablanca to apply for a passport so he could go to France and work.

At Ksar el Kebir, Amin got out with many farewells. He had been a great singer and enthusiastic Bou Jeloud, and a good friend as well. "Chalk up one more despised factory worker in Paris," Joel grunted as the young malim disappeared into the train station.

We were moving north along the coast, coming out of Larache, when I looked up at some monumental ruins atop a mountain-sized promontory between the road and the ocean. I'd noticed the ruins many times, and now instinctively insisted that Joel stop the car. "Why?" he asked. "Do you want to see Lixus?"

"It's not a question of 'want,' " I said. "Something is pulling me up there."

"It's a spooky place," Joel said, pulling to the side of the deserted road. "It's a Roman ruin, but I've heard the site is extremely old, possibly Phoenician."

At road level were well-preserved ruins of thermal baths, similar to those I'd seen in Rome and the south of France. We climbed halfway up the great hill and found ourselves in the remains of a thriving garrison town overlooking the harbor of Larache and the serpentine river Oued Loukos, which meandered spectacularly back into the country, draining the mountain range that contained Jajouka. We walked into a huge, perfectly preserved gladiatorial amphitheater whose tiers of seats overlooked the great river and valley to the east. In the midst of the seats was an immense stone throne. We sat quietly, listening to the wind whistling through the dead city, and I had one of those ineffable sensations that I'd been here before.

"Lixus was only excavated in the 1950s," Joel mused. "That's why it's so well preserved. And nobody comes up here. The Moroccans think it's haunted by the Djinn." At that instant, a small hunched figure appeared out of a niche in the wall. A shiver went down my back. But it was only the old guardian of the place, and he gestured us to come down to the floor of the theater. He turned out to be a kindly faced old man whose livelihood depended on the generosity of the few visitors to Lixus. He guided us over to the wall, where faint red streaks stained the old stones. "He says thousands were killed here," Joel translated. "He says this stuff on the wall is blood."

The guardian nodded vigorously. *"El Roumi,"* he said, using the local term for the Romans. *"El Roumi michi m'zien."* The old man went on, and Joel said, "He's telling us that the Romans were extremely cruel."

I looked in the man's clear, almost pleading eyes. He spoke with such conviction that it seemed he'd been here when men and beasts died in these circular ruins, and that somehow he remembered. I fished into my pocket and gave him the bills that were there. He looked at the money with great surprise, and put it quickly inside his cloak. "That's probably more than he's seen in a year," Joel said.

The old guardian vanished back into his hovel inside the wall and emerged with a plastic bottle of water, motioning us to follow him. He led us farther up the hill, at the top of which stood the columns and walls of a crumbling acropolis.

"I don't believe this place," David whispered as we walked. "It's incredible. Why have we never heard of it? Look at these ruins!"

We filed down a three-thousand-year-old cobbled street and found ourselves in a courtyard, tiled in perfectly preserved mosaic. It took me a minute to realize it wasn't a courtyard at all. "Don't look now," I said, "but we're standing on the main floor of a very lavish Roman bathhouse. This is probably the steam room."

The guardian had uncorked his water bottle and was pouring it onto the middle of the mosaic floor, which had dried out a bit in the sun. What emerged was a fantastic mosaic head of the sea god Neptune, or Poseidon, dripping in contrast to the dry floor around him. The god was depicted with glaring metallic eyes and great crab and lobster claws waving from his thick, matted green seaweed hair. We stood there for a long time, gazing into the eyes of the old god,

"I can't get over that this is just *out* here, unprotected." David was incensed. "I mean, someone's going to come along and steal this thing someday."

The ruined temple above us now beckoned, but at that moment the skies opened and it began to pour, as if the gods had decided we'd seen enough. We scrambled back down Lixus's rocky hill and took shelter in the car, waiting for the weather to change. When it didn't, Joel said, "Next time," put the car in gear, and resumed driving toward Tangier.

Why, he asked, did you want to go up there so much? I told him

I didn't really know, but that I had an intuition that somehow Lixus and Jajouka were connected.

LATER THAT DAY, when the Iberia Airlines office reopened after the siesta on the Boulevard Pasteur, I confirmed my flight to New York, via Madrid. Then, footloose, I wandered around Tangier until twilight, savoring the variant scents of the old city—jasmine and cedar, piss and corruption. Then I met Joel and the Courages in the piano bar of the Minzeh. There we hashed out plans for the Saintly Folklore Association. We would issue Joel's recordings of Jajouka on an album and sell the record by mail to raise badly needed cash for the musicians. Perhaps, some day, we would try to bring them to America.

Joel woke me at seven the next morning. I left the rest of my Moroccan money on my unmade bed for Fatima, said good-bye to the cat and her brood of kittens, and carried my luggage down the garden path of the Villa Elizabeth. Mohammed clanged the gate behind me, and I knew I'd never see this house again. We drove to the airport and ate omelettes while waiting for my flight to be called.

"Safe journey," Joel Fischer said. "I've had a lot of fun; it won't be the same up there without you."

It meant a lot to me to hear those words. "It was good that we connected," I told him. "I never would've been able to pull this off if you hadn't been there."

"Mektoub," he answered with a shy smile. "It was written."

BOOK TWO

The Reckoning of the Generations

PAN (păn), *n.* [L., fr. Gr. *Pan.*]

1. *Gr. Relig.* A god of flocks and pastures, forests and their wildlife, patron of shepherds, hunters, fishermen, etc. The original seat of his worship was Arcadia, where he was supposed to wander through the forests attended by nymphs, playing upon his syrinx, or "Pan's pipes," fabled to be his invention. He was also regarded as causing sudden and groundless fear, the *panic;* the Athenians, believing him to have caused the panic among the Persians at Marathon, established his worship in a grotto in the Acropolis. In later times Pan became a special God of the Orphics (who interpreted his name, probably originally *ho Paōn,* "the feeder," as to *Pan,* the All) as a pantheistic nature god. Pan was represented as having the legs and sometimes the ears and horns of a goat, and this type was often multiplied into a plurality—*panes, panisci*—who became lesser deities or sprites similar to the satyrs, sileni, fauns, etc. By the Romans he was identified with *Faunus* or *Inuus.* His cult survives in modern folk beliefs in the Balkan countries and in Italy.

chapter 5

The Secret of Andaluz

I returned home and was put in quarantine by my doctor. My head was still in Jajouka, but my corpse was back in America. Berdouz had been right about the echoes; for months after my return I could hear phantom rhaitas keening like ghosts of consciousness. Joel wrote to say that Morgan had been asked to leave a week after my departure. They'd had enough cameras by then. Joel and the Courages stayed long enough to make a few more tapes, and then left.

When the hepatitis wore off, I wrote my story for the *National Geographic*. They hated it, but Morgan's photographs were well received, and a big layout was prepared after I had turned in several drafts. Then I settled down to wait for the story to be scheduled.

One day, a few months after my return, the phone rang. It was Brion Gysin and I nervously stammered something about wanting to meet him.

"Good," he said. "I understand you've just come back from Jajouka. Can you come to lunch at my sister Felicity's this Sunday in New York?" He gave me an address in the West Twenties, and I said I'd be there. I immediately called Joel Fischer at his apartment on Riverside Drive and invited him as well.

Brion Gysin opened the door himself when we arrived. "Ahhh," he said with gently patronizing bemusement, "here are the intrepid journalists from the *Geographic*. But not as I expected. Their hair is too long!"

He swirled his whiskey glass and his blue eyes shone like ice. I fell for him immediately. He was over six feet tall, in his mid-fifties, and as ruggedly handsome as a Swiss mountain guide. He led us into a sunny dining area with a table set for brunch. An eminent musicologist, a famous poet, and several others were already there. His "sister" Felicity turned out to be one of his dearest friends, belying Gysin's reputation as a world-class misogynist. "Tell us everything about Jajouka," he demanded. "What did you find up there?"

As we told him our story—Hamsa's exile, the theft of the djellabas and their replacement—Gysin's brow began to furrow. Clearly, he didn't like what he was hearing. At one point he interrupted and asked, sounding annoyed, "How can you say Hamsa *stole* the djellabas? He bought them in the first place."

Joel tried to reason with him. "That may be true, but he bought them with money Jajouka was paid by Brian Jones. And the Malimin swear they never saw any money Hamsa received from you or the Stones."

"Sounds typical," the musicologist said. "Musicians never trust their managers. Probably shouldn't either."

But Gysin was incensed. "Look, Hamsa *saved* Jajouka. It is doubtful the musicians would even *exist* anymore if Hamsa hadn't intervened by taking people up there. If they crossed him, of course he retaliated." The blue eyes flashed as Gysin leaned his big frame forward in emphasis. "I mean, how can anyone say he *stole* those things?"

"That's what they told us," Joel said. "And that's what Hamsa did. The guy's a thief."

"The guy—as you call him—is an *artist*," Gysin said. There was silence for a minute. "I'm going to pee," Gysin sniffed, and walked out of the room.

Felicity spoke next. "You boys must understand Brion. He *loves* Hamsa. They're soulmates. Hamsa opened Jajouka for him, and to hear of this argument must be very upsetting for Brion. I'm sure Hamsa's done everything you said, but when Brion comes back, try to change the subject, please." Her tone, very sensible and *veddy* British, brooked no argument.

When Gysin came back, it was with another whiskey and a freshly rolled joint of tobacco and hashish. "Now then," he said, ready to forgive. "Where were we?"

"We were discussing Hamsa," I said. Felicity looked at me darkly.

"I'm not saying what you describe didn't occur, but I do wonder what will happen to the village if Hamsa is persona non grata. They obviously need him. Just look what's happened. Many of the best young kids have gone to the cities or off to Europe to work. You think they'll come back? Never! And only the son of a Master Musician can really become one, so they can't go out and *recruit*. What will happen to the esoteric knowledge handed down through the generations? It'll be *lost*, I'm telling you. The musicians are rather aristocratic Arabs in a Berber society. The Spaniards, when they took over that part of Morocco, recognized this, and the moral authority of their saint. They were smart enough to realize that the music Jajouka plays comes from the courtly music of Al-Andaluz, the Moorish part of southern Spain that was destroyed when Ferdinand and Isabella threw out the Muslims and the Jews in 1492. Maybe you've heard that the Spaniards found a couple of Stradivarius violins when they first got up there, in the 1920s. It's true!"

"What happened to them?" I asked.

"Oh they were sent to Madrid, along with the originals of the seven royal decrees allowing the musicians certain rights over the king. But where was I? My point was that the Spanish allowed Jajouka to continue to *tithe,* to take part of the annual crops. But lately this has fallen apart. A few years ago fights broke out when the musicians went out into the fields to collect. Plus the musicians are taxed for each of their instruments, maybe six dollars a year, while their annual cash income might only be ten dollars apiece. So, without Hamsa, how will they survive? Maybe he did keep most of the money for himself. But isn't that normal in the music business? They *need* somebody like him, or the whole thing is going to go to hell, I *promise* you." Gysin took a draw on the joint and passed it.

WE ATE right after that—salad, eggs mayonnaise, very cold white wine. Someone asked Gysin about taking Brian Jones to Jajouka, and the monologue continued:

"They came back to Tangier in, I think, the summer of '68. It was Brian, his girlfriend Suki—I can't remember her last name but she's dead now anyway—and a very good sound man, George Chkiantz. They wanted to record Bou Jeloud's music during the Aid el Kebir, but of course it wasn't that time of year, so they said they'd settle for whatever they could get. I tried to get them to leave the girl behind in Tangier. I told them it was no place for a woman, but she wouldn't listen and absolutely *insisted* on coming. So I had her cut her hair, and she dressed in pants to try to look like a man, and off we went. We arrived late in the day and set up the tape machines and they played until four or five in the morning. At one point all the dogs in the village started to bark, and Jones got upset that the dogs would spoil the tape. So Hamsa had them round up the dogs and move them off somewhere.

"It was the first time any serious recording had been done up there, apart from my little Uher, and there was some uncertainty among the musicians. The older ones were sure it was a big mistake, but they went ahead because Hamsa bullied them. But some of the younger kids were *very* eager. They loved putting on the headphones and listening to the playback. It was the first time some of them had ever 'heard' themselves. In general, there was quite a commotion because they thought that Brian Jones was very funny and not really of this world, with his long blond hair and furry hippie togs. Remember, they'd never seen anyone like this before. It was very new to them, right?

"Anyway, we finally crashed around dawn. This was before I built the madrassah for them, and we were in some house Hamsa had commandeered. The three English kids slept in one room and I lay down under a couple of djellabas on the porch outside. We slept for the rest of the morning, and I suppose the musicians became impatient. At about eleven o'clock the whole group gathered in front of the house with their rhaitas and blew one tremendous blast. Then they ran away, falling over each other in laughter. It was our wake-up call."

Later, something strange happened.

"I was sitting on the ground with Brian and some of the younger musicians, who were really digging this Rolling Stones cat in his red long-haired Afghan coat. We sat under the eaves of a thatched farmhouse where we were going to eat supper, which was being prepared by four or five musicians working a few feet away in the courtyard, where the animals are kept. Two musicians came along, leading a snow-white goat. Off into the shadows the uncomprehending animal disappeared with the two men, one of whom was holding a long-bladed knife. Catching the glint of the blade, Brian Jones realized the goat was being led to the slaughter, and he staggered to his feet and made a funny choking sound and gasped, 'That's me!'

"And everyone there immediately picked up on it, and said yeah, okay, right, it does look just like you. Because it was too perfectly true. The goat had this fringe of white hair hanging down over its eyes, and I could only say, yes, of course, *that's you.* And Brian turned white, as if he'd had some kind of premonition. Twenty minutes later, we were eating grilled chunks of this goat's liver on skewers, and it was never mentioned again.

"We spent the rest of the day doing further recording. They put on a little synthetic Boujeloudiya, so they could get a taste of it on tape. It wasn't really authentic, you might say, but Brian Jones was ecstatic. It was all he needed, I guess. Later in the day, we left for Tangier, so we were only there for one night. But it was enough. He had his tapes."

I asked what happened next.

"Well, not much," Gysin said. "We went back to Tangier. Brian Jones was very intrigued, and spent his time at the Hotel Minzeh listening to the tapes."

Did Brian Jones pay the musicians?

"Well, Hamsa got paid, but we've already been over that, haven't we? Of course I kept on going back to Jajouka and they always asked after Brian. They wanted him to come to the Aid el Kebir in early 1969, but the Stones were in the recording studio and we couldn't reach him. Brian tried to interest the band in Jajouka, but they didn't want to bother with it. And a few months later he was dead of whatever—drowned, ODed, murdered . . . who knows? You've heard all the stories. 'Whom the gods love die young.' We pestered Jagger and the others until they put out *Brian Jones Presents the Pipes of Pan at Jajouka* in 1971, with all that electronic stuff in there, quite unnecessarily in my opinion."

Eventually the talk devolved into other matters, and I was content just to sip my wine and listen to Brion Gysin. He was extremely learned and opinionated in a charming, sophisticated way. He was funny and bitchy and preoccupied with money and not having it. In sympathizing with Hamsa, Gysin seemed to know what was happening in Jajouka and was determined to stay out of the war between his dearest Moroccan friend and the tribe that had adopted him.

Before the party broke up, he cornered Joel and myself. I had worried that Gysin might have felt we were encroaching on his territory, but instead he was obviously pleased we were interested in his discovery. "Tell me," he whispered with a soupçon of conspiracy. "Is Malim Ashmi still alive?"

Yes, I told him. And he asked where you were.

"He did?" Gysin was pleased. "He's a wicked old man, and I believe every word he says. Did he tell you about his love life? About the boy that looked like a jewel? The story was this: At a big festival in Jajouka, many years ago, a group from a neighboring village brought a boy more beautiful than anyone had seen in the mountains in decades. The kid was a *peach,* and when he danced people went wild. Anyway, the men of his village guarded this boy very closely. When he went to sleep in Jajouka that night, they slept in a ring around him, after surrounding themselves with a blue cactus fence. But at dawn they found young Ashmi cuddled with their jewel, both sleeping blissfully. In the night Ashmi had cut through the cactus and taken his prize. If it hadn't happened in Jajouka, Ashmi would have been killed. It was a scandal in the hills for *years.*" Gysin laughed with pleasure.

"I'm going home to France soon," Gysin told us. "The cultural commissars have given me a flat in the Cité Internationale des Arts. Come see me next time you're in Paris."

WE SPENT THE REST of 1974 ironing out the details for the Association Sherifiya Folklorique incorporating in the state of New York. Joel Fischer brought out his album, *The Master Musicians of Jajouka,* a splendid ethnosonic record that hit every main facet of the music, from rhaitas to dance rhythms, sanctuary music to Bou Jeloud's panic modes. The album also featured several unusual tracks, such as one of Berdouz's fervent group prayers, along with splendid versions of "Brahim Jones" and "Jajouka Black Eyes." But the best track was a few minutes of women's music recorded by Joel's former girlfriend Anastasia, who had waded with a microphone into a crowd of women "teasing" Bou Jeloud during the Aid el Kebir of 1973.

I made sure the album received good reviews in the press, which wasn't hard since Brian Jones now had his own cult among writers who covered music. Red Courage set up a post office box at Planetarium Station in Manhattan to handle orders for the record, which sold well enough to earn several thousand dollars for Jajouka over the next few years.

"WELL, OF COURSE the Moroccans have never had much of a problem with homosexuality. They're not Christians. The answer's as simple as that."

I was interviewing William S. Burroughs in a motel room on the Fenway in Boston for a local newspaper in late 1974. A longtime friend and collaborator of Brion Gysin's, he had visited Jajouka several times and had incorporated elements of the Boujeloudiya into his fantastic novels, *The Ticket That Exploded* and *Nova Express.*

"The best thing about the Moroccans is that they never had Saint Paul telling them what they could and couldn't do. They don't have the same attitude as Christians on homosexuality or any other sexual matter. Their sexual attitudes are more, shall we say, casual. No uptightness, no guilt, no complexes—nothing like that." Burroughs paused for a moment, thinking. About sixty at that time, he was wearing a checked tweed jacket with a shirt and tie under a Moroccan vest, set off by a pair of bright yellow high-top basketball sneakers. That evening he was to give a benefit reading for a literary group called the Good Gay Poets.

"Wait a minute," Burroughs continued. "I don't want you to have the impression that the Prophet Mohammed said 'it' was all right—homosexuality—which he didn't. But I believe he regarded it as a minor matter. Very minor."

More interested in his experiences in Jajouka, I asked when Gysin had first taken him up there.

"It wasn't Brion I first went there with. I had met him in 1954 in Tangier, but we didn't see much of each other then because he was running his cabaret, The Thousand and One Nights, using some of the Jajoukans as house musicians. Later I got to know him in Paris in 1958 and that's when we became very good friends. We were living in the same hotel. Brion introduced me to Hamsa, who took me to Jajouka in 1964." Again Burroughs paused. "Of course it's changed since then; they've replaced the thatched roofs with tin and built all these new houses. It seems like a much bigger place now."

Do you think the music, the magic of the place, has changed also?

"Ummm, no. Still plenty of magic in Jajouka. Lots of it. They're still living, to some extent, in the magical world. Did you ever notice the odor when the musicians are really cooking? It's like a crackling in the air, a mixture of ozone and incense. They're probably related to the Persian poet Farid ud-Din Attar, who wrote a wonderful philosophic poem, *The Conference of the Birds,* sometime in the twelfth century. They can produce this scent with their music. To me, *that's* magic. Not that they can do this always. But I've smelled it myself."

Someone knocked on the door, and Burroughs said it was time to go. I inquired after Brion Gysin and was sorry to hear he was quite ill and living in London.

When asked what was the matter, Burroughs's face went ashen. "I'm afraid I just can't talk about it," he said. "It's too upsetting."

Later, Burroughs's assistant told me that Brion had developed rectal cancer, but was responding very well to treatment.

JOEL FISCHER WROTE to me from Morocco at the end of 1974 to say he had been to the village briefly. The Masters sent their regards, and the sad news that the cook had died. I remembered how well he had looked after us, and wondered what would happen to his little dog.

UP UNTIL 1975 Morocco was thought of as just another sleepy post-colonial regime dominated by a Francophone elite who ran things solely in the interest of their own pockets. But nobody really grasped the cultural and physical strength of the Moroccan people, national traits that had not been tested for more than sixty years. All that changed when the Spanish dictator Francisco Franco died. Spain was the only country in the world where a new government run by a king could be called a move to the Left.

It was in 1975 that Latin colonialism in Africa began to crumble, most notably the abandonment by Portugal of its vast colonies in Angola and Mozambique. In his capital at Rabat, Morocco's King Hassan decided that the so-called Spanish Sahara—an immense hunk of empty desert under which lay potentially rich phosphate deposits—should revert to Moroccan control, from which it had slipped after 1860. In a brilliant and theatrical coup, Hassan announced that Morocco would not reclaim its lost southern territory by force of arms. Instead Hassan orchestrated the epochal Green March, in which tens of thousands of ordinary Moroccans would assemble on the old Saharan border, then walk in and occupy the land. Spain withdrew its military garrisons from the old mud-walled desert forts, and the Green March took place. In partnership with neighboring Mauretania, Hassan reasserted his sovereignty over the Western Sahara.

But not without a long and difficult guerrilla war, fought by disgruntled tribesmen fighting under the banner of the *Frente por la Liberación de Saqiat al Hamra y Río de Oro,* the Polisario Front. Supplied by Algeria and riding Land Rovers instead of the camels of their ancestors, the Polisario fighters demanded independence from the Moroccan king and began to kill his soldiers.

All this reminded me of Nasser's famous remark that the bravest of the invading Islamic warriors who had raged westward from Arabia in the eighth century had wound up in Morocco. It also reminded me that some of my younger Jajouka friends had left to join the army, perhaps to fight in the Sahara.

I WENT TO New Mexico to visit Joel that year. He was building a restaurant in the desert suburbs, a perfect domed and crenellated replica of a saintly tomb one sees in the distance across the rolling Moroccan countryside. Architecture wasn't the only thing Joel was importing. He had procured a passport and visa for Mohammed Yusufi, our friend from Tangier, who would serve as chief cook. "It's beautiful," I told him. "The whole *idea* is great. What are you going to call it?"

"El Djebala," he said.

A year later, in 1976, I ate there. The ceilings were painted like those of the madrassah at Jajouka: red, blue, and yellow geometric whorls. The waitresses were very pretty, and the flat rounds of crusty bread were almost perfect. Mohammed had quit, but the food was excellent, spiced a bit differently for the Southwestern palate.

Joel was living in an adobe house on an old cavalry fort. We stayed up all night, listening to Jajouka tapes, nodding at transcendent passages, laughing when we heard Berdouz pretending to go into a coughing spasm after some brain-beating jam banged to a halt. If the Navaho carpets, descended from the Moorish saddle blankets of the conquistadors, could have turned into flying carpets, we'd have left for the foothills of the Rif that morning at dawn.

WE FOUND OUT, Morgan Robbins and I, that our story—in greatly truncated form—was scheduled to run in the July 1976 issue of the *National Geographic*. Now titled "The Goat God Still Dances in Old Jajouka," the piece was only ten pages of text and photographs, but at least it told the story and put Jajouka on the map.

Then, to our dismay, a month before the issue went to press, the story was killed, rubbed out, with no hope of a reprieve. I was blown away. Later, we heard the editor had squashed the piece because of the descriptions and pictures of marijuana smoking. So much for the diffusion of geographic knowledge.

I thought about all the times we had boasted to the chief that we were going to make Jajouka famous in the most important magazine in America. Jnuin would simply deploy his sad, kindly smile and murmur, "Insh'Allah."

154   He'd been right all along. It was written.

A few weeks later I received a letter from him. Written in French, it said:

> From the Zahjouka Folklore Association to our true friend, it is with great joy that we take this moment to present our happiest salutations from all the musicians and their president, as well as the little musicians [the boys and young men]. We hope that our letter to you finds your life in the best conditions possible.
>
> We call to your attention a letter sent to us from Miss Susan Small of the National Geographic Society. This letter says that the article which was written by you was not accepted. We truly regret this business, but wish to express our hope that God will guard you, for your family, and for our young association.
>
> Thank you for the great effort that you have accomplished for our association. Please come to pay a visit soon.
>
> Finally, pass our *bonjours* to your friends and colleagues.

I wrote back to the chief, saying that I would see them again someday.

IN 1977 ORNETTE COLEMAN released *Dancing In Your Head,* an album containing some of the experimental music he had recorded at Jajouka five years earlier. The music came with an artistic manifesto called the Harmolodic Theory, and ended with a track called "Midnight Sunrise," which featured Coleman improvising over a cut-up jumble of Jajouka's music—drums, flutes, rhaitas, gimbris—all played at once in a mad salad of noise.

Hearing this new music coincided with a faint but persistent psychic broadcast from Jajouka. *Come back and visit,* whispered the telepathic beam on the Sidi Hamid Sherq channel. Joel Fischer called from New Mexico to say he was picking up the same signal, loud and clear. So in February 1977 we met in New York and flew to Madrid. Then an Iberia 727 dropped us onto the windy seaside tarmac of Tangier's airport, where date palms lashed wildly and clacked their stiff fronds in the warm winter breeze off the Atlantic.

Morocco was a different experience without the *Geographic* behind me. The expense account, lovely villa, fleet of cars, and dago-dazzlers were gone. Now we rented a veteran yellow VW microbus and checked into the ultra-modest Villa Mouneriya, former high temple of the expat Beats of 1950s Tangier, secluded down a sinister alley in the upper town. It was run by a pair of middle-aged Englishmen. There was a brothel across the street and a Spanish social club next door, from behind whose walls came the incessant clacking of continuous games of *boule*. Joel and I took the two bedrooms at the top of the house, which shared a private bathroom and a terrace with a splendid view of Tangier Bay and Spain looming across the strait. Jet-lagged, I closed the curtain and slept for hours.

A soft knock woke me up. "It's me," Joel said through the door. "I'm going down to Yusufi's. Want to come?"

Give me five minutes, I said.

The late winter light was dwindling as we walked along the Boulevard Pasteur. Tangier was very quiet and clean, and the cafés along the avenue were empty of tourists, scared away by the war Morocco was pursuing in the Western Sahara, far to the south.

We walked downhill toward the medina, through the big oval of the Socco Grande, crimson with Moroccan flags festooned to celebrate the King's Coronation Day, *Aid El Arsh,* and the feast of *Mouloud,* the Prophet Mohammed's birthday. We entered the medina through the gate of the Siaghines and hurried through alleys and passageways until we reached the tiny courtyard with its skewed beige walls boxing a patch of dark blue sky. The green wooden door opened, we received a kiss from Aisha, and followed her up the green walled stone staircase into a sitting room with red cushions and a tiny daughter named Fatima Zohra.

Whatever had transpired between Joel and Mohammed over the

restaurant was safely in the past. The Moroccan still wore his clinically depressed mien; the family was suffering financially because Tangier was empty of tourists. "The war kills between eighty and a hundred Moroccan soldiers every day," Mohammed whispered, as though the walls had ears, "but this is not official. How do we know? Radio Algiers. Talk on the street. People find out."

Over dark mint tea he told us stories of the portentous events in the city of Meknes:

"A woman cast a spell on her son so he would not be able to lie with a woman, whether out of jealousy or not . . . nobody knows! The woman then died, was wrapped in her shroud, carried off to the cemetery, and buried. The next morning she was discovered lying on top of her grave. They buried her again, but the next morning she was found on top of her grave again.

"When her son came that afternoon with the sherif, he was counseled to stay and observe the grave, do what he was told, and then leave and not look back. That night he heard his mother's voice. She told him that she had buried a packet of herbs and a clasp knife, closed on a paper charm, under a tree, and if he dug it up he would be able to lie with a woman again. As he was leaving the cemetery he heard his mother scream his name. He turned his head halfway before he remembered what the sherif had said, but it was too late. Now his neck is paralyzed."

Mohammed paused to let this sink in, but Aisha prodded him to tell the other story. "Also in Meknes," he said, "two men were trimming a row of eucalyptus trees by the side of the road. When they cut into the last one, it began to bleed profusely. Red blood! One of the cutters collapsed and died right on the road. The other one expired in the doorway of the hospital."

Joel and I looked at each other and said nothing.

Mohammed also mentioned that the kif supply was of national concern because it had been raining for three months. Roads had washed out, houses collapsed, people had died. He took out his sebsi and gave Joel a fresh-cut supply wrapped in cellophane.

That night, Mohammed took us to a café hidden deep in the bowels of the medina, one of the few places left that had live Andaluz music every night. As the violins and treble flutes soared like birds, smokers exchanged lit sebsis by spinning them across the room, where they would be caught and inhaled on the fly. Joel was delighted. "I thought I'd seen everything," he smiled, "but never flying sebsis before."

A FEW HOURS LATER, as the rising sun outlined the faraway Rif in jagged black, we checked out of the Mouneriya, provisioned at the market in the Rue Fez, and drove south out of Tangier along the wide Atlantic beach. Everything was gauzy blue with surf spray and slanting light. Joel remarked, as we drove slowly through a tough gendarme roadblock, that King Hassan seemed to have Morocco more firmly under his authority than ever, the war in the Sahara having rekindled feelings of nationality and patriotism. "Besides," Joel said, "Yusufi swears that Hassan was protected at birth by a powerful spell that prevents him from suffering a violent death. That's why both the bloody coup attempts against him failed."

The heavy rains of the past winter had turned the farina and sugar-beet fields of northern Morocco a surreal green, and as we turned inland, past mysterious Lixus and Larache, the landscape appeared to be tinted with all the possible variants along the blue-green spectrum. This glowing verdure was only broken by distant, white-domed *qobas,* burial places of saints that lay in the folds of the land, well off the roadway.

North of Ksar el Kebir these agrarian vistas were interrupted by a new industrial complex, whose steel towers and stacks shone in the sunlight. Traffic slowed as we approached this behemoth, surrounded by several hundred conical white tents and several thousand people encamped on a great meadow. We drove through Ksar, and turned northeast toward Tatoft. There, in the distance, halfway up the mountain, gleamed the tin roofs of Jajouka. But when we

158   stopped to register with the caid at his utterly empty fort, the lone
soldier on guard pointed back toward Ksar. "Everyone's at *la fête*,"
he shouted.

So we drove back to the huge festival on the great field surrounding what turned out to be the new sugar refinery. The government
would dedicate it the following day, coincident with the feast of
Mouloud. We parked the bus by the mule corral and tramped
through the muddy pasture. Night was falling now, bonfires were
alight, and clusters of robed men were drumming and dancing in
rhythmic abandon. Someone behind us shouted my name and we
were instantly surrounded by familiar faces, old and young, leaning
into us to kiss and be kissed. We were marched to a pair of big white
tents next to the reviewing stand, where Jajouka would entertain
during the dedication ceremonies. In the larger tent sat the village
hierarchy—the chief, Fudul, Berdouz, Malim Ali, and the rest.
They were very surprised to see us, and close questioning ensued.
Joel told them he had brought several thousand dollars, representing
their royalties from the album he produced. "M'zien b'zef," the
chief said. "And where is this money now?"

In my suitcase in our van, Joel told him, adding that he had
brought them cash, exchanged for dollars in Tangier at a favorable
black-market rate procured by Mohammed.

In the car? Jnuin's eyes widened in worry. He barked some
orders and a cadre of tough young men frog-marched us back to the
bus before any of the hundreds of thieves they swore preyed on the
festival got the idea to smash the windows and steal everything.

Back in the tent, gas lamps threw soft shadows on the white
canvas walls. We traded sebsis of our Tangier kif (quite m'suss, they
commented on its high tobacco content) for pipes of the Masters'
home-grown finest. The delicious smells of chef Megaria's open-fire
cuisine filled the air as tables were opened, hands were washed, and
a great supper of spiced mutton grilled on skewers, lamb and
chicken tagines, and loaves of crusty bread for gravy-sopping was
served. The chief told us that Jajouka had accompanied the caid of

Tatoft to help open the new refinery, which would process beets from all over the area into cones of blue-wrapped sugar.

At about ten o'clock a muezzin called the hour of prayer, and the older men trooped out of the tent to prostrate themselves. Around midnight, the lamps were turned down and the older musicians cuddled up to sleep in a bunch, with Joel and me almost buried in the middle. I tried to sleep but instead lay awake the whole night in anticipation of the days ahead.

AT ABOUT NINE the next morning, the musicians assembled in rhaita and drum lines in front of the reviewing tent, luxurious with divans and carpeting for the local gentry and caids. I stood behind the chief, wrapped in a djellaba, with a Sony TC-224 strapped to my chest, taping the performance as they began an hour-long medley of martial rhaita airs. Thousands of people crowded in behind us, attracted by the music and colorful display of religious flags in honor of the Prophet's birthday.

After half an hour, some dignitary led in his own band, a small Djibli ensemble dressed in black djellabas and red fez; they were three rhaitas and a brass trumpet, along with military-style trap drums and a big green bass drum. This group sat down and was ordered, by their patron, to begin playing while Jajouka was still wailing away across the little space in front of the VIP tent. Quite shamefaced at their plight, this second group began a loud counter-march. The two bands playing at once were caterwauling and hilarious. Dignified in their embroidered djellabas, the ones we'd bought three years earlier, Jajouka kept on playing. Soon I realized this amazing mishmash sounded familiar. Let's see: two different rhythms, with tempered horns and untempered reeds playing two different songs at two different tempos. It sounded like . . . Ornette Coleman!!

After an hour, a frantic official waved the musicians to a stop as loudspeakers blared martial music from Rabat. This was followed by

160   a program of religious and patriotic messages, followed by an address from the king himself, speaking from his palace in Marrakech.

The Master Musicians of Jajouka hurried back to their tent during a midday pause in festivities. Everyone slept for a half hour after lunch before going back to work. Large numbers of country people had been trucked in for the occasion, and when the rhaitas fired up again I was swept up into the swell of a panicky Moroccan throng. A Bou Jeloud, not from Jajouka, came out to dance as the Priests of Pan played his music. He was good, this goat dancer, kicking like a ram and arbitrarily rearranging the masses of onlookers with threats and slashes of his long flails.

What do you think of him? I asked Joel in his capacity as an *aficionado*.

"Lacks the *duende* of Abdallah," Joel replied deadpan, referring to Jnuin's third son, a very elfin and frenetic Bou Jeloud. "But quite excellent all the same. I wonder where he's from. Could be anywhere from here to Wazzan. It just goes to show that Bou Jeloud isn't alive only in Jajouka."

The day's festivities ended and it was time to head for Jajouka in a bus crammed with seven musicians and all the baggage. Of course we immediately bogged to the axles in the soupy pasture mud, and had to be pulled out by a passing tractor after the Malimin threatened the reluctant driver with the retribution of an outraged Sidi Hamid Sherq. An hour later, we ground along up the outrageous mountain track. The town was dark as we drove through, but the somewhat musty madrassah was immediately opened and prepared for our stay. Brian Jones beamed at us from his framed photo on the wall.

"I'm famished," Joel said, and at that moment a big platter of fresh couscous arrived, despite the late hour and apparent slumber of the village. It was explained that the sherif of the sanctuary had seen our headlights and sent the food on learning the identities of the visitors.

Despite the chill in the night air, we ate by lantern light on the terrace, while Malim Titi's son Ahmed fumigated the musty madrassah with a Flit-gun. "Insh'Allah, it'll stun the fleas for a few weeks," Joel murmured under his breath.

IN THE MORNING the sky was blue and brilliant. My spirits felt like they had been unbridled and unbound, as if we had arrived at the apex of the world.

We washed and shaved in front of an old auto mirror that had been cemented in one of the whitewashed walls, and were served coffee on cushions set out on the terrace. We noted there were fewer young men around. Abdallah Attar and Achmido, who had been the village's star dancing boy, had joined the army for twenty-year terms. Other familiar faces were also absent. Some had left the village. Some were away at school. One or two had died.

"Where is Tahir?" I asked. There was an embarrassed silence, until Berdouz said, "Alcazar." There followed a conversation in Arabic that I couldn't follow. Later, Joel explained.

"They say that Tahir left about a year ago; he's playing music with his own group in Alcazar. There's controversy about his departure, apparently. He was brought to the village by Hamsa in the first place, but stayed after Hamsa left. I gather they're not too happy, since Tahir seems to have taken some business from them lately."

Devastating, I thought. Like losing your lead singer *and* lead guitar all at once.

That evening, when they played music after supper, they proudly gave a bravura performance to show us that Tahir's absence meant nothing. The chief's wonderful, ascetic son Amin had not made it to France after all. Something wrong with his papers, he told us sheepishly. Good for Jajouka, I thought, because Amin was playing the violin that Ornette Coleman had bought for Jajouka during his visit, and was handling the lead vocals as well.

JAJOUKA WAS TRANQUILO; it was off-season. The Aid el Kebir had passed by some months before, so there would be no Bou Jeloud dancing in the late afternoons. The priests of Pan tended their gardens and flocks and smoked a little kif. We rose late, took walks, and sat around waiting for the music to begin at night.

"Does something seem different about Jajouka to you?" I asked Joel one morning.

"Yeah, it's the cook," Joel said. "You know what I mean? A lot of warmth and hospitality emanated from his kitchen." This was true. As visitors, we were lavished with food and affection, but in Skirkin's absence the kitchen was a dark, grungy den in which the usually unkempt Megaria nevertheless produced excellent tagines and couscous. Other absences were readily apparent. Malim Titi, the great singer who farted on his tobacco, had died as well. When I gave his son a print of Titi I'd had made from one of Morgan's slides, the boy clutched it to his chest and ran off in tears. Also gone was the master flute and rhaita player Mohammed Stitu, or Little Mohammed, who was living in Alcazar. Some said he was ill. Some said it had to do with Hamsa, who was Stitu's wife's nephew.

We were sitting with Ali and Fudul on the terrace where they were repairing instruments. I asked if Malim Ashmi was still alive. Yes, we were told, but he no longer comes out of his house. Ali, Ashmi's great-grandnephew, promised to relay our greetings to the 117-year-old man. While he talked, Ali replaced the skin on the big gimbri. He affixed the fresh skin with metal studs, and then handed it to Fudul, who punched holes corresponding to the f-holes in a guitar body with a red-hot skewer from the clay brazier. Another small hole punched in the gimbri's side served to let out the Djinn.

After a few days, we grew attuned to the seductive torpor of Jajouka in the winter. Days went by slowly; incidents seemed to happen in strobe light. Hours were spent propped up on cushions, reclining on a reed mat on the porch, accepting pipes and glasses of hot mint tea. Sometimes I'd read, or we'd search for the BBC on the miniature short-wave radio I'd brought. Mostly, I lay back on those pillows watching the clouds and the hooded figures glide over the horizon.

Early one Friday morning, I lingered by the gate of the sanctuary as the musicians were finishing the heraldic anthem that concluded the day's religious observations. The pipers filed out the back door into the graveyard, and the sherif, a fierce old white-beard, came out and shook my hand in his gruff but affectionate way. Everytime I saw him, he tried to communicate something to me about Jajouka, but we had no common language, and I knew he was frustrated. There was something he wanted to explain.

Down in the valley below the sanctuary, a fog bank rolled in like a flock of golden brown sheep. Then the sherif of the shrine of Sidi Hamid Sherq did a strange thing. He put his hands on the temples of my head. The fog vanished and I saw stark images of old wars and famines in the valley, while Jajouka remained somehow serene and provisioned, literally above the fray. He took his hands from my head, and the picture vanished. The incident lasted only a few seconds, but took my understanding of the village to another level. Somehow, Jajouka is *protected*.

That night, after supper, in the hissing gas light of the madrassah, Berdouz led a prayer; the Malimin filed in, sat down, and cupped their hands. Berdouz prayed for the brotherhood, their friends (a long litany of names), their land, houses, families, and animals. After every phrase, they responded "Amin." Then Berdouz prayed for Sultan Moulay Hassan, the caid, and the caliph. At the end, the company recited a low unison prayer asking for individual guidance and protection for the tribe Ahl Sherif. After the final Amin, there was a burst of applause.

TWO KIF TRAFFICKERS had passed through the village late in the afternoon. Each grizzled mountaineer carried a hundred kilos on his back. They had already walked the fifty miles from Ketama in the Rif, and said they had another seventy-five to go, using old smugglers' trails through the mountains, avoiding main roads and the police. They were greeted as friends at the madrassah and given tea, nourishment, and a place to rest. One had his thick leather hiking slippers repaired by the village cobbler.

During their hour's sleep, Fudul explained: "Once these same two hid out in Jajouka while the police searched for them. Three gendarmes drove up in a Jeep and asked the Malimin whether they had seen anything. They said no! Anyone would, praise be to God! But these same two were hiding in the madrassah. No, no, we all said. We didn't see anything or anybody! Since that time, these same two drop a kilo or two on their way through our town. Every time!"

That night it rained like crazy and the music was fast and wild. As the drums began to kick in during the second number, Abdinde leapt through the doorway in a blue silk dress and red belt cinched around his hips—country-girl drag—and began to shimmy seductively. It was hilarious and beautiful at the same instant. "Eewa!" yelled the Master Musicians. "Eeeewwwwwaaaaa!!!" Abdinde wiggled over to us and produced an astounding hot shake that stretched the dancer's skill and blurred our powers of observation. The Masters looked on approvingly. Achmido Twimi, the sober and dignified young piper who was Abdinde's father, sang lead in his piercing high tenor, almost shouting to be heard over the bum-churning syncopation of the drums.

Then the vocal dropped out and the dancer feinted away like Syrinx, his feet darting through mesmerizing half-steps as he swayed back toward the musicians. My hands hurt from clapping along to the irresistible time they were keeping. I looked again and the knotted tassels on Abdinde's belt were swinging like mad. When it was his turn to sing chorus, Abdinde stopped moving and leaned into the pulse of his uncles and cousins, wailing old Andaluz in a penetrating soprano that cracked in the higher notes.

When this brilliant performance finally crashed to a halt, the feeling in the room was ecstatic. "Berry gut!" shouted the irrepressible Berdouz as he lit his sebsi. "Berry much! Eberryting outasight!"

ONE EVENING, after a long roundabout to Bou Jeloud's cave, we found the Malimin huddled in brown djellabas around braziers on the terrace of their house. When I returned from the hammam Joel asked, "How do you feel?"

"Tired, but still kicking."

"Good, because tonight there's a festival in honor of Sidi Hamid Sherq's family and we're going to be up all night."

At eight o'clock we were taking mint tea and enjoying fresh night air on the terrace when the sherif dropped in, raving about all the pilgrims and lunatics he had on his hands in the saintly precinct awaiting Sidi Hamid Sherq's curative blessing. He pulled the musicians up from supine positions, roughly, some by the hoods of their robes. The festivities were about to begin. Joel and I slipped into djellabas, pulled the hoods over our heads, and followed the musicians into the black night.

Three rhaitas (the chief, Malim Ali, Mezhdoubi) began to play in the darkened town plaza. Two drummers joined a moment later. I couldn't see anything but stars and the shadows of buildings until Mohammed Attar joined us, carrying a gas lantern on his head. Our musical procession followed him into the walled compound of Sidi Hamid Sherq's family, the Rotobe. As we filed through the arched gate, a spine-tingling yodel came from a cluster of white blankets in a doorway. *Yuyuyuyuyuyuyuyuyuyuyu!* reverberated off the walls and into our heads. To the high and mighty music of the rhaitas, the saintly flag was brought out for display: a bright sherifian green banner bordered in golden thread, containing a red square and a gold square combining to form an octagon, in the midst of which, stitched in crimson, were the words *La Illa La Allah.* Women now rushed forward to kiss the hem of the flag before it was raised again; some tried to tie their silk scarves to the staff for baraka.

Suddenly the crowd scattered as a big apprehensive black bull was manhandled into the courtyard. Amid great approval, the beast was displayed and blessed. It smelled its own blood in the air.

Bashir and some others wrestled the bull to the ground. A long curved knife was produced, but deemed unsharp. Another knife ushered in the moment of slaughter. Mustapha Rotobe, a friendly ''enemy'' of mine from the soccer field, offered to cut *my* throat. ''Baraka!'' I pleaded, and he laughed, gathering the folds of the bull's throat and cutting. The animal's brown eyes bulged out.

An assistant saint forced a tea glass into the pumping jugular vein, filling it with hot blood. This glass was whisked away to the sanctuary. Meanwhile the collection and prayers and chanting continued, the prone bull gave a few kicks, and ever-jolly Mustapha asked, with up-country humor, if I was *sure* I didn't want to be next.

Later, as morning approached, the bull's heart was grilled on skewers, with spices.

As the sky began to lighten, with barely time for coffee, we were again led off to witness a sacrifice. The same three rhaitas formed in the plaza and began to play, moving to the sanctuary to again fetch the flag. Then the procession went to the chief's house, for prayers and further offerings. As two bulls and two goats were led into Jnuin's courtyard, one of the animals kicked and bucked and seemed as though it were trying to fly away, like a bull in a Chagall painting. But it was quickly caught and subdued. The other bull simply lay down in the dirt, quite sensibly I thought; it rose again only after much prodding. The goats were carried out of the courtyard. Then the rhaitas led the congregants to the cemetery for some further praying, and the animals were quickly slaughtered on the broad plain between the government school and the madrassah. Soon glaring pools of blood gathered in the green grass as the sacrifice in honor of Sidi Hamid Sherq came to a close. Later, all the meat was auctioned off to villagers and pilgrims.

THAT AFTERNOON, as the warm sun reigned over the world, we followed Abdsalam Fudul down a hedge-and-cactus path behind the musicians' house, and descended into a sparkling green valley planted in wheat. We walked over a small arroyo and through a hundred yards of scrub. In the distance above us loomed the haunted granite escarpment that held Bou Jeloud's cave. At the bottom of the valley we found the *piscina* Abdsalam had promised, a natural rock pool under a waterfall.

Abdsalam stripped down to shorts and plunged in, as if he were taking a thermal bath. I stuck my foot in and shivered with the icy contact. "Aisha Hamoka inaya," Abdsalam called. This was Crazy Aisha's spring! Joel was lighting his sebsi. "Good," he said with his bemused, ironic smile. "After all the blood in the last twenty-four hours, I was feeling in a stone-age mood anyway."

So we had a cold bath, shaved in a scrap of mirror, and spread towels on flat rocks to dry in the sun, watched in total silence by three shepherd boys and their flocks. The boys waited for us to leave, and plunged into the pool themselves.

There was great music that night, hard Afro-Moorish rock with soaring choruses anchored by Berdouz, who was playing bass lines on his drum. Hourglass drabougas and tambourines and flat bendirs syncopated the beat so that the muscles twitched in sympathy, and even I got up to dance as verse and chorus built to an impossible finale. "Why yeh, why yeh," they sang. "Jajouka, you are my black-eyed lover."

THE NEXT AFTERNOON, an extraordinary thing happened. A *sherifa,* a middle-aged woman of extremely saintly lineage, trundled across the low wall and plumped herself in our midst on a cushion that was hastily inserted so her holy bum would not be profaned by the terrace of the musicians. She was the only Moroccan woman I'd seen inside the madrassah's walls, except for Haimu, the chief's sister. From the folds of her white blankets, Sherifa produced a tomato can full of fresh orange blossoms, which she gave to the cook for tea. Her face was uncovered under her mindle, and she stared into my eyes like a soul-ophthalmologist.

An hour later, a familiar figure stepped through the gate in the wall. "Look who's here," Joel said with surprise. "It's Tahir!" And there he was, smiling and shaking hands and kissing us, dressed in a natty checked suit and a red shirt, more handsome than ever, his eyes flashing from his round face. My name sounded like music when he said it, and I was very glad to see him. He said he'd left Jajouka two years before to help his family in Ksar el Kebir, but now he was working as a waiter and musician at the Hotel Ibn Batuta in Tangier. He had a little group with dancing girls—*mujeres,* he whispered conspiratorially—and they were here to play a private party in another part of the village. He finished his tea, bade us an affectionate farewell, and left amid general grumbling.

"The old men don't like him now," Bashir told us. "His girls dance with tea trays on their heads and they think it vulgar and unreligious."

LATE IN THE DAY we decided a hot bath was a good idea, so we said a temporary good-bye to the Masters and arrived in Tangier in under three hours.

The next morning was cold and fresh. A big white cruise ship had docked in the port overnight, and the town was crawling with its Italian and English passengers. I found Joel at the Café Paris sitting with a tall, horse-faced American with long hair and a gold ring in his left ear. "Meet Skip," Joel said. "We knew each other in Ibiza."

"Skip Early," the other one said, extending his hand. "Last time I saw Joel was in 1970. He had a leather shop and I had a little band. Then I migrated to Formentera nearby, where I met Sandra, my

English rose. She has a son with a guy whose main trip was running guns and smuggling hash for the IRA. Can you dig it? Are you with me?''

I was rapt.

"This IRA cat was totally hip and had unlimited cash, okay? About ten years ago, maybe 1967, he buys an old palace here in Tangier, called Ben Abou. Sandra didn't want to live in it, so he bought her a farm in Wales instead and disappeared. That's when I came in. Sandra and I got together, right? Now we want to live here in Tangier so I can get a band together and her kid can go to the American School in town. I'm trying to sell Ben Abou so we can buy a little house on the mountain. And I show up here for coffee and run into Joel. Small world.''

I asked how he planned to sell a palace.

"Ain't easy, take my word for it. Been empty for two years. There are broken windows, man, and birds and the weather have gotten in. There's this one guy that seems interested, but not at my price. Hey, wanna see the house? Let's go.''

The Palais Ben Abou was at the top of the casbah, the fortified rampart of old Tangier. Before a carved wooden door set in a pointed Moorish arch, Skip produced an archaic iron key from a leather pouch at his belt. We walked into a dripping Orientalist fantasy of romantically decayed Moorish splendor. As my eyes adjusted to the gloom of the unlit house, I noticed magnificent tiled walls, Corinthian columns fifty feet high in the atrium, carved latticework and tracery everywhere, and giant wooden doors that led to successions of apartments and suites. In the middle of the sunny atrium was an old fountain, now silent, its carved alabaster bowls filled with rainwater from the shattered glass ceiling.

We stood in silence. Skip exhaled. "It's a *trip,* don'tcha think?''

"Yes," I said in total awe. "A trip it is.''

We spent an hour exploring the derelict palace's warren of harems and chambers. "This is amazing," Joel said. "It's a shame it has to be sold.''

"I hear you, man." Skip sounded regretful. "But it's been empty two years, and you can see what three months of rain has done to the house. It needs a rich man to come in and restore it."

"I hope it'll be someone who appreciates its historical value," Joel said. "And its spirituality. I felt it as we were walking around just now."

"There's no doubt this house has magic in it," Skip said. "Listen to this. Once, when me and Sandra were livin' here, we had a big party and invited a lot of important people from town. The police commissioner brought twelve Gnaoua with him to play music and do their baraka thing. When they arrived, the leader of the Gnaoua, an old man, kissed the floor near the fountain. The boys in his band started to snicker, but he told them off. 'This is a *palace,*' he told them. 'This is a place where I'll be able to *dance!*' "

Before we closed up the house, Skip took us around, showing off secret doors and hidden galleries used for eavesdropping. There was an old escape tunnel that once led down to the port, but it had been bricked up a few hundred years ago and turned into a cistern. Then we climbed to the roof for a spectacular view of the rooftops of the medina, hidden gardens, rounded green domes of mosques, surprised young girls cavorting on the open rooftops in colorful slit dresses they'd never wear in the street. Beyond was the broad beach along the bay and the jagged black Rif in the distance. "Yep," Skip said. "It's a *trip.*"

WE LEFT SKIP at Ben Abou and walked through Casbah Square with its famous sultanic courthouse, then down steep stone flights of rock-hewn steps to the labyrinth of Yusufi's neighborhood. Eviction for nonpayment of rent loomed at the little green house. Mohammed had been earning a little money cutting kif in the café, but continual rains had caused a severe kif shortage.

I wanted to have a couple of burnooses made for my girlfriend, so I asked Mohammed to accompany us to the market to buy cloth. As we walked, Joel asked, "What did you think of Skip?"

"He's like a hippie time capsule from 1967," I said.

"That's probably the last time he was in America."

"Let's take him to Jajouka," I suggested. "I bet they'd like him."

"Insh'Allah," Joel said.

With few tourists, business was bad. Our progress through the market was accompanied by a litany of whispers from the shops and stalls: *My friend . . . come look . . . half price . . . spécial pour vous.* I bought one bolt of wine-colored cloth and another of light brown camel's hair. We took them to an Arabian Nights tailor about to go to mosque in his red fez, baggy patched pants, and spectacles perched on the tip of his nose. His twenty-year-old son sat in front of a sewing machine while his small grandson kept the bobbin in place. Much haggling occurred, and we agreed on fifty dirhams per burnoose. I paid the tailor in advance and gave Mohammed enough to make his rent.

When we returned to the Mouneriya, we found that Skip had moved in downstairs from us. "Didn't like the Continental," he said as he lit a joint in Joel's room. "A kid tried to rip me off on the street in front of the hotel last night. Kid says to me, 'Ah fok you modder.' So I showed him this." Skip took a gleaming six-inch Buck folding knife out of its belt sheath and displayed it. "Kid took off, but I don't wanna see him again. Besides, it's quieter over here, and there's girls across the street."

Later that evening I ventured into the Mouneriya's quasi-gay bar that occupied the basement rooms where Bill Burroughs wrote *Naked Lunch.* Presiding over the bar was Eddie, one of the English proprietors, who kept things going with a 45-rpm record changer and a little microphone through which he delivered risqué quips. He kept playing "Tie a Yellow Ribbon Round the Old Oak Tree" over and over again to a cozy room half full of British tourists. I had one cognac and watched a stone-drunk bunch of teenage rough trade, all heavily rouged, cruise the place with noisy menace.

I retired to bed around ten, after listening to the BBC news, and began reading *The Sheltering Sky,* which Joel had recommended to me that afternoon. At midnight there was a knock. "It's Skip," a voice said.

"Hey man," he said when I let him in. "I was just across the street."

"At the brothel?"

"You got it! Dig this: the girls with the veils are *tattooed*. Tribal tattoos, on their cheeks. *And shaved pussies!*"

"Skip, you madman. How much?"

"Hundred dirhams. She gave me an alcohol bath; I gave her fifty dirhams as a tip. Ain't that a trip? Hey, goodnight! Sorry to bug you, man. I'm going to bed now."

Life imitates art, I thought, as I plunged back into *The Sheltering Sky*.

IT RAINED HARD the next day, and Tangier was bathed in a chilling grey fog. The cafés were full, their glass windows steamed with smoke and humid breath. Inside, people read newspapers or stared at the soccer game on Spanish TV.

"When I was a boy," Mohammed said, "all the cafés had music."

"What kind of music?" I asked.

"Andaluz," he said. "Moorish songs. Very old."

"Music from Spain," Joel put in. "What was played in, say, Córdoba or Granada prior to 1492 when they threw the Muslims out of Spain."

I wanted to hear this music and make some recordings.

Mohammed spoke in Arabic, Joel translated. "There is an Andaluz music school in the medina; Mohammed says they're *very* private. But he knows most of the musicians, so maybe we can approach them."

"Insh'Allah," the fatalistic Mohammed murmured under his breath.

. . .

MOHAMMED ARRIVED AT our hotel at six o'clock that evening. "Hurry up," he told us. "They say you can come to the Andaluz institute." I packed up my tape recorder and mikes and we dashed up to the boulevard and caught a *petit taxi* to the Socco Grande. From there we hastened through the streets of the medina until we arrived at a modest house at the foot of the casbah in a neighborhood of movie theaters and Jewish shops. Up a narrow flight of stairs, we were greeted by a dark old tea-maker in a red fez and long white duster. We were then shown to a room lined with divans and furnished with tea tables, blackboards, instruments, and photos of old masters hanging on the walls. After a minute mint tea with citrus blossoms was served, and a beautiful, bent old man, Malim Mustapha, entered carrying an antique oud in a cloth case. Under his elegant burnoose, Mustapha wore a suit and white shirt. He listened carefully as Mohammed explained that we had come to learn about and, Insh'Allah, make a *magnetophone* recording of some classical Andaluz. The old man looked at us and nodded silently.

Others came up the staircase and retreated to an adjacent room when they saw that there were strangers in the salon. An hour passed, then another. We kept drinking tea, and tried to make polite conversation. Finally, Malim Mustapha explained that not enough musicians would be present that evening; if we returned the following night, perhaps our wishes could be accommodated. Before we said goodnight, Mustapha unwrapped his oud and tuned it with a series of deep, Andalusian airs that described the most ardent of loves in the most lost of worlds. This music was so beautiful, so penetrating, and the insistent thump of the bass string soon realigned my heartbeat to the oud's own vibration.

Walking back uphill through the quiet medina, Mohammed mentioned that the song Mustapha played was more than a thousand years old.

WE RETURNED TO the Andaluz institute the following night, and the place was packed. Anticipating an evening of sonic time-travel to medieval Spain, I requested and received permission to set up a stereo microphone. There was a bustle outside the room and rows of men parted to make way for someone important, a tough-looking man of maybe fifty years, in a good double-breasted suit with close-cropped grey hair. He was introduced to us as Si Muhammed Larbi. As he sipped his tea and spoke with Mustapha in Arabic, Joel leaned over and informed me, "This guy is the high commissioner of police in Tangier." I sat up a little straighter, and stopped wondering why, with all these musicians present, no kif was being smoked.

It turned out that Joel knew this guy. Two years earlier, during a visit to Tangier, Joel had been accosted on the streets by Hamsa, who accused Joel of stealing Jajouka from him. Joel and Hamsa wound up at the Tangier *comisaría,* in front of this official. "He listened, threw Hamsa out of his office, and apologized for the inconvenience," Joel said.

Si Larbi wasn't about to let me start taping. He spoke in French, conducting an interrogation: Who were we taping for? Would there be an album? This could cause problems, he told us, pointedly referring to Joel's previous difficulty with Hamsa. I interrupted, explaining that we were recording for our own pleasure, to study an important mode of music that was little understood in the non-Islamic world.

Si Larbi bought it. *"D'accord,"* he said. "But first you must comprehend the frailty of our music. Once it was the only orchestral music in the world, but today it is threatened with extinction! Only dedicated amateurs like these men keep it alive."

Dozens of musicians nodded gravely, and listened as Si Larbi, who revealed himself as the official patron of the school, delivered an analysis and historical discourse of Andaluz music while I struggled to take notes.

He reiterated that Andaluz represented the courtly, formal music of Muslim Spain, where ancient knowledge was nurtured and preserved during the long Dark Ages of Europe. In the five centuries since the Moors were expelled from Spain, Andaluz has survived, he said, through eleven basic strains, each with its nearly infinite variations. "That ghibli music you like up in Jajouka is a *folklorique* type of Andaluz—something the mountain people play."

Andaluz didn't have to be forced on people, he assured us. "Once one has heard it, the music becomes an addiction.

"Look at me," he said, letting his shoulders hunch into a Gallic shrug. "I toil as a simple fonctionnaire to support my family. If I were a millionaire, I'd spend it all on music." His tone became somber, and the room grew quiet. "All of us are condemned to death," he said sadly. "Why do we bother to do anything with our lives except create and preserve beauty. Why?"

No one said anything. The tough-cop look returned. "The answer is within the question," he said, quoting the Koran.

We were instructed to remember that classical Andaluz was an adaptation of the most antique Grecian modes of music, preserved first in Baghdad and Egypt by the heirs of Alexander and later in Spain by the Moors. After the expulsions of 1492, the cream of Andaluz musicians, the most orthodox schools, settled in Tangier and Tetuan. Most had come from Seville. Some lower classes of musicians filtered to Algeria and Tunisia where their style of Andaluz was later suppressed by the Ottoman Empire, although lately there had been a revival of the music in Tunisia.

I asked about the lyrics of the songs. Si Larbi said that the lyrics were mostly preserved within the human memory, and that they were being lost as older masters died. The problem was compounded because the lyrics were in classical Arabic, while the Moroccans spoke a dialect called *Darija*. "Today our most important project is to increase what is currently preserved in writing. And please note that our notation is circular. There are no bars and staffs as in European music. Andaluz is a circle. It has no beginning, no end. It never stops, you see? It just goes on.

"Think of the tragedy for the world if Andaluz music disappeared," he pleaded. "What if baseball didn't exist in America in a thousand years, and only a few people remembered it? If the American West were paved with concrete and the cowboys were finished, it would be the same!''

Tea was served, and Mustapha began to tune his oud. Other men began to sing the old song he was playing, and then a violin joined. Even Si Larbi picked out the waterfalling riff on a four-stringed banjo. It was beautiful, and I couldn't bring myself to turn on the tape. Noting this, Si Larbi told us to return the next night, ready to record.

THE ANDALUZ SCHOOL was again crowded. Si Larbi had organized three violins, two violas, oud, banjo, drabouga, tambourine, and twenty singers. There were middle-aged men in brown djellabas and a few young men in dungaree jackets; one had a Led Zeppelin patch sewn on his back. Several wore the red fez, others wore Moroccan zoot suits with lapels as wide as the Nile. Si Larbi was the undisputed producer of the session. He directed the microphone placement next to an old amphora on a metal tea table. Before the performance, he wanted to make a few more points.

"I desire you to understand that the Andaluz orchestral form is similar to the European. We play an overture, and build through *adagio* and other movements.

"We always say that Andaluz music is like walking a high wire; we are the acrobats. One shift of balance, even slight, and everything ends in failure. So our rule is that if a musician should play a wrong note, the orchestra stops. And then we recommence. Understood?''

With that, the lead violin, Achmed Bichuela, raised his bow, nodded to the others, and a slow overture began. The tempo increased into a cantering Moorish romp over a soundscape of breezy strings and earthy percussions, while the rhythm was kept steady by the oud and the banjo. After a slower section, the chorale came in, rising in lovely, dramatic lamentation. The plaster walls of the room gave the music a soaring, echolike sound. When I closed my eyes, I felt as though I was riding a mystic beam into the very soul of Andalusian orchestral music.

When the last tones of the suite faded away, there was silence. Si Larbi looked at me and nodded, a telepathic order to stop the tape. The musicians breathed, and tuned their strings. "There was a dissonance in the third section," Si Larbi said. "We shall record it again."

"The whole piece?" I asked.

"No, just that section. Rewind it please."

"But Si Larbi, this simple machine has no editing capabilities. If the new part is longer than the original, it will ruin the whole tape."

"Do not worry," the policeman said, and hoisted his banjo to the ready. Achmed nodded again, I pressed the record button and they replayed a long *legato* segment. When it was finished, Si Larbi ordered a playback. To my astonishment, the new piece fit properly, to the microsecond.

"He really pushes these guys to perfection," Joel whispered.

The old *qaouaghi* in the fez and white duster brought in tea. Si Larbi looked pleased behind his hooded dark eyes. It was as if Kojak were conducting the New York Philharmonic.

"The lyrics of this song," he explained, "are very old fragments of verse, the lamentation of the poet who has been singing all night, and his sorrow at the rising sun." Within this group, he told us, were smaller mystico-religious cults that preserve special parts of the music in vocal *a cappella* format. "It is impossible for me to reasonably explain to you how important our music is," Larbi said. "For me, it is the basic dictionary of all non-Asian orchestral music. I believe, for example, that Strauss unconsciously stole the waltz tempo and many melodies directly from some Andaluz notation he had found. Even some of your American songs—like 'My Darling Clementine'—are *pure Andaluz*." Joel and I exchanged dumfounded glances.

Si Larbi continued: "We know that many of the great violinists

178 in Europe between the 1492 *Reconquista* and 1800 were Moors. Did you know that three violins by Stradivarius were discovered in Morocco by the Spaniards? One of them right in your village up there in the Djebel . . . Jajouka. Yes. How did they get there? Musicians brought them home, of course.''

I asked Si Larbi how this music had arrived here from Baghdad.

''In the ninth century of the Nazarene calendar, there was a Persian musician called Ziryab. He lived at the palace of Haroun Er Rashid in Baghdad. Haroun was the sultan of the Thousand and One Nights, *n'est-ce pas?* A very cruel ruler. In any event, Ziryab's skill and intrigue got him into trouble and he was forced to flee. He came to Andalusia and—because of his fame—was welcomed at the court of Sultan Abderahman II [822–852]. What a man! Ziryab knew the words and melodies to ten thousand songs. Once in Spain, he added a fifth string to our lute, which increased its sweetness. He introduced new styles in clothes, etiquette, and epicurean dishes— spiced meatballs, asparagus, the fricassee. He invented a new drainage system for our cities. But to answer your question: It is Ziryab we remember as the father of our music.''

We finally thanked Si Larbi and the rest and made our way back through the darkened medina, well after midnight. With us was Mustapha, the old Malim, who insisted on escorting us. ''Si Larbi is quite a man himself,'' Joel said to him in Spanish.

''*Sí,*'' the old man agreed. ''I was starving five years ago. I was playing in cafés for tourists. Si Larbi rescued me and made me a professor in his school. H'amdullah! God be praised!''

BACK IN JAJOUKA, the Masters accepted Skip right away. He played some of his hippie ballads for them, and they smiled nervously as he sang. I could tell they hated it. ''Berry gut!'' Berdouz cried when Skip finished. ''Bee-oo-tifool! Outasight!'' Berdouz gently took the guitar from Skip and started cuffing the strings like a drum, dancing around, drawing attention to himself. ''This cat's a trip,'' Skip marveled.

I could smell the fresh sardines we'd bought in Alcazar frying in olive oil from Megaria's kitchen.

During dinner, Joel wondered if we'd have any dancing boys tonight in honor of our return. Skip said he had heard of a famous dancing boy in the south of Morocco. This youth was so handsome and supple that gendarmes were assigned to patrol the places where he performed, lest the crowds go wild. When this boy was brought to Marrakech, Skip avowed, the king had to assign bodyguards so this dancer wouldn't be kidnapped in the streets.

There *was* a dancing boy in Jajouka that evening: Abdinde, dressed in silks and chiffons, performed a rattlesnake shake that eventually had the whole room on its feet, dancing in a circle around the undulating figure of this boy in a dress.

Later that evening, we played them the Andaluz music we had recorded in Tangier. They listened carefully, with rapture. When it was over, so was the music for the evening.

THE NEXT DAY was a Friday, and I was awakened by that haunting, distant sound of rhaitas skirling in the sanctuary. I walked alone across the broad village plaza, the sound of the rhaitas growing louder as I went. Once inside, I found nine rhaita players and four drummers, playing the holy anthem they called "The 55." Dozens of visiting pilgrims were camped with their mules and burros under the metal canopy. Children played on the fringes, as local women watched the ceremonies from the steps and windows of the sanctuary. Everyone's eyes were on a mad girl dancing in a trance, unveiled, her black hair wet and stringy, eyes bulging and blank. A shiver ran down my vertebrae as she turned toward me. What was behind this anguished mask, whose features were as distorted as one of Picasso's cubist attacks on his women? Twining and twirling a long blue scarf, the girl stopped and rotated to the beat of the drums. After ten minutes, another woman—the girl's mother?—moved in with a blanket to cover the dancer, but was fought off. The girl continued to spin. The older woman gave up and appeared

180 distraught. Perhaps Sidi Hamid Sherq and his musicians were her last hope.

Another young woman sat on the roots of the five-thousand-year-old olive tree in the courtyard, wrapping herself in the old chains that seemed to grow out of the bark. Other women began to dance, and I pulled the hood of my djellaba a bit farther over my face, hoping not to be noticed.

Just then the band stopped. Berdouz slung his drums around his back and stepped out to lead the prayers. A tall woman with a crutch emerged from the crowd and prostrated herself on the ground in front of the musicians. As Berdouz recited his formulae, the musicians went over to the woman, slipped off their shoes, and pressed the soles of their feet all over her motionless body. Then they carefully laid their instruments on her, leaving them in place for a minute.

She lay there until the musicians began playing again. Slowly she got to her feet and began to dance, her previously stiff leg now supple and strong.

I swallowed, hard.

Then the first girl resumed her frantic gyrations. A farmer in a white djellaba—her father?—tried to cover her with a blanket, but she pushed him away, too. Then she walked over and began to undo the belt of the woman who'd had the instruments laid on. Berdouz intervened. I began to feel as though I shouldn't be there, so I slipped out the back door, left a couple of dirhams with the local tramps, and headed up to the madrassah.

Something about the healings I had witnessed at the sanctuary bothered me. Was it witchcraft? A survival of an old religion, older than history? I remembered tales of faith healers and holy rollers up in the hills of my childhood. Was this how Jajouka was perceived by the caid and other Moroccan bureaucrats?

I FOUND A sunny spot on the terrace and watched the fig trees sprouting in the gentle spring weather. Then all of a sudden the warning bell went off in the back of my mind. "I've been here long enough," I said to Joel. "Let's start thinking about home."

Something in the tone of my voice must have alerted Berdouz, and he asked Joel what I'd said. Joel told him we would leave in a day or two, and Berdouz became concerned. "Are we not treating you well?" he asked me. I started to protest, but it was useless. Berdouz became mock-agitated.

"Perhaps the music could be better?" he cried. "Or the food! Don't leave us. We like it when you come up here and make your recordings and write in your notebook. H'amdullah!" The tiny drummer picked up his sebsi and pretended to play it like a flute, hopping around on one foot, singing a goatish pipe song in falsetto. Then he peeled the guitar off Skip, who was laughing at these antics. Berdouz began to whack the strings, singing obscene parodies of Spanish songs. Next Berdouz began to dance with the instrument, caressing its curves. Berdouz's brown flesh was moist from exertion, but on he proceeded, sitting cross-legged on big Ali Ayashi's lap and lampooning the ornate hand-gestures of the famous Blue Women of Goulemime, far off in the southern desert.

Everyone had a good chuckle. Achmido Twimi, Mohammed Mujahid (whose name meant "Holy Warrior"), Mohammed Ben Aisha, Fat Mohammed Attar, Mohammed Ben Ali, and Mohammed Titi, Jr., all giggled, half with mirth, half with eye-rolling embarrassment. Delighted to have been the center of attention, Berdouz finally threw himself on the divan and called for another pot of tea. He opened up his bobcat-skin mutwi and proudly displayed a *mujood* of fresh kif, which he sampled with continued show and relish.

THAT NIGHT WAS pitch black, devoid of the star canopy and moon lantern that usually illumined the mountain plateau after dark. Feeling *triste* about leaving, I spent some time in the kitchen with the chief, who was sitting against the wall on a reed mat with his knees drawn up under his djellaba. The chief was in the kitchen because three of his sons were inside wailing on "Jajouka Black Eyes" and "Brahim Jones." Rules are rules.

Jnuin said his eye was bothering him, and asked me to look. By the light of my flashlight I could clearly see a cloudy grey cataract. "It's not too serious, Moqadem," I told him. "It's very operable, and if you need some money for the surgeon, we'll try to arrange it." The chief thanked me profusely and asked for some aspirin. Ten minutes later he felt much improved. "The governor at Tetuan," he said in Spanish, "has told me, personally, that if Jajouka gets any kind of contract to play in America, we can have our passports for fifty dirhams. That's fifty! Hamsin! You comprehend? Fifty, *todos!* That's all. Safi!"

Five minutes later he told me the same thing again, as was his way. Then he told it to bored Megaria, who was washing dishes, and to Abdsalam Fudul, and then to me again. I noticed the chief was no longer wearing his heavy silver earring. What did this mean? I couldn't bring myself to ask him.

A BLAST OF hard rain on the tin roof woke me early. Skip was asleep, but Joel's bedding was already packed and the door was open. I found him squatting in the kitchen with the chief. They were drinking bitter black coffee and spooning marmalade from a can onto toast grilled on the *mizhmar.*

For the next hour I packed my gear and loaded the bus. Meanwhile the walled enclosure began to fill with musicians, all wearing the "dress" djellabas that we had bought for them three years earlier. "Looks like they're going to send us off in high style," Skip said when he saw the preparations. Just then the sun came from behind a cloudbank, and the cool misty day immediately turned hot and steamy. Nine rhaita players and nine drummers formed up at right angles and started to roar. After five minutes Bou Jeloud himself appeared and began to butt and strut. As soon as he emerged from behind the madrassah, it started to drizzle again. But Bou

Jeloud didn't care; he wiggled and waved his oleander branches and frightened the women and children huddled on the wall in a cluster of heaving white blankets.

Suddenly Fudul grabbed me and threw me into a ring-around-the-rosy with the rhaita players. Joel too. After circling, ecstatically, for the rest of the song, we filed into the madrassah, where Berdouz issued forth a long prayer of thanks and benediction. Amin, amin, amin, prayed the Master Musicians of Jajouka. Then we all kissed each other and our party piled into the bus. Down the awful road we bumped, stopping at the bottom of the village for Abdsalam Fudul, who was waiting for us. Half an hour earlier he had danced as Bou Jeloud. Now, penniless, he wanted to go to Tangier to sell some red coral necklaces for cash.

After a very fast ride through the wheatfields and melon patches of northwest Morocco, we arrived on the outskirts of Tangier. We let Abdsalam Fudul out near a new neighborhood of concrete houses, and he disappeared into the crowd of djellabas and motor-scooters and donkeys, the goat god loose in town.

"I woulda bought those coral pieces from him," Skip said. "But he wanted more than I could pay."

"Red coral is becoming scarce in Morocco," Joel said. "Moroccan women say it brings good luck in childbirth, and now tourists want it."

"Yeah man, no kidding," Skip said. "About ten years ago I knew this rich English hippie couple who were touring Morocco in their Rolls-Royce. They had it all down: they'd park the Rolls outside of a town; they'd walk in, dressed in, like, *rags,* and have lunch, mosey around, ask if anyone had any old coral necklaces they wanted to sell, and they'd buy 'em up. For *cheap.* Silver, *medieval* pieces for maybe five or ten bucks, dig? I heard these two cleaned out southern Morocco within a couple of months."

We checked into the Mouneriya and walked up to the boulevard for the papers and some café con leche. A bit later, walking through the medina toward the tailor's shop to retrieve my two burnooses, we were waylaid by a drunken young hustler in a narrow alley. Skip told him to fuck off, and the hustler went berserk. Then he and Skip squared off in totally pseudo–kung fu poses. For thirty seconds this absurd tableau was absolutely silent. Then my tailor's son came around the corner, noticed the scene, grabbed the big scissors out of his belt, and went after the hustler, who dropped the martial arts bit and began to beg forgiveness.

He grabbed the young tailor's hand and planted a wet, sloppy kiss on it. The tailor recoiled in disgust and the hustler began to cry. "My name is Mohammed," he sobbed. "You have seen me in the street, in the Socco Chico. My mother has died and my father has died and all I wanted was ten dirhams, Insh'Allah." The proud Moroccan walked by him as if the kid were dirt. "I will have the Mafia kill you all tonight," hissed the hustler as we followed the tailor. This punk bothered us all the way to the Socco Chico, where Joel paid another hustler ten dirhams to drag the first one off.

I WAS UP LATE that night, listening to the click of the steel balls in the *boccie* court next door. At 3 A.M. I finished *The Sheltering Sky*.

In the morning, I decided to visit Paul Bowles, the American writer, expatriate in Tangier, who wrote *The Sheltering Sky* in 1948 and had lived there ever since. I had Bowles's address, but it was a post office box. The Villa Mouneriya's management was of little help. "Oh your Mr. Bowles," Eddie said, "he doesn't mix much. No, can't really tell you where he lives."

Late in the morning, Joel and I stopped at the Café Paris and ran into Skip, who was sitting with a well-dressed man named Omar. "Paul Bowles?" Omar said. "I know his driver, Abdelwahid. Pay the bill and I'll take you to Paul Bowles's house right now." A green mini-taxi screeched to a halt in front of the café and we piled in and headed uphill toward the Old Mountain. Omar knew Bowles's driver because he himself drove for a famous expatriate named James Marshall, a retired British naval officer who used a disguised

Arab dhow to blow German U-boats out of the water in World War II.

The mini-taxi zigged right at the new mosque, zagged left past the Inter-Continental Hotel, and sailed by the compound of the U.S. Consulate, finally stopping before a squat grey bunkerlike apartment building with a little grocery on the ground floor.

We drove to the back of the building. "Señor Bowles is at home," Omar said, pointing to an immaculate burnished gold Ford Mustang convertible, vintage 1968. A Berber woman sitting in the concierge's booth directed us to the fourth floor, number 20. I knocked, and a minute later Paul Bowles cracked open his door and peered at us. "Oh," he said. "I thought you might be someone else. I haven't had my breakfast yet." The scent of kif wafted mischievously into the hall while I introduced myself as a journalist and asked for an interview at a later date. "Come back in two days," Bowles said. "Four o'clock will be fine."

AT THE AGE of sixty-seven, Paul Bowles was the great forgotten man of modern American literature. *The Sheltering Sky* had been a main inspiration for the postwar existentialists and the so-called Beat writers, as had his fervent expatriation in Tangier. Back then he was obscure and almost unknown. His wife, Jane Bowles, had died in 1973. She had gone mad, according to Tangier expat legend, after being poisoned by her Moroccan maid (and lover), to whom she had previously willed her house in the medina. Since then, Bowles had published very little. He was now principally known for two small volumes of kif lore, *A Hundred Camels in the Courtyard* and *M'Hashish,* the latter a translation of dope stories supposedly related by his illiterate young protégé from the Rif, Mohammed Mrabet.

On the appointed day, at the appointed hour, Joel and I drove around to the back of Bowles's building, and parked behind the gold Mustang. Behind the door of number 20 was an impressive stack of steamer trunks and suitcases, and a set of heavy purple drapes.

186   Through these we found a cozy, fire-lit flat and a small party. Bowles was taking tea with Mohammed Mrabet, who waved a little sebsi in the air as he spoke. Bowles greeted us cordially, dressed in a brown English suit, waistcoat and tie. He first wanted to know who we were and what we wanted. So, we explained our relationship to Jajouka. Bowles said nothing. It was Mrabet who reacted. He laughed when told that Hamsa had repossessed Jajouka's old djellabas. Red-eyed as a Rastafarian, Mrabet made various disparaging remarks about Jajouka and their dealings with foreigners like Gysin and Brian Jones. At this point Bowles suggested to Mrabet, in Spanish, that he take a walk. He left and Bowles's driver came in and sat down.

"Did you bring a tape recorder?" Bowles asked me. I said I'd brought two. "Good," Bowles said, "because someone has given me a cassette of Jilala trance music, and my own machine is on the fritz." He gave me the tape and I slipped it into my spare recorder. Suddenly the paneled sitting room, stuffed with books and textiles and paintings and more books, erupted with the impassioned drumming and formulaic ranting of a Jilala team in full cry. Bowles sat back and smiled, smoking. Soon the canaries that lived in the dense greenery of his balcony garden began to warble and sing in counterpoint to the crazy rhythms coming out of the box. I switched on the other cassette and pressed RECORD:

". . . A few days ago," Bowles was saying, "my driver here came back from the country with tales of a female demon called Aisha Kandisha having been seen in his village. Eh, Abdelwahid? Isn't that right?"

The driver spoke up in Spanish. Yes, he had seen her himself in the form of an arc of light emanating from the central well in the village. Within a week several people dropped dead near the well. A shiver went down my spine. Aisha Kandisha! Fierce blue-breasted goddess who lurks near water and tempts men to their deaths.

"We used to have a maid," Bowles mused. "If you even said the name 'Aisha Kandisha' out loud, she would leave the room."

I asked if Bowles believed his driver's story.

"*Of course* I believe him! I believe that he believes it. Yes. Without a doubt."

But do *you* believe in Aisha Kandisha? I asked him.

"Well . . . no. If your question is, do I believe that there is such a physical presence as Aisha Kandisha? Naturally not. How could I? No. But when a Moroccan says he saw something . . ." Bowles trailed off, meaningfully. "To me there's no difference between belief in a legend and belief in the thing itself. Once many people believe in something, it becomes part of the truth. Don't you think?"

But what about Morocco's mystical brotherhoods? Joel asked. Music of the kind we were listening to is often accompanied by acts of self-mutilation that seem to heal spontaneously. How can one not believe in that?

Bowles sipped his tea. "Well, you're quite right. Take this Jilala music, for instance. The Jilala like to go into trance and hack themselves with knives, or drink boiling olive oil, or walk on red-hot coals. Once in Meknes I saw them eating scorpions and live snakes. Poisonous snakes! They bit off their heads and spat them on the ground. The next day?" Bowles smiled. "No scars. No nothing.

"But then Moroccans have a completely different consciousness from ours," he continued. "There are those who are able to, as they say, leave themselves behind. They just go out of the house, as it were, and leave the door open so their saint can get in. We can only formulate that. I don't think we could possibly experience it. Not without having been brought up a devout Muslim, I'm sure."

Bowles stopped talking, and the Jilala clatter-and-wail music continued.

"Tell me, have you ever been frightened by anything you encountered in your travels through Morocco?"

"No," Bowles said, and then thought a moment. "Frightened? No. *Delighted,* mostly. I always *expected* to see what I saw, self-mutilation and the like, because I'd been seeing it from the moment I arrived here in 1931.

"But I never felt frightened because I never felt that that violence was directed toward me in any way. I never thought I had anything to do with it at all. I felt like a complete outsider! I didn't even believe in the reality of my being there! And there's another thing: I never felt that any possible hostility could take hold because the things we're discussing are religious organizations. These were religious ceremonies, and I always felt invisible at these affairs; not physically invisible but spiritually invisible. Nonexistent. Because I have no soul, according to the orthodox brotherhoods, I'm not really there at all. So, I'm no danger.

"Nowadays, it's another story." Bowles exhaled, shifting his weight against a red textile flat-woven in dizzy geometric glyphs. "Nowadays, it's not religious, but political. Whatever hostility or animosity you might encounter here isn't directed at you as a Christian or a non-Muslim, but as a member of their archrivals, the Europeans."

Joel asked, "What about the stories of Christians or Jews who have wandered too close to these street rituals and have been sacrificed on the spot?"

Bowles frowned. "Well, I've heard these stories, of course, but none has ever been substantiated. The Moroccans love to tell them because it makes them appear more dangerous. I know the brother-hoods do tear apart live sheep and goats from time to time; and we heard they did it to a French woman at Sidi Kacem one year, but I somehow disbelieve it. I don't know . . . Maybe my imagination isn't lively enough. Certainly they *have* done some incredible things to Europeans, but for reasons other than religion. There was the case of Dr. Mauchamps, a French surgeon who had founded a hospital in Marrakech in the early 1900s. They cut him into many tiny pieces in the street outside his front door, because they didn't like the *idea* of the hospital. They felt it was a place that existed to kill people and slice them up! I remember Marrakech in '31: People still wouldn't walk down the street the hospital was on. It was always empty, because they said people were waiting by the gate to reach out, and grab you inside, and cut you right up.''

Bowles paused for laconic effect.

''And of course there was the case, for instance, many years ago where they killed every European in—where was it?—Oued-Zem, I think. Eighty-seven people killed in an hour and a half. So I know that sort of thing exists, but to answer you, I never felt any violence was about to be directed at me at a religious ceremony. It's not really recommended to kill a lot of people at a religious ceremony. Is it?''

We talked for another hour, and I relished every minute. Before we left I asked Paul Bowles if he would ever go back to the United States.

''No, I don't think so,'' he said. ''I haven't even been back to visit since 1969. When I get homesick now, it's for Tangier.''

THE NEXT FEW DAYS were sunny and dry. We spent them mostly on the beach at Cap Spartel, where the red sand crunched under my feet and the soft azure waves broke with a soft, sucking sound. I'd put my head back and stare into the blue sky of North Africa, and dread the long journey home, through the clouds and western winds.

On Saturday we said good-bye to Mohammed and Skip, then flew to Madrid, and from there to New York. We whiled away the hours in the rear of the 747 playing Jajouka songs on the new gimbris we had bought near the sebsi market in the Socco Grande.

''Ah, Brahim Jones, Jajouka really stoned . . .''

chapter 6

The Dancing-Boy Wars

*T*wo years passed.

I continued to earn my living as a journalist, mining the rich cultural vein that was Jamaica in the late 1970s. I spent time with Bob Marley, the gangster king of reggae music. I visited remote areas in the mountainous central district of the great tropical island, populated by so-called Maroon tribes, the descendants of slave warriors who had battled British redcoats to a bloody draw three hundred years before. I spent hours drinking white rum and smoking ganja cigars with the tribal elders before driving all night back to Kingston to keep an interview appointment with the socialist prime minister first thing in the morning.

This was also the time when I married, turned thirty, and had my first child. My valiant wife delivered a baby girl on a frosty winter's night in early 1979. It was the happiest moment of my life, on a par with the day we had formally presented the Malimin with their new djellabas.

With all that in mind, I named the baby Aisha.

Of course, I couldn't get Jajouka out of my mind. The tapes I had recorded there were always playing in the house. Reactions of visiting friends were varied: Some went right into trance, while others ran howling out the door. Gradually, word got out that I had become obsessed, and this was probably true, in a positive sort of way. My greatest frustration was that Jajouka remained unpublished in the *National Geographic.* I thought it was a crime that those photographs of the goat god and his priests of Faunus in their mountain lair were hidden away in a steel drawer in Washington. I was *determined* to somehow get Jajouka published here in the United States.

Then, once again, Fate dealt her cards.

The unknowing agent of fortune was Fela Anikulapo Kuti, the Nigerian musico-politician and father of the Afro-beat movement. He had been arrested, tortured, and jailed by Nigeria's military junta in 1978 and was languishing in prison. I wrote an article about him in the *Saturday Review,* which ceased publication right after the Fela piece appeared. The editor with whom I'd worked was quickly hired by a new monthly called *GEO,* and was told to come up with some stories about Africa. Because of the Fela story, this editor called me. *GEO* turned out to be the American start-up of a well-established German natural history magazine, known all over Europe for stunning photos and interesting text. They had an office in a glass tower on Park Avenue and a corporate parent willing to spend plenty of deutschemarks to crack the U.S. market.

Over curries in an Indian restaurant in midtown Manhattan, my editor asked for African story ideas. I told him about the resurgence of tribal secret societies in Sierra Leone that was starting to alarm some of the Peace Corps people working there. And I told him about a tribe I knew of in Morocco that preserved Arcadian rituals thousands of years old.

Sounds great, he said, sipping his mango shake. I want both. Where do you want to go first?

Morocco, I said.

I CALLED JOEL in Santa Fe to tell him to pack his gear. But he told me that urgent business considerations would prevent him from making the journey. I almost decided to go to Sierra Leone first; Joel changed my mind.

"I got a letter a few weeks ago from the chief," he told me. "It was a request for some cash, and it seemed pressing somehow. So I got some money from the record people and kicked in a bit of profit from the restaurant. I was going to send it to them. But now you can carry it and save them the hassles of cashing an American check, right?"

SO IT WAS BACK to Jajouka! The Mystic Mountain was beckoning!

Was I exhilarated? Yes. But I was apprehensive as well. With only two weeks to prepare, I wrote to the chief and asked permission to visit. I knew their reply would not reach me in time. I also sent a letter off to Skip Early, with whom I had kept in touch.

The next day I dialed Brion Gysin's number in Paris. "My dear boy!" he called out. "You must be on your way to Jajouka!"

How *did* he know? I invited him to meet me in Tangier and accompany me to Jajouka. "It has long been an ambition of mine," I told him, "to be in the village at the same time as you." There was a silence over the line and for a moment I listened to the roar of the satellite transmission through space.

"My dear," Gysin said, "that's a very kind invitation, but I fear I must decline. My health has been questionable of late, and I told a good friend the other night that the next time I get to Jajouka may be when someone carries my ashes up there in a box . . . but look, let's not be morbid. Why don't you come to Paris when you leave Morocco? We can have supper together and I'll help you with your story."

Just before I left, a letter arrived from Jnuin:

Cher ami, all the members of the Club Musical de Zah-
jouka go each Friday to Sidi Ahmed Cheikh and pray to
God to protect you and to give you success in your work,
and to look after your beloved family. This Friday they
pray "The Fatiha" to Sidi Ahmed Cheikh so that you will
have a safe journey when you pay us a visit. We await your
arrival with joy.

That was all I needed to hear.

I WOKE WITH a start in a dark room early in the afternoon, having
forgotten where I was. Then I heard the haunting call of the
muezzin, saw the yellow light filtering through the drawn curtains
of the cool bedroom, and my memory resurfaced. I remembered
everything from the night flight over the ocean to the Benz taxi that
carried me into town, down the Boulevard Pasteur and through a
series of hilly switchbacks that led to the Rue Magellan and the faded
comfort of that famed Beatnik landmark, the Villa Mouneriya. Since
I had an expense account, I had gone whole hog and booked both
bedrooms on the top floor so that I'd have the bathroom and terrace
to myself. This cost *GEO* eighteen dollars a night. I had spent a
jet-lagged hour on the terrace with a pot of mint tea, gazing with
stupefaction at the Spanish mountain ranges that loomed in a blue
haze across the strait. And at noon, I fell asleep, feeling very alone.

It was around three o'clock when I pulled myself together,
dressed, and went up to the boulevard. I drank a glass of blood-
orange juice in a café and felt my blood sugar begin to rise. Time
to cruise the medina before setting off to find Skip's house on the
Old Mountain. I turned into the Socco Grande and was stopped by
a man in a fez. "I know you," he said in French. "You came to see
our orchestra two years ago." I recognized him as one of the
violinists of L'Orchestre Larbi Siyaz. "Come and visit us while you
are here," he said, and disappeared into the flow of the crowded
street. Then a kid sidled up while I was crossing the Socco Chico

and whispered, "You're from America? You're working on a book? Come see my father's shop," he implored. "Two minutes from here. You want carpets?"

"Minbad [later], Insh'Allah," I told him, shaking my head in wonder. The kid persisted. What did I want? "Some kif," I said softly. "Dangerous," he whispered, and walked away fast in the other direction. This was rather brazen of me, but I had already visited our old friend the sebsi dealer in his stall near the Socco Grande, and he had let me sample his fresh-cut mix. I trudged up and down flights of steps cut into the living rock of the medina until I found Mohammed Yusufi's house. A strange woman peeked through a crack in the door as urchins played soccer with a tin can that reverberated in the little stone courtyard. Mohammed, Aisha, and Fatima Zohra, she said, were all gone. Finish. No, she didn't know how to find them.

THE RUE D'IFRANE was a lovely path winding up the Old Mountain. No one was home at the address I had for Skip. The old caretaker thought Skip was in France. He smiled toothlessly and said to come back later and speak to Señor Skip's neighbor, pointing to a huge pink Art Deco mansion just down the hill. The taxi driver took me back to the Café Paris, where I downed a café con leche before crossing the boulevard to the Avis office. I picked up the keys to the Renault 12 that *GEO* had reserved for me and drove back to the Rue d'Ifrane. In front of the pink mansion, a gardener named Achmed was weeding a concrete planter. Hearing I was a friend of Skip's, he motioned me into the gardens to await the return of the owner. Just then, a little white Honda Civic with Moroccan plates pulled up to the garage. Out stepped an American, about my age with a head full of curly hair and a beard, a beautiful young Englishwoman who was his wife, and two children—a girl of about seven and a baby. These were Skip's neighbors, Sam and Iris Kramer, and their daughters Violet and Daisy.

"Friend of Skip's?" the man asked. "C'mon in. We've been

196 expecting you.'' I followed them through the pink painted wall via a heavy wooden door in an arched gateway. I was overjoyed at the chirping of the children and the sudden bustle of family life. It was a relief not to feel alone, so far from home.

SAM KRAMER WAS in the hashish business. He told me right up front. ''Skip said to tell you he was sorry he couldn't be here, but he had some urgent business abroad. Actually he needed money and is working for me, running a load into Holland.''

Where are his wife and kids?

''They went with him. We like to take the stuff through customs with loads of squawling English babies making a big commotion. It's worked for ten years. Come on, I want you to see the horse.''

For the next hour we walked around the walled hillside estate. Ascending various levels of terraces and gardens, we passed the small cottage of the gardener and his family and strolled down paths whose borders were bursting with carefully tended tropical flora. My host was starved for company and eager to answer my questions. He had met his hazel-eyed Celtic wife in Afghanistan. ''I was buying Punjab hash by the quarter ton and shipping it home in tribal rugs. Iris was a mule; she worked for someone else.''

A mule?

''A courier,'' he said with a snort. ''First time I met her, she had a pussy full of heroin, triple-wrapped in condoms. Just look at her. How could I *not* fall for her?''

Iris was indeed smashing.

''She's been a bit mad lately,'' Kramer confided. ''Been having spells, almost like seizures. She blanks out. I had her tested for *petit mal* but the results were negative. And there's no psychotherapy to be had in Tangier. Actually, Skip is the one who's been able to talk Iris down from these . . . whatever they are. Skip is the one she listens to.''

I wanted to play penny psychologist and suggest that trafficking was

a fairly anxiety-provoking trade, but I kept my mouth shut. We had
come to the uppermost boundary of the estate; a sleek brown Arabian
horse was chewing on a flake of hay in his paddock. "I call him
Runaway Bay, which is a place in Jamaica, right? When we bought him
he kept running away, so it seemed like an apt name for him. He was
flown here from Lebanon when the civil war started up." The horse
walked over to us and nuzzled Sam's hand. A woman's voice called
from the house. Supper would be ready shortly.

The house itself was a stucco masterpiece, with black Deco
flourishes and a red tiled roof. There were carpets and textile
pillows everywhere, all flat-woven in tribal designs. A state-of-
the-art stereo unit in the corner purred out an old Al Green tape,
which Iris soon changed to Dire Straits. "They're my favorite,"
she said, and asked me to send her their new cassette as soon as I
got home. Supper was a fresh harira soup and rounds of bread.
Violet, the charmingly hyper seven-year-old, kept chatting about
her visits to her American granny and life at the American School.
"Eat your soup, lovey," her mother told her, smiling at me, a
shy expat princess, mistress of her pink palace on the Old Mountain. When the children had been put to bed, Sam crumbled some
hash into a sebsi and remarked that he and Iris had always wanted
to go to Jajouka.

"I'm surprised Skip didn't take you," I told them.

"Skip hasn't been there," Sam said, "since the time he went
with you. He and the chief's son seem to have something going,
though, because Bashir comes here sometimes and plays music with
Skip and his friends from England."

It was late on a Sunday evening, and the lights of Tangier winked
across the valley. In the distance we could hear steady drumming.
Around the house it was deeply quiet except for the night birds
perched among the hovering branches of the palms. The air was
clear and seemed charged with an intoxicating floral scent. I told
them they could come to Jajouka with me on Tuesday, if they
wanted to. Sam and Iris looked at each other with satisfaction. I

thanked them for their hospitality and we arranged to meet the following night in town for supper.

I parked in the hotel's lot, gave a couple dirhams to the guardian, walked to the all-night grocery for a bottle of Sidi Harazem water, returned to my rooms, and fell into an exhausted sleep as the wind came up and Monday morning crept in with the fog from Tangier Bay.

AT NINE THE MOUNERIYA's surly porter banged on my door with *café complet,* and I spent a dazed hour watching the bulbous LNG tankers in the strait with my binoculars. Then I was off, up to the boulevard. The war in the Sahara was dragging on, and the Moroccan economy was paying for it dearly. Tourists were scarce, and the old city seemed shabby and threadbare. I detoured and had a pipe with the little skullcapped sebsi dealer; when I stepped back into the crashing African sunlight of the socco, my head began to reel so I ran for the shelter of the reputedly oldest tree in Morocco, a colossal banyan behind the wall of a municipal building, whose genial guardian let me sit in the shade. He even brought me a glass of tea, and refused the dirhams I offered him.

Farther down in the medina, I visited an *expéditeur* I had used before to discuss shipping some carpets back to New York. This man, Bouhantit, was also a musician who played with the Andaluz orchestra. He agreed to be on the lookout for the old-style, flat-woven carpets I was seeking. Then I picked up the car and drove to the airport for that time-honored ritual of the tourist in Morocco—the luggage search. No, the long-suffering Iberia Airlines clerk told me, the flight wasn't in yet. Come back later. So, I lunched on a good omelette at the airport's restaurant, and then drove to the beach at Cap Spartel. Missing my wife, I tried to communicate with her telepathically, sealing the message with a wave west, across the ocean. Then I drove the cliffside route back to the Old Mountain, skirting the Pillars of Hercules and whizzing past the big walled estates of the sheiks from the Persian Gulf who were establishing themselves in Tangier now that Beirut was finished.

"Oh! It's you. How lovely. Please come in. Violet wants to know if you play checkers." Iris Kramer let me in her arched gate and we walked up through the hanging gardens. Iris seemed her usual blithe spirit, but there was a hint of tension in her voice as she said, "Sam's not here, you know. He had to go talk to the police."

I said I hoped there wasn't a problem.

"Well, I'm afraid there could be," she said. "There's been a bust, you see. Not our people, but they wanted to talk to Sam anyway."

"Do they know about him?"

"Of course," she said with a sigh. "Hash is a big business in northern Morocco. Everyone's in on it, and things are usually cool as long as everyone gets paid. Or paid off, as the case may be. . . . Now tell me, has your baggage arrived yet? Well, why don't you have a bath and a shave here, and borrow one of Sam's shirts. Don't thank me, just play checkers with Violet until her dad gets home. Do you mind terribly?"

Violet beat me six games straight, while her baby sister gurgled on her back in her playpen. I left before Sam got home, arranging to meet them later at the Nautilus restaurant near the Boulevard Pasteur. When I returned to the airport, my missing duffle had miraculously arrived on a Royal Air Maroc flight from Casablanca. But, I assured the clerk, I hadn't been to Casablanca. No problem, he said; sign here.

On the way back, I stopped at Paul Bowles's building, the Immeuble Itessa, and rode the lift to the fourth floor. The door to Number 20 was opened by Bowles himself. "Yes, I do remember you," he said. "Did our interview ever get published? Please come in and have some tea." Sitting at a low table, tapping his sebsi into a ceramic ashtray, was Bowles's protégé, Mohammed Mrabet, "totally kif-ed," as Bowles put it. I explained I only wished to say hello now, but to return on the way back from Jajouka. "That would be fine," Bowles said. "Come on Friday if you can. I've just been working on these." He indicated a stack of galley proofs for his new *Collected Stories*.

I asked Bowles if he wanted to come to Jajouka, and he and Mrabet chuckled to each other. "Oh, I don't want to go up there anymore. I'm almost seventy years old! Too old to sleep rough." Bowles excused himself and went into his bedroom for a moment, and I got up to inventory the contents of the mahogany bookshelves, crammed with first editions and translations of his novels, travel writing, nonfiction books, and volumes of short stories. Gore Vidal had recently written that Bowles's short stories were among the best ever written by an American. "Paul Bowles opened up the world of Hip," Norman Mailer wrote. "He let in the murder, the drugs, the incest, the death of the square . . . the call of the orgy, the end of civilization." I said good-bye and left, totally in awe.

The Kramers were waiting for me at the Nautilus. Sam was in an open white shirt, Iris looked spectacular in amber and red coral. Her nervousness had lifted, and it appeared, without anyone saying so, that everything was cool again. We were enjoying *crème caramel* and espresso when a quite striking Moroccan man entered and was shown to the head table. He was well dressed and improbably ugly, with a prodigious nose like a gnarled potato. Sam and Iris looked at each other.

Who's that? I asked.

"Camel Face," Sam said softly.

"That's what we call him," whispered Iris.

"He's the guy who bought Ben Abou from Skip and Sandra," Sam said. "Got a great deal too, although I don't think he's paid them the price he agreed to. I also hear he's spending a fortune fixing the place up." Camel Face looked in our direction; Sam waved, and the man nodded with a barely perceptible smile.

GEO picked up the tab, and we arranged to meet at their house the following day.

That night, I was so excited to be returning to Jajouka that I couldn't sleep. Instead, I listened to Om Kalthoum on Radio Cairo and waited for dawn to break over the jagged black Rif Mountains.

.   .   .

A FEW HOURS LATER, while most of Tangier slept, I slipped out of the Mouneriya and drove to the Fez market to provision with fruits, vegetables, chocolates, and coffee. Driving around post-dawn Tangier was a pleasure, and I sped down the hill to the Socco Grande for kilos of whiting and sardines. When Madame Porte's tea salon opened later in the morning, I picked out a few cans of exotic imported teas and several dozen batches of petits fours.

Our little caravan headed out of town, at about ten o'clock. I was driving my Renault with Violet seat-belted next to me. She was a funny girl, chattering away about how much she envied the Danish schoolbag I was using as a rucksack. Her parents and baby sister were behind us in their Honda. It turned out that Vi's class at the American School was putting on *The Sound of Music,* so we warbled "My Favorite Things" as we skirted Asilah and turned inland at Larache. At Ksar we turned off onto the pitted two-lane road to Tatoft just as the *lycée* was letting out for the day; the street was filled with well-dressed, attractive kids carrying their books and calling to each other merrily. Here and there I thought I recognized the tall figures and lean faces of Attars or Rotobes from Jajouka, but I couldn't be sure. We eased through the throng of kids and picked up speed on the outskirts of town. A woman waved to me from the counter of her little grocery stall. I waved back, recognizing the eyes of Tahir's sister. They were the kind of eyes you never forgot. Bokazar eyes.

We left our passports with the caïd's assistant at Tatoft, much to Sam Kramer's discomfort, and proceeded up the dirt road into the blue hills. At the entrance to the village, the road had eroded almost beyond viability; immense boulders seemed to block passage into the plaza just beyond, where Bou Jeloud danced during the holidays. A shout went up as the car appeared over the ridge and suddenly a dozen *Malimin* were pushing and carefully heaving the car somehow up and through a narrow defile between the rocks. At the madrassah the older musicians launched into a boisterous and tearful greeting with impassioned kisses and great rhetorical flourishes by Berdouz, the text of which I couldn't understand but instinctively felt quite good about. The Kramers, who arrived on foot after leaving their Honda parked under an olive tree at the foot of Jajouka's road, were recognized at once by young Bashir as friends of Skip's from Tangier, and were immediately accorded the respect due a visiting trafficker and potential patron.

Within ten minutes, I felt like I was home again.

"THAT WAS THE WORST road I've ever been on," said Sam Kramer an hour later. We were sitting on the terrace, having been served tea and kif. The baby was asleep in the spare bedroom and Violet was beating the heretofore-invincible Malim Ali at checkers.

"That's good," I said. "The worse the road gets, the less likely that tourists will ever get up here." And I told the Kramers what Gysin had once told me: if electric wires ever climbed to Jajouka, Bou Jeloud would be finished. Old gods don't mix well with light bulbs and television.

Berdouz, whom I wasn't aware had much understanding of English, was evidently monitoring the conversation. He spoke to Sam, who translated: "Berdouz says you should never worry about the road up the mountain. If you ever get stuck, he'll get his best mule and pull you up with a rope himself." You *had* to love this man.

At about five o'clock the chief arrived. Jnuin looked older and more frail. He still wore his authoritative golden turban at a rakish angle and held my hand affectionately while we talked. He accepted the cash Joel Fischer had sent, and handed it immediately to Ali, under whose djellaba the envelope disappeared. Many questions followed about the album, but I regretfully told them I knew nothing.

While the Malimin spoke among themselves, I took a silent inventory. No one had died in my two years' absence this time, not even Malim Ashmi, although he was said to be pushing 120 years of age. His son—or grandson, although the man was at least 70— told me Ashmi still smoked his sebsi every day. The main demographic difference of Jajouka in 1979 was that most of the young men—Berdouz Jr., Abdallah Attar, Achmido the dancing boy, and many others—were away in the army. Before I had much time to ponder this, a commotion arose from across the terrace. Ali, Mezhdoubi, and Mujahid were speaking crossly to each other, and Violet came over to Iris in tears.

"What is it, darling?"

"It's *that* man, Mummy," the little girl said, pointing to a shame-faced Mezhdoubi, who was being berated by the others. "He's *cheating."* Somehow peace was restored, and Violet was persuaded to return to the other side of the terrace and take on Malim Fudul, who proceeded to cheat even more blatantly than Mezhdoubi.

A moment later, after conferring with the other musicians, Berdouz came over to me and asked if I'd drive the chief and Malim Fudul to the Moroccan capital at Rabat the following day, so they could apply to appear at the annual Marrakech folklore festival the following month. I told the old drummer that I would do whatever the Malimin wanted, and they thanked me relentlessly in advance. Looking at Jnuin, I could tell the chief was relieved he wouldn't have to spend two dusty days on a lurching bus so he could discharge the duties of his office among the cultural bureaucrats of the capital.

With night closing in, we adjourned into the madrassah, where tables were being set up for supper. I stuck my head in the kitchen and Megaria smiled over his stewpot full of steaming chickens and platters of our fresh fish frying in green local olive oil. I explained to the Kramers that I had to drive the chief to Rabat the following day, and they said they would go back to Tangier then and see me on my return.

"We've always wanted to come here," Iris said, "but traveling with a baby is difficult without running water." I knew what she meant.

After supper, Amin Attar took out his fiddle, flanked by his brother Bashir—now a mustached, handsome young man—and rotund Malim Fudul, both playing gimbris. Everyone else had drums, and from the start the beat was hot and the dancing tumultuous. Several new dancing boys made their debuts, all dressed in

204   crisp, frilly dresses and belts. Berdouz, now sixty-one years old, still
got up and danced like a dervish, his feet darting over invisible hot
coals, his toothy smile pasted on his rough, mountaineer's mug.
They made Iris dance; she was accommodating and graceful considering she'd given birth only a few weeks before. Then Sam danced,
then me, and I felt so high that while I danced to the throbbing
meter I somehow stepped outside myself and was able to look back
upon the poor fool in my clothes who kept spinning . . . spinning
. . . spinning . . .

Much later, I brought a divan out onto the terrace, and slept
under the painted tin roof and the winking stars beyond, with only
a djellaba thrown over me. The night air of the Djebala in May was
indescribably soft and warm.

MEGARIA NUDGED ME awake just past dawn. The chief and Fudul
were drinking black coffee on the other side of the terrace. Soon
Bashir, dressed for the city in a new djellaba, came through the gate.
He told me softly he would be coming along and wanted to help
with the driving because he had gotten his *permis*. So, an hour later,
after inching down the mountain track myself, I gave the wheel of
the Renault to Bashir, who motored gingerly along the dirt road to
Tatoft and then on to Ksar el Kebir. When we reached the highway
to Rabat, I asked Bashir to stop at the café next to the train station
where I bought large tumblers of fresh orange juice for our traveling
party and then asked Bashir for the keys, citing insurance problems
with the rented car.

Two hours later we were in Rabat, driving from ministry to
ministry looking for the officials who had the proper stamps for the
musicians' papers. "Agi," said the chief, getting in the backseat, his
brow furrowed in frustration. "Come on," Bashir told me. "We
will go to see our friend."

Hajj was a middle-aged businessman, who lived on the wind-
blown beach out of town in a comfortable, rambling concrete ranch.
Even though we dropped in on this guy, out of the blue, within ten

minutes Hajj had put out a platter of delicious fried eggs and olives, followed by a lush bowl of fruit. Then this kind man showed me to a guest room, where I slept for an hour, dead to the world.

We had the papers properly stamped by 4:30, and duly set our course north for Jajouka, roaring up the empty, nearly straight roads at a steady hundred kilometers an hour. At the decrepit toll booths that had marked the old border between French and Spanish Morocco, we were pulled over by gendarmes. Get out of the car, they told me, and come with us.

They took me into a little shack and frisked me. "You smoke kif!" the gendarme shouted.

"No," I lied calmly. "Never."

He grabbed my hands and sniffed my fingers. *"Donnez-moi cin-quante dirhams,"* he said.

"Talk to the Malimin," I told him, and motioned for my companions that it was time for them to intervene. They jumped out of the car. As soon as he took in the approaching Jnuin, with his gold turban, the cop knew he was beaten. They were all over him, talking about the baraka of Sidi Hamid Sherq, assuring him that he would be taking money directly from their vengeful saint if he shook me down for even a few dirhams, never mind the fifty he demanded. Just let us go on our way and we'll pray for you. Baraka l'aufic.

I drove on to Ksar in a furious cloud. We stopped at a roadside grill and stuffed ourselves with lamb chops, *frites,* and cola before young Bashir gleefully took the wheel and slowly navigated his way between the immense potholes in the road that ran toward the village looming somewhere up above us in the night.

Jajouka seemed dark and deserted. The Kramers' car was gone from the bottom of the hill, so I figured they were probably back in Tangier, putting the children to bed. For an hour I sat by myself in the madrassah and wrote an entry in the venerable guest book that sat on the table at the end of the long room, along with candlesticks, ashtrays, and the copy of Bob Dylan's book, *Tarantula,* that had lain there undisturbed since my first visit five years earlier.

Eventually, a few people showed up to spend the evening. Bashir,

206   his brother Amin, Tall Mohammed, and Achmed Titi jammed and grooved at the other side of the room, composing love songs for my daughter Aisha while my tape recorder rolled.

IN JAJOUKA IT WAS instrument repair day, and several of the rhaita players had their horns out for a spring tune-up. I took the opportunity to inspect one of these mystic folk oboes. It was half a meter long with fifteen note holes, top and bottom. The bell was covered with leather that was supple from constant oiling. Like all rhaitas used in Jajouka from time immemorial, this instrument had been crafted in Wazzan out of apricot wood. Several spare reeds hung by a string from the metal mouthpiece, and the whole item was transported in a gay cloth bag. (Jajouka's drums came from Chaouen, and were made of cedar; the large hammer-headed stick that hit the top of the drum was made exclusively of orange wood, while the slender bottom stick was wild olive.)

One of the goals I had set for this voyage was to learn the secret of "circular breathing." Five years earlier, I had timed one note, held by the young rhaita player we called Fat Mohammed, at nearly twelve minutes during the peak of the Boujeloudiya, and some of the rhaita drones seemed to carry on even longer. When asked about this skill, the musicians seemed embarrassed.

This, of course, intrigued me even more.

A couple years earlier, I had come across a book called *The Voice of Atlas* by Philip Thornton. Published in London in 1936, it was subtitled "In Search of Music in Morocco." Thornton wrote the following:

> The Moors have a very strident oboe called Rai'tah (pronounced Ry-eta), which appears at marriage and circumcision processions. The technique of playing it is a guarded secret, as the thread of melody seems to be absolutely unending, and the performer appears never to

take a breath. But the secret is simple and surprising. The professional rai'tah player has two small holes pierced through his neck behind the ear. Through these he breathes while playing incessantly. The mortality amongst the children who have this operation performed is naturally very high, but those who survive this ordeal earn a handsome livelihood by their playing. This may sound a fantastic explanation of the technique, but I have seen the scars on the neck of a man who was persuaded by my music teacher to let me examine them. When not in use, the holes are kept plugged with two small wads of cotton soaked in a mixture of bitumen and gum arabic. In size they are large enough to admit the passage of a knitting needle. I imagine that the punctures are made with a red-hot skewer, but no information on that subject was forthcoming.

So, there I was, lounging on the terrace, languidly accepting an occasional sebsi while trying to unintrusively peer at the necks of the rhaita players. All the older men had large patches of scar tissue behind, and just under, their ears. But there was no sign of holes filled with wadding. Could the scars be masking mere slits that would admit air from behind the throat? It seemed unlikely, regardless of what Thornton said he had seen nearly fifty years earlier. Somehow, these musicians had learned to breathe in and out at the same moment.

Bouchikhi, one of the French-speaking teachers at the school in Jajouka, came to the madrassah that afternoon and sat with me, accepting tea and refusing kif. I wanted to know what this secular Arab socialist thought of Jajouka.

''I like Jajouka very much,'' he said after some thought, adding that it was hard for him to be away from his wife, who didn't want to live with him in a remote place with no electricity or television. I asked him what he made of Jajouka's reputation as a place of myth and psychic healing. Glancing around to make sure none of the younger French-speaking Attars were around, Bouchikhi whispered:

"Some say Attar was just a shepherd, a peasant, four hundred years ago. Sidi Hamid Sherq was a great personage who settled here, from Spain—though, perhaps, the family itself is from Arabia. Why he chose this remote place no one knows. Perhaps he wanted to get away from somebody or something. Anyway, he was a cultivated musician who taught the Attars to play the rhaita so they could earn a living. Tu m'as compris?

"The saint told them that if they continued the tradition of playing the rhaita, they would never have to work. He told them that when he died, they and their descendants should play the rhaita every Friday morning at his tomb.

"And this is what *intrigues* me so," Bouchikhi said. "Because it is usually forbidden in the Arab world to play music on a Friday. This is the only religious manifestation of music on the day of prayer. *C'est extraordinaire!*"

THAT EVENING, after supper, one of the best bands I've ever heard assembled in the madrassah to bang out some muscular hard rock. They pounded out "Jajouka Black Eyes" as if to bring down the walls of the building, chorus upon chorus of propulsive dance grooves. Amin struggled valiantly to make his violin heard above the polyrhythmic din and the impassioned singing, and the atmosphere was filled with the same smoky perfume that always occurred when the music was hotter than hot. Old Berdouz seemed almost ecstatic, calling out and vocalizing and whooping with glee. My recorder was perched on a table away from his bass drum, and when he got up to dance he leapt over this table several times, once while balancing a tray full of glasses on his head—an old dancing-boy trick.

I was so pleased with the tape I made that night that I asked the musicians to sign the back of the cassette before they left at the end of the night. Ten musicians wrote their names in tiny spidery calligraphy: Malim Hamid Attar, Mohammed Berdouz, Mohammed Taira, Mohammed Kadida, Malim Fudul, Amin Attar, Mohammed Attar, Bashir Attar, Achmed Ayashi, Achmido Twimi.

At the end of the list (and I didn't realize this until later, because I don't read Arabic), someone inscribed one additional name, their invisible patron: Sidi Hamid Sherq.

I stayed up very late, talking with the Attars and the young teacher; he told us the government would soon build a much bigger school that would bring students from all over the Djebala to Jajouka. Things are going to change here, he said.

It was three o'clock when the heavy wooden shutters were closed and a few of us settled into the madrassah for the night. I lay there for an hour, unable to fall asleep. I would be leaving Jajouka later that afternoon, and the kif began flooding images onto the screen of my semiconscious state. I saw Brian Jones slumped in a corner, comatose under his headphones. I watched William Burroughs and Brion Gysin laughing and drinking whiskey with Hamsa. Malim Ashmi, leaning on his stick, cackled about sheep tongues and the pick of the litter. Dancing boys in frilly pink dresses whirled as tambourines rattled like snakes.

A FEW HOURS LATER, Megaria grunted my name as a shaft of light pierced the gloom. I remembered it was Friday morning and walked down to the sanctuary to make an offering on behalf of the magazine. Ten rhaitas and five drummers were progressing splendidly through the movements of "The 55." Berdouz prayed and, when indicated, I went forward, trying in vain not to be conspicuous, and put a thousand dirhams in his hand. Then I slunk back into my corner and suddenly it was over.

Back on the terrace, I had coffee with the young men. I wrote in my journal for a bit, with old Mohammed Kadida looking over my shoulder in kif-ed amusement as I paused to watch the breeze shake the hot-green spring wheat that grew in verdant carpets all around the area. At noon a tagine of fresh goat was served. I ate with the chief, who kept assuring me that somehow, someday soon, they would see me in America, Insh'Allah. One of the boys brought me a big chunk of crumbly, brown hashish. They were making it back in the hills, he said, adding that maybe he would see if Sam Kramer wanted to do some business with them.

After lunch, all the men and boys crowded into the madrassah. Prayers were said for the departing guest, each man cupping his hands as he intoned his response. I looked around. There seemed to be fewer of them with each visit. So many had enlisted in the army, and others were leaving for Europe.

I hugged them all, loaded up the car, and drove down the slippery rock trail. Near Larache, I parked by the side of the road and wandered through the upper precincts of the ruins of Lixus, the ancient Phoenician redoubt. As the salty sea wind whistled through the remains of a massive temple, I looked inland and tried to ponder the mysterious relationship between this place and that other powerful plateau I had just left. But Lixus would not give her secret to me that day. I continued up the coast, through miles and miles of green wheat, past the beaches after Asilah, until the Pillars of Hercules loomed over my windshield and I turned the car east toward its home in Tanja.

IT WAS LATE in the afternoon when I reentered the Villa Mouneriya. The two chattering fatimas were glad to see me; Zohra took my hand and showed my wedding ring to Haimu. I showered, changed into fresh clothes, and headed up to the neon twilight of the boulevard. I bought day-old London newspapers, confirmed my flight with Air France, and sank into a seat at the Café Paris to watch the sun set behind the French legation across the street. Tangier was poor and bereft of visitors, but to me the city never looked more raffishly beautiful, nor seemed more dangerous.

Later, I drove up the hill to say good-bye to Paul Bowles. He was with several Moroccan friends and retainers in his snug, fire-lit flat. He made me a cup of tea, served with a wedge of lemon, and asked after Jajouka. Very quiet, I told him.

I asked if he had ever heard of a young American named Sam

Kramer, who lived on the Old Mountain. "You can probably see his place from here," I said. "There, that big pink house with the terraces." Indeed, from Bowles's bedroom the great villa with its gardens, pool, and stable stood apart from the smaller properties and estates that surrounded it. "Hmmmm . . . *that* place," Bowles said. "We've been wondering who lived over there."

I KNEW SOMETHING was wrong as soon as I parked the car and knocked at the massive wooden door in the pink stucco wall. Normally, the gardener's five children and Violet would be riotous, the houses and grounds would be lit, and taped music would be wafting from the cushioned bay windows that overlooked the strait. But the place was dark, silent, and watchful. Some kind of defensive curtain had descended. What had happened?

Hard Berber eyes glared at me through the peephole in the gate, and I was finally admitted by Achmed. I found Iris by herself in the kitchen, crying quietly as she peeled vegetables for supper. The story fell out between the tears.

There had been a *big* hash bust in Kenitra, down the coast, the day before: several tons of hashish from the Rif, many heavy trucks, inflatable rafts to ferry the stuff to waiting ships. Although Sam and his network were not involved, the hash police had come for Sam at noon.

"It's the same bloody thing every time a big load is intercepted," Iris said, regaining her composure. "Sam and Achmed bury any dope we have in the garden, and we're clean. We send Violet out to friends before the hash police show up. They ask us if we own this house, how we paid for it, how we support ourselves. Then Sam has to go down to the gendarmerie with them. He drops a few names, pays some baraka to the inspector, and is home by supper. It's not really a big deal anymore, I suppose." I could see the terrible strain in her shaking hands.

"Why be upset," I asked, "if it's so routine?"

"Because . . . look, if you're a foreigner living here, the Moroccans go out of their way to let you know your status is fragile. They want you to feel that you live here on borrowed time. There's a wide chasm between them, the faithful, and us infidels. They never let you forget it."

The young mother finished her chore and stared out the window above the sink, looking toward the faint lights of Spain in the distance, but her eyes were focused much farther away, somewhere beyond the solar system. It was poignant to see so beautiful a woman so troubled, and with good reason. A couple of years later she and Sam and their girls were busted aboard a sailing yacht in the English Channel with a half ton of Ketama hash oil in the hold. Sam had been sold out to Interpol by his Moroccan partner, or so one heard. The British cops let Iris and the kids go, and sent Sam to Dartmoor Prison for five years at Her Majesty's pleasure. When he got out, the Kramers weren't allowed to return to Morocco, and the pink villa had to be sold.

"Je suis un journaliste."

This is what I told the kepi-hatted French customs cop who pulled me over as I shouldered my way through NOTHING TO DECLARE at Charles de Gaulle airport outside of Paris. He checked my passport, asked the purpose of my visit, and wished me good luck. An hour later I changed clothes at the Hilton, where everything was saturated with Lancôme perfume, and then caught a taxi that sped down the Right Bank, turned left at the Marais, and deposited me as close as possible to Brion Gysin's new studio at 135 Rue St. Martin.

This address was on the vast cobblestoned plaza of the Plateau Beaubourg, the site of the brand-new Centre Georges Pompidou, a futuristic art museum whose mechanical elements wrapped and coiled around the mammoth blue and red building like a high tech exoskeleton. Seeing this for the first time was astounding, like a space station crash-landed in the middle of a quaint Parisian neighborhood.

It was late on a Sunday afternoon in May, and the Beaubourg was buzzing with people, thousands of them, mostly young, from all over the world. They were clustered around acrobats and fire-eaters, into whose eager hats they threw coins. On one side of the plaza a Peruvian panpipe band whistled and cooed, while fifty yards away a polyglot bongo team of Francophone Third World types competed for their share of the crowd with bombastic rhythms and dancers.

The ambience was both electric and medieval, a perfect place to find Brion Gysin in residence.

His pad was on the third floor of a venerable old apartment house that the City of Paris leased to important foreign artists-in-residence. On his way to answer my knock I could hear him shouting something about V. S. Pritchett. The door flung open, and Gysin appeared. *"You're* not V. S. Pritchett, are you? *Of course you're not!* You're my dinner date, and right on time, too. I hate people who are late, don't you?"

I followed Gysin into his sitting room, which was furnished with drawing board and lamp, books everywhere, paintings stacked against each other, piles of archives and files, and an extremely hip Miles Davis tape in the background.

For the next hour, as the rain plinked against the windows, Gysin recounted how he met the Master Musicians; how he found Pan the goat god alive and dancing in the Djebel; how he brought them to Tangier as the house band at his club. After he served a superb cheesy-onion brioche and cold, very alcoholic Alsatian beer, Gysin delivered a hilarious account of the Rolling Stones' first visits to Morocco and Brian Jones's subsequent transfiguration after his pilgrimage to Jajouka.

I sat at Gysin's feet, enraptured.

Later, we walked in the rain to Les Bains Douches, a new restaurant and nightclub in an old bathhouse nearby. Gysin spoke wistfully of the old Tangier, before what he called the "cunt invasion" and the "twat parade" into Morocco in the 1950s. "It was disgusting, take it from me," Gysin sneered. "You'd go into your favorite kif café and the sebsis would have *lipstick* on them!"

Gysin was received like a king at Bains Douches. He ordered champagne and good wine, and rolled a big hash joint that he smoked like an after-dinner cigar, to the amusement of nearby diners whose noses twitched at the sweet organic scent of cannabis in the air. We were soon joined by the manager, a slim Spanish brunette named Violetta; good reggae—Burning Spear—came over the sound system, and Violetta kept ordering fresh carafes of the house rouge. Gysin rolled another joint. A big one.

AT TWO-THIRTY on Monday morning, on the wet sidewalk outside the restaurant, Gysin waited with me for the taxi dear Violetta had summoned. "Thanks for dinner," Brion Gysin said. "I hope I have enlightened you somewhat."

I looked at him—tall, close-cropped, tremendously handsome even in middle age, drunk, and managing it beautifully.

I decided to take a chance. "You're holding something back from me," I told him. "I can sense it. I want you to tell me what you *don't* want me to know about Jajouka."

Gysin thought for a moment. He looked at me carefully. "All right," he said, sounding weary, as a Citroen cab pulled to the curb. "Come tomorrow, and I may show you something interesting."

THE NEXT DAY, Gysin was somber as he led me into his studio. Right away I noticed some files out on the table. "I've been doing your homework for you," Gysin called from the kitchen. He poured us both some scotch over ice.

"As you know," he said, "I have been interested in Jajouka for thirty years now, and I have done a great deal of research on the subject. That they preserve elements of antique Greco-Roman rituals is well established. That they serve a prominent Muslim saint is well established. That their circular breathing is a form of the Sufi *Zikr* is well established. But what else? Some other aspect of Jajouka was, I intuited, still a secret.

"Look at Jajouka's site. Have you ever noticed the ruins beside the road leading down from the village? These were defensive works of some kind—probably Byzantine. At one point, Jajouka was fortified, perhaps even partly walled. Why? Who were they keeping out?"

Gysin stopped and thought for a moment.

"In the old Moroccan army, you know, the rhaitas called the soldiers to battle. That drum roll you hear when they play the 'Kaimonos' in Jajouka? It's meant to call the army to attention . . . Back in the fifties, I knew quite a few old people who had seen the harka—the Moroccan army—on the move as it followed the king. Many of the soldiers had their boyfriends traveling with them. It was like Thermopylae!

"But where was I? Ah, yes. Let me tell you about the first time I heard them. It was at Sidi Kacem, which was basically a very beautiful white tomb on a big dune. The dune was an ancient Phoenician sacred grove, a *very* powerful place. One of those pagan spots the Moroccans call Sidi Mon Arraf, or 'Saint Who-Knows.' This meant the place was very old and holy even before Islam took over. In Phoenician times, there was a festival during which the high priests and priestesses became sacred prostitutes. It survives to this day at Sidi Kacem, where they set up greenleaf cafés, and a sort of licensed promiscuity is tolerated.

"I was with Paul Bowles when I heard this piping. I've told you about it already. I heard the Masters starting to play, but their presence was apparently unauthorized, and I just managed to catch a glimpse of them as they were being unceremoniously bundled out of the place by the officials.

"Now you know about Hamsa. He *is* one of them. When I met him in 1950, he was a very special person in the village, because he was the son of the most beautiful girl the Attar family ever produced—or so it was said. Hamsa's mother was a *famous* beauty; they made up a song about this girl, and the lyrics said something like you couldn't live with her, but you couldn't live without her.

"I remember we took the little train to Ksar el Kebir, which had been a sophisticated Moorish city when London and Paris were

216 muddy towns. They were demolishing the crumbling medieval city walls as I arrived. It was the Aid el Kebir, and a Bou Jeloud was dancing in the streets of Ksar. That's where I saw him first—not Jajouka.

"Anyway, I walked up to Jajouka that first time. In those days the village was invisible until you came right upon it, because the roofs were thatched. You'd hear rats running through the thatch at night. Jajouka was all whitewash and cactus lanes and wild morning glories in bloom everywhere. I was beside myself when I heard the rhaitas and realized this was the music I had heard, briefly, at Sidi Kacem. I told them I wanted to hear this music every night of my life, and they suggested I open a café in Tangier they could play in.

"Which reminds me: In 1955, at the height of political tension in Morocco, the nationalist Istiqlal declared a musical strike when the French kidnapped Mohammed V and exiled him to Madagascar. It looked like the restaurant was doomed. I got word to Jajouka and they came from the hills and played for seventy-two hours straight. The place was *packed.*

"Anyway, I quickly realized what was up there. A cult of priests of Faunus, the Roman god who struck the balance between city and country and kept the flocks fertile and the women pregnant. One could trace the various folkloric dances and characters all the way back to the ritual processions of the Dionysian Mysteries, if one were so inclined.

"And the Attars also had this Sufi breathing of theirs, something that had migrated west with them from Iraq a thousand years ago. Then Sidi Hamid Sherq came up the mountain and they gave the rhaita to *him*! Why? They attached themselves to him to survive, because he was powerful. He could heal crazy minds! He brought good business to Jajouka.

"I also discovered I was *by no means* the first Christian in town. The Spanish arrived in the 1930s, after Raisouli had surrendered. The Tyrant of Asilah! Jajouka had very old papers that identified them as a royal *appenage,* with certain extraordinary rights over the sultan. Moulay Hafid was the last sultan they played for, then

Raisouli hired them to increase his prestige. When he fell, the Spaniards showed up and confiscated Jajouka's seven royal decrees as part of the suppression of Raisouli. They took the documents to Tetuan, but they wound up in the national archives in Seville, *where I found 'em.* And the uptight, constipated Spanish librarians wouldn't let me make copies, either.

"But by then, I was convinced that Jajouka had been some kind of monastery at one time—a militant priesthood that harbored esoteric antique practices. I felt this way even before I heard about the Dancing-Boy Wars.

"I *thought* you would find that interesting. Remember, this is very obscure stuff. And it may not even be true! The only reason we know about any of this is because a nineteenth-century French *arabiste* was passing through and took a prurient interest in the subject matter.

"It seems that there were tribal wars fought over stolen dancing boys in the Djebel a hundred years ago or more. Jajouka was reputed to be the center of these conflicts. Evidently, boys were bought, sold, stolen, and taught to dance, and great rivalries developed. These boys were considered the flower of their tribes, and pitched battles were fought over kidnapped youths. Jajouka is still a haven for them; one always finds boys and young men in the village who have attached themselves to the Malimin, but who are not of the local families."

I had been listening to Gysin carefully, occasionally making notes so I wouldn't forget anything. He paused and looked at me.

"Jajouka had a very unsavory reputation, you know. In some circles it still does. Come over to the light—I want to show you something." Gysin took a photocopy out of a folder and laid it on his drawing table.

"I found this in the Bibliothèque Nationale, only last year; I haven't shown it to anyone yet. It's an account of what this self-styled Arabist called 'the horrors of homosexuality in Zahdjouka.' I'm unsure when it was written, but it was published in Paris in 1899."

I leaned over and tried to read, scanning quickly. Zahdjouka was described as the home of *"cent joueurs de hautbois et son corps de ballet"*—oboe players and dancers. Two sentences later the village was described as *"une vaste coïtatorium."* A few lines later, I translated: "The pen actually trembles in my hand when I think of the unimaginable iniquities that have been perpetrated in this village of Zahdjouka."

Gently, Brion Gysin took the photocopy from under my gaze and returned it to its folder, making sure the name of the author and the title of the book were covered. "I don't know whether I'm going to circulate these documents," he said. "Who knows how reliable this material is?"

My head was spinning now. I thought of Malim Ashmi's funny stories, and the smiling boys who twirled in their frilly dresses. What was Gysin saying to me?

"For years I considered only three main aspects—the Roman Bou Jeloud, the Sufi techniques from the old Persian world, and the cult of Hamid Sherq. But think of this: Lixus was a great center of Phoenician worship and ritual. At some point it was destroyed. Maybe by the Romans, perhaps by the Beni Hallal, a fierce Arabic tribe whose self-appointed mission was to vandalize Roman and pagan religious sites during the migrations west. Remember, there was a Christian bishop in Fez in the third century A.D.!

"So, the hierophants and their musicians had to leave Lixus at some point. Where to go? Deeper into the winding valley of the Loukos! Up there! Where the mountain plateau is! It turned out to have many springs and wells, and they settled in with their secret religion and their 'unspeakable practices' and absorbed everything that came along—Roman gods, Islamic saints, Moroccan kings, the Rolling Stones . . .

"Now you want to know—'how can he be sure?' *But it's right there in the name of the place.* 'Jouka' means owl! 'Dja-jouka' means Owl Mountain! 'Jajouka' means the way to Owl Mountain. Aisha Hamoka is an owl—with grey eyes like Minerva. And they *always* told me she was there in the village, *long* before Bou Jeloud . . . do you see it yet? The owl is the symbol the Phoenicians used for their mother goddess—Astarte. It's the Old Religion, older than human memory. That's why they were at Sidi Kacem, that old Phoenician place! Lixus is the missing link.''

A trumpet blast from the Beaubourg plaza below rent the twilight outside Gysin's studio windows. Inside it was dark, and Gysin snapped the reverie of his speech by switching on the lamp over his drawing table. His own grey eyes were hooded, and he seemed fatigued.

"I've told you almost everything," he said. "I don't want you to publish this material, at least not while I'm alive. Men and boys no longer sleep together much in Morocco, I'm told. It went out of fashion some time ago."

"Did you have sexual relationships in Jajouka?" I asked.

"Ha! What an American question." Gysin laughed. "Yes, some of them were my lovers," he said with a hint of pride. "But I won't tell you which ones."

"Brion, are you sure you won't give me the citation for the *'vaste coïtatorium'* material?"

"I'm sure. Now run along back to America and write your story. Stay in touch and come see me when you're in Paris again."

WHEN I GOT back home, the chunk of hash that the Jajoukans had given me fell out of the shoes in which I had inadvertently packed it, having traveled through a Moroccan exit search, French scrutiny, and American customs. If I had known the contraband was there, I'd probably still be in jail.

I wrote my Jajouka story for *GEO*. The editors liked it, but the Germans pulled the plug on the money-gobbling magazine before the story could be published. In the end, Joel Fischer sent me a postcard:

"This must be Allah's way of telling you to get a job!"

chapter 7

Pandemonium in Kensington

During the summer of 1979 a rumor reached us in America that Jajouka had played in France under the auspices of some international cultural exchange. "Incredible," said Joel Fischer over the telephone from New Mexico. "Does this mean that Bou Jeloud has been let loose to dance in Europe?"

Later that year, Brion Gysin sent me a clipping from the French daily, *Midi Libre:* FROM THE RIF TO LA CHARTREUSE, the headline read, OR THE EXTRAORDINARY VOYAGE OF JAJOUKA'S MUSICIANS. And, sure enough, there was a grainy photo of old Bou Jeloud, Father of Flocks, flailing away in the crowded cloister of the medieval monastery of Chartreuse as the Master Musicians piped away behind him. They were wearing what the paper described as "their traditional costumes"—the djellabas we had provided six years earlier.

Yes, Bou Jeloud was out and about; I had the feeling some new epoch was beginning for Jajouka.

IN APRIL 1980, I received a long letter from Ricky Stone, whom I knew only by reputation. He was a young English friend of Brion Gysin's who had lived in Jajouka for many months, back in the early 1970s. He obviously had a very distinctive style of dancing, because the eccentric moves of "English Ricky" were still being imitated in Jajouka many years later. Ricky was writing to say that he had been working for a year to book a European tour for Jajouka, toiling with various government cultural organizations and, after much slogging, the International Music Council of UNESCO took on the project. Its Extra-European Arts Committee offered Jajouka concert dates in France, Germany, Holland, and Belgium, with the possibility of Switzerland. Then Ricky booked a tour of England, starting in Scotland in August and finishing in London in September. In October Jajouka was booked to play two concerts in the main UNESCO conference hall in Paris, to be recorded live at the expense of an organ called the International Fund for the Promotion of Culture. UNESCO was also going to finance a documentary film.

Ricky had managed to secure the cooperation of the Moroccan Ministry of Information, which resulted in the fairly speedy approval of twenty-six passports, exactly the number needed for Jajouka's current touring party. These precious documents were waiting at the governor's office in Tetuan.

> I took the Hadjj [the chief, Jnuin, who had recently been driven to Mecca by his older Euro sons, and now bore the coveted honorific of one who had made the sacred pilgrimage] and Mh'lm Fudul with me to Rabat for all these meetings. They are excellent ambassadors for Jajouka. In fact, they've developed rather a taste for it, and have since returned a couple of times to waft serenely around the corridors of power. It looks as if Jajouka might begin to be considered 'chic' by the ministerial echelons of Moroccan

society. Now, if only Royal Air Maroc could be persuaded
to give us 26 airfares! In lieu of that, I'm trying to get
Moroccan business interests in England to buy us a bus.

I was breathless. Ricky was thinking big. "This project must be
considered a noble experiment," he went on.

There are 27 people in this troupe, with me being the
27th. Every member of the Serifya Association is taking
full and equal responsibility by contracting to fill his individual role within that Association. Hopefully, this will be
the foundation upon which a 'new era' might begin in the
history of Jajouka.

The letter concluded by asking me to contact the Rolling Stones,
now resident in New York, in order to ask them to reissue Brian
Jones's Jajouka album and hopefully lay a hefty, baraka-laden cash
advance on the Master Musicians.

Why not? I thought.

THUS ARMED WITH a mandate from the Association Serifiya Folklorique and its ambitious new agent, English Ricky Stone, I called
up the Los Angeles offices of *Oui,* the magazine I was contributing
to at the time, and suggested I do an interview with Keith Richards,
the Rolling Stones' cubist guitar player and songwriter. I thought
Keith would be more interested in Jajouka than Mick Jagger, and
figured that one Master Musician might do a big favor for another.
Besides, the Stones had recently opened their own label, Rolling
Stones Records, to outside artists, like the reggae star Peter Tosh.
Why would a reissue of what could be considered the original
"World Music" album be anything less than a great idea and a
tribute to the late Brian Jones?

These, at any rate, were my tactics.

224   The magazine went for the idea, and I sent a request for an interview to Keith Richards in care of the Stones' office in New York.

Nothing for two months. Then one day the telephone exploded. It was a famous Los Angeles rock-and-roll publicist: "We're gonna do your interview! Keith likes your book! He's nuts about reggae! He's got a house in Jamaica! Be at 75 Rockefeller Plaza at two o'clock tomorrow! Keith will be there!"

The next day, I was there with my little Sony TCS-310 tape recorder, rarin' to go. The ostensible purpose of this journalistic deployment was to discuss the Rolling Stones' deplorable new album, *Emotional Rescue,* which fused late disco styles with urgent reggae techniques—and was a real mess. Industry gossip had Mick and Keith in one of their periodic feuds. Reflecting the tastes of the label's proprietors, the music that boomed in the vestibule of Rolling Stones Records was not the Stones' latest, but the limpid crooning of Gregory Isaacs, current champion of roots reggae. I waited in the reception area for ten minutes. Then Keith Richards lurched into the picture, a wineglass in one hand, a lit cigarette in the other. It took a full five seconds to take in the whole carefully assembled gypsy/pirate effect: spiky greying hair, old man's wrinkled face, big silver death's head ring, steel manacle bracelet, torn and frayed suede boots, big flick knife tucked in the waistband of his jeans.

"Are we ready then?" he asked. I got up. "Follow me." We walked down a corridor. Keith Richards reeked of his own legend. For ten years he had been billed as the next rock star to Oh Dee. And now the so-called "human riff," the composer of "Satisfaction," "Paint It Black," and "Get Off of My Cloud," was sitting across from me at a table in an office with a view of the granite monoliths of Rockefeller Center. He was, as far as I could tell, stone drunk.

The interview started off pretty well. We talked about reggae for a while. Then he pulled the knife from his waistband. "That looks like a German ratchet knife," I said, "like the ones the rude boys use in Jamaica."

"Yeah," Keith said. "But this is a French one." He tried in vain to open the large knife with a flick of his wrist. The ratchet stayed shut. "See, that's what happens if you let chicks fuck with them . . . this one was hand-made in France. *This* should do it." He lashed out with a savage stroke of his sinewy playing arm, but the ratchet was stuck shut. His bony fingers grasped the knife's steel ring and the arm lashed out. This time the knife unfolded with a chilling slash and an authoritative click. "There," he pronounced. Satisfaction! "This is a knock-off of the German knife, the Okapi. See? Good bone, good reproduction."

"Do you believe," I asked, "that some knives have lives of their own?"

"I don't know about that," Keith said, "but I've been in situations where I've had a knife or a gun, or just a knife without even them knowing about the gun . . . and the knife alone puts the fear of God in 'em. Yeah . . . cold steel, people don't like." He looked at me. His eyes had a no-limits cast to them.

I found myself liking this man.

Then he produced a glass vial. It was filled with a glittery substance that sparkled as if a dozen large diamonds had been minced to silicate perfection. He poured the contents on the table and put a slender straw in it. Then I did, too. *"Wish* I could wake up," Keith said. He got up and wobbled around the room a bit. Then he slipped out and came back with a framed picture of drummer Charlie Watts, which he reverently placed on the table in front of me.

"What was that pill?" he asked.

What pill?

"One you gave me. Pretty good."

But Keith, I protested. I didn't give you any pill.

"Must have been Ron then," he said without missing a beat. "Lemme go get him so he can talk for me."

Please Keith, I begged, let's just tape a few more minutes.

He seemed surprised and dazed. "Okay. Sure. You're doin' good. As I was saying . . . I've never had a problem with drugs . . . but I *have had* problems with the police."

This seemed funny to me. I laughed. We had some more of the Devil's dandruff just as the L.A. publicist stuck his head in the door. His eyes widened at the glowing lines. "Keith!" he shouted. "What the hell are you doing? This guy's a *journalist*. He's gonna write about this!" Keith obviously didn't give a shit, and collapsed into a chair. The press agent, correctly assessing that Keith was in a voluble, sharing mood, waded right in himself. I had another go, and the publicist sighed with feigned relief. "Now that he's been corrupted," the man from L.A. said, "we can continue."

We talked some more about the Stones, Keith got more and more out of it, and I stepped out of character, so to speak, and started talking to him about Jajouka. Halfway through, I realized this was useless. It was like trying to speak to someone through six inches of plate glass. He could probably see my lips moving, and that's all. Finally I got the question out, "Keith, would you ever consider rereleasing Brian Jones's Jajouka album?"

He thought for a moment. His speech was now very slurred. "Not me," he said. "No. That was Brian's idea. I thought he did very well on that." Then he mumbled something that sounded sorrowful, but I couldn't make out his words. We talked for a few more moments, so that I had enough for a magazine article, and then he graciously bade me good-bye, gathering up his paraphernalia, his portrait of the drummer, and several cassettes along with his wine-glass, and backed out of the room.

I sat there, feeling numb. My mission for Jajouka had failed. But wait! Here was *another chance*. The press agent came in, followed by Mick Jagger. Rather than the studied rock buccaneer look of Keith, Mick was dressed in a yellow cotton shirt, chino slacks, leather sneakers. I gave him the Jajouka rap, and he grimaced. It seemed as if hearing the name Brian Jones gave him a pain.

"We can't release that album again," he told me with a shrug. "It would be too expensive, no one knows who has the rights to it, and besides, no one cares about it anyway."

Mick Jagger walked out of the room. "Guess you said the wrong thing," the publicist snorted.

I WROTE BACK TO English Ricky and told him what happened. He sent me the tour schedule by return mail, and fortune had it that some business I had planned in London for late September coincided with Jajouka's five-night residency there. Just the thought of seeing the goat god cavorting in sleepy London town made my liver quiver. I called Joel to give him the news, but his brother answered the phone. He and Joel had sold their restaurant to some Arabs, and Joel was in Morocco. I guessed he'd find out soon enough.

In early September I received the following letter from him, postmarked London:

Sahibe,

I am still in shock as I write this quick note to clue you in to the events of the past two weeks. Everything you ever thought, or felt, about Jajouka is now topsy-turvy, loop-the-loop, on its ear, whatever. Consider the following: a fortnight ago I was in Tangier, where I ran into Ricky Stone on the Boulevard. He was on his way to Jajouka with a bus to pick up 'the boys' and drive them to England. Invited along, I wound up my business a day later and took a Benz taxi to Alcazar, and then another one to Tatoft. I ran into some Jajoukans at the market and we walked back to the village via the old donkey trail up the mountain. The big grey bus Ricky had bought had been left at the bottom with a guardian, awaiting its precious cargo.

Well, the village was in an uproar. The madrassah was a scene of riot and tumult, with the musicians arguing about what and whom to take along. A new crop of eleven-year-old dancing boys had come along since my last visit, and these lads were being auditioned and rehearsed to exhaustion. The whole tribe was nervous and excited. There was an energy in the village I've never felt before, like a war party was leaving, and you've got to credit

Ricky Stone for this wonderful renewal. You can't imagine the effort this cat has expended over the last few months.

Ricky arrived an hour after me, with the scenery he had commissioned: exquisite variants of the *heiti,* the traditional hangings depicting Moorish arches that adorn the salons of wealthy houses. He also had the *passports,* and a delirious scene of shouting and singing ensued when these priceless documents were passed around to their new owners.

We left the following morning, early. First, there was a send-off and blessing at Sidi Hamid Sherq's HQ that I found deeply moving. We walked down the old mountain road, rhaitas blazing, the mists rising in spirals from the valley below. There was another cheer when the Malimin laid eyes on their bus, a clunky but generally road-worthy French colonial autobus with a few bunks and a little sitting area in the back. We drove to Tangier, everyone really psyched, with much singing. Sitting in the back with Ricky and the Haj, as they now call the Chief, heading north on ol' Moroccan Route One, I thought I had passed on to my own personal heaven.

"The only problem was—no kif. Nada. Ricky laid down the law. If one of us gets busted, they'll deport all of us. Everyone was abstaining, or smoking tobacco, but it didn't really seem like a big deal to anyone but me.

We crossed the Strait on a ferry to Algeciras, drove up through Spain and France and arrived at the English Channel after three days. At Calais, our bus broke down at the quay alongside the English Channel. We spent 24 hours there, waiting for the bus to get fixed. I kept looking at the choppy sea, hoping the crossing would be smooth.

Well, it wasn't. I had noticed that Bashir Attar had been acting strangely toward me ever since I'd arrived in Jajouka. The little boy we used to know is now an intense young cat with an attitude that he is the force to reckon with in the band. So, in the middle of a meeting while we were crossing the channel, Bashir began to pick me apart. He accused me of ripping off Jajouka with the record I recorded. *Where's all the money?* That's what he kept asking. I explained that the record had sold only a few hundred copies, and that all the money that had come to Jajouka, supposedly from the record, was actually out of my own pocket, as a kind of offering.

I could tell Bashir thought I was bullshitting them. It was frightening. I'd never seen this assertive, even combative side of Bashir's personality before. Ricky, I could tell, supported me but didn't want to get involved. The older musicians remained passive, looking at me. I was really crushed—a horrible feeling.

We were met in Dover by Ricky's English contacts and Ahmed Attar, Jnuin's son, who drives a cab in Paris. Ahmed had his own car, so I rode with him behind Jajouka's bus as we made our way from the coastline toward the site Ricky had prepared. Ahmed is a fairly sophisticated guy, and I explained the problem I was having with Bashir. I think I convinced him, because later he explained things to his father and some of the elders, and got me off the hook.

We arrived at this lodge house in the New Forest in Hampshire around five o'clock. It belonged to a friend of Ricky's who managed this estate. The place was wired for sound, and here Jajouka met its English road crew. For the next three days, we worked on getting the band used to playing amplified music with microphones and speakers. A weird scene.

Made even weirder by Bacari, whom I don't believe you've ever met. He is Jajouka's #1 gimbri genius—he plays on the album I made—but he hasn't lived in Jajouka for years—actually he lives in Rabat, where he's a highly sought-after cabaret *gimbriste*. Anyway, Bacari is mad and always has been. He took to England right away, running off with a blond farmgirl the first night.

Then we went on tour, a series of late-summer music festivals in the idyllic English countryside. Imagine this: Glastonbury Tor, a humungous crag in Somerset, in the evening mist. This is where King Arthur is buried! Jajouka is playing, Bou Jeloud is dancing, the sun is setting red and dozens of *bare-breasted* English hippie girls are dancing in front of the musicians, like a scene from an old Druid epic. I had to shake my head a couple of times. And did the pretty girls faze the musicians? Not a bit. They played better than I'd heard them in years. They loved it!!!

For a week we traveled through England, getting good press, preparing for Jajouka's assault on London. Bashir apologized to me, privately, and I felt a bit better. Now Ricky's taking heat over uneven food and huge expenses. I don't know how he's going to be able to hold this thing together. It's a Herculean task.

By the time you receive this, you should be ready to leave for London. I'll be back in the States by then. Jajouka is expecting to see you there. I don't have the address, but I know that Ricky has them staying in the abandoned Cambodian embassy, wherever that is. Good luck, and let me know what happens.

Joel

My cousin Dan picked me up at Heathrow airport on a sunny English Saturday morning and drove me to his house in St. Peter's Square, Hammersmith. I tried to track down the Master Musicians of Jajouka, without success. There was no longer any Cambodian government to maintain an active embassy in London, and no one I could contact on a weekend who could tell me where the old

embassy had been. It was terribly frustrating to think that somewhere in this metropolis of crescents and squares the Malimin were
resting in anticipation of their upcoming five nights at the Commonwealth Institute in Kensington, a series of shows billboarded in the
London press as the triumphant progress of the late Brian Jones's
mystical Sufi protégés.

To work off the frustration, I walked along the Thames for hours,
noting the beauty of the children, the cheery names of the softly lit
waterside pubs, and the smell of the river at low tide. When I
returned to my cousin's terraced house, I was relieved that his
rambunctious kids were there.

The next morning was Sunday, and over breakfast I stumbled
across an article about Jajouka in the *Observer* magazine. THE
WORLD'S OLDEST ROCK'N'ROLL BAND described the author's visit to
the village in the days of Ornette Coleman's "not entirely successful
fusions." There was a picture of my soccer buddy Tall Mohammed
playing the drums and singing as his uncles piped away.

"There is a lot at stake on this tour," the story reported.

> The long-term plan is to get the musicians so well known
> that they can give concerts anywhere in the world for a
> month or two each year, and re-establish their respect and
> reputation back in Morocco. They used to be aristocrats.
> They last worked for the grandfather of the present king,
> and they'd like to be invited back to the palace.
>
> But Ricky Stone says the musicians don't want to be
> thought of as a relic. "They are just extraordinary enter-
> tainers, and they are bringing Pan to thrash the people of
> Europe," he says. After my memorable experiences back
> in Joujouka, it will be intriguing to see how Boujeloud
> plays the Commonwealth Institute.

On Monday morning I drove with Dan down the Westway to his
office near Baker Street to continue the search for Jajouka. I walked

over to number 221B to see if Sherlock Holmes could be of any assistance, but the site of his lodgings was now occupied by a bank. A call to a friend at one of the music papers revealed that the Malimin had played an impromptu show in Hyde Park the day before. So, resigned to not seeing my Moroccan friends until the evening's performance, I spent the rest of the day interviewing an Anglo-Jamaican dub poet in the offices of a radical black magazine in Brixton. Four white cab drivers in central London refused to drive me there, before one old cabbie grudgingly agreed to take me to "where the nig-nogs live."

I returned to my cousin's office in the middle of the afternoon. In the streets, the newspapers were announcing that Led Zeppelin's drummer John Bonham had died after a drinking binge at a Zeppelin rehearsal. I'd met and liked Bonzo, as he was called, and felt sad.

Later, I walked across Hyde Park and Kensington Gardens to my rendezvous with the priests of Pan. Kensington, where Peter Pan had frolicked with Wendy Darling before the fated voyage to Never-Never-Land. Perhaps Lord Peter, now an old man retired in one of the great mansion apartments overlooking the park, might hear the music of the rhaitas skirling up the avenue later that evening.

Peter Pan . . . meet Bou Jeloud!

The Commonwealth Institute was an impressive modern struc-ture on Kensington High Street. Posters out front advertised the Master Musicians of Jajouka, but inside no one was to be found, beside the custodians mopping out the large auditorium where the shows would be held. I went back out to the street to wait, and at 5:30 an incongruous French bus, battleship grey and spewing black exhaust, pulled into the institute's courtyard. I stood there dum-founded. In the windows I could see the chief, Fudul, Berdouz, and a bunch of the boys. Someone in the bus yelled my name and then they were all waving and calling to me. I ran over to the bus and greeted them as they piled out. There were Ayashi and Mezhdoubi, Aribou and Mujahid, Young Titi, and most of the Attar brothers—

Amin, Abdallah, and Bashir. I was introduced to Bacari, a very tall Attar clone with eyes that seemed focused somewhere beyond the asteroid belt. (A young blond English girl, dressed as a gypsy, also got off the bus. She seemed to belong to Bacari.) Everywhere were familiar faces—Achmido Twimi, Fat Mohammed Attar, Megaria the cook, Abdelatif Ayashi—but it was incredibly disorienting to see them in London. We went back to the dressing rooms and had a great reunion as they prepared for their 7:30 gig. They were both exalted by their adventure and exhausted by its rigors. If the state of their tour bus was any indication, their slog through Europe had been anything but uneventful.

But, first things first. The chief—now called the Hajj—sat down next to me and inquired after my family. Then he told me who they had lost: old Mohammed Ben Aisha, a great rhaita player; Tall Mohammed, my young friend, who had died of a fever just before the tour; and their old mentor Malim Ashmi, who had finally joined Allah at the age of 121. Hamid Attar, an old friend, whose hands had withered after a mad dog had bitten him and he developed tetanus, had gotten a space on the bus only because his nine-year-old son Abdelaziz was now the star dancing boy in the little "corps de ballet" that Jajouka had brought along. These were several fifth-graders in brown djellabas, who were helped into their headdresses and gowns by Megaria and Ayashi. Lighting a menthol Dunhill, the chief also explained that many of the young men were fighting in the Sahara and couldn't make the tour. Abdinde was in Mauretania, Abdel'ila was in Tan-Tan, Berdouz, Jr., was in Meknes, etc.

But I was having a hard time getting over the news that Tall Mohammed had died. Hadn't his picture just appeared in the *Observer*?

Just then Ricky Stone breezed in with an entourage of journalists and creditors. He and Bashir had a few unfriendly words. Bashir had his own entourage, English friends that he had met at Skip's old place on the mountain, who loitered in a corner, apart from the Malimin.

I introduced myself to Ricky and received an embrace and an immediate plea to help him in the wings that evening. About thirty-five, he had dark curly hair and a pointed English nose; a crimson kerchief at his throat set off a Regency velvet jacket and cool black boots. The effect was theatrical. The manner was urgent. "I just need someone to get them on and off stage between their segments," he told me breathlessly. "So glad you've come aboard. I was unhappy when Joel Fischer split. You can see it's *bedlam*. Hope you don't mind mucking in."

And he dashed off, trailing young aides. I looked at Jnuin. "Ricky . . . ," he said, smiling and shaking his head.

AT SEVEN O'CLOCK Ricky's people set up tables in the lobby where the audience could buy programs, posters, or cassettes that Ricky had produced from recordings done earlier that year in Jajouka. At 7:15 the dancing-boys' wardrobe was inspected a final time by the chief, whose new gold turban stood out against the crowd of snow-white turbans around him. From my spot in the wings I peeked into the sold-out hall filling up with hip English kids, old Brian Jones fans approaching middle age, and excited Moroccans in a mood to party.

At 7:30 the house was full and the Master Musicians of Jajouka, in new white woolen djellabas, were crowded behind me in the wings, stage left, waiting to go on. As the lights dimmed, the chief and Malim Fudul walked out alone to great applause. As this pair of rhaita virtuosi played a formal fanfare, the rest of the group filed onstage, and the piece became a rich, flamboyant "Kaimonos" whose movements and countertones were enhanced by the good acoustics of the room and bored deeply into the minds and souls of those lucky enough to be there.

When the piece was finished, they filed offstage, and a smaller contingent starring Bacari took over. Playing a big four-stringed gimbri, Bacari did his basic Rabat cabaret act, playing the shit out of the folk lute and hoofing to his own astral rhythms as the drummers poured on funk around him. Bacari had the tall Attar physique, and the eyes of a shaman—someone you shouldn't get too close to. But I could see that no one, not even the great Tahir, could *touch* him as an adept of the gimbri. Even when Bacari hopped away from the microphone, his instrument boomed its goat song out into the room.

Beside me in the wings, Berdouz intently whispered instructions to dancing boy Abdelaziz, who then swayed onstage in his frilly dress to great cheering. (I knew the English would *love* this part.) As Bacari's Djibli band tore it up, Abdelaziz performed a totally devastating shake, much more sensual and suggestive than anything I'd ever seen a boy do in Jajouka.

"This is *it*," a low English accent whispered in my ear. I turned to find Ricky Stone right behind me. He nodded toward Abdelaziz. "This is the real thing."

I tried to tell Ricky that this was an incredible experience and that I was in awe of his organizational skills and of the generosity that prompted it, but his attention was riveted onstage as other dancing boys came out to slither and shimmy. Moroccan ladies got out of their seats and walked onstage to stuff fivers and ten-pound notes into the woven red belts of the boys. Some of these ladies were encouraged by Berdouz to stay and dance, and one glorious Moroccan woman let down her hair and inflamed the musicians into a hard-rocking beat that ran wild before she had to run back to her seat, spent.

Next Amin Attar slid up to the mike with a bendir drum and began to sing, wailing in the high Djibli style as the band burned away behind him. Again, people got up to dance, and the music became as raucous as it could in London, without any kif.

After an intermission, eight rhaitas and six drummers came onstage in "my" djellabas. They charged right into the rhaita themes of the Boujeloudiya, and soon it was pandemonium in Kensington. During the interval I had helped dress Abdsalam Fudul in the goatskins they had brought with them. But, instead of olean-der, his switches were willow branches cut from the banks of the

236   Serpentine. As the powerful rhaitas blared forth, some of Ricky's disciples scrambled onstage to "tease" Bou Jeloud, who chased them up and down the ramps of the auditorium in simulated panic. Then the Hajj character came out to dance—Bashir in red fez and bushy white whiskers. This twenty-minute display of the Bou Jeloud was marvelous to watch, but at the same time a *frisson* came over me. There were only eight rhaitas here, mostly old men, like Sioux warriors in Buffalo Bill's Wild West Show.

Bacari and Berdouz played a little duet that emphasized the hypnotic bass string of Bacari's gimbri, while his adoring hippie girlfriend did a lascivious grind next to me in the wings. Bacari took one look at her and went into gyrations that seemed to propel him into outer orbit. The piece crashed to a halt when this maniac fell over and crashed with a laugh.

The concert ended with flutes and muffled drums. Half the audience responded to Berdouz's beckoning enmeshed with yells of "Outasight!" and "Berry gut!" and "Eberryting!" and soon a worried Ricky Stone was whispering that the stage was going to collapse under the weight of so many players and dancers. I looked out and saw *more* people heading to the stage, which began to shake under our feet. Ricky Stone went pale. I could already see the headline in tomorrow's *Evening Standard:* HUNDREDS DIE IN PAN RITE DISASTER. Tuning in to our anxiety with his acute psychic antennae, the chief immediately looked over, and I made the cut-throat sign. In the next moment, the chief signaled a high trill, and the flutes dispatched the instantly understood message as the drums crashed. The show was over, thank you for coming, time to go home now. The audience onstage applauded itself, and there was a superb atmosphere in the hall, the buzz of people leaving a party everyone had enjoyed.

DOWNSTAIRS, THE MUSICIANS changed into street clothes to receive well-wishers and the press. Then we piled into the bus for the ride to their quarters. I was led to a seat in the back, between the chief and Berdouz, while the former played "Jilali" on the flute and everyone clapped and sang as the grey bus growled past bright Knightsbridge storefronts.

Jajouka was staying in an Edwardian mansion in St. John's Wood, the abandoned Cambodian legation which had been taken over by squatters who had somehow got the electricity and water turned back on. The Masters were living in the large paneled ballroom, under a brilliantly painted blue-and-golden ceiling depicting the zodiac of Chinese astrology.

Megaria had left the show early to prepare the evening meal on gas burners in a little greenhouse adjoining the gardens in back. Sitting next to Berdouz, I was plied with mint tea and hash joints, followed by a meal of potatoes in oil and cumin. Some of the communalists who lived in the place, friends of Ricky's, dined with us, and then Ricky himself came in with a very blond German girl. He gave her a lingering kiss in front of the whole company, and someone started a beat. There was a minute when it looked like a party might start, but the chief and Berdouz hushed everyone, lest the usual chaos disturb the sedate diplomatic neighborhood in which Jajouka was hiding. One of the conditions of Jajouka's residence here, apparently, was a very low profile.

The musicians were eager to describe their adventures on tour. Some of them still wore laminated ID badges from the Festival of Fools they had played in Somerset the week before. Naked girls had danced in front of them, they told me. *Naked!* The chief smiled ruefully. Berdouz turned up his nose disdainfully at these infidel antics, but Ricky told me later that Berdouz had *loved* it, that all the old men were *completely blown away* by this unrepentant hippie fiesta. I looked over at Bacari and his fair lass, who were sitting by themselves in a corner. Bacari was cutting hash and rolling bombers; when he had crafted half a dozen, he spaced out and ended up staring at the ceiling for the rest of the night.

After supper, I went to sit with Achmido Twimi and Fat Mohammed. Twimi, whom I had always admired, seemed worried. His

238   son Abdinde, he told me, was in the Sahara. They were fighting the
Polisario and there were lots of casualties. Someone passed him the
tribe's old radio, one Joel had left behind years before. By some
miraculous manipulation, Twimi tuned in Radio Casablanca with
crystal clarity, and listened carefully to the news from the desert
war. I felt terribly sorry for him, and wished I could do something
to alleviate his completely justified anxiety.

I stayed until midnight, declining the offer of a place to sleep,
promising I'd be back the next evening. As I walked out the door
to look for a taxi, I had the same exalted feeling as when I'd actually
made it up Owl Mountain in days of yore.

"IT WOULD BE DIFFICULT to imagine a more fascinating musical
experience," said the *Daily Telegraph* the next morning, "than is
offered this week at London's Commonwealth Institute . . . Even
the transfer of fertility rites from a remote African mountain village
to a rather arid auditorium in Kensington retained something of the
original magic, with a goatskin-clad Pan leaping about and trying to
sprinkle pregnancies among the audience."

From the review in the same day's *Times:*

> The Master Musicians of Jajouka were, for many centu-
> ries, attached to the Moroccan court; since political events
> deprived them of that function at the beginning of this
> century, they have maintained their high status within a
> rather humbler community, placing their art in the service
> of local ritual, entertainment and spiritual healing.
>
> . . . A brief glimpse of the abandon of the *Boujeloudiya*
> is the centrepiece of the programme which the Jajouka
> musicians are presenting in London. Most strikingly, it
> features eight men who play rhaitas, double-reed horns
> which sound with an enveloping shrillness and whose ve-
> hement attack comes, thanks to the players' command of
> circular breathing, in endless overlapping waves.

They were accompanied by five side-drummers who delivered bafflingly ingenious unison patterns, occasionally giving a hint of superimposed triplets which suggested that this is yet another tributary of the vast river which also gave birth to jazz.

The musicians did not treat their work with undue reverence: they shared jokes and exchanged winks with members of the audience, who were encouraged to participate in several displays of come-as-you-are dancing.

. . . It seems that the future of these musicians is threatened by the usual contemporary cultural imperatives, and that this European tour is a fund-raiser to help secure their continued existence, so it would be gratifying to see the Institute full for the remainder of their short season, which ends on Friday.

The concerts got even better as the week progressed. Most evenings were sold out, and hundreds of people danced to the pipes of Pan. I continued to help out in oblique ways, getting people on- and offstage and dealing with the hordes trying to get in free through the stage door. One night Bashir had a special guest, a long-haired cousin of the British royal family whom Bashir had partied with at Skip's villa in Tangier. This stoned worthy brought an entourage of twelve, all of whom we had to admit. We also let in many young English musicians who came from the shires to pay their respects, but couldn't get tickets on sold-out nights.

The dancing boys in their gauzy dresses were a nightly sensation, easily drawing the most applause as they swayed to the dropping bombs of Berdouz's drum. My heart went out to these sweet little boys, who worked so hard on stage, and then had to serve the old Masters at dinner two hours later, under the starry ceiling of the embassy ballroom.

It was after one of these meals, on the second or third night, that an argument erupted between the musicians and Ricky Stone.

Several things seemed to trigger this event. First, there appar-

240   ently had been some kind of politico-musical upheaval within the Ahl Sherif, and it took several days for it to dawn on me that Malim Fudul was also wearing a golden turban because *he* was now the moqadem. Second, Bashir had been upset and confused about the tour's financial basis from the beginning. Third was the arrival of the Hajj's two eldest sons—Mohammed from Germany and Ahmed from Paris—to mediate the dispute. I had been wanting to meet Jnuin's son Mohammed Attar, also called Hajj (as he had made the pilgrimage to Mecca, too), for years; many people said he was the greatest rhaita player of all, after his father. He looked exactly as Jnuin must have at forty, and carried himself with the quiet dignity of a great poet. His brother Ahmed was shorter and rumpled, with long hair and expensive Italian clothes. He looked like Amin Attar, and soon became the mediator between his family and Ricky Stone after Mohammed calmly asked for an accounting. Soon everyone was screaming. Then Jnuin got up and denounced the bickering with wild contortions and great oaths. Ricky Stone explained the complex structure of the tour with angelic patience, and I knew he'd said the same things to them one hundred times. I, meanwhile, was sitting in a corner, trying to be a fly on the wall, but Mohammed Attar wanted to know who the hell I was and what was I doing there. Berdouz, bless his heart, recounted the story of the replaced djellabas with some eloquence. Mohammed nodded to me. Ahmed shrugged. Big deal, right?

This went on until three in the morning. The boys had been put to bed by Megaria and Ayashi hours before, and most of the Masters were only half-listening. The ballroom was dark except for the candlelit corner where the battle raged. Finally, Ricky Stone finished his defense and demanded their confidence if they wanted to continue the tour. Who should they trust, he asked, if not him?

This session ended at four o'clock, the darkest hour of the night, with a lengthy prayer led by Berdouz.

As I was leaving, Ricky asked if I wanted a ride back to St. Peter's Square. He was on his way to his girlfriend's flat to get some sleep. I asked what he thought of the ordeal he had just been put through.

"They're such children," he said, exhausted. "And because it's a family fight it goes on all the time. There are a lot more factions than there used to be. That's the irony, you know. Jajouka is at this incredible fulcrum right now. On one hand, they're threatened with oblivion, while on the other we face the real possibility of a rewarding future traveling around the world, playing this magical stuff for new audiences. As Gysin says, Jajouka's situation has as much potential as it has danger for them."

Dawn was coming as Ricky steered us through slumbering London. It was the fortieth anniversary of the Blitz of 1940, and in the deserted streets all the buildings were scaffolded for cleaning and repair, giving the sooty capital a nostalgic, post-Blitz feel.

As I lay in bed at my cousin's, trying to fall asleep, I kept thinking about Mohammed Attar. They told me he drove a truck in Germany and made a good living. His wife was from Jajouka as well. I asked if Mohammed would ever return to Jajouka and claim his hereditary place as head of the Master Musicians.

No chance, they told me. His wife would never return.

THE LAST SHOW in London took place on Friday night, and it was uproarious. The Commonwealth Institute was packed beyond capacity with Moroccans who vied with Jajouka's boys for good dancing spots in front of the musicians, and the Malimin consequently outdid themselves.

After the show, the musicians were besieged for photos and autographs as they waited in the night air for their decrepit bus to heave into view. I waited until they were all aboard to say good-bye. I wished that I could go to France with them, but my time away from work had to be short. "Come and see us again in the mountains," Fudul said. "Come any time, dear. You are always welcome." Then the door closed and the old bus roared away down Kensington High Street like a fire-breathing dragon.

It was then I realized that nothing about the Master Musicians of Jajouka, of the hill tribe Ahl Sherif, would ever be the same again.

chapter 8

After Inuin

Brion Gysin wrote to me from Paris a few months later.

What did you think of the Jajouka tour? They still have a huge debt in Morocco and need money. Can you help? Ricky is gone, the victim of the usual misunderstandings about finances. Apparently the UNESCO film money is still available and some California movie people have contacted me, since Ricky can no longer help them. I would take them to Jajouka myself but am about to be operated on here. Can you get them to Jajouka as soon as possible? I have given them your address, and my old henchman Targuisti will escort you from Tangier. Hope you don't mind this not unpleasant chore. Best wishes as usual,

Brion.

.   .   .

A FEW WEEKS LATER, in the spring of 1981, I had a letter from Joel Fischer, who had recently visited Jajouka. I read the letter twice before my eyes began to tear: Jnuin had died in a Rabat hospital. It was still undecided who the new leader of the Master Musicians of Jajouka would be.

It was a bitter spring, that year. Bob Marley also died in May. At the same time, Carl Mendacia, the American producer who had been recommended to make the UNESCO-funded documentary, kept phoning from Los Angeles, asking me to take him to Jajouka so he could get his film rolling. I told him to wait for the Aid el Kebir, which came in October, so he could see Bou Jeloud dance *in situ*. Finally, on October 7, 1981, I flew to Tangier to play my small part in helping the old tradition continue.

I HAD ARRANGED to meet Carl Mendacia at the Villa de France, the old European hotel where Henri Matisse once lived. Since it was very off-season, and they were available, I requested Matisse's rooms at the top of the building and was duly pleased by their late-afternoon views of the city's roofscape with blue Tangier Bay in the background. Gysin had recommended that Mendacia make the hotel the film's headquarters. At six o'clock I knocked on his door.

"Hey, come on in," Carl called. "I'm going to meet Hamsa in an hour and I want you to be there."

I told him that I didn't want to see Hamsa.

"Yeah, I know about all that, but Gysin insists I see him. What am I gonna do? Say no to Gysin? Forget it."

So I arranged to meet him later for supper and went out on foot through the twilight streets of the medina, looking for skeins of red coral beads for my wife, and soaking in the commingled scents and stinks of the souk at closing time. I took a petit taxi to the Boulevard Pasteur where I found Mendacia and Hamsa seated on the terrace of the Café Paris. I sat with a coffee while Hamsa delivered an hour-long monologue on the history of Jajouka, which held Mendacia spellbound. As Hamsa spoke, I tried to study him. He was short and powerful, with swarthy skin and sensitive, beautiful Attar eyes. He looked more weathered than when I had glimpsed him eight years earlier, and his wavy hair was just beginning to grey. He was probably just over sixty years old. Once he had seemed mad and dangerous to me, but now he was older and calmer. When he smiled at me and spoke about Joel Fischer, whom he felt had stolen Jajouka from him, I sensed he was sorrowful for his long exile from his mother's village. He seemed to indicate that Jnuin's death might mean a chance for peace between him and the Malimin.

As Hamsa spoke, I began to feel sorry for him. He was a charmer. And he was, after all, the hero who had broken through thick walls to bring Jajouka out of its own exile and into contact with the rest of the world. Somehow, I felt I owed this man something I'd never be able to repay.

I explained this to Carl Mendacia over a late meal at Claridge's. "So, if Hamsa's so great and knows everything, why can't we take him up to the village instead of Gysin's other friend . . . whatshisname . . ."

"Targuisti," I prompted.

"Right, except he calls himself Idrissi these days."

I told Mendacia that I didn't think Hamsa had been welcome in Jajouka since he made off with their djellabas years before. He couldn't go there, even if he wanted to.

"Targuisti's coming to the hotel at nine tomorrow morning," Mendacia said. "He wants me to rent a car from a friend of his, and then we'll leave for Jajouka. Gysin said he wrote to them, so they should be expecting us."

The tiled courtyard of the Villa de France was deserted at midnight. I lifted the iron key from its hook behind the front desk and walked up three flights of stairs. I had left the window open, and Matisse's bedroom was damp with salty dew from the Strait of Gibraltar. For the next hour I sat—mesmerized—as the BBC

World Service described the day's assassination of Anwar Sadat, president of Egypt, by army troops who had been passing before him in review.

THE LEGENDARY TARGUISTI turned out to be a distinguished gent in his mid-sixties: tall, in a grey suit and tie, crowned with a red fez. Gysin's young henchman was now reincarnated as a reputable but still formidable senior citizen. He was magnificent, and one could easily see why Gysin had loved him as a youth. Si Mohammed Idrissi, as he was now called, had brought along a relative eager to rent Mendacia a dusty little Fiat for our trip to the hills. Mendacia paid, in cash, as I wondered if the wheezing heap would actually make it.

We left Tangier and its new suburbs of boxy tenements and drove out into the immense brown African continent. On the roads, the Moroccan peasants seemed more wretched than ever as Targuisti made grumbling noises about the continuing war over the Western Sahara. Now and then huge flocks of sheep and goats blocked the Atlantic highway. Despite the impending joyous holiday of Aid el Kebir, Tangier seemed less festive than in the past, as if something was terribly wrong this year. When I mentioned this, Targuisti explained. "Few months ago," he said, "price of cooking oil and bread go up. You have *manifestation*, bread riot, in Casablanca. Police machine gun, three hundred people—finish! So king says on radio to people, we not make sacrifice this time, because Morocco people is mourning."

"This might not have been the best time to come here," Mendacia said. But I had a feeling he'd see Bou Jeloud, despite the king.

I sped the little Fiat through the rolling contours of inclining harvested hills, over long bridges spanning broad aquamarine rivers draining into the sea. Then great forests of citrus and cork, with giant eucalyptus trees lining the shaded road for miles. Storm clouds overhead, and slow trucks with their flatus of black exhaust to be doubled. At Asilah the earth turned from brown to red. At Larache, I pulled over to photograph the ruins of Lixus from a distance as the dead Phoenician fortress loomed over the riverine gateway to the Djebel like a gigantic billboard from the past, advertising unfathomable mysteries and impenetrable secrets. I drove on to Ksar el Kebir, where we stopped to provision under Targuisti's strict supervision. "I know these men forty years," he told us. "I know what they like for eat!" And with the tempered deliberation of the connoisseur, he carefully picked the right vegetables, fruit, fish, and live poultry to take up the mountain. Meanwhile, I bought a case of bottled water and about five pounds of Spanish chocolate bars.

When we reached Tatoft, we stopped to leave our passports with the caid, who was elsewhere. The soldiers on duty knew class when they saw it; they saluted Idrissi respectfully and told him that Aid El Kebir in Jajouka was *canceled*. In the back of the Fiat, Mendacia looked morose. Targuisti laughed and told him not to worry.

The gravel piste that led east through the hills was in much better shape than the mud-bath I'd seen two years before, and soon the roofs of Jajouka were visible. Then we were past the easily defended hairpin curve that disguised the trail before it became a steep incline, which I quickly realized was in terrible shape, worse than ever. "Everyone out," I yelled, and somehow got the tightly packed car up through the ruts and jutting boulders. Instead of the pilgrim-swollen tent town I had expected to see amid the village, Jajouka was quiet, somber. There was clearly no celebration of Aid el Kebir.

Then a shout arose. In the rearview mirror I could see Mendacia and Targuisti walking round the bend. Then a couple of woolen bundles in a doorway rose and became Mezhdoubi and Aribou. The plaza came alive with musicians and kids and I felt like I was home again.

Ten minutes later our party was comfortably ensconced on divans and cushions on the terrace of the madrassah. Berdouz unrolled his wildcat-skin mutwi and proudly displayed a batch of

248 fresh kif, gleaming with oily bract. The tea tray was out within moments, and the atmosphere was thick with sugar and mint.

I took a deep breath. It was good to be back.

IT WAS A RELIEF to find that none of the old rhaita players had died, beside the old chief. Fudul told me that Jnuin had been taken to the hospital in Rabat and had not returned alive. Now the leadership of the Masters was split. Mohammed Mujahid, the best rhaita player, had some authority as an Attar, but Berdouz was nominally the chief, and Fudul now served as unsmiling enforcer. Bashir had calmed down and was as sweet as ever. Malim Ali was semi-retired and had stopped smoking kif. Like Fudul, he was diabetic, and both took their tea from a separate pot with much less sugar.

A nearby rooftop had sprouted a TV antenna, and I asked Titi's son if there was now electricity in Jajouka.

"Batería," he said. I was relieved.

We slept a bit after lunch. It was bliss, after the morning's journey, but I woke up feeling melancholy, and explained to Mendacia that the rate of attrition among the musicians was disquieting. Most of the younger generation were away in the army or at work. Of the old men, fully half the rhaita players we'd bought djellabas for were gone. Their old cloaks now hung limply on pegs like textile memorials among the old photographs and instruments on the walls of the musicians' clubhouse.

There was a big discussion about Mendacia's movie. I translated Mendacia's proposals into French for Targuisti to pass on to the musicians in Arabic. This took forever. The musicians were promised a sum of money in return for their cooperation.

They had discussed the idea with Ricky Stone who was—"God be praised"—no longer representing them. They said they wanted to own the film themselves, and Mendacia agreed to this. The deal was done, and everyone seemed pleased.

There was good music that night after supper. Berdouz still

anchored the band with his rub-a-dub bass drum, but a new violinist named Hassan was also very hot. The Afro-Moorish polyrhythms combined with the new crop of dancing boys into an uproarious evening. After one long song crashed to a halt, Berdouz shouted, "TANKS YOU BERRY MUCH. YOU ARE WELCOME!"

Later that night, preparing to sleep after the musicians had gone home, I asked Targuisti what he thought of Jajouka. He thought a bit before replying in French.

"Everything has changed. Listen—I met these people with Gysin in 1952. They used to work for him at The Thousand and One Nights. Each week, a different team came down from the village to Tanja, and played music. When we closed the restaurant, we kept coming up here. These are *good* people, and the music was always first class.

"When did it change? I can't remember. The younger ones began to mix modern music in with the original music of their grandfathers. Then the old style went away. Then they went to Europe. Then they lost the ability to play it the old way. And so forth. They're still good people, but they've stopped playing the *real* music."

I said that I was still hearing some of the things I'd heard long before Jajouka went abroad, but Targuisti simply sighed and covered himself with his blankets. Within minutes the old bandit was snoring like a lord.

THE NEXT AFTERNOON I followed the sound of wedding rhaitas to the lower plaza, where I found Aribou and the sherif of the sanctuary sitting by the entrance to Sidi Hamid Sherq's. Eventually, the wedding parade passed by. First came a ragged queue of kif-smoking young men in djellabas, chanting religious phrases quite merrily. They led the teenage bride on a white mule. Her body was wrapped head to foot in white, her headdress was bound by a black cord, and her face was covered by two pennants held by retainers who walked on either side of the mule. Earlier the women had prepared her for her husband and covered her hands and feet with red henna to ward off evil spirits. Both bride and groom had been feasted at separate affairs, with much singing and dancing.

The groom came next, or "Moulay Sultan" as he was called during the days of his nuptials. About twenty, he rode a big brown mule and sat under a small brocade canopy to protect his "royal" head from the sun. A couple of his male relatives rode behind him on little donkeys. Then came three rhaita players on mule-back, Fudul, Twimi, and a player from the groom's *tchar* (hamlet), back into the mountains. Bringing up the rear was a white-blanketed covey of women, young and old, ululating madly. The parade took its time winding through the saintly village, displaying the newly-weds, fulfilling Jajouka's age-old tradition of blessing through music.

Later the sky turned amber, and they lit a lantern on the terrace of the madrassah. Empowered by fresh kif, the boys put on a thumping display of Djibli music that night, mountain drums and soaring choruses that lasted until the wee hours, interrupted only by the arrival of a large lamb couscous and the surprise appearance of young Mohammed Berdouz, home from the army for the holiday. My old friend was as warm and voluble as ever.

"Sadat finish," he said, solemnly. I nodded.

"Reagan?" he asked. No good, I told him in Arabic. He said he had liked Jimmy Carter. As we spoke, young Berdouz made it plain he was glad to be home. He was in the army for ten years, he said, and played the bugle. Proud, loquacious, and as charismatic as his father, he plunged into the flute and rhythm airs of his resident cousins and stayed up with us all night.

ON FRIDAY MORNING I assumed there would be the usual service at Sidi Hamid Sherq's shrine. I washed and shaved and left the madrassah, only to find the sanctuary empty. Instead, because this was the first day of the Feast, there was a public prayer and sermon in an open spot near the cemetery, looking down the valley, the traditional spot where Sidi Hamid Sherq came to meditate and pray. From a distance I watched a fqih in a white djellaba as he led the chanting and spoke to the townspeople seated on the ground around him, their heads covered by the pointed tips of their hoods. The low, passionate humming of *Allahu Akbar* drifted over the field, the only sound beside the far-off bells of goats. I was extremely moved by the simplicity of this outdoor service.

After that, we had to go down the mountain to show ourselves to the caid and ask permission for Bou Jeloud to dance, despite the sultanic decree. Targuisti and I put on our jackets and ties; Targuisti had his red fez as well. Being from southern California, Mendacia had no tie. Fudul came along, as did the goofy-looking Mujahid, who was now chief musician, which meant he was considered the best rhaita player as well.

I made them all get out and walk down the hill before we hit the worst of the pitted track. They climbed back in by the giant cork oak that shaded the resting place at the bottom of the mountain, and I drove on. I asked Targuisti if he had known the fathers of the present older generation of musicians. Yes, he said, most of them. They were great men, Targuisti sighed. They smoked a lot of kif and played music all day and all night. The late Jnuin's uncle, Zakana, was moqadem then. Malim Ashmi? Already old and long retired by that time. As we bounced along, Targuisti discoursed authoritatively on the myriad villages perched like condors on the the hills in the neighborhood. It seemed that he and Gysin had visited them all in search of clues to the misty history of the Djebel.

At the caid's, we were held outside by a young sergeant until the official was ready to see us. This was a new caid, very different from the leather-jacketed fixer I'd met years before. Short and serious, this caid was respected in the area as uncorruptible and just. He wore a light cotton djellaba and a blue shirt open at the neck. After listening to the musicians' plea and consulting with four white-turbaned elders who sat off to the side, the caid gave his assent. Then he summoned the sergeant, who took our passports. Muttering effusive thanks and gratitude, we backed out of the caid's office. Mission accomplished. There was a market going on, and Fudul and Mujahid spent an hour arguing with a spice seller before we were allowed to point the Fiat back to Jajouka.

THE AFTERNOON WAS very hot, and I slept fitfully back at the madrassah, until the flies got bad. Drinking tea with Berdouz, my thoughts ran to home, the red maple woods of New England, but also to the ties of friendship and wonder that kept bringing me back to this village. Someone announced that Mohammed Stitu had died yesterday in Ksar el Kebir, and would be buried tomorrow. Another rhaita player gone, I thought sadly, remembering the avian flute duets he and Jnuin had played.

Shortly after four o'clock the musicians piped themselves over to the main plaza, where they began to play Aisha Hamoka's seductive rhythms. A crowd of locals gathered as the sun sank behind the blue hills, the white cluster of women on one side, the brown cluster of men on the other.

Little boys began to dance first, a trio of kindergartners flicking their wrists and twitching their bums with puerile grace. Then from the men emerged handsome Abslimou, a famous Bou Jeloud alumnus from ten years earlier (he had danced for Brian Jones), who kicked off his Spanish loafers and danced in front of the line of musicians until his smart civilian clothes were limp with sweat. Someone handed 'Slimou a pair of oleander switches, with which he danced in the goat god style, holding them over his head and behind his back as he hunched over. The younger men, I noticed, were watching him very carefully. He was a *famous* mover. Some of them got up to dance themselves, clearing room by chasing smaller kids from the fringes of the circle. The massed horns roared away, as strangers passed fresh pipes over, and the moon rose clear and snow white through wispy clouds. The bonfire was lit, and 'Slimou chased the teasing children a little faster, and hit them a little harder when he caught one. Soon the real Bou Jeloud would be on the scene in all his ragged glory.

Suddenly! There he was! *"Hunh,"* he grunted in a dusty whirl-wind, brandishing stout oleander whips and herding people into smaller clusters, threatening children who dared to get close to his shaggy satyr's wriggling body. The rhaitas broke into his panic music, wild as the wind. If I hadn't already known it was Abdsalam Fudul under the floppy yokel's straw bonnet, I certainly wouldn't have been able to tell. Bou Jeloud was on the loose! The old god danced, with permission from the caid.

The music got crazier; other dancers began to quiver. Then Bou Jeloud stopped and looked at me. He shimmied over and gave me a clout on the head with his whip. *Purified.* Achmido Twimi leaned over and said, "B'saha"—congratulations.

The performance continued for ninety minutes, the music becoming faster and more shrill as the white disk of the moon rose higher. Eventually, the dancers exhausted themselves and the skirling rhaitas geared down into a ragged coda. Bou Jeloud and the big drum held by Berdouz Junior disappeared into the crooning cluster of women. Mendacia asked what was going on, and I explained that Bou Jeloud was purging the women of impurities so they could conceive, so the village's fields and flocks would be fertile. It was pure Lupercalia.

LATER BERDOUZ AND I walked up the darkened lanes to the madrassah. On the terrace we found the younger Fudul, his foul skins cast away, nursing his torn feet and waiting for his bath water to warm. I gave him some ointment for his wounds. He seemed dazed, as if in some psychic interzone between human and godling. Seeing an opportunity, I turned on the TCS-310 and conducted an interview with Bou Jeloud as he was becoming a man again:

Who are you now?

Abdeslam ben Mohammed Ghailani.

Where is Bou Jeloud?

Safi. Finish.

What do you feel when you put on his skins and hat?

I go crazy when I dance him. I'm nervous. Tense. Can't eat. When I hear the music I go wild and beat people. If someone gets in my way, I hit him.

Then what happens?

I go wild. It's not me anymore. I'm sick. Crazy. Very nervous. I hit children. Bou Jeloud hits anyone near him—woman, man, child. They say things to him, and he tears his clothes and kicks and butts people and hits them with his whip! Then he races back to the rhaitas. Then he goes to the people, and then back to the rhaitas as fast as he can. He is wild. He is amok. He is a savage. That's all.

Wait. What else about him?

There is baraka in him, like a spiritual power. When he comes, they tease him, but some of those he hits become healthy because of his baraka. If someone is sick, he becomes healthy when the fear strikes him. The fear flies out of him, and he is well.

Tell me what it feels like to put on the skins.

When I dress in his clothes, I feel like a mighty demon! Then the tune scares me—I don't have any choice about it. I hear the music; I have no control; I become confused. *He* is enchanted by this . . . yes . . . and confused. His poor mind becomes angry. The music is in his head and he likes it. He goes crazy. There's power, I'm telling you, an *ugly* power. Like ten people inside me instead of just one. Then he gets wild. He flies over the rocks and through the fire. When he jumps it is like flying. That's the power he gets when he hears the music of Bou Jeloud! He speaks to the people—*"Hhhuuurrrrrr!"* The children come and he runs

after them, top speed. *Hhhuurrr!* And he hits everyone as
if he didn't recognize them, even if it's his own son. He
strikes out at anyone who comes near, as though he
wanted to kill them!

Later, we heard that during the previous year's Aid el Kebir,
another boy had died in Jajouka after dancing in Bou Jeloud's skins.

THERE WAS GENERAL SATISFACTION that evening. Bou Jeloud had
danced, the Americans would be coming back with money to make
their film, and unity prevailed among the Masters. There did seem
to be some underlying concern among the musicians as to how they
would survive the death of their old chief, Jnuin. Yet there were
also those, Fudul among them, who weren't among Jnuin's deepest
mourners. But all of this was more innuendo than fact.

The next morning, Saturday, I rousted everybody out of their
beds and reminded them I had a plane to catch in Tangier. It had
rained during the night, and the air was clean, like pure oxygen. We
had coffee, and Berdouz said a prayer for our safe journey. A mass
of tribal warmth enveloped us as we piled into the Fiat, and various
familiar personages ran up to say good-bye as we rolled through the
plaza.

On the road to Tatoft, we came upon Malim Fudul, riding on a
big mule with a little girl in his lap, going to Ksar el Kebir for the
funeral of Little Mohammed. I insisted that Fudul come with us, and
he handed the mule to its owner, who was walking behind (the old
moral authority again). Back on the road, I asked Fudul why he
alone was going to see his old comrade into the ground. Perhaps he
thought the question impertinent, because he didn't answer it. I
dropped the big tribesman at the entrance to a shantytown along the
railroad tracks at Ksar, and watched his broad back and white turban
disappear into the crowded slum.

Two hours later, I pulled the car over by the lower ruins of

Lixus, and took Mendacia up to see the mosaic Poseidon in the baths below the amphitheater. We walked silently through the dead city with its decayed temples, shrines, and barracks of monumental granite blocks. A few minutes later, in the great acropolis temple with most of its arched roof and brutal columns intact, I heard the building groan; it sounded like the yawning ache of centuries.

We headed up the coast to Asilah, which was very spruced up for a festival. The old Barbary pirate town was in the process of becoming an artists' colony and cultural center. Targuisti pointed out a white house built into a medieval wall overlooking the ocean where he and Gysin had lived with Paul Bowles thirty years before.

I had some time when we got back to Tangier, and decided to go see Bowles. I said good-bye to my comrades at the Villa de France and took a taxi to Bowles's building. He opened the door with a start. "Oh! I didn't even know you were here. I was just going to the post office, but I suppose it can wait."

"Are you sure?"

"Yes, come in. Leave your bags in the hall and have a cup of tea. Have you been in Jajouka?"

I told Bowles about getting permission to stage the Boujeloudiya. He listened intently, puffing on a filtered cigarette in a black holder. He was now seventy, his hair white, his face wrinkled and full of his famously implacable detachment. I mentioned that the film people would probably want to interview him when they returned.

"I can't imagine what I could tell them about Jajouka that they'd want to hear," the old writer said.

I asked what he meant.

"Well, I don't think you can have it both ways with a place like Jajouka. People want the old mysteries to be preserved there, but at the same time they want it to be improved and modernized. You know, I hear all these schemes about 'saving' Jajouka by bringing a busload of high-paying tourists up there, things like that. People think they can get back what they've lost by using what they've gained. Ha! Not possible.

"And I tell them that I don't think you can regain the irrational, the very old instincts, once you have been educated. Education contorts the human mind, which loses something it can't ever get back. That's all. You can't have everything. It's like driving out one nail with another. We Westerners have already lost our most important intuitions, and I don't think we can ever go back. I'm not even sure it's desirable, but that's another matter. Now—finish your tea, and my driver will take you as far as the post office, and you can find a taxi to the airport."

The officer at exit customs did a complete body frisk, looking for hashish, on my way to a British Caledonian DC-8 with Scottish stewardesses, cold lager, and a load of daft English tourists. I had a stunning twilight aerial view of Tangier against brown hills and the blue strait. The plane flew over the mountains of Spain and the Bay of Biscay to London, as the waxing Bou Jeloud moon glowed in the dark October sky.

chapter 9

Jajouka Rolling Stone

I followed Jajouka's progress through the 1980s, from a distance. I kept meaning to get back up the mountain for a
spiritual refill, but work piled upon work and kept me away. I had
news of them every few months from Joel Fischer or Brion Gysin.
When I could, I sent a little money in care of Berdouz, asking them
to pray for me and my family on Friday mornings. On stressful
occasions, like taking off or landing in large jet aircraft, I'd shut my
eyes and mentally chant Sidi Hamid Sherq's name, as if he were my
guardian angel holding up the wings of the plane on his saintly
back.

ANY CHRONICLE OF the recent history of the Master Musicians of
Jajouka must begin in 1982, when they returned to Europe to play
another tour of summertime cultural festivals under UNESCO aus-

pices. Ahmed Attar gave up his Paris taxi to serve as tour manager and images of a whirling, ecstatic Berdouz were broadcast on French TV.

BRION GYSIN WAS now in his mid-sixties, the hippest man in the world, the doyen of the expatriate avant-garde in Paris. Semi-supported by the French government, he painted in his studio opposite the Beaubourg, and frequented the current clubs of the day. His favorite was a disco called The Palace, where decadent Kuwaiti princes appeared half-naked with dog collars around their necks. Gysin also wrote song lyrics in his permutated, cut-up style, which he recorded on several albums with Steve Lacy's neo-bebop ensemble. I saw Gysin for dinner whenever I was in Paris, and every few months received a long funny letter containing the news, or lack thereof, from Jajouka, as well as requests for new books unavailable in Paris and bitter complaints about the publishing and art worlds.

In 1983, a notice appeared in *The New York Times* that a New York-based Moroccan named Jaffar Wakou was presenting a dance piece called "Jajouka," with proceeds going to a little North African village whose musical heritage was threatened with extinction. I sent the clip to Gysin, who wrote back immediately:

> Mohammed Idrissi has just been through here, followed by Ahmed Attar, who says *he* is the manager of Jajouka. He intends to streamline everything and grind out some money. Maybe he will. Do watch out for Wakou, a mean little thief who induced Idrissi into stealing pictures of mine, which he sold and, of course, I got nothing. Wakou may be the one Moroccan who can't dance, but he can do the rest. Ahmed Attar is a match for him. Don't get caught in the cross fire. There's going to be a row very soon in Jajouka, and I intend to stay out of it. Civil wars can be

nasty. Send me a line before your next trip to Paris so I'll know you are coming.

Love, Brion.

LATE IN 1984, I stopped in Paris on my way to Tangier, where I was planning to meet Joel Fischer. Joel was taking his new wife and their young son up to Jajouka for a blessing from the Masters. He was starting his own import business, selling Berber textiles in the crafts-hungry markets of the American Southwest. Moroccan flat-woven carpets were extremely popular in Taos and Santa Fe, and Joel was prospering. .

It was November in Paris, and a cold rain washed the grey streets around my little Right Bank hotel. I called Brion Gysin before I unpacked. He answered in a coughing fit. How are you? I asked stupidly. "Breathless," he replied.

We made a date for dinner the following night, and he told me that Bashir Attar was now staying in Paris with an ex-boyfriend of Gysin's named François. I called Bashir, who asked me to come over that evening to an address near the Place Bastille. François was a young wannabe-Moroccan wearing traditional Rif peasant garb, while Bashir was in cowboy boots. Bashir was now thirty years old and seemed much wiser. He spoke sadly of Jajouka and said he would stay in Paris because in Jajouka, there were only old men left.

"I went back to Jajouka after living in Paris for some time," he told me. "I went back to devote myself to the rhaita. I sat and played the horn for one whole year, and now I know all the old songs my father knew. I became completely *committed* to this music. I think about it. I think about my grandfathers, and how they suffered for this music. Still, today, we suffer for it. It is *magical.* You understand? Even if I am just sitting here with you, drinking a tea, I get a strange feeling—a popping in my head, telling me that I must continue to learn the music.

"But I was the only young man left who would devote himself

262 to the rhaita. No one wants to play it anymore. I came back here to make some arrangements, and Insh'Allah, the Masters will come here and make a tour in April.''

For a moment, Bashir was silent. Then he said something about Fudul being in the hospital with diabetes. Then he simply said, "Five years."

What do you mean, I asked.

"In five years, Jajouka is *finished*. Who will play the rhaita when the old Masters die?''

I didn't have an answer. Bashir's question made me dizzy. I told him that I was going to Jajouka, and he said not to bother; it was raining too hard in Morocco right now. I said goodnight and made my way through the winter mist to the Bastille station of the Métro. Scrawled on the tiled wall in red paint was the racist slur on the Africanization of Paris—INVASION NÈGRE.

I TOOK A CAB to Brion Gysin's studio the next evening. I found him quite drunk, talking about Jajouka to a couple of documentary filmmakers from California. "It all goes back to the Phoenicians," Gysin was saying. "They had a big Astarte cult going in Lixus, and when Lixus was captured, the goddess's priests must've retreated to Jajouka . . .''

After he had rolled a big hash joint and completed what he termed his "whiskey fix," the film people departed and Gysin and I walked to a trendy postmodern restaurant nearby, Magnetic Terrace.

Over a good bottle of wine, I tried to speak of Jajouka, but Gysin said he was lately very deeply affected by memories of his life in Morocco. Recently news had come from Tangier that his old friend Hamsa was in the hospital. "Hamsa's father went mad too,'' Gysin said with a groan. "In the end, he drowned himself in a holy well.''

Gysin pushed back his plate of beefsteak and put his head in his hands. I thought Brion was going to weep, and almost started myself, but he recovered. He made a remark about some of the older men in the village having been his lovers when they were all young and beautiful. A bit drunk myself, I asked him which ones. "I'm not going to tell you," he laughed. Then Gysin sighed. "You know, the whole world is turning to shit. Everything real is dying out and *no one can stop it*. Soon the entire planet is going to be a pathetic theme park. It's a real shame, man. A bankrupt fucking *theme park*. And that's the truth. I'm glad I'm not gonna be around to see it."

I called for our check and Gysin eyed our bare-chested teenage waiter appreciatively. I asked him about the fathers of the Masters, men who were already old in 1950, when he first went to Jajouka. Brion grimaced, making it clear that Memory Lane was an address he was now finding uncomfortable. He shook his head sadly, and said, "They were *magic*. That's all. They had very little to do with the reality of this world."

THERE WAS LITTLE NEWS out of Morocco for a long time after that. King Hassan won his war over the Western Sahara when Algeria withdrew support for the Polisario rebels, and the Moroccan army built a fortified sand berm around the entire phosphate-blessed territory the king wished to defend. Somehow, it worked.

I continued to correspond with Brion Gysin, but his letters were filled with less news of Jajouka and more news of his worsening condition and his work. In September 1985 he wrote:

> I have contracts with Faber in UK and Grove in the US for my novel, now titled *The Faultline,* with such miserable advances that together I couldn't live a month in Paris. I'm permanently an invalid attached to bottle of oxygen and dread the winter. This summer past, I painted my last big picture: 16.30 metres long over 10 canvases called *Calli-graffiti of Fire.* Maybe you'll see it one day.
>
> Best wishes, Brion.

Another letter from Gysin, written in early December 1985:

No news of Jajouka. Glad to hear you are coming in the Spring, and hope to see you but am tempted to add: if I'm here. I now have a permanent nurse and am tied to a bottle of oxygen but hope to get to the Ministry of Culture on Dec. 18 where they are to dub me *Chevalier de l'ordre des Arts et des Lettres.*

I am leaving my paintings to the Musée d'Art Moderne de la Ville de Paris. They may get embalmed in there but there is no afterlife for them out on the market as I have no gallery or dealer to push them. Who knows what is going to happen to all of this rubbish anyway?

My novel is done, and gone to the printers. I am very lucky to have an ''angel'' and young friends to look after me. Hope to hear from you and see you soonest.

Best wishes, Brion.

Gysin did indeed make it to his ceremonial induction into French artistic knighthood. He lived for seven more months in his studio as lung cancer debilitated his tall frame, in the care of a loving male nurse who would travel the length of Paris by Métro to find denatured wines that Brion could drink without discomfort. On his last evening, in July 1986, he dined in his atelier with friends on clear broth and gelatin. By candlelight, the old chevalier was begged to put on the ribanded medallion of his order. He sat for a while, smoking against doctors' orders, proud and content. During the night, his soul left his body, which was disposed of according to Brion's will. First, the corpse was eviscerated, then displayed for a week by candlelight in its former owner's studio while verses were chanted from the Tibetan Book of the Dead. Then the body was cremated. Gysin had often told friends that he wanted his ashes strewn into the winds around Jajouka, but we heard later the remains were scattered near the Caves of Hercules by Cap Spartel.

A few months later, Gysin's novel was published, posthumously, as *The Last Museum*.

Brion Gysin was very influential, and many people were devastated by his passing. Friends remarked that the best conversation in the world had died with Brion. He was a living link to the romantic Orientalism of the nineteenth century and beyond, through the bottomless well of the past. The world seemed diminished by his death.

I HEARD NOTHING from Jajouka for months after Gysin died. Joel Fischer moved his base of operations to Marrakech, the ancient red-walled caravan terminus at the edge of the Sahara, under the mighty arms of the Atlas Mountains. He started a factory that produced beautiful leather goods and clever faux Berber trinkets for markets in the American Southwest and beyond. His business was successful, and Joel continued to "tithe," sending Jajouka money whenever he made a profit. For a couple of years we heard little, except that all was quiet in Jajouka.

Too quiet, as it turned out.

In June 1988, I received a letter from Joel, postmarked Medina, Marrakech:

> You won't believe this—just returned to Marrakech from US in time for the annual folk festival, held every year in the ruins of an old palace. We hadn't thought Jajouka would be there since they weren't listed on the program—but I was watching a TV promo for the festival and saw Berdouz! We rushed over to the old palace and were directed to the musicians' encampment outside the city walls. The place was tightly guarded, but somehow we got in and had a joyful reunion with the small group—ten musicians and the cook—from the village. It turned out they alternated years at the folk festival with another rhaita

band from the Djebala, and only ten players were allowed to come.

Much news: Bashir is out—some kind of split over touring—I hesitated to pry as feelings seem to be running raw. Berdouz is now chief, and most of the regulars were here with him. Not Fudul, ill with diabetes, although he might also be in the 'Bashir faction' now.

After a big hassle we got permission for the musicians to leave the compound—their movements are tightly controlled within the city walls—and I gave them a big feast at my Banana Tree House. Much music, all the neighbors came, and Berdouz blessed the house with a special prayer.

The next night we went to their show at the folk festival—a glitzy production staged by French technocrats. They had rhaitas wailing and Bou Jeloud dancing amid *day-glo laser beams* splitting the darkness. As Skip used to say, what a trip!

Love, Joel.

Six months later, another letter arrived from Joel in Marrakech:

We have just seen Bashir Attar, who came for a visit here in the south, and there is news of Jajouka. While the old men were here for the folkloric festival recently, Jajouka was taken over by Randy Weston and a movie crew of 200 Frenchmen filming a TV series about African music. Bashir had arranged the contract in Paris, and thought everyone would be happy, but the Masters decided to go to Marrakech instead. So Bashir assembled a band of his brothers Amin and Mustafa, plus Fudul (who can't travel) and Bacari (from Rabat) and auxiliaries from nearby hamlets. In the end they had five rhaitas and five drummers, and the film got made.

But the result was a tremendous schism in Jajouka.

Bashir complains the old men just want to sit on their mountain and smoke kif all day, while Bashir wants to take Jajouka out into the world. The final split came when Bashir presented the old men with a lucrative gig at a big peace festival in Jerusalem. They told Bashir they would do it, then changed their minds after the arrangements were complete.

Anyway, Jajouka is suffering. Bashir and his faction occupy the Madrassah. The Masters are in another house. I asked who was playing for Sidi Hamid Sherq on Friday mornings and was told . . . *no one.*

Bashir was very upset about all this. He is being accused of trying to steal the name Jajouka from the Masters, but all he really wants is to hold it together. I feel for him—he has become a Master himself, and is seeing it all slip away. He met a young American photographer in Tangier—a Paul Bowles protégée named Cherie—and they plan to marry and come to New York for awhile. Please visit them when they call you.

Love, Joel.

The telephone rang, and a voice boomed, "This is Bashir Attar!" followed by a long laugh. Bashir was in New York, living on the Lower East Side with his wife. The mystical Attar family had attained its first footfall in America; I realized a new era was at hand.

I drove to New York to see them the next week. I found Bashir and Cherie living in Moorish bohemian squalor on East Eleventh Street, their tenement digs beautifully done up like a flat in the casbah of Tangier. A large gimbri reposed in its leather bag on a cushion in a corner. I hadn't seen Bashir for five years, and there were many passionate Moroccan embraces before we could exchange a word. We had been through a lot, both together and separately. I noticed that while I had aged, Bashir looked like he was getting younger. His English was very good, quite Americanized.

He held me at arm's length and said, "We love you. You're the same family as Attars."

Bashir disappeared into the kitchen and I looked at Cherie's photographs of the expat community of Tangier. They were black-and-white portraits, and they were very good. She had been taking pictures of Paul Bowles one evening when Bashir showed up at Bowles's flat. It was love at first sight. Bashir returned with a delicious harira soup and loaves of crusty bread he'd baked after the sun set. While we ate, he told me the score.

The numbers were pretty grim. The rift among the musicians was serious. When Bashir returned to Jajouka from Paris, he moved into the crumbling madrassah, which Gysin had built on his father's land. Berdouz and the Masters told him: "You sit in one room, and we'll sit in the other." Bashir said he had ten good musicians, including his brothers, Bacari from Rabat, even Berdouz Junior when he retired from the army.

Things were not good in Jajouka. Achmido Twimi had died, Bashir said, and suddenly his delicious soup tasted bitter. Old Mujahid was out of it, he went on, and couldn't play the rhaita anymore. Malim Ali was similarly retired. Mezhdoubi could no longer travel because he had injured his leg. In town he had kicked an auto that had brushed too close to him as if it were a mule, and was now semi-crippled. And the madrassah was in terrible disrepair and would fall down soon if nothing was done. Cherie showed me a recent photo of Fudul, and I could see the old ruffian had aged dramatically.

I looked at Bashir, who glowed with the tremendous vitality of a young musician in his prime. He had the Attar smile, the Attar magic, and was beginning to build a career of his own. He had just played the rhaita in an off-Broadway production of "The Night Before Thinking" by Ahmed Yacoubi, and was playing a gig that week at the Knitting Factory with various denizens of the Down-town Manhattan avant-garde. It seemed that while Jajouka was unraveling at home, Bashir was about to take off. "Have you heard him sing and play the gimbri?'' Cherie whispered to me while Bashir cleared the table. "It's *legendary*."

We drank some tea then, and smoked a bit. Bashir said that his father, Jnuin, had indeed changed Jajouka's music by composing new material, but it had been his right to do so. I mentioned the late Malim Ashmi as the teacher of the old Masters, but Bashir corrected me, saying their real teacher had been his father's uncle, Zakana Attar. "Now I have all my father's music, right here," he said, tapping his head. "This is where it is."

Before I left, Cherie told me she had written to the Rolling Stones, concerning the possibility of Jajouka appearing on their forthcoming album. "Good luck," I told her sagaciously. "It's a real long shot."

BASHIR CALLED ME a month later, very late at night.

"This is big secret," he said, stifling giggles. "Don't tell no one. *I'm playing with Mick Jagger!*"

I started to sing into the phone: "Ah, Mick Jagger, Jajouka Rolling Stone" to the old tune of "Brahim Jones." Deep laughter came back over the line.

"The Rolling Stones are flying us back to Morocco. We record with them in Tangier next week. I want to say good-bye!"

SO GOOD-BYE, Bashir, and Godspeed.

By 1989, the Rolling Stones were in disarray. Mick Jagger launched a solo career in the mid-eighties after his old band seemed played out. He refused to tour with the Stones after the release of a so-so album, *Dirty Work*. Instead, he went to Japan and Australia with a new band to promote his own career, which eventually subsided due to abysmal sales. This enraged his old partner, Keith Richards, who responded by making a pretty good album of his own. The two Stones traded bitter remarks in the press for several years.

In 1989, they made up. The Stones needed money and credibility to survive into the 1990s as greying priests of rock music. So Jagger and Richards met in Barbados and wrote some songs. One of these was an Arabic-sounding chant whose working title was "Speed of Light." Keith listened to the melody, which Jagger had composed, and mentioned something about maybe getting Jajouka to play on it.

A week later, Cherie's letter arrived, notifying the Stones of Jajouka's availability. Mick Jagger wrote back. Then he and Bashir met in New York and rehearsed "Speed of Light." Within days, Bashir and Cherie were on a plane to Morocco, with orders to assemble the Master Musicians of Jajouka in Tangier in ten days' time, ready to record with the Rolling Stones.

Bashir returned to Jajouka and put out a call for musicians. This was unheard, or ignored, by those allied with Berdouz, and none of them showed up. So he assembled as many of his brothers as he could find, plus the Fuduls, plus the brilliant Tahir from Ksar and several rhaita players from neighborhood hilltops. His final tally was seventeen musicians. Up on Owl Mountain, they rehearsed "Speed of Light" over and over again by lamplight in the open air, recording on a cassette machine powered by an auto battery. Meanwhile, Cherie stayed in Tangier, trying to find a suitable studio.

Bashir had given her the name of an acquaintance who was said to be a large property owner. This turned out to be Camel Face, who had bought the palace Ben Abou from Skip's wife, years before. He had also bought Sam Kramer's villa when the Kramers had to leave Morocco after Sam got out of Her Majesty's prison. Camel Face took Cherie to Ben Abou, which he had restored to its former Mooresque glory, and said he would be pleased to serve the Rolling Stones during their stay in Tangier. They had their studio.

The Stones' ultra-tech studio equipment arrived early in June, accompanied by technicians and a programmer/arranger ready to "sample" the shit out of any exotic tone that came his way. The Stones arrived shortly afterwards, separately, and checked into the venerable Hotel Minzeh. It took a few days for them to settle in, and right away Bashir and Cherie noticed some strain. Jagger kept inviting them to dinner every night, so they had to visit Keith and Ron Wood in their hotel rooms since they didn't hang out with Mick. It was "You sit in this room, and we'll sit in the other" all over again.

Bashir's musicians arrived the next day from Jajouka, and several hours were spent arranging microphones and TV lights around the tiled blue courtyard of Ben Abou. Flanked by several boom mikes, the seventeen musicians lined up in traditional L formation, rhaitas at a right angle to the drums. Jagger, dressed in a long white *gondura* and pointed yellow slippers, walked around with wireless headphones, directing things. Keith and Ron sat off to the side, sipping tea and smoking. The musicians, dressed in brown djellabas and gold turbans, spent a long afternoon trying to play along with the prerecorded track. "Love comes," droned the taped lyric, "at the speed of light . . ." In a darkened room off the courtyard, the Stones' young programmer listened raptly through headphones, his eyes riveted on the dials and lights of his machines. The tape was rolling.

Mick Jagger ran a tight ship. He worked the young men from Jajouka hard all afternoon. Bashir did a lot of solo work with rhaita and flute. Drum tones were sampled. Friends of Camel Face came in, photographers showed up, Paul Bowles stopped by to say hello. Eventually, Jagger and the engineers were satisfied they had enough tape to return to London for mixing, and the session evolved into a jam. Long after the track had drifted off the speakers, the Moroccans kept a devastating sonic undertow in the air for sheer pleasure.

Later, in an upstairs sitting room open to the breezes from the harbor, Jagger reflected on Jajouka for a reporter:

"I remember Brian [Jones] playing the tapes he made up there," he said. "We had this engineer we were working with, George Chkiantz; he was one of the first people to be heavily into phasing, which was like the 'scratching' of the middle sixties. So Brian took all of the Jajouka tapes and put them through phasing, which was

272   really quite before its time.'' Jagger paused, then added: ''I always
felt the Stones were quite adventurous in that way.''

Asked why the Stones had called upon Jajouka, Keith Richards
replied: ''I thought, 'Yeah, we need something like this'—the
unification of what this band is about. It really pulled a string in
me.''

Bashir told the reporter he had been seven years old when Brian
Jones had visited Jajouka, and was quoted: ''I became a musician,
in a way, because of the Rolling Stones. When Brian Jones came,
I listen for the first time to music from outside Morocco. It gave me
the wish to play this music—to someday play with his band. I was
little, and it was a big dream for me.''

The reporter then noticed that Fudul, ''a stately gentleman of
seventy-five and a veteran Master Musician who actually performed
for Brian Jones all those years ago,'' wanted to say something.
Bashir listened, and then translated: ''He says this is *big* music. He
means there are big things in this music. And he says we need more
of it!''

THE ROLLING STONES stayed in Tangier for a day or two after the
sessions, the objects of much social heat. The French cultural at-
taché had begged Bashir and Cherie to be allowed to give a party
for Mick Jagger, and Mr. Jagger had consented. Soon hundreds of
Tangerines were disgruntled at not being invited. Bashir, in turn,
begged Jagger to visit Jajouka. The day after the party, Jagger
informed Bashir that he would go to Jajouka for only a few hours,
since he had to be in London for a costume fitting the following day.

This was how Mick Jagger came to Jajouka, twenty years after
Brian Jones. By June 1989, the old road had become impassable,
and Jagger and his escort left their cars at the bottom of the
mountain and walked up to the village. They were taken to the
madrassah, now in need of repair, and made comfortable on the old
shaded terrace. Tea was served, some music was played, and pipes

were passed around. In their quarters elsewhere in the village, Berdouz and the old Masters seethed with chagrin and regret.

Mick Jagger never knew the difference. He flew out that night with his own Jajouka tapes, intent on the reconquest of the world.

AS PREDICTED, the Rolling Stones released *Steel Wheels* later that summer. The album was a great success. By far the most interesting track was entitled "Continental Drift." This opened with a rhaita playing the melody, then some singing—"Love comes . . . at the speed of light"—followed by a long tonal collage whose swirling gyre recalled an abstract version of the Bou Jeloud music on Brian Jones's old record. After minutes of this dark vortex, the sweet rhaita came in to break the spell, and then two twirling lira flutes fade to black.

I kept punching in the track, over and over again, trying to unearth its secrets. What was it? An homage to Jajouka? A pandering stab at trendy World Beat? Wasn't it strange, twenty years after fallen angel Brian Jones thought Jajouka's rhythms could revitalize the Rolling Stones, that the Rolling Stones and Jajouka should recharge each other?

The ironies were murder.

IN SEPTEMBER 1989, while the Rolling Stones were stadia-storming through North America, opening their shows with Jajoukan "Continental Drift," I received a telex from Joel. It was marked URGENT.

BASHIR IN JAIL. JJKA IN DIRE STRAITS. MEET ME VILLA DE FRANCE, TANGIER 9/25. REPLY SOONEST. JF.

I cabled back that I'd be there.

I flew out of New York aboard Royal Air Maroc. Also flying east that night was a team from *Vogue*—star lensman, coltish models, crew and stylists. Eight miles high, a Manhattan makeup gal with frizzy hair told me that Morocco, especially Tangier, was going to

274   be very in, very soon. Malcolm Forbes's big international party in Tangier the month before, starring Elizabeth Taylor, was only just the beginning. Didn't I know that Bernardo Bertolucci was filming Paul Bowles's novel *The Sheltering Sky* in Tangier before moving into the desert? The *Vogue* squad was to capture Tangier's new energy as a backdrop for this winter's resort wear. Did I know, she offhandedly queried, of any interesting expats or hangouts in Tangier?

A swirl of faces came to me—Gysin, the Masters, Skip, the Kramers, Bowles, the boys at the Mouneriya, Camel Face, Si Larbi and his Andaluz orchestra, Hamsa, Targuisti—and then vanished as the 747 dipped and I gripped the seat-top for balance. No, I told the woman. It had been eight years since I'd been to Morocco. I'm out of touch.

The airport in Tangier was deserted that hot Sunday morning. My lungs inflated with warm North African air; what a feeling to be back! The first person I saw was . . . Bou Jeloud! This was Abdsalam Fudul, mild-mannered *portero* who had been working the airport on alternate days for ten years. I was greeted by the goat god himself! He pulled me out of line, kissed me on both cheeks, led me through customs with a wink (much to the envy of the jet-lagged magazine people whose every chic grip and alloy camera case was being assiduously rifled by customs agents on a feeding frenzy), and delivered me to Joel Fischer, waiting with a sleepy grin by the kiosks.

"Thanks for coming," my old friend said. It had been some years since I'd seen him, and his black hair had gone slightly grey. "We have some work to do together."

The younger Fudul reappeared with my valise, and asked if we were going to Jajouka. Yes, we said. "Say hello to my father," he said, "and tell him the children are well and that I'll see him soon. Get them to stop fighting with each other. They will listen to you, God willing."

Joel told me what he knew, as we drove into the sparkling white and yellow suburbs of Tangier. There had been a big row in Jajouka, and Bashir had been jailed on as-yet-unknown charges leveled by the Masters. Now Bashir was free and somehow involved with Signore Bertolucci's film, which had taken over Tangier. Our self-imposed mission was to find Bashir, visit Jajouka, and try to reconcile the two factions so that Jajouka could continue.

"It's the least we can do," Joel said, "for all the baraka they've given us. And besides, we owe it to Brion Gysin. Don't you think? Do you want it on your conscience that Jajouka self-destructed, and you didn't try to do anything? I don't."

As we entered the town, I could see Tangier was much different than the last time I'd visited. The new petrodollar expatriates— elite Saudis, Kuwaitis, rich young bloods from the Emirates—had bought up the old villas or built new palaces of their own, and now clogged the boulevards with their huge white BMWs and Benz limos. The debacle in Lebanon had restored Tangier to some semblance of its old glamour, for the time being.

We checked into the Villa de France, whose tiled courtyard gleamed in the morning light. I asked for Matisse's room, but it was taken. Later, on the terrace of the Café Paris, everyone was connected to, or discussing, the filming of *The Sheltering Sky*.

We had to find Bashir and Cherie; they were somewhere in Tangier. "So where do we look?" Joel asked.

"Paul Bowles," I said.

It was the only logical place to start, since they had first met at Bowles's flat. The woman at the door informed us that Señor Bowles had left early in the morning and was expected home shortly. We could, she said, go upstairs and wait. We squeezed into the tiny lift. I knocked on the door marked 20. It was opened a crack by Mohammed Mrabet, Bowles's protégé, who seemed to recognize me. Mrabet led us past the old steamer trunks in the vestibule, through the heavy purple curtains into Bowles's sitting room. Paul Bowles, he told us, was off working on the film, but would soon return. I got up to eyeball the Bowles library.

"A man from California comes here," Mrabet said solemnly, "and offers Paul fifty thousands of dollars for these books." Mrabet looked incredulous. He said he was having some trouble with his liver. The week before, Bertolucci had given a cocktail party for Paul and the movie people at the Minzeh. "I have *one drink,*" Mrabet said with pride. "Then I go to café and throw up vomit two, three liters!" The doctors were prescribing something for him, he said, but he preferred the folkloric method—olive oil and honey. Then Mrabet went into a tirade about his French publisher. Since 1967, Bowles had recorded and translated a dozen volumes of this Rifian's tales and pipe dreams, which had been reprinted in many languages. Mrabet was illiterate, yet here he was, complaining bitterly that all publishers were bastards and thieves whose souls are possessed by the most malevolent of Djinn.

Just then, there was a bustle at the door—and through the curtain stepped Paul Bowles, wilted from a blistering day on the set. He looked like an old god—Mercury at eighty. He was impeccably dressed in an English tweed suit, matching suede oxfords, white shirt with silk tie knotted at the neck. I noticed quickly that, despite two operations, he looked octogenarically healthy, if somewhat exhausted and startled to find visitors. I apologized profusely, and we got up and made for the door, but Bowles said, "No, please don't go. Good to see you again. How long has it been since you've been here? Let's all sit down." Bowles dropped into a nest of blue pillows that lay under a reading lamp. Quite gruffly, in appalling Spanish, Bowles ordered the wasted Mrabet to get in the kitchen and put the kettle on.

"Oh, I'm very tired," the old writer said with little strength in his voice. "When they first told me about this movie, they didn't inform me I was expected to *work* on it. Now Bertolucci has me on the set as an advisor; and I'm recording some voice-overs, like a narrator. And he's got me appearing in several scenes—just, you know, walking through. But he likes to shoot them many times and has just informed me—Mrabet? Are you listening?—that they want me back on the set *at 8:45 in the morning!*'' This was spoken as though the hour was unthinkable; nothing happens in the morning in Tangier.

Mrabet returned with cups of tea, lemon slices, and sugar. He chatted about his liver while we drank. Soon, stimulated by the strong black tea, Bowles was recalled to life, his blue eyes alert. He said he was amused that the film crew spent a day laying tracks near the bottom of the Casbah so an old trolley could rumble through a scene. ''As far as I know, no streetcar ever operated in Morocco,'' he mused. ''But then I don't really see why they're filming here in the first place since the actual story is set entirely in Algeria. It's the same thing with your friends from Jajouka.'' Bowles looked up to see if we were interested. ''Bashir is very charming and I've always respected Jajouka for what it is—but I'm against their being in the movie, and Bertolucci has hired them. The music the characters hear on their voyage should be Algerian. It's ridiculous, the whole thing. There aren't even any sand dunes in Morocco!''

At five o'clock, Bowles's flat quickly filled up with friends and we decided to make our exit. An English woman with a house in Tangier and an art gallery in Paris presented Bowles with a copy of Bertolucci's screenplay for *The Sheltering Sky,* a hot black market item in Tangier. Somehow, she gloated, one of her servants had obtained it. An American writer came in with his wife and fired up a joint. ''Mrabet's finest,'' he said with satisfaction.

''We're filming at the Hotel Continental tomorrow,'' Bowles said as we left. ''Cherie's mother has a house nearby in the Rue Dar Baroud. That's where you can find them. If you go to Jajouka, come back and see me before you leave Tangier.'' We stepped out the door into the hallway. ''Don't fail,'' Paul Bowles said, and closed the door behind us.

WE CONTINUED OUR QUEST the next morning in the Rue Dar Baroud. Cherie's mom turned out to be a friendly, beautiful woman

278   in her mid-fifties. She received us on the third floor of an old house
with a long view of Gibraltar, dressed in a silk morning gown like
the heroine of an unproduced Tennessee Williams play. We chatted
a bit before Cherie came in from a hard session negotiating with the
film people for the rights to two songs that Bashir's band had
recorded for them the previous week. "They're tough bargainers,"
she told us plaintively. "I'm not a business person. There are no
music lawyers here. What should I do?"

Take the money and run, we suggested.

Cherie sat down and informed us of the sorry situation in Jajouka.
The split between the two factions was now the subject of some
controversy in the Djebala, and the authorities had been called in.
It was the Old Originals versus the Rock & Roll Gang, and nobody
was happy.

Berdouz was now the moqadem, and had brought Ahmed Hamsa
back into the tribe. The Masters saw that Bashir's contacts with the
Western world—Randy Weston & Co., the Stones, *The Sheltering
Sky*—were bringing in business, and they, who saw themselves as
the *real* Jajouka, were not getting any. The best Hamsa could do for
them was a gig greeting Malcolm Forbes's exhausted revelers as
they landed at Tangier airport.

After Jagger's visit to Jajouka, Berdouz and Hamsa went to the
caid in Tatoft. Bashir, they screamed, is passing himself off as *us*!
They told the caid that most of Bashir's so-called Master Musicians
were riffraff from other villages. Then they charged Bashir with
being a thief.

What, the caid wanted to know, has Bashir stolen?

Mick Jagger, Hamsa said. *The Rolling Stones,* Berdouz added.

It was a replay of the Dancing-Boy Wars that plagued the Djebala
of the 1800s, with middle-aged Mick Jagger in the unwitting role
of Best Boy in the Mountains.

But it was also more serious than that. In essence, they were
saying: This kid is killing us.

The caid took it seriously. The following day, gendarmes arrived at the madrassah, now occupied by Bashir and his family. They arrested Bashir and dragged him off to jail. It took Cherie and Bashir's younger brother Mustapha three days and many trips to various bureaus and fonctionnaires to get him out. And while Bashir was in jail, Cherie alleged, Hamsa broke into the madrassah and tried to seize the building and its contents on behalf of the old Masters. But Bashir had papers that proved the madrassah was built on land owned by his father, Jnuin. So Bashir was allowed to reoccupy the property.

And there things seemed to stand. The caid hammered out an agreement that separated the musicians into two groups, two bands. "So that, supposedly, there would be no problems," Cherie laughed. "But nobody's talking up there, so I don't really know what's going on, except that I think it's impossible for people like us—you know, Americans—to solve a quarrel between Moroccans. They're very stubborn, and seem so dead set against each other."

I asked where Bashir was. "In Jajouka," Cherie said. "He's expecting you."

"So are Berdouz and the Masters," Joel told me later. "I wrote both sides to say we were coming."

THERE WAS NO ANSWER when I knocked on Joel's door at five o'clock. I walked down the hill and ordered mint tea at the Café Paris. Then Abdsalam Fudul walked by. We were due in Jajouka the following day so I grabbed him and made him tell me who was on whose side in the battle for Jajouka. He and his father were with Bashir, he told me, as were many of the younger men. The old men, he said, were with Berdouz; he ran down their names and those of their sons.

A few moments later Joel joined us, and the sun set behind the verandah of the French legation across the street. Neon billboards winked on above the Place de France: SHARP   IBERIA   COCA-

COLA. Joel wanted to visit the perfume shop down in the medina, so the three of us ambled down to the Socco Grande, whose sooty bus terminal had been relocated, leaving the great square more pleasant. The Cinema Rif was showing Pakistani kung-fu films, and young petrocrats in checkered *kafiyas* and sleek white German cars sought places to park.

The medina was brightly lit for the evening's shopping. Every merchant was open, every stall crammed with clothes, shoes, electronics, ancient crafts, anything. Cafés blared televised soccer. After five minutes swirling through this maze we reached the Parfumerie Sliman Madini, a shop full of glass bottles and exotic scent: amber, jasmine, musk, oil of rose, as well as Madini's perfect knockoffs of French brand names—Opium and Paco Rabanne. We had been here fifteen years before, I remembered, but old Madini was dead, his place taken by his son, who proudly informed us he had a branch in Woodstock, New York, and it was doing quite well.

We walked back uphill for supper and retired early to our rooms. Later Bou Jeloud returned to the hotel with a fat ball of hashish oil, whose scent was as impressive as anything at Madini's.

The night was sleepless, and at five o'clock in the morning we heard the muezzin's aria-like first call to prayer.

A BLAZING NORTH AFRICAN sun beat down on the harvested brown landscape as we drove south later that morning. It threw down solar flares like scourging bolts from Zeus, burning the world, forcing humans and animals to seek shelter from the empyrean wind.

As Joel drove the Renault down the oldest road on the oldest continent, I feared this might be my last journey on its Atlantic path.

In Ksar el Kebir we shopped for tomatoes, carrots, green peppers, white radish, squash, onions, potatoes, bottled water, sardines, and chocolate, then fled the dry heat for cold orange juice and delicious *kefta* sandwiches under the awning of a café.

Back on the road we noticed a sign: CHAOUEN 100K. "That must mean this road has been paved all the way through the mountains,'' Joel marveled. Soon we could see the tin roofs of Jajouka on its own plateau, more than halfway up Owl Mountain.

You have to know where to look.

WHEN WE EMERGED from the car at Tatoft it was like stepping into a kiln. ''Unbelievable,'' Joel muttered as we moved through the Tuesday market-day tumult toward the caid's. Waved through the gate by soldiers, we made our way through the crowd of Moroccans who stared at our American clothes and our unfamiliar faces. Someone murmured, barely audibly, ''Jajouka.''

This caid was a formidable, grey-eyed fifty-year-old with a military bearing and a khaki shirt. He eventually removed his glasses after scrutinizing our passports like a jeweler examining emeralds, and asked us, ''Which group do you wish to visit? Bashir? Berdouz?'' There were murmurs from the local notables seated along the walls like spectators at a trial, straining to hear the verdict.

Joel disappointed them. ''The last time we visited,'' he told the caid, ''Jajouka was one group, one family, and so we intend to visit *all* of our friends up on the mountain.''

There was silence. I heard a flock of goats passing under the open window behind the caid. He put his glasses on again, looked at us briefly, and handed our passports to his major-domo, who placed them in a drawer. You may pick these up when you leave, he said.

''We're probably lucky,'' Joel said. ''I was half afraid that Jajouka might be closed to foreigners because of all the trouble.''

The new blacktop to Chaouen began to climb the blue conical hills, traced by lines of sheep browsing in the freshly turned soil. I drove slowly, following a blue *colectivo* taxi crowded with farm people returning from the market.

The almost hidden track to Jajouka was so indistinct at its beginning that I drove by it at first, and was dismayed to realize that I might have missed it completely, if Joel had not been with me. So

282 I backed up a few feet and turned onto the "Phoenician" road, now
so eroded that I gave the wheel to Joel and got out to walk. I quickly
fell into conversation with an Achmed on a donkey. He was
wrapped up in his djellaba despite the hundred-degree-plus heat,
coming back from the market with goods for his mother in the
village. He lost no time in telling me that he was aligned with
Bashir, and as I walked along he described, in gossipy detail, the
schism among the Master Musicians.

Rounding the hairpin turn at the bottom of the mountain, we
could see that, near the top, the road had deteriorated so that cars
could no longer drive up to the village. So we left the car in a
brush-enclosed goat corral kept by a cranky old peasant, and
climbed up the mountain on foot.

When we got to the central plaza, I noticed loudspeakers atop a
refurbished building, freshly painted blue. Then we were swept up
by Berdouz and Malim Ali in many embraces and fervent kisses.
"You poor thing!" Berdouz exclaimed upon seeing my grey hair.
"You've gotten old!" I was laughing and crying at the same time,
pounded on the back and carried off by other Masters—Ayashi,
Aribou, Mohammed Ben Aisha, Mohammed Bad Hands. They led
us to the Masters' new headquarters, since the madrassah was
controlled by the other faction. We were ushered out of the burning
day and into a cool blue room furnished with fresh mats, cushions,
and pillows. Exhausted from the journey, I was happy just to sit
there with my tea, breathing deeply while getting used to the
altitude, contemplating the enormity of distance traveled and the
shock of being in Jajouka again.

HOW OLD WAS Berdouz now? Seventy? He was getting tinier, and
his animated, birdlike face looked like an old pharaoh. He was going
on in Arabic to Joel, saying how, since they were expecting us, he
had spent the last several days doing nothing but cutting fresh kif.
He took out his wildcat mutwi—which I'd seen once in a *High Times*

centerfold as an example of world-class paraphernalia—and un-rolled its leather tongue. He shook out fifty grams of gleaming kif fresh from the drying shed, proudly displaying Jajouka's bounty like a ribbon winner at a county fair. I noticed a UB40 button had been added to the famous charms of the veteran kif pouch.

We chatted for an hour as musicians came in to say hello. Several times Joel tried to steer the conversation toward the rupture in the village, but Berdouz kept insisting that everything was m'zien b'zef and tranquilo.

Although the heat outside was stifling, I wanted to see the "other" Jajouka before dark if possible, without offending our hosts. So I snuck out at five o'clock, when I thought everyone was napping, and headed across the old soccer field toward the ma-drassah. Then I noticed one of Berdouz's sons strolling discreetly behind, keeping an eye on me.

There were a lot of changes in the village. The government school was now ten times bigger and walled off, and Jajouka itself had grown considerably. Traditional mountain clothing had nearly disappeared. Villagers wore jeans and sneakers, and I saw a ten-year-old shepherdess in a Madonna T-shirt. As I turned into the madrassah's enclosure, my chaperon caught up with me. He took my sleeve and said, "No, please," wagging his finger and looking quite pained. I told him in French that I was friends with everyone in the village; he turned on his heel and walked quickly in the direction of the Masters. Whitewashed rocks spelled out J A H J O U K A along the path. A faint trill of flute music was sub-audible nearby, and I knew I was home.

Over the years I'd heard that the house Brion Gysin had built for the Master Musicians had begun to crumble, but Bashir had recently put some movie money into repairing the building, so it was still standing. As I walked on the terrace, two prone bundles of sleeping wool revealed themselves to be Mustapha Attar, Bashir's brother, and Malim Fudul. When they recognized me, they sprang to life. Two teenage boys appeared from inside the madrassah. As Fudul introduced his sixteen-year-old son, also a Mustapha, I realized that I'd met this boy as a rollicking baby back in *National Geographic* days.

It was good to sit on the terrace again, just like old times. The air was cooling and the boys chatted excitedly about Mick Jagger's recent visit. "He sat right *there,*" Mustapha said, "the same place you're sitting now. He smoked, drank some tea, no problem." Everyone smiled at this pleasant memory.

The light was beginning to fade, as Mustapha played some Andaluz on a guitar. The old white-clad sherif of the sanctuary came by for tea, and was surprised to see me. His remarks were translated into French for me by a young Mohammed who had been two years old when I first came here.

Before I left, I asked Mustapha if I could see the inside of the madrassah. Grimacing, he explained the building was still in disrepair, but didn't hesitate to unlock the antique green doors that led to the main chamber. Recalling all the magic I had witnessed in that room, I held my breath as I stepped through the portal . . . and found only a dark, dank cell that smelled of drying cement. No carpets, no divans, no guest-book, no old instruments or pictures of Brian Jones hanging on the walls; only a sodden pile of rags lying in a corner, which turned out to be part of Bou Jeloud's costume and a piece of moth-eaten djellaba whose embroidery identified it as one we had bought in Tetuan many years before. The old galley where Achmed Skirkin had performed savory miracles with goat and vegetables was also bare. Nowhere was there any trace of the Master Musicians of Jajouka, save for dear old Fudul. The madrassah was now a musical crash pad for the older village boys who wanted to play in Bashir's band.

It was hard for me to be there. It felt like a recurring nightmare I'd had where I returned to Jajouka over the lost horizon and found nothing there anymore.

I gave Mustapha a letter that Cherie had sent along for Bashir, and explained that we would be meeting her train in Ksar the following evening. Mustapha, gentle like all the younger Attars, promised we would see his brother when we returned.

BACK AT THE MASTERS' headquarters, I related what I found to Joel, who told me that he had been trying to persuade Berdouz and the old guys to find some compromise with Bashir and Fudul. "They didn't relate to this idea at all," Joel said. "They kept insisting everything's cool with two separate groups, so why worry? Meanwhile, that new building in the plaza with the loudspeakers is a mosque. I'm having a hard time getting it straight, but it looks like there's no more music at Sidi Hamid Sherq's on Fridays, either."

I didn't say anything. Joel groaned. "It looks like Jajouka has changed more than we thought."

I walked outside and sat down with my face toward the breeze. I heard Malim Ali pouring tea behind me. The old champion of social rituals and ex-Franco soldier handed me a glass and casually asked, "How long has it been since we have seen you here?"

I looked up and saw he was studying me carefully, perhaps to verify I was the same young traveler he had befriended long before.

I answered, "Eight years, Malim Ali."

"That's a long time," he said. "It's good to see you in Jajouka again. H'amdullah."

From that moment on, I felt better about being there. I was no longer under the slightest illusion that we could help the musicians sort things out. My shoulders suddenly relaxed, as if relieved of some horrible burden, and I followed Malim Ali into the cool blue room and fell asleep for an hour.

THE MUSIC BEGAN about nine, well after dark. Fat Mohammed and two others on cane flutes, Berdouz and Achmido Titi on drums; it was "Brahim Jones" from the top, *threedle-dee-dee* from the flying flutes, light-footed stomp from the drums. Joel and I looked at each other and knew the music was great, and who feels it knows it.

The music of Jajouka was still alive.

At one o'clock I left the yellow glow cast by the musicians' gas

286   light and went out back to look at the stars. It was so clear; the
Milky Way was cinched around the vastness of the universe like a
studded belt. Suddenly two hooded men loomed by me and I
shivered. Somewhere else in the village, a maniac was raving in
horrible explosions of fury. They were merely teenagers, but they
got very close and asked for money and kif. The lunatic was
screaming louder at the same time in what I took for a murderous
rage. For the first time ever in Jajouka, I felt danger.

I bolted back to the fireside, where three dancing boys in brown
djellabas were entertaining.

Eventually, I distributed some good chocolate, appreciated particularly by the old men, and we turned down the lamps and went
to sleep.

THE CONSTELLATION THE ARABS call the Belt of Fatima had still been
visible when I'd fallen asleep. When I awoke, not long after dawn,
the sky was a matte white haze with no sense of depth. A few hours
later, before noon, it was nearing a hundred degrees. Joel was
trying to reason with the old men, begging them to reach some
compromise with Bashir and his faction so the tribe could be unified,
as in olden times. Listening to this, my first trip to Jajouka fifteen
years earlier now seemed like ten thousand light-years away. It's
been torn apart, I thought, and will never again be the same.
Perhaps it was written.

I walked over to the madrassah to see what was happening. Two
kids were practicing the flute in the damp main room, while Fudul
slept on a mat in the corner. He rolled over when he heard my voice
and invited me to sit with him. I gave him news of his son and
grandchildren in Tangier and then asked why he, alone of his
generation of senior Malimin, had joined Bashir.

Big Fudul laughed dejectedly, like an old gangster, and explained
that he and Bashir were kicked out together for the crime of wanting
to take Jajouka's music to the whole world. The old musician's

diabetes was bothering him, he said, and soon he wouldn't have to worry about the survival of the tradition anymore.

Joel came along a bit later. I asked him, "Any luck with the Masters?"

"Are you kidding?" he replied. "They can't even bring themselves to say Bashir's name, let alone work with him."

The autumnal heat was appalling, and the blue hills of the Djebel were still and soundless, as if the landscape had been stifled. As we walked through the village, we could see Bou Jeloud's cave in the distance. We paused in the shade of the wild olive trees that overlooked the cemetery and the valley below. There were, I noticed, many fresh graves.

After lunch—the grilled liver of a freshly killed young goat—I took out an old Jajouka red-tipped cane flute, which Little Mohammed had made for me years before. It was barely in tune with the new aluminum flutes the locals now played, but a couple of musicians took the time to teach me the slightly different way they were playing "Jajouka Black Eyes" and "Brahim Jones" these days. Then someone passed a pipe. Feeling exalted, I sang a line from an old Djebala song I used to hear in the village, which Berdouz found hilarious. "We could give you a job," he teased. "You could be a professional Malim, like we are. We could tell everyone you were an infidel café-singer!"

After that, I shut up.

AT FOUR O'CLOCK the following afternoon, Joel and I took Megaria's grocery order and trod down the mountain on the antique paving stones, discussing our evident failure to unite Jajouka or even to get anyone talking. We retrieved the car from the thornbush corral and drove to Ksar in the dusty twilight, the road empty except for the occasional farm truck. We guzzled cold orange juice in the station café, where we waited for the six o'clock train from Tangier to arrive. Cherie was dressed as an elegant expat gypsy, and looked relieved to have ended a crowded journey. We gave her orange juice, shopped for vegetables under strings of bright white lightbulbs, and drove out through the suburbs of Ksar toward the indigo darkness of the mountains.

We climbed into the little hills, along which now ran fragile-looking pylons that would someday bring electric power to the Valley of Ahl Sherif and maybe even Jajouka itself. At the turnoff to the village, our headlights picked up two Bashir-boys waiting with a lantern and a donkey for Cherie to ride up the trail. We locked the car and struggled uphill after them on foot, as Venus sparkled like a pearl in the western sky and the Big Dipper materialized in the north. Ahead of us, I could make out the dark form of the American woman, riding the little donkey toward Jajouka.

TO AVOID OFFENDING our hosts as much as possible, Joel returned to the Masters' house while I followed Cherie's caravan to the old madrassah. The porch was alight with gas lamps, and a tape of Bashir jamming with his downtown colleagues played under the stars like an urgent fax from the future.

Bashir greeted his wife and me wearily, and asked when Joel would be coming. *Momentito,* I assured him, then turned to see who was tapping my shoulder.

Tahir!

Here was the legendary Bokazar Tahir, former godling, now middle-aged with thinning hair, but still utterly radiant. It had been fifteen years since I had seen him, this splendid musician who had been Jajouka's shining star.

Tea was served, and Tahir began to whisper into my ear in a polyglot of Arabic, Spanish, English, and French. For years, he said, he'd had his little band in Ksar, with girls that danced with tea trays on their heads. Now, he was playing with Bashir again, like the days when we all were younger (he nudged me conspiratorially), but what he *really* wanted was to take his troupe to New York so the whole world could see how great they were.

He took his violin from its case and began to tune up. Joel appeared out of the night, and for the next hour we tried to help Cherie in her financial dealings with the soundtrack producers for *The Sheltering Sky*. Now the producers were demanding world rights to the music in perpetuity, for which they were offering six hundred dollars.

"Unbelievable," Joel said. Cherie looked at me, and I shook my head.

Cherie said, "The truly terrible thing is, we have so little money that we could be forced to sign this contract."

Tahir chose that moment to start a medley of his greatest hits, and the others picked up hand drums and eased into a groove. Soon the pace began to swing, and then it got good. At the height of this performance, the drumming slowed, and old diabetic Malim Fudul got up and danced a subdued version of his familiar jigging stomp. I looked up, saw a shooting star flash across the northern sky, and made a wish that the Master Musicians of Jajouka might reunite some day.

FOR REASONS OF ETIQUETTE, we thought it best to decline the offer of supper. We walked back over the hill as Tahir & Co. resumed their Djibli/Andaluz fusion; at the same time we could hear the flutes of the Masters piping in their house just over the crest of the hill. Two groups now, playing in the cool of the evening.

Five pipers and four drummers were wailing on the porch of their house. It was a glorious cry, and the rhythm turned my legs to rubber. I danced myself into a lather as Berdouz shouted encouragement. Then he got up and danced until the thing crashed to a halt. Saturated, I excused myself to the hammam, where a big metal bucket of cold water was waiting to be poured over a steaming body. A dry towel and fresh clothing felt like heaven.

Old Mujahid Attar, titular moqadem of this bunch (but in fact retired from the rhaita and living in Ksar) had arrived. He was wearing his golden turban of authority and hadn't aged a day from

1973. His only English words were "panny kut," which meant very good, and he said this over and again to much hilarity from his fellow duffers. Unfortunately his lovely brother Mezhdoubi (who'd slammed a car door on my hand) remained in Ksar, where his youngest son was in school. I missed seeing his handsome, slightly crazed mountaineer's face.

When Joel emerged from the hammam, a goat tagine was served, hot with cumin, with crusty bread for scooping. Then kif and rumination, followed by more flutes and three dancing boys in brown djellabas, their delicate fingers tracing invisible arabesques above their heads. Spirits and music ran high for hours, flashbulbs popped, and the scents of mint tea and Spanish chocolate mingled in the night air. We retired to the blue room at midnight, but it was still too hot. I got up, spread my blanket on a grass mat on the porch, and gazed at the stars until I finally slept. At dawn, a cat walked on me.

WE HAD PLANNED to stay through the Friday morning healing rite at the tomb of Sidi Hamid Sherq, but we were informed that this ritual was no longer performed, that any religious observance in Jajouka now occurred exclusively in the new village mosque.

So much for Sidi Hamid Polytheism.

"Let's go then," I told Joel the next morning. "They'll get it all sorted out eventually, and our being here may be more divisive than helpful."

While one of the Rotobe boys loaded our gear in the baskets of a donkey, we said good-bye to both groups of musicians. As we made our way through the sun-scorched village plaza, where Pan the goat god used to dance on cold nights, a toothless old man lounging on a ramshackle porch began to wave and shout praises for Jajouka and the hill tribe Ahl Sherif. We waved back, and I wished I could have told him how much I agreed with him.

A pack of kids braved the heat to follow us halfway down the mountain, and then we were alone on the yellow brick road, our donkey's unshod hooves slipping on the broken Phoenician cobbles. We transferred our luggage to Joel's car, paid off the disgruntled guardian, picked our way carefully down the piste to the paved road, and were soon on our way. I looked at the electricity pylons, as yet unwired, and wondered if I would ever again pass through these little blue hills to see Pan in his natural element.

We arrived back in Tangier at three o'clock, exhausted by the three-hour journey that had turned the Renault into a steel oven. I went up to the boulevard for cold water and the English papers, and then collapsed in my darkened hotel room and slept until the call to evening prayer.

LATER, OVER SUPPER at Romero's, open to the street and filled with smoke, gangsters, film people, and Spanish prostitutes, Joel and I began to try to figure it out.

"It's like having the whole problem of the modern world laid out right before us," Joel said, over a plate of squid in its ink. "It's the elemental conflict between the traditional and the modern, the folkloric and the commercial, the local and the global, the sacred and the profane . . . the old and the new. It was right there for us to see . . . *and it hurt!*"

Joel sat back and looked at me. "It was hot up there," he sighed.

"AH, YOU'RE BACK from Jajouka," Paul Bowles said the next day, as Mrabet let us into his sitting room. "Tell me, how was your stay?"

Bowles was stretched out on his nest of comfortable pillows, his mail, reading, and tea close by. He held out his hand and shook mine warmly.

"It was a bit of an ordeal," I said.

Bowles wasn't surprised. "*Of course* it's an ordeal," he said crisply. "That's why I don't go up there anymore."

"At least," I ventured, "it was an *ecstatic* ordeal, once the music started."

Bowles said, "Well, I can believe that. When a group of them came down last summer to play with the Rolling Stones, I visited the recording session and surprised myself by quite liking what I heard." I took this as a great compliment, since Bowles was famous as a connoisseur of Moroccan folk music, whose field recordings had been issued by the Library of Congress.

Mrabet began to choke and cough, exhaling a spastic lungful of spent kif smoke. Speaking in Spanish, he proclaimed that he can't understand why anyone—Bowles, the Stones, Bertolucci, me and Joel—likes Jajouka's music. "It's just peep-peep-peep," he laughed. "Look at me. I'm Moroccan, and I don't like it!" He nodded toward Bowles, who regarded him with passive bemusement. "Look at Señor Bowles," Mrabet snorted. "He has lived here for sixty years and *even he* doesn't understand Morocco."

There was a silence. "No Nazarene can understand Morocco," he went on. "Not possible. Never."

I ROSE EARLY in the morning and drove over Cap Spartel to the Atlantic beach by the Caves of Hercules. Except for the fishermen, I had miles of smooth sand to myself. The surf was cold, but I needed a wake-up call. Drying off under the rising sun, I looked to the west and pondered flying home over this ocean in a few days' time. I wondered if I could still count on my personal copilot, Sidi Hamid Sherq.

On the way to the airport, we had to stop at a roadblock with a dozen other cars because the gendarmes had closed the road for the king's arrival from Spain. We saw his military jet land, and then watched his motorcade turn south, once again snubbing Tangier, which the king is careful *never* to visit because of a lifelong grudge against the city.

"Sa Majesté," one of the gendarmes said reverently, as the king's limos sped away.

When we were finally allowed in the airport, Bou Jeloud was waiting for us. He humped our bags over to Royal Air Inter, checked us in, disposed of our rental car (the owner was a pal), and walked us through exit customs with a wink. He led us to a waiting area filled with uniformed authority—gendarmes, customs police, airport security, local cops—and casually lit a *big* joint.

Joel turned purple. This was suicide! "What are you doing?" Joel hissed in Arabic.

"No problem," Bou Jeloud laughed. "These mens are my friends." I looked around, and no one seemed to care.

Our plane was an ATR-300 prop, with the belly slung under the wing. It climbed up over the beach with a smooth lurch and flew out to sea a mile before turning to port and continuing to climb. Once in the air, the pilot announced in French that his usual route had been altered since no air traffic was allowed over the mainland while the king was en route to his capital. As we flew parallel to Africa's autumn-brown coast, Asilah and Larache appeared like white mushroom clusters amid the stupendous coastal landscape.

"Look," Joel said. "A bit inland you can see Ksar." And beyond that, stretching into the dusty haze, began the foothills of the Djebala rising toward the invisible mountains of the Rif. Somewhere in that cauldron lay the valley of the Ahl Sherif, somewhere overlooking that valley sat a village called Jajouka.

After an hour, the plane turned inland, and flew on to Marrakech.

Epilogue

My story would have ended there, but for the tenacity of Bashir Attar, who was determined that his father's music live on, and that Jajouka be reunited.

After I left Morocco, Bashir and his troupe of younger Jajoukans appeared in the movie *The Sheltering Sky*. Then Bashir and his wife Cherie returned to their pad on the Lower East Side of New York City, trying to connect with the American music industry. Meanwhile, in Jajouka, the older Masters allied themselves with their old cousin Hamsa, who claimed to have a secret letter from the king saying that he, Hamsa, should lead Jajouka. By 1991, the musical and spiritual energy was so low in Jajouka that no rhaitas played during Aid El Kebir. Bou Jeloud did not dance.

But in Manhattan, Bashir was blowing the rhaita with a drummer and a good guitar player at the alternative clubs on East Houston Street. He called his group Hamduolillah—"Praise God"—and

296 they *really rocked.* Bashir's playing was so soulful, even away from the context of Jajouka, that I went to hear him every chance I got. At the same time, immigration officials were trying to deport him for having no visible means of support. It was my honor to sign an affidavit saying that he was one of the most important musicians in the world.

One night I took David Courage to see the group. David, now divorced, was still working in television in New York, and he and Bashir reconnected. A dinner party was arranged at which Bashir Attar was introduced to a New York producer, who resolved to sign Jajouka to a recording contract—just in time to save Bashir and Cherie from eviction, as they'd been too broke to pay the rent.

All the while, fate continued to play her tricks. In July 1991 Bashir received a plane ticket to London and a request to appear at ceremonies marking the fiftieth birthday of the late Brian Jones. Bashir played the rhaita in Cheltenham Cathedral, with Brian's lookalike drummer son Julian, in commemoration of the founder of the Rolling Stones. Thus the sons of Brian Jones and Abdeslam Ahmed Al-Attar achieved a second generation of musical synthesis, and became friends as well.

In the fall of that year, Bashir and Cherie took a crew of technicians to Jajouka, where they recorded a compact disc. Bou Jeloud danced through the embers of a bonfire, and Bashir gave his fifteen young musicians one thousand dollars apiece, a major payday considering their chronic poverty. This was duly noted by Berdouz and the old Master Musicians, who had been invited to participate, but had passed. One can only imagine their continuing anguish and desperation.

Apocalypse Across the Sky, by a group calling itself The Master Musicians of Jajouka Featuring Bashir Attar, was released on compact disc six months later, to general acclaim. It was the best recorded performance of notoriously skittish rhaita music I ever heard. Its title came from William Burroughs, whose CD booklet notes placed Brian Jones in Jajouka in 1970, the year after he died.

When Bashir returned to Jajouka that spring, the remaining musicians, young and old, who had been allied with Berdouz and Hamsa, came to him and asked to be let into the band. In June 1992, Bashir wrote to say that many lambs had been sacrificed in an old-fashioned Aid el Kebir just held in Jajouka—''without tourists, like in the time of my father.''

Berdouz had been the last hold-out. Jajouka's resident shaman had been too proud to accept Bashir as moqadem, as chief of the Master Musicians. But after the Aid el Kebir, Berdouz found himself alone. He returned to Bashir one night in tears, and thanked him for taking them all back. Reports reached me sometime later of a tremendous celebration of Jajoukan unity and baraka. Friday morning music resumed at Sidi Hamid Sherq's. Only Jajouka could save itself.

The last I heard, The Master Musicians of Jajouka Featuring Bashir Attar were headed to an appearance with Ornette Coleman at a festival in Switzerland. Bou Jeloud lives, and that is how the generations came to a reckoning in Jajouka, Ahl Sherif.

> *It Is Written*
> *Is written on the forehead*
> *For the eye to follow*

(old Moroccan proverb)

ACKNOWLEDGMENTS

I have relied for history and nuance on the following texts: *The Process* by Brion Gysin (New York: Doubleday, 1969); "Joujouka" by Robert Palmer (*Rolling Stone,* Oct. 14, 1971); and *Tales of Joujouka* by Mohamed Hamri (Santa Barbara: Capra Press, 1975). My brief account of the Bou Jeloud legend is loosely adapted from M. Hamri's version. For background I'm indebted to Edward Westermarck's *Ritual and Belief in Morocco* (London: Macmillan, 1926) and *The History of the Maghreb* by Abdallah Laroui (Princeton University Press, 1977). Brion Gysin's letters are quoted by kind permission of William S. Burroughs, literary executor of the Brion Gysin estate.

Thanks to "Johar," Bob Palmer, Howard and Hana, Rikki Stein, Philip Schuyler, Mike Mendizza, the National Geographic Society, Martin Rogers, C. Nutting, Bashir Attar, and all the Master Musicians, then and now.

Love and appreciation to JHA, Lily Aisha, India, L'il Bee, and W.M.F. Magicel. Give thanks: M. L. Helm, J. A. Isaacs, R. F. and Units 1 & 2, and David Vigliano.

Highest praise to the valiant Rebecca Beuchler who survived Mesoamerican microbes and lived on to edit this book.

S.D.

STEPHEN DAVIS's bestsellers include *Hammer of the Gods,* *Fleetwood,* and *Moonwalk.* He is also author of the acclaimed biography *Bob Marley* and other books. He lives in New England.